WHAT WAS LOST

WHAT WAS LOST

Jean Levy

THE
DOME
PRESS

Published by The Dome Press, 2018
Copyright © 2018 Jean Levy
The moral right of Jean Levy to be recognised as the author
of this work has been asserted in accordance with the
Copyright, Designs and Patents Act 1988.

This is a work of fiction. All characters, organisations and events
portrayed in this novel are either products of the author's imagination
or are used fictitiously.

A CIP catalogue record for this book is available from the British Library

ISBN 9781999855963

The Dome Press
23 Cecil Court
London WC2N 4EZ

Printed .A.

It's the right door. Even in the dark I know it's the right door.
But it's in the wrong place.
It's lying across the step. Like a drawbridge.
Icy weeds are poking up through the broken glass
That used to be the window.
Thistles, I think. And nettles. That can't be right.
Where is he?

The wooden panels split and crumble as I step across into the hallway.
Bigger weeds have been growing inside. Pushing the floorboards apart.
All dead now.
I remember wallpaper. Yellow and green.
It isn't there anymore. Just a few dirty traces high up.
Why isn't he here?

Did he tell Grandma he was going away?
Perhaps he's upstairs. But the stairs are not there either.
Just a tall empty space stretching straight up to the sky.
From the bottom of the stairs that are not there I can see the stars.
At least the stars are still where they ought to be.
But I can't remember their names.

In some places, silver moonbeams are breaking through.
Lighting up the dirt and bricks.
I can see a crushed bucket. Empty cans.
A broken book. Its pages torn open.
Its words are all eaten away. All except one.
One word remains: LOST

Episode One

The room was bright. Yet, through the half-closed blind, the world outside was still black as night. I watched the nurse arranging my tray. A flash of red interrupted her busy fingers.

'You wanted a ruby!'

The young woman paused, her empty smile becoming uncertainty. 'Yes, that's right! I brought your breakfast. Yesterday. Scrambled eggs. Like this.' She checked her watch then hurried round to adjust the bed. I could feel myself becoming higher. 'You wanted a little salt, remember?'

I reached for the salt pot, then pulled back my hand. 'How much did I want?'

'Just a little.'

I shook out a few grains. My fingers seemed strangely disobedient. I changed hands. That was better.

She handed me a spoon, watched me as I ate, then stepped round to the end of the bed and lifted a chart that was hanging there out of sight. She checked her watch again. Time was important. She nudged a china mug towards the front of the tray then fetched a small beaker from the side table. I watched it approach, removed the two yellow pills and swallowed them, each with a mouthful of tea. The tea was

3

terrible, worse than yesterday. I remembered yesterday's less-terrible tea. But I knew I was in no position to complain about tea, so I drank it and put my empty mug back on the tray. I hoped I wasn't making a face. The pills had left a bitter aftertaste that even the terrible tea couldn't wash away.

She removed my tray then pulled a chair over and sat down beside me, her hands together in her lap. 'Can you tell me anything about yesterday, Sarah?' she said.

I knew this was a test, I knew I had to say something, so I tried to recall things before today, looked again at the red stone, surrounded by a circle of tiny, sparkling diamonds:

'Your ring.'

She turned the ring on her finger and smiled. 'Anything else?'

I searched the room for inspiration. There was not much to see. Another chair, the side table, a lamp, a jug of water, a glass, a painting on the wall, a window.

'I remember the sun.'

She smiled. 'Yes, it was sunny yesterday. Anything else?'

Anything else? Yes, there was something else but I didn't want to talk now. I wanted to concentrate. But my thoughts were giving way to the hum of the lights. To the distant laughter of a child. Ridiculing me. I felt myself becoming lower. A heavy door closed. Then footsteps. Two shadows alongside the nurse. One tall and wide. One short and thin. I tried to focus as the ruby-ringed fingers secured the sheet too tightly over my arms. I tried to listen as the same-as-before nurse spoke to the shadows, informed them of things beyond my hearing. As if only they were entitled to know. That today I remembered yesterday.

Episode Two

As far as I remember, the day began with waiting. Of course, I had by now come to realise that cats care very little about the passage of time. Only people care about that. So I stood patiently and watched the black and white cat sniff the newspaper around the outside of the plate, lick some invisible scrap of tuna from the newsprint, re-sniff the plate and then, without casting even a glance in my direction to offer some gesture of humble gratitude, pad purposefully towards the cat flap and nose its way through. I had no idea who that cat belonged to. If it had a name I was not aware of it. In fact, my association with this animal depended entirely upon the fact that the door that opened from my dank backyard into my kitchen included this special, cat-sized flap. I had considered resealing it. Parcel tape would probably have been enough to stop the ungrateful animal nudging its way through. But there was always the worry that the parcel tape might turn up at its edges and look a mess and then I'd regret my decision. There was also the possibility that I might miss the cat. Sometimes it purred. I might have missed the purring.

I watched the flap for a few moments then hurried over to the window to catch a last flash of black tail as it disappeared over into the yard next door. The cat was gone. So I turned my attention to the list on the work surface, took a pencil and added the word TUNA, folded the slip of paper into my jean's pocket, replaced the pencil and walked over to the back door to confirm that the two bolts were secure. I checked that my wallet, driving licence, notebook with attached pencil, mobile phone and car keys were in my bag, touched the kettle and washing machine plugs three times each, rechecked the back door then hurried out of the kitchen before any doubts might set in. I knew it would be all right once I was in the car. I was always all right in the car.

*

The supermarket was anywhere between ten and twenty minutes away depending on traffic, and all the way there I played over the morning so far, from the point when I'd been ready to leave and that black and white cat had popped in through the flap and purred. So now it was after nine and the car park was busy. Too busy. But I knew that driving straight back home would not have been the right thing to do.

*

Inside, the aisles were still sparsely populated. So it would probably be OK. I grabbed a trolley and navigated it straight through the opposing rows of crisps and biscuits towards the central walkway. A sharp left took me into the tea and coffee aisle, which stretched deep into the rear of the supermarket. Then, avoiding the stack of Easter eggs abutting the central aisle, I pushed on to cereals, halted my trolley and observed the choices before me. So many choices. So many rectangular boxes, diminishing off into the distance. An intimidating range of nuts, dried fruits, seeds, wheat/no wheat, oats to absorb cholesterol, low salt, low fat, high fibre, additives/no additives stretched out before me. I threw myself into reading labels, studying carbohydrate contents, pushing my trolley further in past illustrations of happy, healthy other thirty-five-year-olds, whose lives were perfect because they consumed the correct breakfast cereal. The happy images began to coagulate into one multi-coloured muddle of good advice, manufacturers' commitments, occasional warnings. I could feel myself diffusing into the options that surrounded me. The familiar stirrings of panic were rising up from just below my diaphragm. I controlled my breathing, observing the oat-coloured floor tiles, the matt surface of a shoe. Its partner shoe was hovering slightly off the ground. My eyes traced up the many-deniered tights to a woolly hemline, thick, wintry cloth, grey hair, an outstretched arm, an aged hand reaching hopelessly for a small packet of cornflakes on the top shelf. My own crisis was suddenly dwarfed by the plight of this diminutive shopper. I watched her sag in frustration and help herself to a family-sized box from the shelf below. I had no choice but to intervene.

'Shall I try and reach?' I whispered.

The woman glanced round. 'Oh, would you, dear?' She replaced her family-sized box and turned to me, wobbling her head slightly as she watched me ease one of the smaller boxes from the top shelf. I handed it over. She thanked me. I smiled graciously and watched her round the end of the aisle before stretching up, taking an identical box and placing it into my own trolley. I stood for a moment staring back along the aisle of wasted opportunity then, clenching the handle of my trolley so hard that it must have looked as if my knucklebones might burst through my skin, I hurried away from cereals. Justifying my decision. Cornflakes are good for you.

There was a feeling of openness about the fruit and vegetable terrain. Here the produce was arranged on long, sloping stalls. It was like a huge, sterile homage to those fairy-tale markets, where ragamuffins stole peaches and a boy might trade his cow for a handful of magic beans. I brushed past a tall stand of fresh herbs and the air filled with the lush, calming fragrance of basil. A startling yellow and black promotion demanded: BUY ONE GET ONE FREE. I ignored it, hurried on past strawberries and grapes, grabbed a bunch of green bananas, then wheeled my trolley back and helped myself to a pot of basil, re-read the promotion, selected a second pot, put both pots in my trolley, picked one of the pots up and put it back on the stand. Why would anyone want two pots of basil? One's enough. Why on earth was I getting myself wound up about a pot of basil?

But it wasn't really about the basil. Or the cornflakes. I knew that. It was about deciding. Not just about deciding what to choose. It was all those other decisions about what *not* to choose. Because every choice involves not merely the possibility of choosing the wrong thing but an endless number of possibilities of not choosing the right thing. Too many decisions about *not* choosing. Dr Gray always insisted: 'If there are too many decisions, just take a deep breath and walk away.' So I had walked away. I'd walked so far away that there were now six mountainous banks of food between me and those unchosen boxes of cereal. I took a deep breath, fumbled in my pocket and pulled out my list:

BANANAS

CEREAL

CAT BICUITS

TUNA

I read it several times to make sure. Then, just as I was folding it back into my pocket, I glanced up and noticed a perfect red and green apple rolling towards me. Arcing towards my foot. Impact was inevitable. Inevitable. And that's when it all began. Well, just some of it began. Although, in truth, it really did all begin with an apple.

*

I stared at the apple resting against my shoe. It was probably a too-red Bramley, perhaps a too-green Gala. I can't remember now. But I do remember that, even after everything that had happened, everything I had lost, I could still remember the names of apples. And I could still remember Granny Clark's stories: how apples came to be called this or that. Barnaby Smith's old grandma used to hide those hard green apples in a box under her bed so that the night fairies would never find them. Annabel Bramley had been disappointed that only one of her apple pips germinated although she wasn't to know that trees from that one tiny seedling would one day provide fruit for the best apple pies in the world. I was writing all those stories into picture books. Doing the illustrations myself. In fact, I'd been thinking about Orange Pippins that very morning. Before the black and white cat had purred in through the flap and demanded tuna.

I stooped to retrieve the unsolicited fruit, lifted it to my nose and was briefly overwhelmed by a memory of pumpkins and autumn sunshine. I read the name on the round, sticky label. Was Braeburn in Scotland? Perhaps that was something I once knew.

'I'm sorry, I didn't aim that at you!'

I looked up. He was smiling. The man who had not aimed the apple was smiling. He was, perhaps, early forties, tall with some very pleasing russet stubble, specked golden in the artificial light. His eyes were green: not apple green, more pastel green, like husky eyes made white by the snow. I offered him the apple. 'It seems OK,' I said. I really liked the colour of his eyes. Mine are just brown, like most other eyes. 'But you ought to put it back. In case it's bruised.'

'Then someone else might finish up with a bruised apple.'

I felt myself smiling. That in itself was brave of me. 'Shall I put it back for you?'

He made a display of coming to a decision. His smile disappeared. But the tiny creases beside his eyes didn't. 'No, never get anybody else to do your dirty work. I'll take it to a member of staff and explain.'

'They'll put it back when you're not looking.' I was amazed at my own boldness.

'Yes,' he said, 'but at least my conscience will be clear.' He took the apple, hovered momentarily, then his face broke into a broad smile. 'See ya!'

I watched him return to his trolley, replete with vegetables, grabbed a grapefruit I didn't want, pulled off my scrunchie and reorganised it, then hurried away towards canned fish, where I loaded a dozen small tins of line-caught tuna in spring water into my trolley, before collecting two bags of cat biscuits and wheeling on towards the checkouts. Did tuna live in spring water? I couldn't remember. I joined the nearest queue and thought about Orange Pippins, remembering what Granny Clark used to say: if they rattle they're ripe. I could remember her holding those yellow-red apples to my ear and shaking them. I could remember them rattling. I could remember back then.

'Fancy a coffee?'

I spun round. 'What?'

'Coffee, do you fancy a coffee?' The apple man. He was right behind me in the queue.

I caught my breath, recovered. 'I have to get back. I'm writing a book. For children.' I noticed a slight flicker of awkwardness in his pastel-green eyes. 'But thanks, if I didn't have to … Do you come here often?'

He laughed away the awkwardness. 'Excellent line! You're clearly a world-class author.' He took a very obvious deep breath. 'Mostly Thursdays. Occasionally Saturdays. Not usually as early as this. The name's Parry. Matthew Parry.' He offered his hand.

'Can I help?' The checkout operative sliced through our conversation.

'Oh, sorry,' I said and hurried four tins on to the conveyor belt.

'Do you need help?' He lifted two tins and my box of cornflakes and aimed them at the till. 'Are the cornflakes for you or your cat? I presume you have a cat.' He scooped up the cat biscuits. 'Either that or you have a strange taste in biscuits.'

I forced myself to smile and quickly transferred the rest of my shopping before he could offer further assistance, pushed my trolley past the checkout and hurried everything into my bag, handed the woman my credit card, punched in the number that was written across my wallet, glanced towards the exit and waited.

'I'd like you to have this as a deposit.' Again I was forced to look round. I was being offered a familiar red and green apple. The shop assistant tutted. He addressed her directly. 'It's weighed and included in the price.' He demonstrated the sticker on his bag of other red and green apples. 'Do you want to check it?'

The assistant rolled her eyes and ripped my receipt from the till. 'Next!' she instructed the conveyer belt, which was already filling with vegetables.

I accepted the apple, surprised at my lack of embarrassment.

Perhaps I'd forgotten how to feel embarrassed. He continued to unload his shopping. 'Perhaps this Saturday? Same time, same place?'

I popped the apple into my bag and said nothing – which was pretty much a reflection of what was inside my head – left the supermarket in a blur and drove home, wondering who he was, what he did, where he lived. What he would think if he knew.

I pulled into the residents' parking zone, parked in my allocated space, being careful not to reverse into the builder's skip that was occupying the two visitor parking spaces, hauled my shopping off the passenger seat and stepped out of my car. The black and white cat emerged from under a nearby van, rubbed past the back wheel of my dilapidated Escort and threw its ear against my leg. I hurried inside. The cat knew not to follow.

Secure in my kitchen, I pulled a tin of tuna from my bag and emptied its contents onto a clean plate. I glanced up as a familiar black and white head purred through the flap, watched as the indifferent animal lapped systematically around the outside of the tuna flesh, savouring the spring water, before attacking the main course. The purring intensified. I washed my hands thoroughly then emptied my shopping onto the work surface, snatched up the apple as it rolled away and tried to remember whether apples ought to be kept in the fridge. It didn't look as if it did. So I put it in the fruit bowl with the grapefruit and bananas. I stacked the rest of the tins and the cat biscuits into the cupboard under the sink and then returned to the small box of cornflakes, carried it over to the cereal cupboard, and took a deep breath before opening the door and inserting the fresh box alongside all the other identical boxes arranged two deep on all three shelves of the cupboard.

Episode Three

The black and white cat had clearly decided to stay for the morning and was now asleep on a dining chair pushed halfway under the kitchen table. Its right ear was perhaps two inches away from the ridge of wood that ran between two table legs. It must have had to squeeze itself underneath, yet it was sleeping peacefully. I envied the way that cats were able to be comfortable in such uncomfortable circumstances. But then, cats have small heads containing small brains that have no room for the kind of worries that could congeal into frantic dreaming or reasons for not sleeping. I watched its fur breathe. What a declaration of confidence in my benign hospitality that this animal, so able to roam free, should sleep so soundly on my kitchen chair.

I stepped over and slid out the tray from beside the dresser, fetched two china mugs and the empty biscuit tin. Half-filled the sugar bowl. Checked the kitchen timer. Forty-five minutes. Filled the kettle. Forty-three minutes. I wandered through to the lounge at the front of the house. My desk was beneath the window that looked out onto the road outside. On its surface was a lined notepad open at the first page. A brief list was pencilled halfway down:

PIP

PIPPIN

PIPPED

It annoyed me, so I took a pencil out of the pencil pot, one that ended in a smudged eraser, and scrubbed out the bottom word. The eraser transferred its smudge to the paper. Now I was really annoyed. I ripped out the page and noticed that the page beneath still bore the imprint of the three words. I pulled that one out as well, screwed them both into a tight ball with that bottom word locked deep inside. I heard something, glanced up, and noticed movement through the narrow slits in the blind. I bent lower to get a better view of the pavement outside. It was old Miss Lewis from next door. And a woman, short and thin, exhaling cigarette smoke as she spoke. She was pointing her cigarette up towards the empty flat above mine. Miss Lewis was leaning away from her, shaking her head. I looked up at the ceiling. Sometimes, there were noises. I reached over to pull the blind closed, slowly so that no one would see it move. The woman was walking away towards a silver-grey car. Miss Lewis was watching her go. I glanced again at the ceiling then hurried back into the kitchen and threw the paper ball into the recycling box. Thirty-one minutes. The house phone rang beside me. I waited for the ringing to stop then copied the last incoming number onto the telephone pad, detached the sheet and hid it underneath the pile of tea towels in the tea towel drawer. Twenty-seven minutes.

When the timer said ten minutes I turned it to zero, went through to the lounge, sat down on the larger of the two sofas and watched the minute hand on the wall clock jolt towards twelve, then down towards the one. The doorbell rang. I hurried over and peered through the small peephole. A tiny, cone-shaped Mrs Parkin was on the other side; she moved her head towards the outer part of the peephole and her eye became bigger than the whole rest of her body. I opened the door before things got any worse.

'Hello, Sarah,' said Mrs Parkin. 'I've had to park miles away. It's a bit of a liberty those builders taking up your visitor parking like that. We ought to complain. How are we today?' She always said that, but I don't think she ever expected an answer. She stepped inside and waited for me to close the door. 'Shall we have some tea?' This was Mrs Parkin's usual opening gambit. She probably imagined that it created a friendly atmosphere. It made me cringe each time she said it, which, at the moment, was every Monday and Thursday.

'I'll put the kettle on,' I said.

She nodded her approval and followed me into the kitchen. The black and white cat was nowhere to be seen. I watched Mrs Parkin remove her coat and drape it over the back of a chair then investigate her bag for my case file. She was a tall, tight-skinned woman with bony hands and big feet. She invariably wore flat shoes, presumably to offset her height, but the shoes made her feet look even bigger. The overall effect was awkward. She also had a wide mouth, even when she was not smiling, which was most of the time, and, at some point in the past, she had ill-advisedly had her thin hair bobbed into a kind of choir-boy basin cut. She was probably about fifty but looked older. I turned away, emptied out the filled kettle, refilled it and switched it on. When I turned back Mrs Parkin was opening her folder onto the work surface.

'So, how are you today, Sarah?'

'I went to the supermarket.' My eyes strayed towards the fruit bowl and the incriminating Braeburn, only inches from Mrs Parkin's folder. I pointed to the windowsill. 'I bought basil.'

'How lovely. Did you speak to anyone?'

'No.'

'No little panicky episodes?'

'No.'

She made a brief note. 'Have there been any calls?'

'No.' The kettle flicked off. I made tea.

Mrs Parkin watched me for a moment before removing a packet of biscuits from her bag. 'I thought we'd try something special for a change. Chocolate gingers.'

I took the biscuits, emptied them into the biscuit tin and placed it on the tray, then carried the tray the short distance to the table. Mrs Parkin picked up her folder and sat down.

'And how was your consultation yesterday?'

'Dr Gray was pleased,' I said.

'And Dr Williams on Tuesday?'

'Fine. I had a note from the Indian restaurant on the corner, about removing a gate and re-fencing. I showed it to Dr Gray.'

Mrs Parkin checked her information. 'Hmm, Dr Gray feels it's best if your mail continues to be redirected.' She glanced down a list. 'There hasn't been much. Mostly bills. And they'll continue to be paid from funds. Is your allowance proving sufficient?'

'Yes. I bought a microwave.'

'I noticed.' She helped herself to a biscuit. 'Have you been able to use it?'

'Yes. I'm OK with instructions. Mrs Parkin, I think my road tax disc has to be renewed at the end of the month. Will the funds cover *that*?'

She flicked a few pages. 'It's already seen to. As I've said before, we have arranged for all these things to be dealt with. According to your agreement. Shall we pour the tea?'

I poured. I could feel my blood pulsing past my throat. I needed to ask.

'Mrs Parkin, I can't expect to be paid for like this forever. My car, my rent.' I handed her a mug. 'Does my landlord know about me?'

Mrs Parkin helped herself to sugar. 'Dr Gray is optimistic about your recovery. In the meantime there are sufficient funds.'

'What funds? Is it the money from my books?'

'Sarah, we have discussed trust, haven't we?'

'But there must be people who know what happened to me. What happened to make me not remember. Where are all the people who knew me?'

'Trust, Sarah!' Mrs Parkin sipped her tea. 'Now, what about your writing?'

I resigned myself to not knowing. 'I did some this morning.'

'Good! That's a good sign, I'm sure. Do help yourself, my dear!' She leant over and took another chocolate ginger, bit into it and left a trace of pale, ill-chosen, pink lipstick deposited across the surface of the chocolate. I helped myself to a biscuit and took a modest bite and instantly experienced the strong sensation of what must have been ginger, curling around my tongue in advance of the luscious, dark chocolate. I closed my eyes and tried to remember these tastes from before but Mrs Parkin interrupted, asking me if I'd thought of leaving the house other than to visit the supermarket. 'We could arrange an outing. To buy clothes or ...'

'I have clothes. And lots of shoes. I must have liked shoes.'

'We could go back to three visits a week, if you'd prefer.'

Good God, no. 'No, I'm fine,' I said, trying not to sound ungrateful.

Mrs Parkin wrote notes. 'Have you made contact with any more of the neighbours?'

'No. Just Miss Lewis next door. Then there's the house with the builders and the people next to that are still not there. She talks about the weather. Miss Lewis.' I took another small bite of the chocolate ginger. 'Does she know what happened to me?'

'Enough not to mention, which is for the best at the moment. Dr Williams thinks it's essential for recovery. I think I'll have a top-up.'

I refilled Mrs Parkin's mug and handed her the milk jug, watched her fill her mug almost to overflowing then zoom in to suck up the first mouthful before it could throw itself over the side, watched her bottom lip deposit a pink smear across the china.

'Today I remembered how my granny used to rattle apples,' I said.

Mrs Parkin looked up from helping herself to sugar. 'And why exactly did she do that, Sarah?'

'To see if they were ripe!'

Mrs Parkin's mouth puckered into a smile. The pink lipstick was now restricted to the peripheral regions of her lips, the rest was either consumed along with the chocolate, or left on her mug. I felt the need to look away.

The allotted hour staggered to a close. Mrs Parkin checked her watch.

'Now, Sarah, as always, please contact either myself or one of the doctors if anything changes. You must keep our numbers with you at all times. And if you feel yourself remembering anything at all, call us straight away. That's what we're for.' She closed her folder: 'So, we've had a nice little chat. And I get the impression you're feeling a little more relaxed about everything, so that's super-duper. Next time we'll ...'

'But, Mrs Parkin, I still don't understand how I can do the things I can do, but I can't remember most of my life.'

Mrs Parkin glanced again at her watch. 'Sarah, Dr Gray has explained the difference between remembering how to do things and remembering your own personal experiences, hasn't he? You really must trust his expertise. We can discuss this during next Monday's session if you are still concerned.'

I realised that any further questions would achieve nothing, so I contented myself with watching Mrs Parkin pulling on her coat, walking her to the front door and watching briefly as she strode off in the direction of the Indian restaurant. I closed the door, paused for a moment to compose myself, then wandered through into my bedroom and on into the bathroom. As I stepped inside, I caught sight of my face approaching in the mirror above the sink, a pale face that offered me no explanation, apart from perhaps a sadness in the eyes. I stepped forward to take a closer look. I could make out an old chickenpox mark on my left temple, which was usually masked by my hair. I studied it and tried to capture some echo of a childhood sickbed, of warm tears and calamine. But there was nothing there. I brushed my hair smooth then stepped over to the wall cabinet, took out a slim make-up bag and sat on the edge of the bath to investigate its contents. Everything was unused. I poked around to find a thin maroon tube with gold writing: *Autumn Kiss. Non-smear.* I eased it open and returned to my pale face in the mirror and carefully applied a smooth covering of dull brownish red, snapped up a tissue and closed my lips over it. I assessed my appearance and watched myself smile. It suited me. It complemented the flashes of amber in my light-brown hair. Again, I closed my lips over the tissue then flushed it away, took another look at myself and then returned to the kitchen. The black and white cat was back, sleeping soundly, presumably taking advantage of any residual warmth left by Mrs Parkin's thin bottom. I hurried to clear away the tea things, then picked up the biscuit tin, walked over to the sink and tipped the remaining rich, chocolate gingers into the organic waste. Ginger was probably something I didn't like.

Episode Four

Friday came next. And, as on every Friday throughout that unusual springtime, Annie Dickson was to spend the two hours between ten o'clock and midday cleaning my lounge-diner, kitchen, bedroom and bathroom. I assumed that Mrs Dickson answered directly to Mrs Parkin and suspected that she wasn't really a cleaner at all but rather some kind of middle-aged spy, obliged to report back each week concerning my state of recovery. But I didn't mind the deception too much because Mrs Dickson changed the sheets and did all my laundry and ironing. She was much nicer than Mrs Parkin and not that intrusive, for a spy, although I remember always making sure I was in the same room as her, apart from when she went to the toilet, which was invariably just after she arrived and just before she left. I enjoyed our weekly chats about her last several holidays and her three grandsons and even her troublesome menopause. In fact, that Friday I was really looking forward to seeing her.

'Hello, dear,' said Mrs Dickson. 'Can't seem to make its mind up whether to rain or not. How've you been this week?'

I stepped back to invite her inside. 'I've been fine. Shall I put the kettle on?'

'That would be lovely, Sarah. I'll just spend a penny, if that's all right.'

21

By the time Mrs Dickson joined me in the kitchen, the tea was ready to be poured. She pulled out a chair and sat down. 'No puss today? Just one sugar, please, Sarah, same as usual. Shouldn't really but I like a little bit of sugar and those sweeteners leave a nasty taste in your mouth. Not that you'd know, slim as that. I wish I had your figure. Mind you, poor Mr Dickson would never find me if I was as thin as that.'

Mrs Dickson's chatter always reassured me. And I liked the way she puffed her short, portly body around behind the vacuum cleaner, the way she rolled her sleeves up when she cleaned the worktops. I thought that she must be a perfect granny, the kind of granny one might expect to find living in a cottage in the woods, the sort of granny that a red-cloaked granddaughter might rescue from a grisly fate. I handed Mrs Dickson her tea.

'One sugar, same as usual,' I said. It was almost a joke.

Mrs Dickson chuckled, un-spy-like, then she reached into her bag and pulled out a plastic lunch box. 'I've bought us a little treat. I know how fussy you are about what you eat, but I thought we'd try some of my chocolate cake. The little ones love it.' She flipped off the lid to reveal a rectangular slab. Slightly squashed in transit, its surface was covered in a dense layer of chocolate sprinkles interrupted by an occasional silver ball. I froze. There was something not at all right about the way those little balls were embedded in the chocolate. They couldn't possibly be edible. I'd be bound to breathe one into my lungs and suffocate. And Mrs Dickson would have to try and save me. I felt my fingers knitting together, tried to pull them apart but they were inseparable.

'What's the matter, dear? I thought you liked chocolate. We can put it away if it's upsetting you.'

'No! I do like … but I'm not hungry and …'

Mrs Dickson placed a fat hand on my arm: 'Is it the little balls?' She pushed the lunchbox away. Reproachful. 'I should have known that would be a mistake. The balls, I mean. My boys always pick them off and throw them at each other.' She patted my arm. 'Why don't you fetch us some tea plates and by the time you get back there'll not be a single ball left.' She frowned. 'You do like sprinkles, don't you?'

I went over to the dresser and selected two china plates, held them close to my chest, waited to hear the loose flap of the waste bin then got to my feet. Mrs Dickson was sitting the same as before. In front of her was a completely ball-less slab, its surface pockmarked with a few irregular craters, surrounded by sprinkles. It was excellent cake.

Annie Dickson commenced her cleaning routine. I followed her from room to room, listening, chatting. Perhaps four times in two hours was too many times to thank a person for a cake, but Mrs Dickson seemed pleased, so I felt it must have made amends for the problem with the balls. She was forcing the linen into the washing machine when the phone rang. It rang four times before she mentioned it:

'Would you like me to answer it, Sarah?'

'It's nobody!'

The ringing stopped. Mrs Dickson glanced through the kitchen window and lowered her voice. 'Did Mrs Parkin tell you not to answer the phone?'

'She said it would be someone trying to sell me something.'

Annie Dickson nodded. 'I'll put the kettle on. Then I'll do your bit of ironing.'

It was twenty past twelve before Mrs Dickson pulled her things together and prepared to leave. 'I'd best visit the bathroom before I go,' she said. 'Don't want to be caught short on the way home.'

I waited by my desk. The blind was open. Mrs Dickson always opened it. The traffic could be seen streaming past on the main road. I tried to imagine Mrs Dickson being caught short on her way home. I wondered where she lived. She often mentioned her husband's allotment but I didn't think Islington was known for its horticulture ...

'Ah well, another week over.' She was pulling on her coat.

I stepped away from my desk. 'Do you have far to go?'

Mrs Dickson paused, a brief indecision seemed to silence her.

I caught my breath. I had said a wrong thing. 'I mean ... do you have to catch a bus or something?' I had made a mistake, crossed a boundary that should never have been crossed. 'I'm sorry. I was just worrying. It might rain and you'd get wet. I ...'

'The number forty-one takes me right outside my door. Hornsey. Just past the High Street. Not far if you fly.'

Hornsey? A ripple of fear passed through me. I caught my breath. 'Oh! I don't know it.'

She frowned. 'Anyway, Sarah, don't you worry. A little bit of rain doesn't hurt no one. It'll make my hair grow. Not that I need any more hair. More than you can say for poor Mr Dickson. Bald as an egg.' She picked up her bag. 'Next week we'll give the fridge a good clean. You never know, we might find some crumbs in there.'

I hurried to hold the door as Mrs Dickson stepped through, closed it as quietly as possible then rushed back to the window to catch a last glimpse of her as she disappeared from view. I noticed a silver-grey car pull away behind her. Was that the same car as before? I couldn't make out whether the person driving it was a man or a woman.

I snapped the blind closed, strode back into the kitchen and wrote

HORNSEY faintly on the cover of my shopping pad and was startled by another blast of fear so intense that I had to catch hold of the work surface to prevent myself from falling. I fought to control my breathing, took two, three deep breaths then turned towards the laughter. A child's laughter. I'd heard it before. Always from a long way off. But this time it seemed to be coming from the street outside. Had I accidentally left the front door open? I pushed myself upright and peered cautiously through the lounge. No, the door was closed. I went to the window to check the pavement outside. There was nobody there. Another deep breath. I looked around me. What had I been doing before the laughter? Oh yes ... I went through to the phone and copied down the last incoming number, but as I slipped the small notelet beneath the tea towels, I could feel the bad thoughts breaking through: bad thoughts about things I couldn't remember, intangible things, lost things, things I ought to worry about if I only knew what they were. Bad thoughts about places I didn't know. And people watching, knowing things about me that I didn't know myself. So I took my afternoon pill half an hour early. So that the worrying wouldn't happen.

*

That afternoon I decided that I really would start writing, so I readjusted the blind to allow just enough light to fall onto my desk then went back to the kitchen to fetch my mug of tea. The black and white cat still wasn't there. Some days it didn't appear until the evening. I stepped over and checked through the kitchen window. Sometimes it sat on the wall, close to Miss Lewis's, catching the sun. But today it was overcast. I wandered back into the lounge and sat on the sofa, sipping tea and observing the parallel strips of light falling across my desk. My eyes strayed to its single long drawer. A very old drawer, with a brass keyhole. Unlockable. Its key had probably been lost years ago, thrown away in a pinafore pocket or stolen by a magpie like in a story my granny once told me. Granny Clark. A little like Mrs Dickson.

I finished my tea, placed my mug on the coffee table then strode purposefully to my desk, sat down, removed a slim cardboard folder from the drawer, and read the declaration on the front cover:

Grandma's Apple Stories

I opened the folder and, not for the first time, stared at the top sheet. A sketch: watercolour and faint pencil lines, barely visible. Neatly done, a fat grandma sitting in her armchair, a green apple perched on her lap, just beneath her slipper a title, scratched in red ink: *Annabelle Bramley*. The next sheet was a half-finished sketch, a small girl, colourless apart from her golden curls, holding a green apple up to the sun. At her feet a small pile of apples was coloured yellow. The caption read *Colour them delicious*.

I turned back to Annabelle Bramley, pulled my notepad closer and, for the next twenty-five minutes, failed to write anything at all. For some reason, despite the very clear fable marked out in my head, I was unable to write down those opening sentences about Granny Bramley and her cat, and Farmer Joe's orchard where all the apples turned sour. I had forgotten how to write. I was perfectly able to speak and think and read. I could write down single words. Could even take a run at phrases. But joining the words into sentences was a whole different thing.

After a few moments of hopeless self-loathing, I wandered over to the bookcase set into the shallow recess beside the chimneybreast. Its shelves were bare apart from a flat pile of poetry books halfway down and, below that, a deeper shelf with a few taller volumes, mostly children's literature, an atlas and an elderly dictionary. Among the children's books was a set of eight heavily-illustrated volumes about where things really go when they're lost. I had read these books several times in the last few weeks, each time trying to remember writing them. I eased one out: *The Lost Red Mitten.* Inside there were thirty-two pages, which told the mitten story. Thirty-two pages of coherent sentences, albeit sentences appropriate to a child. Nevertheless, sentences into which I had written proper meaning. Yet, for the last few weeks, every effort to write had been destined to failure, doomed to tiny outbursts. I carried the book back to my desk, sank into my chair and once again read its opening narrative:

Jenny Berry opened her drawer and took out her one red mitten. Then she frowned. She stood up on her tiptoes and looked inside the drawer. The other red mitten was nowhere to be seen. She looked under her socks and scarves. She pulled out her woolly hat and her leg warmers. But however much she searched for that other red mitten, she could not find it. It was LOST. Where could it be?

I traced my hand across the bold print and felt a wave of panic rise up through my chest. And then another, stronger. The afternoon pill could never really stop them happening. It could only dull the thoughts that provoked them. I pulled my blank notepad towards me, snatched up my pen and wrote a single word: LOST.

Episode Five

There were nine items on my vegetable list. Two of them were tomatoes. So I went directly to the tomato section, ripped off three flimsy polythene bags and started to help myself to the mini Italian plums. As I loaded thirty, perhaps forty, of the not really plum-shaped fruits into a bag, I assessed the huge beefsteaks in the next compartment, arranged there so that the mini tomatoes would look especially small and the beefsteaks especially large. I don't like beefsteak tomatoes. Too many pips. So I scooped up twenty normal-sized tomatoes, divided them equally into the two remaining bags and knotted them closed. Beetroot next, red onions, carrots, butternut squash, yellow peppers, cauliflower, courgettes. I rechecked my list then did a quick scan for possible omissions. Perhaps a frivolous bag of baby salad leaves flown in from Mexico, half a world away, then drenched in spring water to wash away the taint of foreign grime? Perhaps a bunch of British asparagus, first of the season? No, there's something not right about asparagus. I turned the list over, read STRAWBERRIES, and pushed the trolley towards fruit, pausing briefly to read the name of an apple I did not recognise: Fuji.

'Hi! You also shop on Saturday!'

I caught my breath, turned. 'Sometimes.' I glanced into his trolley. 'You eat a lot of fruit and vegetables!' There I was, being bold again.

'Five a day. And some. And you eat a lot of tomatoes!' He moved closer to me and started to sort through a pile of bagged-up grapes. 'I read somewhere that if you eat a lot of tomatoes your skin turns orange because of the carotenes.' He looked straight at me. 'Obviously not in your case.'

I suffered a stultifying wave of self-consciousness. The lipstick was probably making my skin look even paler than usual. Perhaps the carotenes would have been a good thing. Why was I so pale? It was probably all those weeks under artificial lights. I felt bleached, etiolated. I couldn't work out what to say so I turned back to the contents of my trolley and shunted the onions away from the squash.

'I'm sorry, that was rude of me,' he said. Then suddenly he was abandoning the grapes and walking around my trolley. Towards me. I waited for panic to close my throat.

'Did you finish your writing?'

The panic didn't happen. I just felt awkward. The way anyone would feel. 'Not quite. I've been suffering from writer's block.' I felt myself smile.

He smiled back. 'I've heard a large cappuccino can work wonders with writer's block.' He put his head to one side. 'Perhaps a latte?'

But our exchange was interrupted by a woman barging past and parking her shopping and strapped-in infant alongside my trolley, boxing me in. The child dragged itself round, twisting its head until it looked as if it might snap completely off its neck, and stared at me, scrutinising my face, all the while its mouth opening more and more until, for no apparent reason, it emitted a penetrating shriek of laughter. Laughter. It reminded me of … I caught my breath.

'I have to get back,' I whispered, as my throat closed over.

He glanced at the child then took a couple of paces back to offer me an escape route.

'Just Thursdays and Saturdays then,' he said. 'I find Tuesdays are also great fun. Over by the tins of tuna.'

Another shriek of laughter.

I pushed forward, avoiding the gaze of the wide-eyed infant. The child kicked out repeatedly as I squeezed past, but its feet failed to reach my trolley. I mustered another smile and hurried away, holding my breath. If you repeatedly suspend your breathing, as if you were trying to defeat hiccups, the self-imposed breathlessness can delay the crisis, check the tyranny of panic just long enough for you to make it through the checkout and the driving rain to the safety of your car. Without looking back.

By late afternoon it had stopped raining and the edges of the grey clouds were trimmed with a golden white promise of better things to come. There was something primitive and reassuring about a sky like that and, as I watched from my kitchen window, hope seemed to radiate down onto the flat roof of my garden shed. I swigged down my four o'clock pill and caught sight of the red and green apple, still resting in the fruit bowl, untouched since two days ago. Its skin was perfect, unbruised, nothing that might identify its previous traumatic impact with my shoe, nothing that might reveal its singular history. I thought I might like to paint it. I went to touch it then pulled back my hand as a beam of light burst through the window and reflected off its waxed surface. What an image! I remember thinking that, if I had a camera, I would photograph it and then copy the patterns of light frozen, unchanging. I turned towards the lounge. There were cardboard boxes in the big cupboard, opposite the cramped dining area. Between the kitchen and the lounge. I had no idea what they contained. Perhaps a camera. Perhaps now was the time to discover what I owned. So I left the Braeburn basking in the afternoon sunshine and went to investigate.

I positioned myself in front of the cupboard and, after a moment of breathless anticipation, pulled open its doors and gazed up at the unreasonable amount of china, at the rows of identical glasses. I tried to imagine the banquets such splendid tableware might deserve. I couldn't believe that my life had ever included so many people eating food. That this small apartment could once have housed occasions that required quite so many bowls and platters. A lower shelf was crammed with an assortment of vases. Could I ever have been given lilies, carnations, roses, in sufficient quantities to justify so many vases? I reached up and pinged a long-stemmed glass and listened to the crystal ring clear in my empty life. The sound recalled a moment: honeysuckle, pink rose petals falling on to white linen. Then it was gone.

Lower down there were two rows of black and white boxes: five smaller ones along the bottom shelf and three larger ones on the floor below, all covered in the same disgusting geometric design. I pulled out one of the smaller boxes and read the label stuck to one side: CDs. I decided against opening it. The next box was labelled BRIC-A-BRAC. It contained a mass of unfamiliar ornaments. I eased out a tacky water-filled dome, held it towards the light and watched its chaos of pink and blue glitter snowing down onto a jumbled heap of objects: a tabby cat, a rag doll, a book, an oversized red mitten. Around its base a gold inscription read: *Raggedy Lyme – where your LOST things hide.* I tipped the snow globe upside down, watched its sparkles collect into a heap, strode round to place it on the bare mantelpiece and left the unlikely snow coming to rest around a past I was unable to remember.

The next three boxes were CHRISTMAS TRIMMINGS. I lifted a lid and stared at the network of tinsel and coloured balls, peered round into the lounge and tried to recall a tree covered in all these packed-up things. But I couldn't. I prodded everything back into place then pulled at one of the bigger boxes, read the label half-obscured down one side: BOOKS, pushed the lid upwards and read a few titles: *The Bread Bible*; *Wedding Etiquette*; *The Canapé Banquet*. I had no idea why I owned them. I didn't feel like the kind of person that cooked. In fact, I didn't feel like the kind of person that did anything.

The next box said CAMERAS. Cameras? I eased it out onto the carpet and lifted the lid. So much black camera equipment! I dragged the box nearer the table and started to set out the various bits of equipment. After ten minutes or so I had arranged everything according to presumed function. I selected a small digital camera and poked buttons. Nothing. It probably needed charging. I read its name: Fuji; sorted through the various adaptors until I found the correct charger, plugged it into the camera, carried it through to the kitchen and wiggled the charger plug in next to the kettle. A red light flashed on. Suddenly the black and white cat was rubbing itself against my legs. Without thinking, I bent over and stroked its head. The sensation of my hand passing over its fur took me by surprise. It felt familiar. I watched the animal carry its affection over to the table leg and rub itself against that.

'Do you remember me from before, puss?'

Purring reverberated throughout the kitchen. I watched the animal's dedicated rubbing against the dishwasher. Then I strode purposefully back to the china cupboard and eased a fine willow-pattern platter out from under its matching tureen, carried it back to the kitchen, set it down on the floor and emptied a heap of cat biscuits down amidst the oriental lovers. After a few tentative attempts at stretching its neck, the resourceful animal took up a position in the middle of the vast plate and ate from around its own feet.

Strangely satisfied, I turned to check the camera. The light was still red and the sunlight had already faded. I glanced over at the apple, dull now against the ripening bananas. Oh well, perhaps there would be sunshine tomorrow and, if not, there was probably a flash option. I went to investigate the pile of instruction manuals and discovered a chunky Fuji booklet full of symbols and diagrams of people taking photographs. I carried it into the lounge and started to read, paused, then looked at the mantelpiece, empty apart from its newly-stranded snow globe, at the bare walls, at the bookcase with its barren shelves. I thought of my bedside table with just a lamp and an alarm clock. All that camera equipment and no photographs.

The third large storage box did not contain the ALBUMS its label promised. It contained nothing.

Episode Six

Sunday was always a difficult day but that Sunday began particularly badly. The curtains were still drawn against the night when I was startled from sleep by a shrill burst of laughter. A child's laughter, over as soon as I was aware of it. I sat up and stared at my bedroom door. It was definitely a child's laughter. I might have heard it before. I might have even been dreaming about a child laughing. I couldn't be sure, because if I did have dreams, as soon as I was awake they were beyond remembering. One moment I would be asleep and the next moment I would be completely awake with never anything left of my sleeping, apart from, occasionally, an anxiety. And, that day, a little girl's laughter.

I checked the alarm: 05:34. I didn't want to be awake as early as that; my morning pills were not due to be taken for almost two and a half hours. I slumped back onto my pillows and tried to go back to sleep but the anxiety left over from dreaming grew worse, focussed upon nothing, and became unmanageable. Became fear. I watched the clock change. At 06:01 I wandered through to the kitchen to make tea and get my pills ready. The black and white cat was asleep on the doormat, just below the cat flap. A quick flick of its ear acknowledged my presence. I filled a bowl with milk and lowered it to the floor then walked over to add MILK to my shopping pad. It was then that I noticed HORNSEY written faint on the paper cover. And, for some forgotten reason, I thought of Mrs Dickson.

By eight o'clock I had showered, dressed, cleaned the refrigerator and taken my pills. At some point during all of this the cat must have slipped away, probably when I was dealing with the salad drawer. It was obviously off for the morning in search of the sun. I carried my tea through to the sofa and sat until quarter to ten, when the shops would be preparing to open and I'd be able to wander past their windows lost in the crowd.

*

I made my way towards the High Street, enjoying the fresh breeze and the anonymity. Just by Islington Green I nipped into a newsagent and bought an A-Z, then walked the short distance to Starbucks, bought a latte and sat by the window turning the spiral-bound pages. I found my own street, traced my finger from the Indian restaurant along Essex Road towards the Green then on to the likely location of Starbucks and the map I was currently holding in my hand. I turned pages and for some reason noticed the word HORNSEY written in capital letters. Did I recognise that name? I flicked back the pages. According to the scale, Hornsey was about three and a half miles to the north of where I was sitting, a good hour's walk, probably more. Mrs Parkin had said I should think of going for a walk. Perhaps I would walk to Hornsey. A man in a dirty anorak sat down at the next table. I kept my head down and studied the route that led north from Islington Green. It stretched across more than one page. I opened my bag, took out my notebook with attached pencil and marked the route, a process which demanded a certain awkwardness with the attached notebook. I feared I might be drawing attention to myself. I could smell the man at the next table. It was time to leave.

Turning left out of Starbucks, I started to walk towards Highbury Station, checking my map every so often to confirm the sequence of street names. There were a lot of roads. The walk would take longer than anticipated. I quickened my pace along Holloway Road and eventually came to the junction with Hornsey Road. How convenient those old names were, in the days when things were less complicated, when roads told you where they were going or where they had just come from.

I made my way past the university buildings and then it happened. It might have been the few drops of rain falling on my face or perhaps the noise of the traffic, but all at once the map I was looking at ceased to make sense. Perhaps I had accidentally turned a page too many. But the ones either side were also meaningless and now I was no longer sure which page I'd been following before the raindrops. I spun round to look back the way I had come but recognised nothing. I tried to calm myself: things always look different on the way back. I remember looking down at the thick white coil that was binding the pages together. Pages and pages of meaningless colours and lines, slightly blurred. And when I looked up I had no idea where I had come from or where I'd been going. My head started to spin, lurching first one way and then the other like a toy top that was losing momentum, about to spin out of control. I knew that if I allowed this spinning to continue I would never find my way home, so I threw the useless spiral-bound pages to the ground and tried to hold my head still, placed my hands over my ears then knelt down to feel the earth beneath me. To anchor myself. That was the biggest mistake of all because Miss Grainger had said that all objects in space are in motion and now I could feel that motion, see that motion. I could feel my eyes racing from side to side to keep up with it. I was the only stationary thing in the entire universe and the universe was spinning all around me: the stars, the Earth, the pavement. I had to make it STOP!

'You all right?'

'Is she breathing? Shall I call an ambulance?'

'Did she fall over?'

'I didn't see. I just saw her lying there.'

'I think she fell over.'

'What's going on?'

'She fell over.'

'OK, you lot, stand back, give her some space. You all right, love?'

'What's up, Joe?'

'Looks like she's taken a tumble. Seems to be OK.'

'Where you going, love? Do you know where you're going?'

*

The police car deposited me outside my front door. The policeman called Joe asked me if I needed to contact anyone. I told him I was OK. I hadn't been going anywhere in particular. I had felt faint. I had forgotten to eat breakfast. I hoped I hadn't frightened those young people. Thank you. No, there was no one to contact.

That evening I worked out how to use the flash option on my camera and took several photographs of the Braeburn. Then I peeled it and ate it. It tasted of moss and cream and autumn rain. And a promise of being normal. I cleared the peelings into the organic waste then packed all the camera equipment, including the Fuji, loaded now with its own apple story, back into the storage box, and stowed it away in anticipation of tomorrow's Mrs Parkin.

Episode Seven

Mrs Parkin's Monday morning visit was invariably more difficult than her Thursday afternoon visit, probably because Saturdays and Sundays were two silent days, and I was never really sure, after a weekend devoid of conversation, whether my voice would actually work on Monday morning. It helped if the black and white cat was there first thing: I could practise. But this week was different. Yesterday there had been the conversation with the two policemen. And Saturday I had spoken to the person called Matthew Parry. So today I was reasonably confident.

Mrs Parkin arrived just after eleven. Things were proceeding quite well when, just into the tea-drinking ceremony, I heard myself say: 'I was wondering about my photographs.'

Mrs Parkin withdrew the bourbon that she was about to insert between her teeth: 'Photographs, Sarah?'

I sensed evasion. 'Of my family? And I must have had friends.'

'You had a very small social network, my dear.' She bit into the bourbon and communicated around the crunching. 'Your photographs are in safe keeping. Dr Williams believes a sudden influx of such information might precipitate further crises. He's convinced that a natural recovery of past experiences is the correct way forward.'

I remember swallowing my frustration as Mrs Parkin took another bite. But then I happened to notice a minute bourbon crumb fly out of her mouth and land on her jacket, just below her left lapel. Grateful for this self-imposed blemish, for the disempowering effect it had on Mrs Parkin, I summoned the will to insist.

'But how does he know, Mrs Parkin?'

This time Mrs Parkin allowed her mouth to clear: 'In actual fact, Sarah, nobody *knows*. But Dr Williams is, *as you must be aware*, an eminent neuropsychologist. And a recognised authority in the areas of schizophrenia and hallucinatory psychoses.' She took a deep breath to fuel her appreciation. 'He has published extensively in these areas, and he is very interested in your case. He believes that if you are ever to recall those years of your past that are currently denied you, then it is through your *own gradual efforts* that you will do so. Not through some dramatic exposure to *secondary experiences*.'

I stared into my tea and said nothing. Mrs Parkin continued.

'I suggest that, if you are no longer satisfied with our recommendations, re your agreement, then you must discuss this with Dr Gray. I am only here to help you rehabilitate, help you blend back into society. And I congratulate you on your efforts so far, Sarah. Now, is there anything to report?'

I suddenly felt exhausted. This was a game of language and the rules were beyond me. 'I went for a walk yesterday,' I said.

'Excellent!' She drained her mug. 'Anywhere exciting?'

'No, not far. Would you like a top-up?'

As I handed over Mrs Parkin's refilled mug, I allowed my gaze to fall upon the bourbon crumb still hanging precariously, drawing attention to Mrs Parkin's mean bosom. I focussed on the crumb.

'I remember my Granny Clark from when I was small. Wouldn't it be appropriate for me to see a photograph of *her*?'

Mrs Parkin began to flip through her folder. 'I'm not sure there is a picture of your paternal grandmother. I'll mention it to the doctors.' She helped herself to another biscuit. 'Do sit down, Sarah.' I remained standing. Mrs Parkin wrote a brief note, licking her lips as she did so. 'I see you have a scan scheduled for tomorrow. Now, you know what to expect with that, don't you?'

'There's a button to press if I want it to stop. Dr Williams shows me photos. And tells me things, to see what my brain does when I hear them.'

'Yes, that's right. Now, are you going to sit down?'

I leaned against the refrigerator and sipped my tea, allowing myself a moment's belligerence. 'And will the things he tells me be about what happened to make me forget the last twenty-five years of my life?'

Mrs Parkin rolled her eyes. 'There will probably be some autobiographical detail. I have not been informed as to what will be included on this occasion.'

I watched her reading her notes. The notes about me that I was not allowed to see. Why wasn't I allowed to see them? Why did Dr Williams never include a photo of Granny Clark? They only ever showed me photos of people I didn't know. And there must have been a photo of my grandma somewhere. People don't just die and leave nothing. They leave photographs to help you remember. And I did remember Granny Clark: her curly grey hair and kind blue eyes and … paternal? Had she referred to her as my *paternal* grandmother? I stared at Mrs Parkin.

'Why was she called Granny Clark?'

'Beg pardon?'

'You said my *paternal* grandmother, that's my father's mother, isn't it? She should have had the same name as me. That's right, isn't it? But my name's Blake. It says so on my driving licence. And the books on the shelf.' I could hear the panic in my voice. I banged my mug down on the worktop and felt hot tea slop over my hand. 'I am Sarah Blake, aren't I? That *was* my name in the clinic. On the tubes of blood. She was my granny, wasn't she?'

'Sarah, yes. Try and calm down. I believe there were multiple marriages. Something of the kind. Your grandmother Clark was very active in your life until she died ...' She balanced open the front of her folder, making sure that the pages she was referring to were kept out of sight by the pages that followed. '... just before your ninth birthday. You lived with her after your parents separated.' She looked up at me, her face almost sympathetic. 'I'm sure there *will* be a photograph. And Sarah, my dear, you must try not to work yourself up into a panic like this. I'll mention this little episode to the doctors. It might be advisable to review your drug regime.'

I took a deep breath. 'How old was I when my parents separated? Am I allowed to know *that*?'

Again Mrs Parkin referred to her folder. 'You were two years old. Your father has proven to be untraceable. There appears to be no record of him for the last three decades.'

I felt as if the very will to live was being drained from my body. I glanced at the wall clock: 10:35. Another twenty-five minutes of this awful woman, helping me to blend back into society. And all I wanted to do was go to my bed and sleep until all this was over. I watched Mrs Parkin brush her skirt. The activity dislodged the lapel crumb so that it fell away, along with the greater part of my fragile confidence. But there were still questions to be asked and, if I didn't ask them right then, they would be festering in my mind until Mrs Parkin's next visit.

'Mrs Parkin, when did my mother die?'

She seemed uncertain. 'Sarah, I do think you need to discuss these matters with Dr Gray. Suffice it to say that you had a full and productive life before your current condition, and it is that life which the doctors want to give back to you. You must trust them, my dear. Now, tell me about your writing.'

*

Later that afternoon, my tiredness abandoned, I investigated my laptop. It was a disappointing experience. It turned on. Offered opportunities. But it held no vestige of any previous involvement in my life. So I spent a while playing Spider Solitaire. I realised that I must have played it before. But the trouble with such distractions is that they are not distracting enough and, as I dragged each card towards inevitable victory, I mulled over those two words. Schizophrenia? Psychoses? Did those things take away memories? I turned to my bookcase, fetched the ancient dictionary and turned its unreasonably thin pages. Psychoses? That sounded a bit like 'psychiatrist' so it undoubtedly began with the same deceitful letters. I flicked through the pages until I arrived at **psychiatry**, bold at the top of the page. Scanned down: **psychic – psychokinesis – psychology – psychopath – psychosis.**

Psychosis. That was probably it: 'loss of contact with reality. Delusions or hallucinations'. Hallucinations? I flicked back and the pages fell open at a card. A postcard. A black and white picture of a narrow beach and beyond it cliffs rising out of the sea. There were stranded boats, a few grey people along the shoreline, walking, watching the breaking waves. I turned the card over. Nothing. Just faint legends at the top and bottom:

Sidmouth * Lyme Regis * Seaton * Beer Cove
Beer Cove, Devon.

Places I had never heard of. I inserted the black and white beach back between the flimsy pages and investigated **hallucination** and, after further effort, **schizophrenia**. At the end of my research I was little wiser than before.

BEER COVE

'Why are you doing that, Daddy?'

'Because the fossils are hiding inside and if we bang the shale ... this rock is called shale. If we bang it in a special way, it pops open and you can see where they're hiding.'

'Daddy, can I hold the hammer and bang the rocks?'

'Well, I think it's a bit heavy for you. And, besides, you need to keep hold of Dolly in case she falls in the water.'

'*Daddy*, she's not Dolly. She's Raggedy!'

'Well, you don't want Raggedy to fall into one of those big waves, do you?'

'No! Oh, the rock's broke!'

'Yes, and here, look, there's our fossil. It's called an ammonite.'

'But it's made of gold nearly!'

'Yes. Would you like to take it back home with you?'

'Will Grandma let me?'

'We'll ask her, shall we? Here she comes now. With our ice creams. And after we've eaten them, we can go back to the house for tea. And then we can go upstairs and look at the stars.'

'Through the telenscope?'

'Yes.'

'Will Grandma look too?'

'Yes, she will ... Hi, Mum. We've found a perfect ammonite.'

'It's made of nearly gold, Grandma.'

'Sarah would like to take it home, if that's OK.'

Lily Clark frowned at her son. 'Jack, her shoes are soaked!'

Episode Eight

My appointment was for 11.30 but I always arrived early and used the time to visit the shop in the hospital concourse. That day I bought a glossy magazine, because its cover promised an article about what to wear on a first date. Was I already imagining, hoping there'd be a first date? At 11.45 a nurse escorted me from the bright, unnatural silence of the waiting area to Geraint Williams' consulting room, a much less lavish setting than the private rooms he shared with Dr Gray, close by Regent's Park. Dr Williams was not alone. Two men and a woman, all white-coated, were squashed into chairs alongside one another, to the left of Dr Williams' modest desk. His seat swivelled as he stood.

'Hello, Sarah.' He stepped round and shook my hand.

He always did this so I was used to it. But then he placed a hand on my elbow, which I was not used to, and pressured me slightly in the direction of the three other people. 'Sarah, let me introduce my three associates. If you're agreeable they'll be observing this morning's session. Then in the following weeks they'll each interview you independently.'

I nodded. It didn't occur to me to ask why.

'Excellent!' said Dr Williams. He introduced: Drs Shoumi Mustafa, perhaps forty, who was squarish and black; Sam Clegg, younger, tall and slim, with smiling eyes; and Della Brown, thirty-five-ish, a slight, unrelaxed woman, whose fingers bore the stains from frequent nicotine and whose white coat looked several sizes too big for her. They each stood in turn, shook my hand, mumbled a greeting and sat down. It was a well-synchronised performance. I would have liked to see them do it again.

Dr Williams indicated my usual chair, opposite his, then walked back round to his own seat. He exchanged a few niceties with me then briefed the Associates on my apparent inability to remember any personal experiences beyond my first nine years. I had not heard him refer to my 'apparent inability' before that day and I wasn't sure what he meant by it. He engaged specifically with Della Brown:

'Memories concerning one's personal experiences are processed and stored apart from those which relate to normal everyday function. This is why Sarah is able to continue to live a normal adult life without being able to recall anything that has happened in it. The imaging technique can go some way to confirming this memory loss.'

I wanted to interrupt and tell him that this was not my normal adult life. But I knew that would be inappropriate. Della Brown gave a brief nod, glanced at me, then looked away.

Geraint Williams followed this up with a run-through of the day's imminent procedures, speaking mostly to the Associates and only occasionally to me. I noticed his expression change as he turned from them to me, listened to his tone transform from one of authority to practiced friendliness, watched his smile come and go. It was a handsome smile. In fact, he was a handsome man, probably in his early fifties, clean shaven, almost polished, but I disliked him. There was just something about his confidence that was unappealing.

Perhaps it was the mastery this accomplished stranger had over my life. Perhaps his suit was a little too expensive. Sitting opposite him, I always felt as if I had been fitted out in a charity shop. Even that day, when I was wearing my new boots and leather jacket.

The first scan was scheduled for twelve-thirty. I settled myself on to the flat plinth and felt the pads move to hold me still. I used to hate my head being held motionless in that way, but at least, by now, I had proved that I could lie sufficiently rigid for them no longer to consider the bite bar necessary. I lay staring at the roof of the tunnel, its ceiling some six inches above my nose, and waited for the noise to begin. The instructions then the banging. I always worried that something would distract them and I'd be left in there, unable to wriggle my way out. As usual, they asked me to identify sets of objects: musical instruments, flowers. I liked the flowers, I was good at recognising them, but I was hopeless with the numerous things that looked like violins. And I failed utterly when it came to images of places. The endless sequence of buildings and streets meant nothing to me. Then came the faces. Of course, I recognised the Queen every time, and a couple of individuals from the newspapers in the local shop, although I had no idea why they were newsworthy. There was a pause, and then Dr Williams' voice reverberated inside my ears.

'Sarah, I'm going to show you three photographs of people, each one for ten seconds. I want you to study them carefully and try to hold the images in your mind. Then, after a pause, I'll show you a second sequence of photographs and we'll see if you are able to recognise any of the people from the first batch. Try to relax as you look at the first three photographs. Do you understand these instructions?'

I hated speaking into that microphone. 'Yes!'

The images appeared on the screen: an old woman, a man, then a young woman with long blonde hair. Then the pause. I wasn't sure how long the pause was going to last. I knew I ought to be remembering the three images but I couldn't stop wondering why they never included a picture of Granny Clark. The pause was lasting too long. My mind began to wander: a girl on tiptoes looking for her mitten; a mandarin's daughter fleeing with her lover, his green eyes sparkling when he smiled. The second sequence began. A photo of an old woman. Then a man. That's when the laughter began, just audible above the sound of the scanner. It seemed to be coming from inside and outside my ears. Then to make matters worse somebody's voice, probably Dr Williams', was rattling around in the chamber. The laughter intensified. Then the man disappeared and a new image filled the screen: a young woman, her face vibrating, her long blonde hair scintillating beyond seeing, ejecting electric blue sparks into my tube chamber. The noise was intolerable. I felt the communication button in my hand and concentrated on not pressing it. Then the screen became blank and the scanner became silent and the laughter was gone. Dr Williams' voice rang clear in my ears, asking me if the three photos had evoked any memories of images or sounds, whether there was anything I wanted to mention. I said no, I didn't want to mention anything. There was a pause and then he asked me to observe a further batch of three: an old woman, a man and a younger, fair-haired woman, but I failed to recognise any of the images. The sounds died away and a different voice, I think Sam Clegg's, asked me had any of the images seemed familiar. I told him the flowers and the Queen but, apart from that, nothing.

A nurse took me back to the waiting area, where I was expected to sit and wait for Dr Williams to summon me into his room to tell me that the scans were very encouraging. That's what he always did. But today I had my magazine to occupy me. So I flicked through the glossy pages full of women pouting in their underwear, smearing on make-up, simpering over jewellery. I scanned the article about a first date and then one about losing weight – I was reasonably certain I didn't need to do that. I paused over a recipe for guacamole. Something told me I liked guacamole so I pulled out my notepad and started to copy down the ingredients.

'Have you managed to find something interesting in there?' I looked up. It was one of the Associates. The woman. I recognised her despite the fact that she was no longer wearing her too-big white coat. She was looking down at me, unsmiling. 'Do you take that magazine regularly, Sarah?'

'I don't think so.' I felt awkward. 'I'm sorry, Dr … I've forgotten your name. I wasn't really listening when Dr Williams introduced you all. Too many names all together.'

'I can imagine. It's Brown. Della Brown. Do you think that's the kind of magazine you usually read?'

'I don't know.' She took a seat. Two chairs away from me, although I could still smell her clothes and her stale cigarette breath. 'I'm waiting to see Dr Williams. He usually speaks to me after the scans.'

'Yes, the scans. I was very interested in your responses. Does Dr Williams never ask you about being found unconscious, how you came to be on that particular beach?'

I could feel my nails digging into the palm of my hand. 'Dr Williams knows I can't remember that. I've told Dr Gray everything I can remember.'

'Ah yes, Dr Gray.' She glanced past me then pulled a packet of cigarettes out of her jacket pocket and held them ready. 'I was interested in your inability to recognise the images of people you knew so well. People so close to you.'

I stared her. 'Which people?' But my question was cut off by a burst of childish laughter echoing along the corridor. I turned to see where it had come from and caught sight of Dr Clegg striding towards us.

Della Brown got to her feet. 'Sam, hello. We were just discussing Sarah's magazine.'

Sam Clegg regarded her for a moment frozen-faced and then smiled down at me. 'Dr Williams is ready for you now, Sarah. Shall we go?'

*

On the way home, I persuaded myself into the supermarket, went straight to fruit and vegetables and picked up an avocado. It was as solid as a rock, but by the weekend it would be ripe and I would make guacamole, using the recipe I'd found in my magazine. I took out my notebook and read the list of ingredients, found chillies and a carton of sour cream. Then I went to the bank of cereal, stretched up but withdrew my hand at the last minute. Somebody, just anybody, might notice a too-soon box of cornflakes. But I definitely needed more tuna. I collected twelve small tins then headed for the checkout. While I was waiting I allowed myself a quick look around. Disappointment. I exchanged a few unwelcome words with the checkout woman then wheeled my trolley outside and was just tessellating it back into place, when I became aware that somebody was standing behind me.

'I'll give you a pound for that trolley!'

I turned, exhilarated. 'I'll expect to see your money first!' It was a proper joke.

He laughed, put his hand in his jacket pocket and pulled out some loose change. 'Here, take your pick.' I looked at the pile of coins. There was a pound coin towards the bottom. But it might mean touching. Perhaps noticing my hesitation, he plucked up the coin and handed it over, slipped the rest back into his pocket and stepped forward to claim the trolley. 'I think you've grown,' he said. 'You're definitely taller.'

I laughed. I couldn't remember doing that before. Was laughing something you would forget? I took a step back. 'It's probably my boots.'

He pulled the trolley free then turned to face me. 'Maybe. I take it you're in a hurry?'

'Yes!'

'Too busy to go for a quick coffee.'

'Yes!'

'Perhaps another time.'

'Yes, I will!'

He paused. 'What? You'll come for a coffee another time?'

I was almost suffocating with excitement. 'I'll come now.'

MRI Suite

'Well, Sam, a perfect confirmation. Not only is Ms Blake suffering a progressive retrograde memory loss but she has also clearly demonstrated highly-focussed anterograde amnesia.' Sam Clegg nodded his agreement. Geraint Williams continued, 'Clearly, her memory dysfunction, regarding specific people and events, denies her all knowledge of the December incident, and any detail that might contribute to its recollection. As you can see from the scans …' He indicated the numerous images illuminated on the wall behind him. '… there is no evidence of left or right cerebral pathology, traumatic or otherwise.'

He leaned back in his chair and pressed his fingers together. 'Language areas of the brain demonstrate normal function. Her language skills appear to be slightly diminished but they remain above average. We have been unable to demonstrate any abnormalities: biochemical, physiological or morphological. The angiograms reveal a healthy circulation. Indeed, we have a physically normal thirty-five-year-old woman, yet functional MRI reveals that she is unable both to recall most of her past and to correctly process and retain new memories specifically related to the traumatic incident. She remains convincingly ignorant of exposure to autobiographical information however often it is presented.' He allowed his fingers to interlock. 'This young woman is literally losing her mind before our eyes.'

Sam Clegg frowned. 'Dr Williams, how aware is Ms Blake of the dynamic nature of her condition? She reported that she failed to recognise the three individuals when their images were presented for the second time but the intense cerebral activity would suggest otherwise. And yet when their images were presented the third time, there was no activity and no recognition. And she displays no awareness that she might have forgotten the images previously presented.' He referred to his notes. 'There appears to be no reference to the anterograde component of her condition in any of the transcripts of her interviews with yourself or Dr Gray.'

'Bob has recommended that this information is withheld for as long as the patient remains unaware of it. To avoid confounding anxieties. Although, I must say that I'm convinced that if she were to be told she is forgetting details of her previous life, however many times it is presented, this fact would also not be retained. Indeed, there is a possibility that providing data pertaining to the December event may exacerbate further repression. We believe that the intense activity you witnessed indicates that the process of repression is either occurring or about to occur, heralded, I believe, by the patient experiencing what she believes to be extrinsic noise, an aura, quite possibly laughter, which she either instantly forgets or is unwilling to mention, but which quite definitely accompanies the erosion of new information.'

Sam Clegg's frown deepened. 'Dr Gray believes that Miss Blake is being denied this information by her own mind.'

Geraint Williams smile was quite derisory. 'And what do *you* believe, Dr Clegg?'

Sam Clegg closed his notebook and, for a few moments, held Geraint Williams' gaze. 'I believe that the MRI session I have just observed demonstrated very clearly the dynamic nature of Sarah Blake's amnesia. And the very focussed and repressive activity of her unconscious mind.'

'Quite so, we have all been able to witness its *activity* but, unfortunately, not its essence. Indeed, we are confronting something invisible and intangible. Personally, I prefer my enemies to be visible and removable. Do you imagine, Sam, that you will be able to defeat this invisible foe and save our attractive Ms Blake from succumbing to a completely empty head?'

Sam Clegg was not one moved easily to contempt but, after this and two previous meetings, he was certain that he loathed this man who seemed to be able to find entertainment in the misfortune of others. He paused to consider Geraint Williams' challenge. Then he smiled. 'If I might be so bold as to borrow your metaphor, Dr Williams, I am confident that, if we can fully understand the intention of Sarah Blake's unconscious antagonist, then this invisible foe will have unwittingly revealed itself to us. And, thereby, will have fashioned its own defeat. In the meantime, I tend to agree with Dr Gray that Ms Blake should be spared any knowledge of the progressive nature of her condition.'

Episode Nine

'You'll come now?'

We were beginning to cause an obstruction. He turned and addressed a woman ferreting in her purse.

'Madam, please allow me to present you with this trolley.'

The woman gave him a doubtful glance then continued to scrabble. 'Will you take two fifty pence pieces?' she asked.

'No, please!' He handed her the trolley. 'I have a pocket full of change already.'

The woman gave another doubtful look then accepted the trolley. I waited for her to head off before whispering, 'What about your shopping?'

'It can wait. Where shall we go? There's a little bistro just along the road.'

I hugged my bag. I couldn't believe what I was doing. It was grossly irresponsible given the circumstances. Selfish even. But I was doing it, and that was that.

'Shall I put my shopping in my car?' I said, glancing at my Escort and feeling the need to get inside it and drive away.

*

The walk to the bistro was not too traumatic. He did most of the shouting above the noise of traffic. I tried to respond but found it difficult to make myself heard, so I resigned myself to letting him handle the conversation. After less than five minutes, he steered us off the main road, into a narrow side street. Terracotta pots and broken paving stones were in abundance. The bistro manager seemed to recognise him. He accompanied us to a table towards the rear of the seating area, dimly lit, away from the few other tables that were occupied, and pulled out my chair. I smiled gratitude, sat down and tried to look relaxed. I noticed the man at the bar eyeing us from behind a spike of artificial orchids.

We looked at each other across the vast expanse of red and white chequered tablecloth. He prodded a menu towards me. It proved illegible, so I guessed. 'Cappuccino, please.'

There was a pause, which showed all the signs of becoming awkward, but he hailed the waiter and ordered two large cappuccinos, turned back to me and smiled. And I couldn't help noticing how very bright his eyes were in the dim light.

'So, what shall we talk about?' he said.

My stomach churned. 'I'm hopeless at conversation. You've probably noticed.'

'You could start by telling me your name.'

My stomach churned again. 'I'm Sarah … Blake.'

'Sarah Blake, the author. You know, Sarah Blake, I thought it was going to take a lot longer than this to get you to come for coffee …'

Great! I'd been overenthusiastic. So much for Mrs Parkin's advice regarding blending into society. All that stuff about dress sizes and catching a bus and nothing useful like how many times to say no to a cappuccino. I felt hideously self-conscious and the man behind the bar was definitely watching me.

'So I'm delighted. I was beginning to think I'd have to shop three times a day forever just to run into you. There's a limit to how much broccoli even a committed vegetarian can eat!'

'Are you a vegetarian?'

'Yes. Aren't you?'

'No.'

A frown flickered across his face. 'I hope you're not prejudiced against my kind. I occasionally eat dead fish. And oysters. They're animals, aren't they?'

I laughed, desperate to say something. Something not stupid. Then suddenly, unexpectedly, my mind unjumbled. 'What do you do?' I said. 'I've told you I write so now you have to tell me what you do.'

'Well, obviously something that means I can nip out to the supermarket three times a day and hang around drinking cappuccino.' He folded his arms. 'You're not going to believe this but ... I'm an agent.'

'You sell houses?'

He laughed. 'No, a *literary* agent.' He leaned back in his chair. 'I allow authors to take me to lunch to interest me in their books. And then I get publishers to take me to lunch so I can offer them the books of the authors that bought me the best lunches.'

'It's a wonder you ever need to buy food!' I remember being really proud of myself for saying that, especially when he started to laugh. I laughed too. 'What kind of books?'

Another slight frown. 'Some young adult. Mostly younger.' He paused as the coffees arrived. 'So, Sarah Blake, who do you publish with?'

Panic. Who did I publish with? I watched him sink a sugar lump through the cappuccino froth and, just when it seemed that my only sensible option was to run away, I remembered the name on the citation pages in my collection of LOST stories.

'J.D. Hillier Publishing,' I said. 'Have you heard of them?'

'Of course. The MD's even bought me a few lunches.'

We sipped our cappuccinos. He mentioned a series he had just placed. I listened, aware that my hand might be touching my mouth too many times between mouthfuls. But I couldn't stop myself. I was worried I might be leaving chocolate powder on my face. I had a sudden mental image of Mrs Parkin's diminishing lipstick and checked my cup. No smudges: *Autumn Kiss. Non-smear.*

'Would you like something to eat?' he asked. 'Panna cotta? Ice cream? Stuffed courgette flowers flown in from the Mediterranean with only the tiniest of carbon footprints?'

I took a slow breath. I wasn't sure I was ready to eat in front of this new person because eating in front of new people can be embarrassing.

'I'd like an ice cream,' I heard myself say, 'But only if you have one too.'

'I *always* have ice cream! The pistachio is to die for, although sometimes you … you have to go with the chocolate chip.'

I said yes please, chocolate chip, and would he excuse me for a moment.

Walking past the man behind the bar, I could feel doubts asserting themselves. By the time I stepped into the washroom I was approaching panic, and I hadn't eaten lunch so the thought of shovelling ice cream into my empty stomach was making me feel nauseous. I went straight over to the mirror and scrutinised my reflection for any evidence of chocolate powder, pulled out my comb, smoothed my hair, loose today so my scrunchie wouldn't stick in my neck when I was lying in the scanner. I touched up my lipstick, stood back and reassessed my appearance: who *was* that person looking back at me? And why had this man been so interested in asking me for coffee? I was reasonably sure, even under my current circumstances, that I was attractive, in a thin, retiring kind of way. If such characteristics could be attractive. But he seemed so keen to know me. A look of doubt flashed across my reflection. I noticed the door behind me, the one that led back to ice cream on an empty stomach, and the man at the bar watching me. The nausea intensified. But I knew I had to return.

He smiled as I approached. 'I've ordered some biscotti to help soak up the ice cream,' he said. 'And some Pellegrino to soak up the biscotti. Don't worry if you're not hungry. You can take the biscotti home for your cat.'

I sat down. 'It's not really my cat.'

'Oh!' He looked confused. 'Whose cat is it?'

'I don't know. It just keeps nudging its way through the hole in my back door.'

'But why …?'

The manager interrupted with the biscotti and two tall glasses of mineral water. 'Ice, no lemon,' he said. I stared at my glass.

Matthew frowned. 'Did you want lemon? I could ask …'

'No, I hate lemon.'

The ice cream arrived. The sight of it bolstered my confidence and, fortunately, my swallowing reflex dealt efficiently with the chocolate chips. Things were proceeding well. Then a small dollop of ice cream slithered from my spoon and slid down my sleeve towards my elbow. My reaction caused the rest of the spoonful to fall onto the table. I felt myself become rigid, watched him snatch up his napkin and leap to my assistance, wipe the stream of chocolate from my sleeve, holding my wrist briefly, scoop the melting chocolate chip off the tablecloth with his fingers and deposit it on his plate. I could sense the couple over by the window watching. He remained standing, wiping his fingers on his napkin.

'I wouldn't worry, you always … You always have to test the staff. Sometimes I throw stuff about deliberately!' He hovered for a moment and then sat down. 'It's a lovely jacket. Good thing about leather is that it doesn't mark. You can spill anything down it and it doesn't matter. Apart from paint. That's usually a disaster.'

The manager approached with a fresh napkin. Now I knew everybody was watching.

'I'm sorry,' I whispered. 'I'm always clumsy.'

'I … no, you're not. Eat the rest. I'll race you.'

I felt myself smile. What was it about this person that made the panic go away?

*

We strode back through the suffocating fumes of rush-hour London. The car park was full with people jostling for parking places. He walked me to my car and held the door as I stepped inside, touching my elbow gently as I did so. Not at all like Dr Williams. He asked me when I was going to shop next and would I like to go for another cappuccino. He had a waterproof I could borrow if we decided to throw food. He suggested Thursday about nine. A woman in a Peugeot tooted us to hurry up. I rolled my eyes and closed my door without saying anything else, watched him watch me pull away, managed to avoid reversing into the Peugeot, squeezed past a Range

Rover that seemed to be threatening to use its bulk to snatch the parking space from the smaller car, and made it on to the road without incident.

Driving home, I worried about our fragile arrangement. We had not exchanged telephone numbers or addresses. Our future meeting, if there was to be a future meeting, depended entirely upon next Thursday at nine o'clock. Had I actually agreed to next Thursday at nine o'clock? By the time I arrived home I was frantic that I might forget, so I hurried inside, grabbed my notepad and wrote GO TO THE SUPERMARKET NEXT THURSDAY AT NINE O'CLOCK. I observed the letters arranged into words. It was a whole sentence.

That evening I fell asleep to the sound of crashing waves ...

Episode Ten

It's dark. And cold. But at least the cold is taking the pain away.

Lie still. I can't move any of myself anyway.

I'll just rest here in the dark and the cold and listen to the waves.
And let it be over.

The gulls are screeching. Flying through the darkness.

Making themselves ready.

They know it will soon be daylight.

I think they can already see me. They know I shouldn't be here.

The waves are closer now. Sucking the sand away from under me.

Perhaps a strong wave will come and suck me away with the sand.

Take me out to sea. Away from this place. Take me to him.

Take me to the place where the LOST things hide.

*

I woke with the dawn, gasping for breath and fretting about Matthew Parry. Had he really been shopping in order to run into me? He was too handsome not to have run into someone already, someone more accomplished at eating ice cream. Someone the man behind the bar might expect to see him with instead of me. I was fraught. I wanted to stop thinking about the barman, the ice cream, although I didn't want to forget the things Matthew Parry said. But the problem with memories is that they're impossible to separate.

I wandered through to the kitchen. The black and white cat was asleep on the windowsill. It had never done that before and I wasn't sure whether I approved of such liberty-taking by someone else's pet. The cat seemed to sense my irritation, stretched, jumped down onto the floor, padded over to the doormat and started to groom itself. I felt a pang of remorse. It was not until the door to the under-sink cupboard opened that the ear-and-paw-cleaning ritual was suspended. Then, with an air of negotiable feline disdain, the cat watched biscuits tip onto the platter, watched me hover in repentance, and at last deigned to pad over and purr. I sighed. 'Don't mind me, puss. It's Wednesday. I'm seeing Dr Gray this morning.'

*

Only two of the Associates were waiting in Dr Gray's palatial Regent's Park consulting room, when his secretary showed me inside. My elderly physician stepped round his desk to welcome me.

'Sarah, hello. I gather that you met our two research associates yesterday? Geraint tells me that you're happy for them to take part in these consultations?'

I looked at the two men, each of them noticeably demonstrating a lesser degree of humility here in Dr Gray's elegant and kindly presence than I had witnessed yesterday when Dr Williams was presiding. They mumbled an unsynchronised greeting. I smiled recognition, wondered what had become of Dr Brown then paused: '*Research?*'

Dr Gray's eyebrows rose above the rims of his spectacles. 'Did Geraint not explain?'

I glanced over at Drs Clegg and Mustafa. 'Explain what?'

Dr Gray returned to the laptop open on his desk. I interrupted his reading.

'Dr Williams never mentioned *research*. I would have remembered.'

Dr Gray peered over his spectacles at me: 'I'm sure you would, Sarah.' He walked over to the door, addressing the two Associates as he did so. 'Do you think you could give Sarah and myself a few moments? Denise will call you when we're ready.'

I watched Drs Clegg and Mustafa file out and the door close behind them. I felt awkward. 'Dr Gray, I didn't want you to send them away. I just wasn't sure what kind of *research* they're doing.'

He returned to his chair. 'Sarah, there's nothing to worry about. My young colleagues are working in the field of research psychology, cognitive psychology in particular. Dr Mustafa has established quite a name for himself in the field of psycholinguistics. Sam is investigating memory as a temporal narrative ...'

'Dr Gray, I'm not sure what all that means.'

'Well, you could say they are both investigating memory dysfunction. Your case is worthy of investigation, not only for your benefit but also because, if we can understand the mechanism whereby your past is denied you, then this will tell us much about normal brain function. It is through studying disorder that we may reveal the nature of order.'

'But, how will they research me?'

'They'll interview you. Ask you to undertake a few simple written tests. To try and map any improvements.'

'But there haven't been any improvements, have there?'

'Mrs Parkin tells me you are managing *very* well.'

'But I'm just learning a new life. Learning to be an adult when all I can remember is being a child. And where are all the people I knew? Has everyone deserted me?'

Dr Gray's blue eyes revealed no emotion. 'Sarah, for the time being, our recommendation is that recovery of your memories will be best achieved through your own efforts as opposed to a series of dramatic revelations.'

'Secondary experiences?'

He raised an eyebrow. 'Yes. Telling you what has been pieced together of the circumstances whereby you were found, unconscious, will not reclaim your memories, it will merely replace them, possibly with something inaccurate.' He paused. 'You did agree to this method of rehabilitation. If you no longer feel confident in our recommendations, you must tell us, Sarah. The process requires your complete cooperation.'

I gave a small nod of approval, although I couldn't actually remember agreeing to anything: 'I've remembered more about my grandma.'

'Mrs Parkin informed us of that. You requested a photograph.' He pushed a brown envelope towards me. 'These were taken on your seventh birthday. The date is written on the back of one of them. You were living with your grandmother. Take a look and tell me if you can remember the occasion.'

'Can I keep them?'

'Yes, Sarah, they're yours.'

The envelope was unsealed. I pulled out two snapshots: a small girl, wearing a red frock, blowing out the candles on an iced cake; the same girl, holding a tea plate ready, eyes full of laughter, standing beside the old lady from my mind: Granny Clark, cutting the cake. They were both waving at whoever was holding the camera. I smiled back at them, tears blurring my vision. I recognised that small girl, almost from a dream, from a time before all of this. I held the two thin slips of paper and stared at two moments in time captured from the grey mist of nothing, remembered on my behalf. I fought the tears. Tears were useless. I slipped the photographs back into the envelope:

'I remember red jelly,' I whispered. 'Dr Gray, please ask the Associates to come back in.'

The interrogation began. Dr Gray listened and smiled and never once interrupted. Dr Clegg asked most of the questions. His interview technique was relaxed and friendly, whereas Dr Mustafa maintained a distance. Sam Clegg asked me to describe my earliest memories. So I told him about Granny Clark's garden with the big pear tree. It was near the sea. You could walk to the beach across a field and there were cows that walked towards you with big udders. They were frightening. I recalled moments at school. Story time. A boy who stole my ruler. I remembered a long train journey and Christmas trees with coloured lights. And a red dress with strawberries on the pockets. Not the one in the photos. I paused, having exhausted my resources.

'Was it an earlier dress?' asked Shoumi Mustafa.

I said I wasn't sure. He frowned and then continued with his copious note-taking. Sam Clegg leaned forward. 'Do you remember the stories your teacher told you?'

'Some of them, but I preferred the stories I used to make up with my grandma.'

'What kind of stories were they?' asked Sam Clegg.

'Stories about losing things,' I said. 'And stories about apples.'

*

I spent the rest of that afternoon and most of the evening reading my battered but wonderfully illustrated copy of *Andersen's Fairy Tales*. I remember fetching my drawing pad and sketching my own version of 'The Princess and the Pea', although I made it easier for my princess by placing a melon beneath the twenty mattresses. I've no idea what happened to that drawing, but my desecration of such a revered tale still makes me smile. I remember turning to the dedication at the front of the book:

September, 1927
To Dearest Lilian from your Loving Father

1927: Lilian and her father must have been over and done with years since. And that love was a love long passed. I remember running my finger along the inked words and wondering how this book had come into my possession: perhaps I had spotted it in some charity shop or other, bought it to savour the illustrations, and had inadvertently brought home with me this relic of paternal love. I imagined infant Lilian, sitting on her father's knee, reading the book, newly given, pointing to Dulac's illustrations. Maybe it had been a birthday gift. Perhaps Lilian's seventh birthday. I walked over to my bag and took out the two photographs. Looked again at the little girl and wondered how time could have carried me from that day to this moment. And I wondered what my forgotten time was preventing me from knowing.

MARGATE

Sarah gave her grandmother's hand a gentle push but there was no response.

'Auntie Maisie, will Grandma wake up soon? Because I want to read her the rest of *The Real Princess*. We only got half way through before she fell asleep again.'

Maisie Price lifted Sarah's hand from the quilt. 'Sarah, she's very tired. She needs her sleep. Let's go downstairs and have our tea, shall we? Dr Mason will be here soon to give her some more medicine.'

'But the medicine always makes her be asleep again.'

'We'll talk to Dr Mason about it, shall we? I think he wants to tell you about taking Lily into hospital for a while. To try and make her feel better.'

'But I don't want her to go into hospital. It smells horrible.' She took her grandma's hand again. 'We can look after her here.'

'Sarah, my lovely, they're much better at looking after sick people at the hospital.'

'But how long will she be there? Can I go with her?'

'I think your grandma wants you to come next door and stay with me for a while. I've made up my guestroom specially for you. Then next week Mummy's coming to visit with the new baby. You haven't seen your new sister yet, have you?'

'Will Grandma be back home by then?'

'We'll ask Dr Mason, shall we? Come on, I've baked some of my ginger cake.'

Episode Eleven

I had calculated that if the Escort failed to start, I would still be able to make it to the supermarket within twenty minutes, so I dressed, ate, took my pills and waited until quarter past eight, which gave me enough time to check everything and leave by eight-thirty. I was glad the cat wasn't there, getting in the way. I arrived in the car park at eight forty-two, waited ten minutes before going inside and went straight to cereals, stretched upwards …

'Shall I get that for you?' He reached over me. I could hear my blood pulsing inside my ears. I hoped it wasn't obvious from the outside. He handed me the cornflakes. He was wearing a red scarf that made his eyes look almost transparent.

'Ever thought of trying something different?'

I indicated along the aisle. 'There's too much choice.'

'Yes, I think you might be right.' He smiled. 'So, Miss Blake …'

'You're early,' I said, not meaning to.

'So are you. What else have you got on your shopping list?'

'Just cat biscuits.'

'Goodness, such dedication to someone else's cat!'

'It's good company sometimes. Where do you live?' I couldn't believe I'd just asked that.

'Crouch End. Flat. Second floor. One reception, two bedrooms, one en-suite, additional bog. Pleasant aspect. The bog, that is. Gas central heating. Lift works occasionally. Within easy walking distance of station ...'

'I'm sorry, I didn't mean to be nosey. I don't know why I asked.'

He laughed. 'Perhaps you wanted to know where I live.'

I laughed too. 'Do you joke about *everything*?'

'Only when I'm nervous. Shall we abandon our shopping and make a run for it?'

I indicated his empty trolley. 'You haven't bought anything yet!'

'Neither have you. There's just a box of cornflakes in your trolley. You don't have to buy it. Come on, let's leave our pound coins for someone to find. They'll buy lottery tickets and win a fortune and never know we were responsible for their happiness.'

'Money doesn't buy happiness.'

'Yes, it does. Are you coming?'

'Only if we put the trolleys back.' I handed him the cornflakes. 'And these.'

We strolled along in the sunshine, more leisurely than the previous Tuesday. He suggested we find somewhere serving breakfast because Tony's bistro didn't open until eleven. I confessed that I'd already eaten, so we found an almost hygienic café where I sipped tea and watched him eat a heap of yellow-grey scrambled egg, which reminded me of my weeks in the clinic. Those memories began to override the conversation to the point where I found it difficult to listen and impossible to say anything myself. I was suddenly aware that he was staring at me.

'I'm sorry, Matthew. My mind started to wander.'

'Yes, my conversation often has that effect. Are you all right?'

71

I tried to say yes, but my throat resisted. I saw his hand coming across the table towards me. Felt his fingers close around mine. Heard him whisper, 'What is it, Sarah? You can tell me.'

I shook my head. 'I can't. I don't know you.'

'Of course you do! We've shopped together, done outrageous things with ice cream.' He glanced out of the window. 'Look, there's a bench under the trees. Shall we go and ...'

'What about your eggs?'

'They're disgusting.'

Outside the air was cool and fresh and only slightly tainted by exhaust fumes. He guided my arm across the road, tightened his grip as a bus approached, removed his hand as soon as I was safely across. He indicated a bench that was not too severely covered in guano, took off his scarf and folded it for me to sit on, sat down beside it and stretched his arms along the back of the bench.

'It'll get dirty,' I said.

'Don't care. Tell me what's wrong.'

I sat down on the scarf, slightly forward to avoid resting against his arm. We passed a moment in silence. I knew none of this could continue unless I offered some kind of explanation. So I turned to him and sighed. 'I really like being with you, but ...'

'My God, are you dumping me? Before you've even given me a chance to prove what a fantastic boyfriend I can be?'

'Matthew, I ...' I paused. 'Boyfriend?'

'Do you think I'm too old to be a boyfriend? Damn it, woman, I'm only forty-six. I've still got loads of life left in me!'

I couldn't help but laugh. 'Can't you be serious for five minutes?' I sagged even further forward. 'Look, I have problems ...'

'You should worry, my girlfriend's just dumped me!'

'Matthew! Will you please listen to me! I can't remember anything!'

'That happens to me all the time. Just wait 'til you're thirty!'

I put my hands over my face: 'I'm thirty-five and will you please stop joking and let me tell you something?'

'Is this our first row?' He was grinning.

I took a deep breath. '*Matthew*, something happened to me, last December, I can't remember what. And nobody else seems to know either. But, whatever it was, my mind doesn't want me to remember, so it's made my memories go away. All of them right back to when I was little. So, you see, I don't know much more about myself than you do.'

'Were you hurt?'

'I was unconscious. My arm was broken. They photographed my brain but it was OK.'

I looked down at my lap, fiddled with the strap of my bag.

'I was missing for two days, then a man walking his dog found me lying on a beach. I don't remember any of it. All I can remember is waking up in the clinic, not knowing who I was, or who anybody was. I am Sarah Blake. It says so on my driving licence. And I think I remember that being my name when I was at school. But I don't know anything else about myself. And there's no one from before to tell me. So, it would be wrong to let you carry on thinking I'm normal.'

I looked up at him. He was smiling.

'What makes you think I thought you were normal?'

'What?' I half turned as I felt his arm across my shoulders.

'Really, Sarah, you're far too interesting to be normal. Besides, writers are never normal. When you told me you wrote children's books I was smitten. Let's give me a chance, shall we?'

Good sense informed me this ought not happen, yet there was his arm preventing me from tumbling back into emptiness. I was fed up with being on my own. So I said nothing.

'Is that a *yes*?'

Still I said nothing. He patted my knee with his free hand.

'Look, I don't want to seem forward, but if you ever let me stay the night, probably years from now, will you remember who I am when we wake up together or will I have to start all over again? I don't mind either way but you ought to warn me what to expect.' He pulled me closer.

Spend the night? I knew I ought to panic. But I didn't.

'I remembered you this morning,' I whispered. 'I have dissociative amnesia.'

'And you've lost your memory on top of it. Life sucks, doesn't it?'

I laughed. Then I let myself lean against his jacket and it felt OK. In fact, it felt better than anything had felt for as long as I could remember.

We walked back holding hands. The major part of my consciousness was taken up with this hand holding, so again Matthew did most of the talking. 'Have you a preferred way of meeting other than the supermarket? Because if we carry on like this we're going to be restricted to three-hour parking forever. And some things take longer than that.'

I came to a halt. 'What things?'

He pulled me forward. 'Going to the theatre, choosing curtains, dinner this Saturday. I could pick you up in a cab. If you don't mind me knowing where you live.'

I didn't want him to know where I lived.

'Why wouldn't I want you to know where I live?' I was aware that hysteria might be creeping into my voice.

'I get the impression you're a bit cautious about things like that.'
This time *he* came to a halt. 'So, are you going to tell me where you
live?'

Trying to sound casual: 'Farlington Close … 24.'

'Just north of the Angel, then?'

*

Mrs Parkin arrived in a fluster just before noon. As we single-filed
towards the kitchen, she apologised about having brought no biscuits.
Her schedule was very full at the moment. I said not to worry, there
were biscuits left over from Monday. Then I stopped short in the
cramped dining area trying to remember whether there actually were
any biscuits left over from Monday. Mrs Parkin frowned. 'Are you
alright, dear?'

'Yes!' I took a breath. 'I was just wondering, since you're so busy,
perhaps you only need to visit me *once* a week. There are probably
people who need you more than me.'

I was surprised to hear myself saying that. Mrs Parkin was clearly
shocked. She placed her folder on the dining table. 'Sarah, why don't
you go and start the tea? I just need to check my notes.'

I hurried into the kitchen and was relieved to discover Monday's
carried-over bourbons in the biscuit tin. I made tea then stepped back
into the lounge to say it was ready. Mrs Parkin was slipping her phone
into her bag. Her wide mouth stretched into a smile.

'Excellent! And, regarding your suggestion, Sarah, I'm sure the
doctors would discourage reducing our meetings just yet. You're really
not ready.'

Episode Twelve

Friday came round very quickly that week. Probably because crazy things had been happening and crazy things always make time go faster. As I sat at my desk, waiting for Mrs Dickson to arrive I agonised about whether I should tell her about Matthew. I realised that she would have to report something as significant as that back to Mrs Parkin. And that would mean … the doorbell rang. I hurried over to greet her, pulled open the front door and froze. A young woman was hovering on the threshold.

'Hello, I'm Dawn. I'm standing in for Mrs Dickson.'

Dawn? I was speechless. This person was too thin to stand in for Mrs Dickson. A distant siren fractured the silence.

'Where's Mrs Dickson?'

'She can't come today.' She leaned forward and whispered above the noise of the traffic. 'Can I come in, Sarah?'

I was reluctant to let go of the door, but aware that I had no choice, so I stepped back to allow the thin woman into my home, watched her place her coat and handbag on the sofa, then followed her into the kitchen and watched her walk over to the sink and stoop to open the cupboard. I leapt forward.

'Mrs Dickson doesn't do cupboards!'

She regarded me cautiously. 'OK. I presumed the cleaning products were in here.'

'Oh, yes, they are.' I felt ridiculous: 'Sorry, I get nervous. I'll make tea.'

'I'd prefer coffee, if that's OK. Instant will do. I'll start in the lounge, shall I? Where's the vacuum cleaner?'

I backed into the lounge and indicated the meter cupboard then hurried back to the kitchen to make coffee, which I hadn't attempted since being coaxed through the procedure by Mrs Parkin. Weeks ago. Mrs Dickson never drank coffee. I fetched two china mugs, filled the kettle and waited. I would have to have coffee as well: it would be rude if I made myself tea. I turned as the cat flap sounded, watched the black and white cat pour through onto the doormat, sniff the air, walk over to rub itself against my jeans, then pause and re-sniff the air. I was aware that some kind of feline assessment was taking place and was reassured when the animal padded over and leapt up onto its usual chair.

'Mrs Dickson can't come today,' I whispered.

The cat ignored me, stretched out its claws and licked the freshly-exposed skin between its pads. The kettle flicked off. I added a flat teaspoonful of instant coffee to each mug and carried the kettle over and half-filled them. Mrs Dickson hadn't mentioned anything about not coming. I topped the mugs up with milk and sighed: that didn't look the right colour. I sprinkled a few more grains of coffee into one of the mugs. They floated to the edge and stuck to the china. That would have to be my one. Then, as I was arranging the tray, an unwelcome thought perforated my mind. I looked at the cat. What if Mrs Dickson had said she wasn't coming and I'd forgotten? I didn't think I forgot new things. But then how would I know I'd forgotten things if I couldn't remember them? The cat's ears flattened. I ran into the lounge and shouted above the noise of the vacuum:

'Did Mrs Dickson tell me she wasn't going to be here this week?'

Dawn looked up, then extended her foot and turned off the cleaner. 'Pardon?'

I held my breath. Exhaled. 'Did Mrs Dickson know she couldn't come this week? Already? Did she tell me *already*?'

Dawn looked apprehensive. 'I don't think so. It's a tummy bug.' She extended her arm as if to touch me. 'Are you alright?'

I edged away from her. 'Yes, I ... I'll fetch the coffees.'

*

I set the tray down at one end of the coffee table. Dawn frowned slightly on catching sight of the mugs.

'That's yours,' I said, pointing to the mug without the clots.

Dawn picked up her coffee and sat down on the large sofa. 'You have a lovely home,' she said, swallowing a mouthful and requiring a moment to recover. 'Do you have nice neighbours?'

I carried my mug over to the smaller sofa. 'The lady next door usually says hello, but I don't know about the rest of the street.' I noticed her glance up at the ceiling. 'It's been empty since I came home. I was ... Did Mrs Parkin tell you about me?'

'She said you write children's books.' She took another mouthful of coffee then got to her feet. 'I'd best be getting on or we'll never get finished.'

As she set her mug back on the tray I noticed her perfect long nails, all the same length, thick, cloudy white tips then nail-coloured further down: very different from the nails on Mrs Dickson's stumpy fingers. I sipped my coffee. It was disgusting but I drank it all the same, and watched Dawn slide the vacuum backwards and forwards with her slim hands and her magazine nails, watched her manoeuvre her way over to the bookcase, cut the power and make a display of pulling a duster from her waistband.

'Gracious, are these your books!' she said. 'May I take a look?'

'If you like.' I had absolutely no intention of discussing my writing with this interloper, so I picked up the tray, complete with Dawn's half-full mug, carried it into the kitchen and pushed the door as closed as I could without appearing to be rude. Then I sat down beside the cat and re-read my magazine.

That Friday's two hours took a long time to pass, and Dawn did not make the bed half as well as Mrs Dickson, nor did she do the laundry. I thanked her when she left but I was careful not to give her the impression I ever wanted to meet her again. I really hoped that, whatever was wrong with Mrs Dickson, it would be over with by the following Friday. Alone at last, I made tea and toast and banana, threw the banana skin into the organic waste and recoiled at the smell that escaped before the flap fell back. As I ate my lunch I worried about forgetting new things. Then I worried about Dawn being a cleaner. Did she have ambitions of being something else: a hairdresser or a secretary, perhaps a writer of children's books? I wondered when I had started writing children's books. The earliest LOST story was dated four years ago, so I must have started writing before that, perhaps a long time before that. But then it didn't matter how long ago it was because, if I couldn't write now, it was all meaningless. I had to do something about it. I walked through to my desk and sat staring at a blank sheet. Glanced across at my books. Perhaps when they were being published at J.D. Hillier Publishing I had met the person who went to lunch with Matthew. I fetched my wallet, pulled out the business card he had given me and read the words, written bold across the middle of the card:

Parry & Ashdown Literary Agency

*

By late afternoon I was desperate to think of something or someone other than Matthew Parry. The prospect of an evening waiting for his phone call was making me crazy. So I fetched my magazine and forced myself to read. I came across a full-page spread: a woman in a bath full of bubbles, her hair perfect and dry: 'relax and stay young'. Staying young was not one of my immediate concerns, but relaxing in a bath full of bubbles, perhaps that would help. I went to investigate the bathroom cabinet. It was crammed with unopened bottles: more of the shampoo I used; conditioner; a mass of different bath and shower gels. I wanted bubbles. One of the bottles claimed to be a relaxing foaming bath experience. It was a striking shade of purple. Lavender and bergamot. I remembered a sneezy lavender bush in Granny Clark's garden, always covered in butterflies. But what on earth was bergamot? I read the instructions barely visible against the contents. They did not instruct adequately regarding the amount of the purple liquid that was necessary to provide bubbles and relaxation, so I turned on the bath taps, tipped purple into the gushing water and started to undress.

As the bath filled and the bubbles mounted, I experienced a half-remembered childhood excitement, scooped up great handfuls of foam and blew them into the air, imagining pixies so light that they could leap between bubbles without bursting them. I inhaled the approximation of lavender and something else that was possibly bergamot and imagined a giant with a magic pipe, imprisoning fairies in bubbles of daydream, unfastened my bra, stepped out of my knickers and surrendered myself to the bathwater. As my shoulders disappeared beneath the bubbles, I realised that I'd forgotten to tie up my hair, so now it was wet. I didn't care. I dunked my head backwards and came up laughing and covered in foam. Then I lay back and relaxed and let my thoughts stray again to Matthew Parry.

It was just after five-thirty when I heard my mobile. I sat up straight, causing a tidal wave of bathwater to pour over on to the floor. I hauled myself out of the bath, dripping wet and covered in foam, grabbed my towel, hurried through into the kitchen and snatched up my mobile. I pressed the red telephone. The ringing stopped. I placed it to my ear. Nothing. The ringing started again. I pressed the green phone:

'Sarah, is that you? I'm sorry I think I lost signal. Can you hear me?'

'Yes!'

'Damn, this is a terrible line, I can hardly hear you. It's Matthew.'

I moved my mouth nearer. 'Hello.'

'Oh, that's better. I hope it's OK phoning this early but I've got caught up in some bloody publishing thing this evening. I haven't interrupted anything, have I?'

'No! I was writing.' I pushed back my hair to prevent my phone being covered in bathwater.

'Great. So, if we're still on for tomorrow, I could pick you up at around six. Is that OK? I've managed to get a cancellation at Gusto. In Primrose Hill. We can have a drink beforehand. There's a wine bar next door.' He paused. 'Is six o'clock too early?'

'No.'

Silence. Which he interrupted. 'So, have you had a good day?'

'Yes.' Another silence. 'Was your meeting OK?'

'Not bad. I don't think I can retire on this one, but it will help pay the rent.' He laughed. 'So, what are you doing this evening?'

'More writing probably.'

'OK. Would you like me to ring you again tomorrow?'

'No!'

Pause. 'OK, ring me if you want to chat. OK?'

'Yes … bye.' I heard him laugh.

'Bye, Sarah.'

I put my phone down on the worktop and stared at it for a moment, exhausted. Wet. Then I pulled my towel around myself and followed the trail of wet footprints that lead back to the soapy flood alongside the bath. There was a squeegee mop propped up next to the hand basin. Dawn had failed to put it back into the meter cupboard. I started to transfer the water from the floor back into the bath, squeeze at a time. It proved to be a Herculean task, not easily carried out while swathed in a bath towel. As I squashed out a heavy spongeful of water, my towel slithered down to the floor. I snatched it back up but it was already drenched, so I threw it in the corner and continued naked and cold, until the floodwater was gone. I pulled out the bathplug and walked into the bedroom to retrieve my dressing gown from the other side of the door. It was then that I caught sight of myself in the full-length mirror.

Myself naked: a sight I was not familiar with. In fact it was a sight I had been avoiding, yet I was unable to turn away. I watched myself approach, my arms at my sides, my step apologetic, as if I were creeping up on an embarrassed stranger, caught naked and unable to escape. I came to a standstill about two feet away from my reflected self, far enough away to be sure of staying separate. And looked. She was thin, this other me, too thin; her hipbones were too prominent. And her shoulder blades, full of grey shadow, really did look like blades. Her image was made worse by wet strands of hair that were dripping little rivulets of water down her breasts, her stomach, accumulating in the hair between her legs, then escaping down her thighs. I hoped I didn't look like that. I hoped that this other me had somehow suffered the worst of an unequal deal. But I could feel those streams of bathwater running down my own thighs. This *was* me, and this was the too-thin body that I was going to cover up and take to dinner tomorrow evening. I didn't want to go. I didn't want to do anything that would end up with anybody seeing this bony thing. Because that's what happened when men asked women to dinner. Perhaps not straight away. But eventually it would be expected: nakedness, touching, feeling. My magazine was all about encouraging such things. I lifted my hand and wiped the water from my breast, my thumb brushing across my cold nipple. I repeated it, once, twice, then caught my breath. I couldn't remember feeling anything like that before. But I must have … I looked at my flat abdomen, ran my hand from my hip down the inside of my thigh and let it come to rest a little above my knee. How could I know? Just looking at myself? How would I know what sensations that body might have experienced, what ecstasy, what disappointment? Because those things leave no outward trace. And right now all that I had left were outward traces. I turned away, grabbed my dressing gown from the door and hurried to the airing cupboard to find a warm towel for my hair.

MARGATE

There's a space in a place called Raggedy Lyme,
Full of errors and terrors and wasted time,
Where your lost things can hide until they decide
That you've earned their return from Raggedy Lyme.

from *The Lost Stories of Raggedy Lyme* by Sarah Blake

Sarah sat on the cold, cushion-less window seat, waiting. She watched her unfamiliar mother squash the last of her things into Granny Clark's suitcase, force the zip closed and drag it onto the floor. Sarah's childhood lay sealed inside that case. And now it was over.

'Right!' said Diana Dawson. 'I think that's all you'll be needing. We'll have to get somebody to help carry it between trains.' She stepped over to investigate the bulging koala rucksack Sarah was nursing at her side. 'What have you got in there?' She lifted it up. 'My God, it weighs a ton!'

'It's my keepsakes to take with me. Aunt Maisie helped me choose them.'

'Yes, well, Maisie Price hasn't got to carry them across St Pancras Station in the middle of the rush hour, has she? Let's have a look.'

'Mummy, I want to keep it all. Please, Mummy!'

'We'll see, shall we?' She prised open the koala's back and started to order its contents on to the seat beside Sarah's leg: a small, greyish rag doll with stringy hair, baby-button eyes and a red dress ...

'That's Raggedy,' said Sarah. 'Daddy bought her for me.'

A copy of *Hans Andersen's Fairy Tales* ...

'I read the stories to Granny because her eyes are very bad these days. She 'specially likes the Real Princess.'

84

An old dictionary …

'I need it because I'm going to be a writer when I'm grown up, and Miss Grainger said my spelling is *terrible*.'

'Sarah, we don't need to take this old thing with us. We can buy a new dictionary!'

'But I know the words in this one.'

Diana Dawson rolled her eyes and banged the book down next to Sarah. Then she extracted a small snow globe. 'What's this?'

'It's Snow White. She's holding the apple that's going to send her to sleep so she can be kissed by the prince and wake up. Granny and Aunt Maisie took me to see *Snow White and the Seven Dwarfs on Ice*. And Aunt Maisie bought me that to always remember it by.'

Diana Dawson sighed. 'Right! What else have you got in here?' She pulled out a snack-pack of Jaffa Cakes and, with effort, a large crumbly lump of grey rock, bundled inside a paisley silk headscarf. 'Sarah! Why are you taking this boulder with you?'

'It's got fossils in it. Ambulites. I collected it from the beach with Daddy. When I was little. And that's Grandma's scarf. I want to keep it because Granny's hair smell's in it.'

Diana Dawson threw it down, wiped her fingers on her skirt and felt deeper into the koala's innards. She plucked out a bundle of letters, packed tight with an elastic band. An old black and white postcard was inserted into the top of the pile.

'Those are Daddy's letters to me. He's in Australia now because he wanted to see the Southern Cross and you can't see it in Margate or in Raggedy Lyme or even in the whole of England. Mummy, will he be able to write to me if I live in London?'

'Yes, he will.'

They both looked up as Maisie Price stepped into the room.

'How's it going?' she said. 'Diana, I was wondering whether I should take Sarah to say goodbye to Lily's old place. While you see to the baby. We can have a last look at the garden. The mistletoe on the old tree's white with frost. And we can check the mousetraps under the stairs. And, Sarah, we can have another look for that lost slipper of yours. It must be somewhere. Things don't just disappear.'

Sarah glanced up at her mother then down at her collection of special things. 'Mummy's in a hurry.' She picked up the snow globe and put it back in the koala.

'I'll do that!' snapped Diana Dawson. 'Why don't you go with Mrs Price. Maisie, would you be a dear and help me downstairs with this case. I'm not supposed to lift too much after the stitches. Then you can take Sarah to say her goodbyes.'

Sarah frowned: nobody had mentioned stitches. But the time probably wasn't right to ask, so she slithered off the window seat. Ouch! The backs of her thighs had become stuck to the painted surface. She felt sure that patches of her skin must still be sitting there. But they weren't. She started towards the door then looked back at her things. 'Raggedy goes in last so she's not squashed.'

Diana Dawson listened to the suitcase bumping down the stairs, glanced over at the baby asleep on the bare mattress, then looked down at the letters she was holding. Thin, blue airmail paper. She eased out the postcard and turned it over. Nothing. Just faint legends at the top and bottom:

Sidmouth * Lyme Regis * Seaton * Beer Cove
Beer Cove, Devon.

She turned it back and frowned at the black and white beach, at the cliffs rising out of the sea, the stranded boats, the people along the shoreline, mostly grey. She threw down the letters, slipped the card between the pages of the dictionary and placed both books into the rucksack, tossed the rag doll, the Jaffa Cakes and the scarf on top of them and pulled the zip closed. Then she wandered over to the waste bin and forced the fossil-filled rock and the bundle of letters from her first abandoning husband deep into the bottom of the rubbish, so they would never be seen again. The baby started to stir, demanding attention. Another worthless daughter.

When, eventually, she heard footsteps coming back up the stairs, she scooped up the baby, hurried to hand over the repacked koala and prodded Sarah back onto the landing and downstairs.

'What have you been doing all that time? Has Mrs Price put your case in her car?'

'Yes. Mummy, will baby Arachne be asleep on the train?'

'Hopefully.'

'Will I be able to hold her?'

'Possibly. If we hurry.'

'Mummy, Grandma's cottage was empty of nearly everything.'

'Yes, there's a new family coming to live there soon. They'll bring their own things. All Lily's things have gone to the charity shop. Mrs Price said she told you about it.'

'She did tell me. But, what if Grandma comes back and there are new people there?'

'She won't come back. Now let's get a move on, shall we? The woman from Social Services is coming to the house this evening and I want to be ready for her.'

'Is that the lady who came to speak to me and Granny?'

'Yes, one of the many. Did you find your slipper?'

'No. Aunt Maisie says she'll send it to me when it comes back.'

'Comes back from where?'

Sarah beamed at her mother. 'From Raggedy Lyme, where all your lost things hide. Until you deserve to have them back.'

Diana Dawson shook her head and sighed. Just like her father: another crazy dreamer. She closed the front door behind her.

'Hurry up, Sarah. We've got a train to catch.'

Episode Thirteen

I stood in my knickers and bra and surveyed my clothes, most of which were scattered around the bedroom: on the bed, on the floor. It looked as if my wardrobes had exploded. I remember being amazed at how much space exploded clothes could occupy. I sagged onto the end of my bed and admitted to myself that, after two hours of fitting myself into all possible combinations of the items that surrounded me, I still had no idea what to wear to go to dinner in Primrose Hill. I would phone and say I couldn't make it. No, he would ask why and I'd have no rational explanation. I stretched over and picked up a fluffy blue jumper with a round neckline. It was towards the top of my short list of possibilities. I threw it back on the bed and pressed down on my stomach to suppress the ripples of panic. I'd pretend not to be there when he arrived. No, he would look through the lounge window, walk down the side alley, smell the dustbins that belonged to the Indian restaurant, look through my bedroom window. I would hide in the bathroom. My mobile interrupted my plans. I excavated it from under a pair of trousers and pressed the green phone.

'Hi, just checking everything's OK.'

'I don't know what to wear!'

'What, for this evening?'

'Yes!'

'Well, you can wear what … you can wear almost anything. Not jeans though … I mean, you could wear jeans. And your leather jacket and boots.' He paused. 'Would you like me to come early and help you choose?'

'No!'

'OK, let's think. Start with the jacket and boots. Do you have any trousers that are not jeans? Or a skirt?'

I thought my way through the things distributed over the bedroom floor. 'I've got grey trousers. It says "wool mix" on the label.'

'That sounds good.' He paused. 'So, now you need a top to go under the jacket.'

'I know that!'

'Right. Tell me about your tops?'

'There's a fluffy blue one.'

'That sounds great. And you've got a bag and jewellery, right?'

'What jewellery?'

'I don't know. Something expensive, like pearls or something gold.'

'I'll go and look.'

'No, not now! Sarah, why don't you try it all on, then phone me back?' There was silence. 'OK, why don't I phone you back in a couple of hours? Four o'clock? Then if you're not happy, we'll go to plan B.'

'OK! Bye.'

'Bye, Sarah.'

*

The taxi pulled up ten minutes early, right outside my flat. I had realised by now that hiding in the bathroom would be ludicrous. Something a mad person would do. So I checked myself in the mirror, unplugged the phone then waited beside the sink. After five minutes or so I heard the doorbell. I checked the plugs one last time, and the bolts. Then I rechecked the plugs and hurried through to open the door.

'Shall we go?' He stepped aside, so my path was clear, pulled my front door closed then hurried to help me into the cab. Walked round and got in beside me. As soon as we pulled away I felt him touch my hand. He turned to whisper, 'You look gorgeous. And don't be nervous. Nothing you can possibly do will surprise me, OK?'

'I found a gold locket.'

'So I see. It's very nice.'

'There's no one in it.'

'Good.'

*

The wine bar was full of noise and people, couples that looked a lot like Matthew and somebody else. He ordered drinks: a glass of red wine and a lemonade for me because Mrs Parkin said consuming alcohol was out of the question with my medication. He didn't seem to mind my abstinence, but he did ask the barman to put my lemonade in a stemmed glass. I really liked that. Time passed quickly. I enjoyed listening to him shout above the jumble of laughter interspersed with people yelling at the barman. It meant that he had to lean closer to make himself heard. I liked that too.

The brief walk next door was uneventful. The manager recognised Matthew and indicated our table over by the window, a table with candles and sparkling glasses and apple blossom in a glass bowl. Matthew suggested we freshen up before we sat down.

I stood beside the marble basin and felt in my trouser pocket to confirm the tiny box with the two night-time pills. They had to be taken in less than two hours. I thought it might look weird if I came back in there so soon. But I couldn't take them then and there in case they made me feel sleepy too early. I wasn't sure what would happen if I became distracted and forgot to take them. So I decided to wait and see: if I felt things going wrong I'd make an excuse and come back and swallow them and try to stay awake until I got home.

We were escorted to our table. Matthew hailed the wine waiter and ordered a bottle of Laurent Perrier. He waited for the man to leave before whispering across the blossoms: 'It's my favourite. I beg you to try it.'

Menus arrived. Matthew helped me choose. I watched his confidence, his friendliness when he ordered, his smile as he turned his attention back to me. I really wanted him to like being with me but I was terrified about what I would have to do to achieve that. I attempted conversation.

'Do you come ... often come here?'

His eyes flickered with candlelight. 'Sometimes. I ...' A waiter interrupted with a bucket and stand. A duplicate waiter held out a bottle, semi-cloaked, its label exposed for all to see. I watched my glass fill, watched the tiny bubbles streaming upwards, unstoppable, eager to burst into the air above. I really liked bubbles. How ready they were to be over and gone. I glanced up: Matthew was watching me.

'Try it, Sarah.'

I looked down at my glass: I wasn't supposed to drink alcohol with my medication. But, then, I hadn't yet taken my medication. I lifted my glass and felt the bubbles popping below my nose, took a sip. It tasted unfamiliar, difficult, amazing.

The courses were many and mostly recognisable: mushroom cappuccino, goat's cheese parcels, cucumber sorbet and a scallop amuse-bouche. The honeyed nut roast was delicious but I was flagging by the time the array of minute chocolate puddings arrived. I watched the waiter top up my glass then, when he was safely out of earshot, I leaned forward and whispered, 'Would you like my chocolate?'

'Always!' He held out his hand. 'Can't you eat it?'

I shook my head and passed my plate above the blossoms and, as I did so, his hand touched mine and a fresh wave of panic and exhilaration rippled through me. It was now well over half an hour since I should have taken my pills but I didn't seem to be suffering any ill-effects, in fact the champagne seemed to have induced a strange euphoria.

Eventually Matthew threw down his napkin. 'Would you like coffee?'

'Not really. Would you?'

'No, I'll get the bill.' He leaned back and caught the waiter's eye. 'So, Cinderella, what time do you have to be home before you turn back into a pumpkin?'

I laughed. 'It's the coach that turns into a pumpkin. You know that! And Cinderella's dress turns back to rags. But her crystal slippers never change. So that the charming prince can find the one she lost, sparkling in the moonlight, and search the kingdom for the slipper that matches it, and find his princess so they can live happily ever after.'

He gave a wry smile. 'You love those old stories, don't you?'

'They always have happy endings.' I took a last sip of champagne. 'I shouldn't be late. This is my first night out since the clinic.'

His smile faded. 'How long were you there?'

'Three months, I think. But I don't remember most of it. I still have to visit my doctors on Tuesdays and Wednesdays.'

'Do they think your memories will come back?'

'I don't know. I'm an odd case. I could remember how to drive but I couldn't remember how to cook or make coffee.'

He laughed. 'Did you ever know how to cook and make coffee?'

'I don't remember.'

Outside, the night air was cold and damp and not that interested in summer. Matthew wrapped his scarf around my neck, allowing his fingers to brush my cheek as he did so.

'You'll be cold,' I insisted.

'I've drunk most of a bottle of champagne. I can't feel the cold. Fancy a quick stroll? Or do you want to go straight home?'

I wasn't sure what going straight home might involve, so I opted for a quick stroll. He took my hand and we walked to the top of Primrose Hill and looked at the panorama of lights. I confessed that I didn't recognise anywhere so Matthew put his arm around me and pointed to a few landmarks and I looked up at him and whispered, 'I don't want to have sex with you.'

Matthew's hand hung in the air, pointing down river towards Canary Wharf. He frowned.

'What never?'

'No, I mean now!'

'Good lord, Sarah, this is a bit public even for me!'

'Matthew, I don't mean …'

'Have you been worrying about that all evening? Scared I'd pounce on you? Sarah, I wouldn't do that.'

'You've put your arm around me.'

He plunged his hands into his jacket pockets.

I was horrified. 'I don't want you to stop! I'm sorry.'

He took a step back and shook his head. 'OK, Cinders, I forgive you.' He pointed into the near distance: 'You live just about there.'

I hovered for a moment, watching his hand, then I took a step closer and tugged at his jacket, felt his arm across my back, looked up into his eyes and said, 'Don't you want to have sex with me?'

And that's when he kissed me.

*

I clutched my bag as the cab pulled up outside my flat, and felt Matthew let go of my hand. I reached over for the door handle, but he caught my arm:

'Shall I come in and check everything's OK?'

'No!'

He withdrew his hand. 'Shall I walk you to the door?'

'No!' I pushed open the cab door then turned to smile. 'Thank you for dinner.'

'My pleasure.'

I glanced at the back of the driver's head. 'Mine too.'

He laughed. 'Good. We'll wait until you're inside. And don't bother losing your crystal slipper. I know where you live.'

I hurried inside to turn on the lights and listened as the cab pulled away. Then I went straight through to my bedroom mirror to check what I must have looked like as he sat beside me in the cab, as I stepped out onto the pavement not that far from the nearest streetlight, because that would most likely be the way he would remember me until the next time we met. I studied my reflection: my clothes, my hair. They were the same. But somehow different. My image was almost trembling, blurred, my cheeks flushed pink with all the excitement of a convent girl kissed for the very first time. I wandered through to the kitchen, my head spinning with fresh memories. Memories I didn't want to lose. I poured myself a glass of milk, felt in my pocket for the pillbox. Popped it open. The two-hour-late pills were still inside, waiting to calm me to sleep. But I didn't want to go to sleep. I wanted to stay awake and remember. I clicked the pillbox closed and heard its contents rattle as I banged it down on the work surface. Tonight was going to be different! I strode through to my desk, pulled out the chair and sat drinking my milk and reliving the last few hours, but especially that walk above the lights of London, breathing cold air. After ten minutes or so, I pulled over my notepad and abandoned pen and wrote: KISS

Then I wrote:

> *Granny Bramley was fat and round and she had fourteen grandchildren and a cat called Blodwen. Her grandchildren used to come and visit her during the school holidays. But Blodwen lived with her all the time.*
>
> *Granny Bramley and Blodwen lived in a small white cottage surrounded by pear trees and cherry trees but no apple trees, which was strange because her cottage was called 'Apple Tree Cottage'.*
>
> *Granny Bramley's Cottage was a mile away from the nearest village. So every Monday she used to walk along the road past Farmer Joe's field and into the village to do her shopping. Whenever Farmer Joe saw her walk past he would stop tending his sheep and wander over to say hello. He always spoke about the local football team and the weather and his orchard full of apple trees. Granny Bramley wasn't interested in football. And she said she couldn't do much about the weather so it wasn't worth talking about. But she was always interested in Farmer Joe's apple trees.*

'You wanted to see me, sir?'

Detective Chief Inspector Royston glanced up from the file open on his desk. 'Ah, Sergeant Brown, come in.'

Della Brown stepped into the dingy office and closed the door behind her. After a few silent moments while she stood waiting, the Inspector slapped the file shut and leaned back in his chair.

'Do you have anything further to report regarding the Hornsey incident, Sergeant?'

'I'm continuing to make enquiries, sir, regarding the whereabouts of Sarah Blake both at the time of the incident itself and throughout the subsequent forty-eight hours during which she appears to have disappeared.'

The inspector folded his arms. 'Do you think it likely that any new information will be forthcoming, given that, despite your and DI Broderick's enquiries, not one person has been able to shed light upon those two days, including Sarah Blake herself? Has she been able to remember anything concerning those involved? Anything that would explain the circumstances in which she was found?'

'No, sir, but I remain hopeful that some evidence will come to light. I believe that Sarah Blake's circumstances and the Hornsey incident must be related by more than simple coincidence. And I am not convinced that her alleged inability to remember those days is anything other than denial, possibly some kind of involuntary masking process, to exonerate herself from blame. From guilt.'

'Do you have any *evidence* upon which to base this opinion? Or is this merely some kind of *female* intuition?'

'I have been allowed by one of her physicians ...'

'Robert Gray?'

'No. Geraint Williams. I've been allowed to witness an episode of MRI imaging, which demonstrated clearly that the suspect ... that Sarah Blake does respond briefly to images of the individuals involved in the incident despite the fact that she is unable to recognise them on any kind of permanent basis. If her amnesia ceases to progress, it is possible that fresh information will become available.'

DCI Royston sat forward in his chair.

'Della, time marches on. It has been suggested that to pursue these enquiries further regarding Mrs Blake's whereabouts would be a waste of police time. We have a flourishing under-aged prostitution problem which, according to Mike Broderick, is threatening to get out of hand. This has in the past proved to be your area of expertise, has it not? In recent weeks we have been blessed with two, possibly three, corpses and a wealthy and embarrassed businessman. It does not need to get any worse.'

Della Brown remained defiantly silent.

Detective Chief Inspector Royston looked down at the file on his desk and exhaled. 'Two weeks, sergeant. No more.'

'Yes, sir. Would there be anything else?'

Episode Fourteen

They're arguing.

I think she's asleep she says.

He says stoned more like. You shouldn't have picked her up.

She says we couldn't just leave her wandering. It's freezing out there.

You're just asking for trouble he says.

Just let her sleep she says. I'll drop her off at the station.

He grunts. Throw her out more like.

Walking. Headlights coming towards me.

*

I woke exhausted. After a brief moment of disorientation I sat up and remembered: Primrose Hill. Granny Bramley. I glanced at my alarm: 10:44. *What?* I jumped out of bed and ran into the lounge. The wall clock agreed with the alarm. The morning was almost over. The doorbell rang. I leapt back and stared at the front door, checked the blind to make sure it was tightly closed. Someone moved the letterbox flap.

'Sarah?'

Matthew!

I looked down at my toes emerging from their pyjama bottoms. The bell rang again. I backed towards the sofa then round into the dining area and on into my bedroom. The chaos from yesterday's wardrobe explosion was everywhere, camouflaging my dressing gown; I spotted it half under the bed, dragged it out, pulled it on, saw a shadow pass by the bedroom curtains. Somebody tapped on the kitchen window. Good God! Had I checked the bolts enough times before going to bed? I leapt over to the bedroom door and pushed it shut. Paused. I was being ridiculous. I heard his voice, muffled through the double-glazing.

'Sarah! Are you there?'

I took a deep breath, hurried into the kitchen and came face to face with Matthew, peering in through the kitchen window, shorter now because the backyard was lower than the kitchen floor. If you looked at his head and the floor at the same time, you could imagine he was a dwarf. A dwarf with a frantic expression. He waved. I waved back. Then I hurried over and released the two bolts, fetched the key and pulled open the door. Matthew stepped inside, the right size now. He frowned at my pyjamas.

'Did I wake you up?'

'No, but I overslept. I've got to take my pills. I mustn't miss two lots.'

'Didn't you take them last night?'

'No. I stayed awake to do some writing.'

Matthew looked around the kitchen. 'Where are they?'

I pointed to the toaster, surprised at his concern. And embarrassed: I didn't want him to be here right now. But I didn't want him to go either.

He held up a white tub. 'These?'

'No, *these*.' I stretched past him, very aware of his proximity to my pyjamas. 'I have to shower,' I said.

He stepped back. 'Just take your pills before you do anything else.' He raked his fingers backwards through his hair, which left a couple of strands standing upright. He fetched a glass from the cupboard, walked over to the sink and filled it with water. 'Are you saying you've only just woken up? Has that happened before? You ought to tell …'

'Matthew! I'm all right!' I took the glass and swallowed my pills. 'When I got home last night I could write again. I've written a whole story. I didn't go to bed until nearly four o'clock.'

Matthew took the glass and placed it on the worktop, held my arms tight in his hands, his expression, once again, frantic. 'God, Sarah, do you think you ought to do things like that after being in hospital for three months? What would your doctors say if they knew you were staying up all night?' He let his hands fall away. The two strands of hair were still standing on end. 'I'm sorry. I feel responsible.'

'I'm fine!' I lied. I felt sweaty and too thin inside my saggy pyjamas. 'I'll go get dressed.'

He rallied. 'OK, I'll make tea.'

I hurried back to my bedroom, closed the door, found underwear, ran into the bathroom, locked myself in, unlocked the door, ran back out and found clothing, returned to the bathroom and relocked the door. As I showered I played over the last ten minutes. I remember worrying if this was the way boyfriends usually carried on. It was exhausting! I stepped out of the shower. Perhaps it was the way men behaved when they wanted to have sex with you. The bathroom was too steamy and my towel seemed impervious to water, unable to make me properly dry. I threw it on the floor and stood for a moment, naked in the cold damp air. I grabbed my knickers, dragged them up my damp thighs, fastened my bra, covered it with a chunky jumper, then tried to pull on my tights, a process which demanded sitting on the toilet, and slowly persuading the stretchy fabric over my knees. My skirt went on easy enough but I was now utterly exhausted. And hungry. I needed shoes. I unlocked the door, stepped into the bedroom and took a welcome breath of dry air. The bedroom was a mess but I didn't have time to tidy it, so I found shoes and braced myself for my return to the kitchen.

Matthew was sitting at the table, reading my magazine, his hair flattened back down, all trace of hysteria gone from his face.

'Tea's in the pot. And I've emptied your organic waste into the outside bin. It was about to explode.'

We carried our tea through and sat on separate sofas. I noticed him staring at the mantelpiece.

'Most of my things are packed away,' I explained. 'They didn't want me to be buried in clutter.'

He looked around. 'Where's your … Don't you have a TV?'

'They thought it best if I didn't.'

'Do you like it like this?'

I shrugged. 'It's a bit bare. I might get some cushions. Red and green.'

Matthew's face reverted to seriousness. I searched for something to say that would re-lighten his mood.

'I've got a cleaning lady, who comes every Friday. But she couldn't come last week. They sent another cleaner but she was rubbish!'

'Good cleaners are like gold dust. You like poetry, then?' He inclined his head towards the bookcase. 'And children's books.' He carried his tea over to investigate. 'Are these yours or were they written by a different Sarah Blake?'

'I can't remember writing them. Have you heard of them?'

He turned and smiled: 'Yeah, I seem to remember them being quite popular. Are you writing more?'

'I think I've started a new series. *Grandma's Apple Stories*. They're the stories I used to make up with my granny. That's what I was writing last night. But I'm worried I'm stealing my grandma's stories.' I was desperate for something to eat. 'Do you think it's stealing?'

'Not at all. It's one thing to make up stories and another to write them down and make them last for ever. Besides, you're calling them Grandma's Stories.' He looked at me for a few silent moments then he smiled. 'Show me. I used to be a good editor. Then after you've benefited from my professional expertise, we can go to lunch.'

Lunch? I suffered a sudden mental image of the two morning pills hanging on the inside of my empty stomach for another hour. 'I usually have cereal first.'

He glanced at his watch. 'OK, why don't you show me what you've written and I'll read through it while you have breakfast.'

'It's probably rubbish.'

'I'd *really* like to read it.'

I braced myself then hurried over to my desk and scooped up a dozen or so handwritten pages. 'The writing's a bit scribbly. You probably won't be able to read it.'

I turned. Matthew was beside me frowning. 'Why didn't you use your laptop?'

'I haven't got a printer.'

'They put your printer away?'

'Perhaps I didn't have one.'

'Sarah, all writers have a printer.' He took off his jacket and threw it across the desk. 'Go eat. I'm best on my own. And bring more tea.'

I was pouring the tea when I noticed my cereal box on the worktop. I thought I'd put it away. I realised that I was probably confused because someone was reading my work: writers are notoriously neurotic. Mrs Parkin had intimated as much. Some of my little foibles, she had said, might have always been there. I hurried over, opened the cupboard and slotted the cornflakes into their proper place …

'You realise it will take you years to eat that lot!'

I spun round, closed the cupboard door behind me and leant hard against it.

Matthew walked over and stood right in front of me, imprisoning me between himself and my hidden stash of cereal. My manuscript was in his hand.

'This is a fantastic piece of storytelling,' he said. 'What's with the cornflakes?'

I slithered out and along to my mug of tea, carried it over to the table and sat down. 'My spelling must be awful.'

He placed the manuscript on the worktop and pulled a chair round to sit next to me. 'It's atrocious. Sarah, why have you got a million boxes of cornflakes in your cupboard?'

I concentrated on the table, on the patterns in the wood, on a pale ring left by some too-hot cup from the time before.

'Don't you want to talk about it?'

I could feel my teeth biting hard against my bottom lip, his arm closing around me.

'Hey, come on, don't cry.'

'I'm not crying!'

'Sweetheart, I think you are.' He pulled me closer, so close that his pullover was prickling my cheek. 'Sarah, tell me why your cupboard's full of cornflakes.'

I heard my voice whisper above the sound of my breathing. 'In case I get worse.'

'What? What difference would the cornflakes make?'

The whispering continued. 'Matthew, nobody knows what happened to me to make my memories go away. And I worry that, if I forget new things, forget who I am, then they might give up on me and forget about me, and if I've got my cupboard full of things to eat then I could keep myself alive until someone finds me.'

I remember feeling relieved to have said that. The idea felt lighter. And a little stupid. I became aware that time was taking too long to happen, felt Matthew kiss the top of my head, peered up into his watery eyes.

'Now *you're* crying?'

'I'm not, although I'm quite distraught at the thought of you being caged up in this flat with nothing but cornflakes and tap water.' He wiped his eyes on his shirt cuff. 'You could at least factor in some muesli. Do your minders know about this particular concern of yours?'

'No!'

'Typical!' He got to his feet. 'Come to lunch. And bring your story so we can discuss it.'

We both turned as the cat flap popped open.

'Ah, the cat,' observed Matthew. He watched it pad over and throw itself against his trousers: 'Does he bite?'

Episode Fifteen

The local newsagent opened at seven-thirty. I prepared myself over breakfast and then nipped along there just after eight, stepped inside, nodded to the grubby man behind the counter and politely avoided his two even grubbier customers, one of whom, I noticed, had a poorly-executed dragon tattooed around his neck. The three men were perusing headlines and exchanging obscenities about some sport or other. I walked nonchalantly over to the rack and snatched up this week's issue of the magazine from the hospital concourse. Then I checked that the three men were otherwise engaged before scanning the wealth of periodicals that were unashamedly dedicated to illustrating people having sex. These were desperate times. I needed urgent tuition. I selected the three magazines with the least harrowing cover illustrations, tucked them under the hospital mag and ventured over to pay. The shopkeeper scanned the top magazine while maintaining his sporting dialogue. When he came to the first of the sex magazines he snorted and held it up for all to see. There was grunting amusement. 'You just checking out your rates for a blow job, love?' asked the man with the dragon tattoo.

The three men continued to grunt. But I needed those magazines, so I waited for the laughter to subside then took out my purse, rooted around in the various compartments and then confessed that I only had a twenty-pound note.

'You've not been charging enough, sweetheart!' said dragon-tattoo man.

I ignored him and handed over the note. 'Do you have a bag?' I asked.

I couldn't understand why everything I said caused them to snort.

Back in the privacy of my flat, I spent the morning browsing through a vast collection of photos of naked men and women. I remember being quite overwhelmed by the way the images made me feel. I realised it was probably not appropriate for me to be feeling that way during Mrs Parkin's visit, so I squashed the magazines into the CD box in the cupboard and hurried to the kitchen to prepare the tray.

After handing over a packet of custard creams, Mrs Parkin was quick to inform me that the doctors had advised against reducing our counselling sessions.

'You must remind yourself, Sarah, that this new confidence has *not yet* managed to re-establish two decades of your memories. So, slow, slow, that's what we want, don't we?'

She pulled out a chair and sat down. She was looking insufferably pleased with herself and I found myself wondering whether Mrs Parkin had ever had sex like the women on page forty-six; the very thought of it caused me to snort like dragon man. Mrs Parkin was barely able to disguise her indignation:

'Have I said something to amuse you, Sarah?' she snapped.

'No, Mrs Parkin. I was thinking about something completely different. I've just finished my first whole story.'

'You've written a whole story?'

'Yes, about cooking apples.'

*

Straight after midday, I watched my beneficent counsellor walk off towards the house where no one lived. Then I closed the door and hurried to my desk to re-read Matthew's edits. Perhaps make a start on some illustrations. As I opened the blind to invite in enough light for sketching, I caught sight of Mrs Parkin walking back from her car. I watched her approach but, just the other side of Miss Lewis's house, she disappeared down the side alley that Miss Lewis shared with the house being renovated. I ran to the far side of my desk to get a better view of the pavement outside, pulled my desk chair round and kept vigil. Eventually, after about twenty minutes, Mrs Parkin emerged from the alley. I ducked down and stayed perfectly still and, when I looked up, there was an empty space where Mrs Parkin's car had been. Was Miss Lewis also being visited by a social worker? No, that wasn't likely. There could be only one explanation.

I was desperate to ask Matthew what to do, but I knew that would involve him too much in the weirdness, and I was very aware that, although he seemed to be incredibly tolerant of my unusual circumstances, there was probably a limit beyond which not even a saint could be expected to go. I would have to handle this alone. I resolved not to mention it to him. When he arrived, I would talk instead about my apple characters, Jack Laxton and Toby Pippin. So, when I opened my front door at five thirty and Matthew stepped inside, I was surprised to hear myself say, 'Mrs Parkin went next door to Miss Lewis after she came here.'

'Mrs Parkin, your counsellor?'

'Yes!' I glanced outside then closed the door.

'Well, it's probably nothing sinister. She's probably keeping the old girl up-to-date.'

'But I don't want people talking about me behind my back.' I watched him walk over and place his bag on the sofa. 'Matthew, how do you know Miss Lewis is *old*?'

He turned and frowned back at me. 'Sarah, why are you asking me that? I saw her through the window. Just now.'

I had a sudden mental image of Miss Lewis spying through her window. Ready to report back to Mrs Parkin about unacceptable visitors. 'Was she watching?'

'She was closing her curtains. I waved.'

I threw myself onto a sofa. 'What if she tells them about *you*?'

He sat down beside me: 'Sarah, you're allowed to meet people.'

'But they don't want anybody telling me things.'

'Telling you what?'

'I don't know. But they think my mind made me forget something terrible and if anybody tells me something it doesn't want me to know then it will erase another whole slice of my memories. I'm scared it will take away my new memories as well.'

He closed his hand around my clenched fist. 'God, Sarah, I don't want you forgetting me. I'd have to start all over again. Shopping five times a day. Throwing apples.'

I was successfully distracted. 'You said you shopped *three* times a day.'

'I didn't want you to think I was crazy.'

I leaned against his arm. 'So you did throw the apple?'

'Yes. To introduce myself.'

'To someone with a lost past.'

'I don't care about your past. I care about now!'

'Even though I said I didn't want to have sex with you?'

'Well, I must admit that was a bit of a blow. But Matthew Parry can wait.'

That made me smile. 'How long?'

'I don't know. It's never been tested.'

I started to laugh. 'They'll disapprove.'

'Tell them to go to Hell! Anyway, who are these people?'

I sank back into the sofa and heaved a sigh. 'There's Dr Gray and Dr Williams. And Mrs Parkin. And three research associates.'

'Three research associates?'

'Yes. One of them is investigating my vocabulary. And one of them asks me about story-telling. I don't know what the other one's interested in.'

'Do you … what are their names?'

There's Dr Clegg. And another man, I can't remember what he's called. And there's a lady doctor … I don't think they told me her name. Oh yes, Dr Brown.'

Matthew frowned. 'Dr Brown?'

'Yes. And there's Mrs Dickson, my cleaner, who's really a spy.'

Matthew leaned back beside me and said nothing.

'Then there's you. I can't think what they'd say if they knew about all this.'

He turned his head towards me. 'All what? We haven't done anything.'

'But, what if …' I pulled myself up to face him, suddenly more than ever aware of this large, after-shave-smelling, next-to-me, handsome man. I started to imagine …

He looked apprehensive. 'What's the matter?'

I could see myself reflected in his eyes, tried to imagine being one of the women on page forty-six. But I felt too thin, too trembly, too far away. I moved closer.

Matthew looked even more apprehensive. 'Sarah?'

I dared to touch his thigh and felt a surge of excitement so profound that it made me weak. 'Matthew, I want you to kiss me!'

A smile spread across his face. 'I'm irresistible, aren't I?'

I sagged away from him. 'Do you have to joke about everything?'

'You're making me nervous.'

'I didn't mean to.' I stroked his arm, ran my fingers down his sleeve so that my nails vibrated across the thin tweed, wished to God I'd never bought those magazines.

He watched my hand on his arm. 'Sarah, this is making me *very* nervous!'

'I'm sorry.' I pulled my hand away. 'I just suddenly wanted you to kiss me. Because, when you're with me I feel safe. And when you kissed me the other night, I didn't care what I couldn't remember. And …'

I caught my breath as he pulled me towards him, grasped his sleeve, let myself collapse beneath him. I inhaled the scent of his hair, felt his mouth on my throat, his hand inside my blouse. I felt myself rise weightless beneath him, readied myself for anything … then sank back heavy and exhausted as he pulled away from me. I lay there bewildered, disappointed, angry.

'Why did you stop?'

'Because I'd be taking advantage of you.'

I sat up and pulled myself tidy. 'What?'

'Look, Sarah, I've no idea how much of this you can possibly know.'

I looked at his lap. Shamelessly. 'I know you don't want to stop.'

He glanced down. 'Ignore that. It'll go away in a minute.'

'I don't want ...'

He lifted my hand away. 'Sarah, stop!' He stood up and pulled me to my feet, caught my other hand as I lowered it. Shamelessly. 'Sarah, please! You're not ready for this!'

I pulled away from him. Enraged. I virtually spat the words at him. 'Why does every *fucker* keep telling me I'm not ready!' I threw my hand across my mouth. I couldn't believe what had just come out of it: 'My granny would die if she heard me say that!'

'So would your readers.'

My only sensible option was to punch him and then march off to the kitchen.

'Sarah, wait!' He hurried after me, moving cautiously to my side. I ignored him. He watched me filling the kettle. 'Are you angry because we didn't have sex? I mean ... Well, it's pretty much a first for me. I don't know how to react.'

I nudged past him to get to the refrigerator. 'Shut up!'

'It's not that I don't want to.'

I stamped my foot. 'I feel *stupid*!'

'Well, don't. I think you're gorgeous. It's just that ...'

'*You don't think I'm ready*!' I pushed back past him, snatched two mugs from the dresser, banged them onto the worktop and turned to glare at him. 'Go and sit down!'

He looked contrite. 'In here?'

'I don't care, just sit!'

He sat. 'Sarah, if this is making you upset, I will, I mean, we can ...'

I grabbed the carton of milk and resumed glaring. 'I don't want to anymore. *I might never want to again*!'

I placed such stress upon that last threat that the milk I was pouring arced over the mug onto the worktop. 'Oh shit!'

Matthew leapt up, grabbed a tea towel and caught the flow just as it was about to waterfall onto the floor.

'Love, why don't you let me make the tea … Hey, don't be upset!' He threw down the cloth and put his arm around me. 'I'm so sorry. I was only trying to do … not do …'

'Do you think I'm going to start swearing uncontrollably?'

'What? No, it's my fault. My mother says I'm enough to make anyone swear.'

I was jolted from my melancholy. 'Is your mother still alive?'

'Yes. She lives in Spain. With my father.'

I sighed. 'I don't have parents. My father's untraceable and my mother's dead.'

Matthew took a step back. 'Your mother *died*?'

'Yes.'

'When?'

'I don't remember. I think it was when I was really little. I lived with my grandma.' I was confused by his sudden concern. I had clearly upset him. All that promiscuousness and swearing. 'Matthew, I'm so sorry I behaved like that.'

He shook his head. 'Don't be. Your charming prince will make it right.'

Episode Sixteen

Before leaving for the hospital, I practised texting Matthew on my mobile until I was almost casual about the whole process. I intended to maintain casual during my consultation with Dr Williams. As it was, it was not Dr Williams who greeted me when I stepped into the consulting room: it was Shoumi Mustafa, wearing an expression of academic determination and no white coat. He got to his feet and extended his hand across the desk.

'Good morning, how are you today, Sarah?'

For the first time, I noticed his accent. American I thought.

I shook his hand. Casually. 'I'm fine.'

He indicated for me to take the seat opposite, sat down and adjusted his cuffs. I watched him checking his notes, his hands resting on the buttons of his waistcoat. He was quite stocky and I remember thinking that he looked like a well-dressed bear. The pattern on his tie was too busy, almost threatening. I decided to avoid looking at it.

'Now, Sarah, before we start let me explain. I've put together a few simple lexical tests: word meanings, synonyms, word associations, to see whether your language abilities have been impaired or altered in any way. We ...'

'But how will you know if my language has altered?'

His look was a little too patronising. 'We have documentation from before your incident. And, of course, your writing.' He pushed a sheet of paper and a pencil towards me. 'Shall we begin?'

I scanned the page in front of me: two columns, the left-hand column a series of words. The wider, right-hand column was blank.

'You'll see a series of words on the left. What I want you to do is write a short sentence in each of the adjacent spaces to demonstrate that you know what each of the words means. If you're not certain just put a cross. Do you understand what I'm asking you to do? Be as speedy as you can. There are other exercises.'

I read the words in front of me. It felt like being back in school but with nobody to get better marks than me if I didn't know the answers. I started to write.

Apple: *Sarah bit into her apple and disturbed the family of maggots living inside.*

Stair: *If you stair at the sun it hurts your eyes.*

Wife: *The farmer's wife hated blind mice.*

The exercise took over fifteen minutes to complete, during which time Dr Mustafa made two phone calls, which made composing sentences difficult. I slid the finished sheet towards him. He snatched it up and replaced it with another list of words but this time I had to provide synonyms. I attempted diligence but as I racked my brain to think of an alternative to *Marriage*, it occurred to me to question how these exercises might recover my lost memories. Dr Mustafa was engrossed in annotating my previous test.

'Why am I doing this?'

He glanced up: 'Sorry?'

'I don't know why I'm doing this.'

A brief irritation flashed across his face. 'Sarah, we need to comprehend this kind of memory aberration and the possible effects it has had upon your cognitive processes. Your disorder does not seem to be associated with any form of physical compromise.' He folded his arms. 'The pattern of loss which you demonstrate has left specific memories intact while others appear to have been expunged utterly. I believe Dr Gray mentioned that your capacity for language is my particular concern? I am trying to determine any vocabulary involvement, any acquired language deficiencies, in what appears to be an involuntary suppression of memory.' He paused with a smile as if this explanation should calm my doubts.

I considered this useless burst of information; one phrase in particular stuck in my mind.

'Do I have language deficiencies?'

'Sarah, it is to answer that *very* question that I have devised these tests.'

I regarded him briefly then returned to my task.

Shoumi Mustafa left clutching my exercise sheets. Sam Clegg's interview followed immediately after. He chatted to me about my writing and asked me if I could describe a day spent with my grandmother. Then he asked me to retell that same childhood day but to add another, imaginary, person to the story: an unexpected visitor. I imagined a crazy astronomer. Then he asked me how differently I felt about the two versions of the story. I was not too clear about his purpose although I really enjoyed his session. The third interview started not at all well. Dr Clegg held the door open. Della Brown stepped through and waited for it to close behind him. I sensed an unpleasant chemistry between them.

'Hello, Sarah,' she said, making brief eye contact. 'How are you today?'

'I'm fine.'

She took her seat and flicked through her notes, her pen poised. Her hand was not that steady. 'Just a few questions ...'

'Questions about what, Dr Brown?'

She glanced up, her pale face displaying disapproval. 'About what you can remember.'

'But I've already told everybody everything I can remember. I don't mean to be unhelpful, but I can't remember anything else.'

'I gather you *could* remember how to drive.'

'I could work the car but I'd forgotten most of the rules.'

'Don't you think that's strange?'

'I don't know what's strange. At the moment, everything seems strange. When I woke up I could count and read but, when I tried to write, all I could manage was lists. Then last weekend I could write properly. But I still can't remember writing my books.' I waited for her to stop writing then resumed. 'I'd forgotten what I liked to eat. I could remember colours and the names of flowers and left and right. But I couldn't remember my clothes. I had loads of shoes. I don't like most of them. I couldn't use my mobile phone, not even after Mrs Parkin showed me. I don't remember anybody from before.' I paused. 'I don't know what else to tell you.'

'What about right and wrong?'

'What?'

'Did you remember what things you should and shouldn't do?'

I shrugged. 'Mrs Parkin did keep reminding me not to take things from shops without paying for them. But I already knew shoplifting was wrong. And any other kind of stealing.' I watched the slow and meticulous note-taking. 'And I realised I shouldn't shout in public or go up and speak to people I didn't know.'

I didn't much like Della Brown. In fact, looking back, I didn't like her at all. Even then, when I had no idea who she really was. I remember thinking that she must have missed out on that being-nice-to-patients course in her medical training because she was horrible. It was as if she was trying to trick me by re-asking the same jumbled question until I gave her the answer she wanted.

She glanced up, unsmiling. 'What about not telling the truth?'

'If you mean lying, my grandma taught me not to do that.'

'And what about adultery?'

'I don't suppose she mentioned adultery. Although that usually involves lying, doesn't it? Why are you asking me these questions? Will it help bring my memories back?'

She held my gaze. 'Do you want your memories back, Sarah?'

I was not expecting that. Through all the long weeks since those too-bright days in the clinic, nobody had ever hinted that I might not want to remember my past. The assumption had been from the very start that my memories were hidden from me and that the intention must be to release them from wherever they were imprisoned. I considered my reply.

'Everybody wants their memories, don't they?'

'One presumes so,' she said, still holding my gaze.

'But I'm scared what it is that my mind wants me to forget. It must have been really terrible. But nobody will tell me what happened.'

'Apparently, nobody knows what happened.'

'But they do know some things. They emptied my flat. Took my photos. I know I agreed to this treatment, but they're keeping me away from everyone I knew. And I'm worried that if there were people close to me ...' As I voiced those fears, an additional concern arose in the pit of my stomach. What if there had been someone, someone very close? And meantime I was spending all my time thinking about Matthew.

'The alternative would have been to keep you in the clinic.'

'What?'

'I gather that the preferred treatment involves isolating you from a sudden influx of information. To avoid secondary dissociation. To encourage your recapture of the past by your own means. Dr Williams recommended an extended stay at the clinic. It was Robert Gray who insisted upon your return home with close monitoring.'

'But what if I never remember? Do they expect me to live like a prisoner for the rest of my life, never speaking to anyone from before? What if there was someone special ...'

'But you don't remember anyone like that?'

I shook my head: 'How ... how can I not remember making love?'

'But you don't remember that?'

'No. I don't remember anything like that. But in the last few days, I've had these feelings ...' I wasn't sure why I was telling this unsympathetic woman all this. 'I just ...'

The phone rang. Della Brown lifted the receiver. 'Della Brown ... yes.' She frowned. 'But I was only speaking to him ... what?' She glanced over at me. 'What shall I tell Ms Blake? ... OK, yes ... Thanks, Shoumi, bye.' She put down the phone and watched it for a moment before re-engaging. 'Sarah, Dr Williams is unable to see you today. There's been an emergency.' She glanced over at the door. 'So when we're finished here, perhaps we might continue our discussion over lunch. There's a sandwich bar close by ...'

'You mean outside the hospital?' Something told me that such patient-doctor dalliance wasn't right.

Della Brown hesitated. 'We can go to the hospital cafeteria if you're uncomfortable about leaving the complex.'

'No! I'm OK about it.'

'Right! I'll fetch my things!'

She snatched up her folder, hurried over to the door and stepped outside. Her attention was instantly drawn towards a commotion, a burst of shouting coming from further along the corridor. She quickly closed the door behind her and the shouting became muffled. I waited. After a good five minutes, she stepped back into the room and beckoned me to follow her. As we hurried towards the lift, I took the opportunity to glance behind. Just beyond the consulting rooms two uniformed men were squeezed into a doorway where some kind of altercation was still underway. I tried to pick up snippets of conversation but Della Brown turned to attract my attention.

'I gather your car's in unlimited parking,' she said.

*

It was more an unsavoury café than a sandwich bar, noisy with workers from the construction site nearby. Della Brown strode over to the counter to order sandwiches and coffees; a couple of the workmen watched her checking her phone. I felt very uneasy. So I took the opportunity to check my own mobile. I poked buttons. Watched the screen. Accidentally turned it off. Managed to turn it on again. No messages.

'You can use it now, can you?'

I looked up. 'I'm still hopeless. Every time I try to write a text, I forget how to spell.'

'Did you tell Dr Mustafa that? It's the kind of detail he's interested in, isn't it?'

She sat down and placed her phone face down on the table.

'Yes, he's investigating my language deficiencies.' I dropped my mobile back into my bag. 'What are *you* investigating?'

Della Brown forced a smile. Her face seemed little accustomed to such an effort. 'I suppose you might call it forensic psychology.'

'Because I was unconscious on a beach?'

'You could say that. Were you previously familiar with the Devon coastline?'

I wasn't sure what she meant. 'Did you say Devon?'

'Yes, Devon. Have you any idea why you were found there? How you got to Beer?'

'Was that where they found me?'

'Yes, in Beer Cove.'

'I'm sorry, I've never heard of it.'

'Really? Don't you remember Inspector Broderick and ... Don't you remember the police coming to the clinic to interview you? Asking you about Beer Cove?'

'Not really. The time in the clinic seems to be crunched together. I don't remember any police interview.'

Our sandwiches and coffee arrived. I looked down at my plate and immediately lost my appetite. But I knew I couldn't complain, so I took a large bite of leathery ham and white bread. It was like chewing cotton wool. I noticed Della Brown watching me.

'Do you like ham, Sarah? I should have asked you, but it was all they had.'

'It's very nice. Would you like me to give you some money?'

She laughed. 'No, this is on expenses!'

I forced a smile then struggled on through the disgusting sandwich and the bitter coffee, answered numerous questions about everything from my writing to immigration and waited for Della Brown to suggest getting back. But she suggested nothing of the kind. She pushed her unfinished sandwich to one side.

'Did they arrange your flat to your liking?'

'They took away most of my things.'

'What things?'

'I don't know. You could ask Mrs Parkin if you think it's important.'

Just then Della Brown's phone vibrated. She snatched it up and listened, said, 'Right!' then slipped it into her pocket.

'Shall we be getting back?' she said. 'I have a meeting.'

Episode Seventeen

I checked my bedside alarm, then the wall clock in the lounge, watched the minute hand approach twenty past five, half past, quarter to six. My stomach churned as every jolt of time declared that he might not be coming. I went to the kitchen, cleaned the refrigerator and threw away an avocado that was never going to ripen. When the kitchen clock turned to six twenty, I went through to my bedroom, curled up across my pillows and tried to think of nothing. My eyes strayed around my room: everything somebody else had decided I would need. From where I was lying I could see my entire shoe collection, some pairs still in boxes but most of them squashed together across the floor of the open wardrobe. I pushed myself up on to one elbow and tried to imagine the kind of person I had been, a woman who needed so many pairs of shoes. One pair of sandals was bright orange. I dragged myself off the bed and walked over to take a closer look. For some reason the thought of feet encased in orange made me feel nauseous. So I eased them out together with some pink trainers, two pairs of beaded flip-flops, and some hideously high black patent stilettos with soles that looked as if they had never touched the ground. I carried them all through into the kitchen and threw them on the table, ready for the charity shop tomorrow. The doorbell rang. I ran through to the front door and pulled it open.

'Why are you late?'

'Sarah, I've been phoning you for the last three hours. Your house phone just rings.' He squeezed past me with a bag of groceries and a large flat box, stooped to kiss me.

I glanced outside then pushed the door closed. 'What's in the box?'

'TV. Didn't you think to check your mobile?'

'It didn't ring all day.'

He propped the box against the coffee table. 'That's because we put it on silent so it didn't make a noise during your appointment.'

I hurried over to investigate my mobile. Ten missed calls, two voicemails and a text. Matthew eased it from my grasp, deleted the voicemails and text.

'You seem to have a mental block about this bloody thing. I was held up.' He handed me the phone. 'Tonight I'm cooking skate wings.' He pulled me into the kitchen, emptied the food onto the worktop and walked over to investigate the home phone. 'The plug's out!'

'I always pull it out so the house doesn't catch on fire when I'm not here. I forgot to put it back.' I watched him reconnect me. 'Doesn't it work if it's pulled out? It's got a battery.'

'Yes, but the base unit …' He rolled his eyes. 'Do you remember how to peel potatoes? My God, shoes!'

'They're for the charity shop.'

'Right. Isn't it unlucky to put shoes on the table?'

'Only if they're new.'

He looked at me. 'You remember that?'

'My granny used to say it.'

'Right. Anyway, fetch a bag. I do not cook when there are shoes on the table!'

I fetched a carrier bag. 'Are you cross?'

'No, I'm stressed.' He started to transfer shoes.

I watched the flip-flops and the orange sandals be consigned to someone else's life.

'Because we argued about sex?'

'No!' He held up a patent stiletto. 'Why are you getting rid of these?'

'I didn't think I'd be able to walk in them. Do you think they're sexy?'

He looked at me and sighed. 'Possibly!'

I laughed at his expression. 'In that case I'll keep them.' I went to reclaim my shoe but he lifted it out of reach.

'Sarah, if you mention sex one more time, I will not cook your supper!' He picked up the matching stiletto and handed them over. 'Go put them back in … wherever you keep your sexy outfits.'

I laughed. '*You* said it.'

'I'm allowed. Hurry up and peel the potatoes! I'll set up the TV.'

'What if Mrs Parkin sees it?'

'We'll hide it.'

The skate wings were amazing. I couldn't remember tasting anything so delicious. We cleared away then watched the microwaves inflating our movie popcorn. It was Matthew's opinion that I should take advantage of my current predicament by watching *Home Alone*, and *Jurassic Park* before I remembered that I'd seen them already. And he insisted that no children's author should be ignorant of the emergent wizardry of Harry Potter. The microwave pinged. He put the bowl of popped corn on to the worktop and drenched it in sweet butter. It smelled of happiness. It reminded me of ... of ... No, it was gone like a dream.

I followed him into the lounge. 'Who taught you to cook?'

'My mother. She thought it would protect me from stumbling into an unrewarding marriage just because I needed someone to cook my supper.'

'And did it save you?'

He set the bowl on the table then bent down to insert the DVD.

'Unfortunately not. We'll start you off with cloning dinosaurs. Unless you'd prefer the escapades of a small boy accidentally left at home by his fecund parents.' He backed towards the sofa and pressed Start.

'Matthew!'

'What?'

'You're married?' I didn't want him to be married.

'I *was*. To Maddie. We still see each other from time to time. She's married to a lawyer. Sit down. I'll wind through the trailers.'

I didn't want him to see her from time to time. 'Do you still ...'

'No!' He paused the DVD and sighed. 'We met in college, got married a month after graduation then spent the next two years realising that all we had in common was college, so she went off and married her lawyer.'

'Was her name Ashdown?'

'No, Lucy Ashdown came later.'

'Do you still see *her*?'

'No!'

'Were you married?'

'No!'

'But you lived together?'

'Some of the time.'

'In Crouch End?'

'No, in a desirable detached property in Hampstead and I'd rather not talk about it.'

I watched him not restart the DVD. 'What happened?'

'We screwed around.'

'You mean you were unfaithful?'

He laughed. 'Something like that. What a wonderful word! Matthew was unfaithful! Shall we watch the movie?'

'Yes. What does *fecund* mean?'

He held out his arm. 'Pass the popcorn. I'll explain later.'

*

I was not looking forward to any further conversations with Drs Mustafa or Brown, although I was quite excited about the prospect of doing more of Sam Clegg's storytelling exercises. So, when I walked into Dr Gray's Regent's Park consulting room, I was almost disappointed to discover my elderly psychotherapist sitting alone at his desk. He looked up from his notes.

'Hello, Sarah. And how are you this fine day?'

'I'm good, Dr Gray. I was expecting to see the research associates.'

Dr Gray raised his eyebrows. 'Indeed, but I've decided that today it's more important for us to have a little uninterrupted chat. Sort a few things out.'

'What things?'

'Nothing too serious. Tell me, Sarah, how are you getting along with Mrs Parkin? Do you feel you can discuss your problems with her?'

'I don't really have any problems. Apart from my memory.'

'Do you like Mrs Parkin?'

I wasn't sure how to answer that question. 'Am I supposed to like her?'

Dr Gray laughed. 'Not really. We just wanted you to have somebody to confide in apart from the clinical staff.' He checked his notes. 'And what about your home help ... Mrs Dickson?'

'I really like her. Dawn was quite nice but I prefer Mrs Dickson.'

'Dawn?'

'She came last Friday when Mrs Dickson wasn't well.'

He wrote a quick note then he looked up. 'So, anything to report?'

'I seem to have a mental block about my mobile phone.'

'Any idea why you think that is?'

'Perhaps my mind is worried it might tell me something it doesn't want me to know.'

'Could be.' He paused and sat looking at me. His silence made me feel really uncomfortable. At last he spoke. 'Sarah, would you like to tell me about the gentleman you've been meeting?'

Dr Gray knew about Matthew! All that time I'd been worried that they were spying on me and they actually *had* been spying on me! He waited for my response. But I wasn't sure what to say. In fact, I wasn't at all certain that I would be able to say anything. I tried to swallow but my mouth felt numb. Dr Gray clearly perceived my discomfort and pushed a glass of water towards me.

'Can we chat about it, Sarah? We ought to get our story worked out before you see Mrs Parkin tomorrow.'

I took the glass and sipped tiny amounts until I was sure my swallowing reflex had returned, placed the glass back on the table and took a deep breath.

'We met at the supermarket and we went for coffee. And he took me to a restaurant and I told him about my memory. He cooks me supper. Last night we had skate wings and popcorn and we watched *Jurassic Park*. At my flat.' I noticed Dr Gray was smiling at me. 'I wanted him to stay, but he said I wasn't ready.'

Dr Gray looked surprised. 'My goodness, that sounds very gallant, doesn't it? And do *you* think you're ready?'

'Yes!'

'I see. No doubts about that, then?'

'But, Dr Gray, I *do* have doubts. I'm worried that there might be someone from before. Nobody has told me anything about the years I can't remember. What if I'm hurting somebody by being with Matthew? His name's Matthew Parry. How did you find out about him?'

'Well, Sarah, we wouldn't deserve our enormous salaries if we didn't find out about things like that, would we? But I don't think you should worry about hurting anybody.' He watched me over the top of his spectacles. 'I assure you there are no left-over romances, so, as far as I'm concerned, you are free to get to know this new man of yours. But, Sarah, we would have preferred you to mention this friendship. You shouldn't feel that you need to keep things from us.' He checked his notes again. 'And we had better make sure we're looking after you properly.' He reached for his phone. 'I just need to make a quick call. Then you can tell me ...

'Hello, Geraint, Bob here, I'm just looking through Sarah's notes, and we don't seem to be prescribing any form of contraception. Do you think you could confirm that for me and, if necessary, set that in motion as soon as possible, preferably before she leaves ... I would rather you do it ... Yes, I'm sure you do but our immediate problem is to prevent a potentially worse situation ... I really do not see that as necessary and probably ill-advised given the circumstances.' He smiled towards me. 'If you recall I did advise against it. I gather ... Well, we'll have to accommodate that problem if it arises. The prescription, Geraint, please, we'll discuss the other issues later ... Yes, of course.' He rang off.

'So, Sarah, tell me about your Mr Parry.'

Episode Eighteen

I left the Regent's Park rooms with more pills and a leaflet about sexual health. Driving home I considered the various scenarios through which Dr Gray might have learned about Matthew, the most likely being that Miss Lewis told Mrs Parkin who told Dr Williams. I pulled up outside my flat and averted my eyes from any possible encounter with my elderly neighbour and, once inside, I made tea and sat at the kitchen table trying to rationalise. I wanted to go and ask Miss Lewis whether she'd snitched on me but I was not at all confident in my ability to pull that off tactfully. I turned as the black and white cat stepped through the flap:

'Hi, puss, fancy some lunch?'

The cat threw itself against my leg then padded over to its empty platter and waited. I hurried to tip cat biscuits onto the willow pattern; the last few fell onto the impatient purring head.

'Can't you wait, greedy? Doesn't anyone else feed you?'

And thereby came inspiration: who owned the black and white cat? Tracing its ownership would be a perfectly legitimate reason to go next door and interrogate Miss Lewis. So I spent the next twenty minutes preparing a casual first statement. As it was, when Miss Lewis opened her door, I said, 'Who owns the black and white cat?'

Miss Lewis was a frail, elderly lady, probably in her early seventies, although she looked tired and even older than that, and she clearly wasn't expecting to be challenged in this way. She offered me a nervous smile.

'Hello, Sarah, how are you? Nice bit of sunshine to make us all happy.'

I wondered whether she was going to mention the cat. I prepared to re-ask the question but she saved me the trouble:

'He's a friendly old thing is Alfie. He got used to me when you were away. And he still comes for leftovers. But I wouldn't encourage him, not now you're back home. I do give him milk from time to time. But I'm not trying to entice him away.'

I stared at Miss Lewis, not really sure what she was talking about. She opened the door wider and pointed along the dim hallway.

'He likes to sleep on the kitchen windowsill. I won't let him in if you'd prefer me not to.'

'What?' I said.

'Your Alfie. I just let him in if he cries outside.'

'*My* Alfie?'

Miss Lewis' face fell. 'Oh dear, I ...'

'The black and white cat's *my* cat?'

'Oh, I *am* sorry, Sarah, have I said something wrong?'

I suddenly felt light-headed. I needed to lean on something, reached for the door, misjudged it and stumbled towards Miss Lewis, just catching the letterbox to prevent myself from knocking the startled woman backwards into her hallway. The impact twisted my fingers painfully and the sharp metal frame cut into my thumb, causing it to spurt blood. I pushed myself upright and held my hand against my sweatshirt, which instantly became smeared with dark red on the yellow. The combination heightened the nauseous sensation that was building in my chest.

Miss Lewis leaned towards me. 'Are you all right, dear?'

'I'm fine,' I gasped. I would have run home if I'd been sure my legs would cooperate.

Miss Lewis held out her hand.

'Deary me, Sarah, that looks nasty! Why don't you come in and let me take a look at it?'

Somehow my legs carried me over the threshold, into the hall and on into an unfamiliar lounge. Miss Lewis led me over to a large armchair, a little like Grandma Bramley's in the drawing I had made. She bent over me.

'Let's see how bad it is, shall we?'

I moved my hand away from my chest. The removal of pressure caused my thumb to ooze, but not as badly as before. Miss Lewis pulled a scented handkerchief from her pocket and placed it over the cut.

'You sit there, dear, and I'll go fetch some disinfectant. I don't think it's too bad. Thumbs always bleed a lot. Are you all right for a couple of minutes?'

I held the soft material against my thumb. I could smell rusty blood and a powdery perfume that reminded me of my grandma's bathroom, an artificial essence of roses and violets, sweeter and stronger than any flowers could ever be. I wasn't sure whether the smell comforted me or made me feel sick. I looked at my sweatshirt and thought of salt. I wasn't sure why. Miss Lewis returned, armed with a wet flannel, a bottle of TCP and a bandage.

'Kettle's on. Let's get you cleaned up, shall we?'

I watched Miss Lewis wipe the blood away from my thumb,

revealing the actual injury, which was surprisingly minor given the amount of blood that it had summoned. I winced as the disinfectant was poured directly on to the gash in my skin.

'Only stings for a second,' said Miss Lewis. 'Can't be too careful with all these new germs about. Now, let's get it covered up. I hope it doesn't stop you doing your writing.' She wound an expert bandage, finishing up with two circuits of my wrist and a tuck-in of the loose end. I felt her cold leathery fingers pressing against my skin.

'There! Would you like me to soak your jumper in some salt?'

'Salt?'

'Salt water. To remove the blood.'

'I think my granny used to do that.'

'All grannies used to do that. But you need to do it straightaway.'

'I'll do it as soon as I get home. Did you say the cat was mine?'

Miss Lewis folded the bloodied flannel. 'I'm so sorry, Sarah. They didn't tell me you didn't know.'

'Do they tell you what to say to me?'

'More like what not to say.'

'Do you know what happened to me, Miss Lewis?'

'Not really, dear. I know your memory's not right and that telling you things might be bad. And now I've told you about Alfie.'

'I was a bit surprised. But I'm glad he's mine. How often does Mrs Parkin visit you?' Miss Lewis looked uncertain. I smiled to reassure her. 'I've seen her disappear down the alley. She probably thinks that way I won't see her.'

Miss Lewis looked even more uncertain. She lowered her voice. 'She's a peculiar woman. There's no doubt about that. But I think she has your best interest at heart. She just asked me to keep an eye on you. Make sure you're managing.'

I had to ask. 'Miss Lewis, did you tell her about my visitor?'

'You mean your young man? No, I didn't tell her. There's keeping an eye and there's nosiness.' She placed a hand on my shoulder. 'You used to call me Peggy. Shall we have that tea?'

Before I left, Peggy and I agreed that, for the time being, Mrs Parkin should continue to believe that her neighbourhood conspiracy remained intact. This counter-connivance lifted my spirits so, as soon as I arrived home, I dragged off my sweatshirt, threw it into the rubbish then went through to run a bath. I selected a bottle of rose and jasmine gel and added it to the gushing water, pulled off my clothes and, being careful to protect my bandage, stepped into the bubbles, lay back and thought about my conversation with Dr Gray.

Twenty minutes of soaking later, I dripped through to my bedroom to inspect the bottom drawer I had been contemplating for the past two weeks. I pushed aside four optimistic bras and a diaphanous nightdress too slight for springtime, and slowly closed my fingers around a stash of disgraceful knickers, some of them almost non-existent.

An hour or so later, Matthew arrived bearing strawberries, swordfish steaks, vegetables, prosecco, a vast bunch of pink roses and …

'What's that?'

'An iPad!' He stepped inside and kissed my cheek. 'How did your psycho visit go today? I've got to check a contract before …' He threw everything down onto the sofa and lifted my hand. 'What in God's name did they do to you?'

'I went to see Peggy next door and I cut my thumb on her letterbox. I don't think she had anything smaller than this.'

'Let's take a look.' He held my wrist steady as he unwound the bandage.

I wiggled my thumb. 'It bled loads.'

He scrutinised the tiny wound then let go of my wrist and carried the slightly bloodied bandage to the bin. 'Go find a plaster. I'll start dinner.'

I left Matthew unpacking vegetables and went off to the bathroom in search of a plaster. I could hear him fussing around between the kitchen and the dining area and wandered out to discover my dining table set for two, a vase of pink roses at its centre. One of the roses had been sacrificed to provide the petals that were strewn around the base of the vase.

'Happy Anniversary. We met thirteen days ago. What on earth have you got on your thumb now?'

'Batman plaster. They were all I had. You found the vases!'

He was momentarily caught off guard: 'I ... I've been rifling through your cupboards. There's a box with CDs written on it. Do you fancy some music?'

'Not really, but if *you* do ...'

'No. Go choose a movie.'

As with the previous evening, Matthew instructed me on the complex art of making after-dinner coffee, or, in fact, any coffee. 'That's right,' he suggested. 'See how much nicer it looks when it doesn't have lumps in it?'

I jabbed him in the ribs then reached for the tray. 'Oh, the sugar bowl's empty.'

'I'll do it!'

I turned to instruct him: 'It's in the tall cupboard ... Oh, you found it!'

He was holding a packet of soft brown sugar: 'Lucky guess! Could have been an ironing board. Or cornflakes. I'm yet to rifle through your drawers.'

I instantly recalled my drawer of shameful knickers and assumed what I hoped was an attitude of calm detachment. 'You take the coffees through. I won't be a minute. And put some tuna down for Alfie. That's the cat's name. Peggy said he's mine.'

'That would explain the cat flap. Do you think he'd like to watch the movie with us?'

'No! He's not allowed in the lounge even if he *is* mine.'

'But I am, right?'

I indicated the coffees. '*Matthew*, take them in.'

I left Matthew loading the tray and hurried away to the bedroom. Five minutes later I walked as casually as I could into the lounge to join him, although the four-inch heels made walking casually utterly impossible. Matthew was sitting opposite the TV; he turned as I approached.

'Did you remember to … Jesus Christ, Sarah!'

He leapt to his feet, knocking the edge of the coffee table and causing coffee to splash over the tray. I realised that it was probably not so much the patent stilettos that had caused this startled reaction but rather the fact that all I was wearing besides the shoes was the black lace knickers I had plucked from my drawer several hours earlier, a concealed outfit that I had been obsessing about throughout the entire evening. I continued to walk towards him, praying that one of the skinny heels would not catch in the carpet and blight my performance. He watched me approach. I reached him after what seemed like an age, placed my hand upon the soft cashmere of his sleeve, and steadied myself whilst I stepped out of the shoes: 'These are impossible to walk in!' I let go of his arm and looked up at him.

Finally, Matthew broke his frozen silence. 'I see you've taken your plaster off.'

I showed him my thumb, pushed my hair back away from my bare shoulder, said nothing.

He took my recently compromised hand in his: 'Sarah ...' He exhaled frustration. 'This is not leaving me a whole lot of alternatives.'

I stroked my free hand down his chest and tugged at the waist of his trousers. 'I was hoping there'd be *no* alternatives.' I couldn't believe I had just said that, but as I felt his chaste resolve crumble, I was really grateful I had.

He closed his hands around my arms. 'Sarah, are you sure about this?'

'Yes!' I could hear him controlling his breathing, could see the concern in his eyes. I needed to reassure him. 'Dr Gray said I needn't worry about any leftover romances, so ...'

I felt his fingers loosen. He took a step back. 'He said what?'

Suddenly I felt naked. Folded my arms around myself. 'I told him about you ... Well, he knew already. And I said I was worried there was someone from before that I might be hurting if I carried on throwing myself at you like this. And he said there wasn't anybody for me to worry about.'

Matthew looked at me for a long moment then his confusion broke into a smile. 'So you're throwing yourself at me, are you? With Dr Gray's approval?'

I felt every scrap of confidence disintegrate beneath my black knickers. 'I'm trying to but I'm obviously CRAP at it! What are you doing? Are you taking your clothes off?'

His jumper and shirt landed on the floor. The sight of his bare chest, his shoulders, the muscles in his arms terrified me. Took my breath away. He sat down and pulled off his shoes and socks. Unzipped his zip. I could feel my breath coming in shallow bursts. I feared that I might faint but somehow I managed to speak. 'Are we going to make love?'

'I would think so.' He stepped out of his trousers and scooped me up.

I caught hold of his smooth shoulder, felt his arm strong and warm across the back of my thighs, glanced at the empty bottle of prosecco as it rushed past, the scattered rose petals, my wardrobe door left open. I heard the bed groan to accommodate our weight. Felt his lips cool against my throat. Felt my body move with his. And, that night, I learned for the second time what it was like to make love for the first time.

*

I lay still, listening to my blood pulsing hard to catch up with me, felt my skin against his, my whole body rise and fall with his breathing as if his breathing was all the time that there was. These were the moments I had craved since I first saw him: his fingers stroking, tracing a small arc just above my waist. I felt him kiss the top of my head, shifted slightly and my senses became filled with his fragrance. My hand strayed easily against his shoulder as I pushed myself up to see his face, his eyes glistering in the dim lamplight, almost colourless. It was all too familiar. I felt for his hand, linked my fingers into his and was certain.

'I know you already, don't I? From before.'

Episode Nineteen

I felt his breathing deepen, his heart beat faster, felt the words rise within him.

'I missed you. Sarah, love. I couldn't leave you on your own like that. They warned me not to interfere, that it might make you worse, but I thought they were wrong and I …'

I placed my finger across his lips.

He closed his hand around my fingers. 'You need to sleep.'

'I don't want to sleep.'

*

It was still not light. I felt the duvet being pulled across my shoulder. I rolled over. Matthew was propped up on several pillows reading the iPad. 'It's not time to wake up yet,' he said. 'Go back to sleep. I'll wake you when it's morning.'

I touched his arm. 'What are you doing?'

'Checking a contract. New author. Could be the next Roald Dahl. We've got a meeting at ten, which is about six hours from now.' He pushed the iPad to one side. 'Do you want your pillows back? You threw them on the floor.'

'I always do that.'

'I know. Are you alright? Are you angry with me about not telling …?'

'Yes.' I moved closer. 'Tell me how we met. Do you remember?'

'I'm not supposed to tell you things like that.'

'I want to know! Tell me! Or I'll be *really* cross with you. When was it?'

He put the iPad on the floor. 'I really shouldn't do this …'

I wriggled with anticipation.

'It was May, four years ago. I was just struggling into the third year of the business, sitting in my office, praying for a J.K. Rowling to walk in and throw me a quill-written manuscript …

'Lucy, I don't know what you expect me to do about this. I can't conjure brilliant writers out of the air just because your bloody accessories bill has gone beyond its first million.'

'For fuck's sake, darling, you've had no end of manuscripts …'

'They were NOT good enough!'

'… loaded with all kinds of wizards and dysfunctional families and freak animals. I remember one about unicorns.'

'I have standards, for God's sake!'

'Standards? Matthew, darling, we're talking about children's books!'

'*Lucy*, I am not having this argument again. I'm not going to embarrass myself with wishy-washy crap about wannabe Harry Potters … or philanthropic vampires. Or retro-fucking-Blyton! I'm looking for something different.' He reached over and rotated his desk puzzle 180 degrees. A cacophony of ball bearings reorganised themselves.

Lucy Ashdown watched him ignore her. 'You know, Matthew, you're such an arrogant arse. You think you're some kind of literary gatekeeper when, in actual fact, all you are is another guy waiting to make a buck out of someone else's words!'

He looked up from the ball bearings. 'So you can go and spend that same buck on a pair of Manolo flip-flops!'

She straightened her skirt. 'OK. I haven't got time or the inclination to argue. I'm having lunch with David Marchant.' She inclined her head. 'Hillier's new MD?'

'I know who he is!'

'I was hoping to offer him something.'

'Well, I'm sure you'll think of an alternative to literature. I'll be careful not to wait up.'

He pulled his laptop closer and listened for the door to close, before taking out his mobile and checking messages. He scrolled down until he came to the number he was looking for, read the two lines with satisfaction and replied: 20MINS CANT W8. As his declaration flashed through cyberspace he heard footsteps approaching, threw his mobile into his jacket pocket and braced himself for deceit. The door opened: 'Lucy, I ...'

A flurry of denim, shoulder bag and brown hair rushed into the room. Its owner, a young woman, seemed to be on an inevitable collision course with his desk. But she halted just short of impact and stared straight at him. Then, without introduction, she hauled an enormous red apple from her bag and banged it down on his desk, narrowly missing his Publishers' Association paperweight. And, as if that wasn't enough, she pulled a wad of paper out from under her denimed arm and banged that down beside the unsolicited fruit. Her eyes blazed. Her gaze did not stray from his:

'I'll give you half this apple if you read my book because it's the best *fucking* book in the world and it's worth sacrificing half an apple for!'

He fought for some kind of sentient riposte, at the very least an appropriate reaction.

'Isn't it worth a whole apple?' he asked.

'That's what I want *you* to tell *me*!'

He felt himself nodding. An image of one of those wobble-headed dogs that people kept on the back shelf of their cars sprang into his mind. He needed to respond to this unreasonable behaviour, immediately and cleverly, in a style worthy of his position and expertise. But her brown eyes were searing straight through into his grey matter and transforming him into an idiot.

'What are you going to do with the other half?' he managed to say.

'I'm going to eat it!' she replied, without a moment's hesitation.

He was clean out of neurons. He took a deep breath. 'Have you just escaped from somewhere?'

The brown eyes continued to look at him. 'I wouldn't tell you if I had.'

OK, this was an emergency. He was completely at a loss. He was not used to being the weakest link in a conversation, if this was a conversation, which he doubted. He was also not used to his office being invaded by seemingly unstable aspiring clients, if that's what she was, which he also seriously doubted. So he opted for,

'The name's Parry. Matthew Parry.'

'It doesn't suit you.'

Damn this woman! 'Right. Do *you* have a name?'

She seemed irritated by the question. She pointed her finger. 'It's on the front page.'

Instinctively, he looked down at the papers, the apple, back to the papers: 'It says Sarah Blake. I ... we mostly handle young adult literature. Even younger. Depends how good it is ...'

'It's for young children. And it's fantastic!' she indicated the chair that still wafted Lucy Ashdown's unmistakeable perfume. 'Shall I sit here?'

'Er?'

'While you read it.' She sat down and settled her bag on her lap.

What? He cleared his throat. 'You want me to read it *now*?' He glanced at his watch.

'Yes, or I'll go somewhere else. It's up to you. Your eyes are a very strange colour, aren't they?'

'I had them done to match the bedroom curtains.' *Damn, not that old line!* 'Look, I can't possibly read with you looking at me.' Now he was defending himself. This had to end. 'And I'm meeting someone in …' He glanced at his watch. 'Ten minutes!'

Sarah Blake jumped to her feet, walked back to her previous position and bent over to reclaim the apple. Without thinking, He leant forward and caught her hand.

'Wait!' He withdrew into the safety of his chair. 'I … give me a minute.' He took out his mobile and keyed in a brief message: HELD UP.

She watched him, her arms folded, her eyes flickering with the promise of triumph. Then she smiled. It was a wonderful smile. He rallied.

'Why don't I get you some coffee and then I'll go off and read this and, while you're sitting here waiting for me to come back, I'll send for the people from the asylum and they can take you back to your cell?' He smiled back at her. At last he had regained the ascendancy. But it had been a close-run thing.

'I don't want coffee. Can't you offer your authors anything else?'

This was unbelievable! He picked up the phone and pressed a button. 'Poppy, have we got something other than coffee? … I don't know: tea, chocolate, hemlock …' He looked up from the phone. 'Do you fancy a glass of chardonnay?' He was gratified to see her shrug. At least that was not a complete rejection. 'OK. Poppy, sweetheart, bring glasses.' He put down the phone. 'What's it about?'

'What, my book? It's about what really happens to things when they go missing.'

'Fairies? Ghosts? Aliens?'

'No, something more interesting than *that*! It's about a place called Raggedy Lyme.' She almost smiled. 'Raggedy Lyme where there's wasted time.'

'Wasted time?' He wet his lips. Picked up the slim pile of papers, carried them over to the window and started to read. After no more than two minutes he looked up and reassessed this new person. 'Are there others?'

'It's a series.'

His pocket emitted a grinding noise. He paused to check the message. Gave a small regretful frown. Then he smiled.

'Fancy lunch? There's a nice little bistro not far from here. We can talk about the realities of publishing schedules. There's an art to stringing out a series.' At last he had achieved her silence. And another unbelievable smile.

The door opened and a flamboyant young man stepped into the room, two glasses in one hand and a bottle in the other.

'Thanks, Poppy,' said Matthew. 'Put it on ice would you? We're just nipping out to Tony's. And text Lucy and tell her to buy herself a new pair of flip-flops.'

Episode Nineteen (continued)

'Did I really say all that? What did you do?'

'I got a keypad entry system to protect me from mad people ... I read your manuscript. Then I phoned Hillier and told them a winner had landed on my desk.'

I pushed myself up on to one elbow. 'Are you my agent?'

'Of course I am!'

I rolled over and snuggled up to him. 'When were you going to tell me that?'

'I don't know.' He stroked my hair back over my shoulder. 'You ought to be asleep.'

'But I'm wondering.'

'Wondering what?'

'What kind of apple it was.' I stifled a yawn. 'So when did we become lovers?'

He took a deep breath. 'That is not an appropriate question at four o'clock in the morning. I'll tell you tomorrow.'

'I want to know *now*! Tell me *now*!'

He sighed. 'Well, surprisingly, we did not make love until well over two years later, in Burgundy, on the way back from the Frankfurt

Book Fair. You seduced me with the promise of a new manuscript. Sarah, go to sleep! You'll be tired.'

'Will you stay tomorrow night as well?'

'I'll stay every night. Now, will you … what are you doing?'

Episode Twenty

Before leaving, Matthew helped me compile a shopping list.

'Is this too much for you on your own? Why don't you wait until later? We can shop at five.'

I followed him into the lounge and watched him checking his shoulder bag. 'I always shop first thing to avoid the crowds.'

'But if I'm with you, you won't need to avoid the crowds. I've got to keep this appointment. I'm already risking a staff mutiny because I'm never there.'

'Have I been interfering with your job?'

'You could say that! But they all want to see you again.' He tugged at the sleeve of my dressing gown. 'I'll check with Dr Gray first.'

'Do they know we're together again?'

He laughed. 'More or less. I confided in Poppy and he's told everyone.'

'Poppy?'

'Poppy Abercrombie. He's one of my editors, in fact he's your editor.' He glanced at his watch. 'I've got to go.'

'I don't want you to go.' I slumped on the nearest sofa.

Matthew stepped over and sat down beside me. 'I have to. It's called going to work. Mrs P will be here in a couple of hours to keep you company. Make sure you don't accidentally mention me spending the night. Then if you get lonely after she's gone, go next door and ask to borrow your cat.' He kissed my forehead. 'I'll ring after lunch. What time does Mrs Parkin go?'

'One o'clock usually.' I followed him over to the front door. 'Matthew, if we were together before all this, why did you have a separate flat? Why didn't we live together?'

He turned to face me. 'It's complicated. We'll talk about it later.'

'Is there … is it just you in the flat in Crouch End?'

'Sarah, don't be ridiculous! It's just me and a tribe of very large spiders. Look, love, I have to go. I really will explain later, I promise.'

As he went to step outside, I caught hold of his sleeve. 'But you used to stay over, right? Then I just disappeared?'

He exhaled. 'I'll explain. Trust me. If you don't hear from me, meet me at the supermarket, OK?' He paused. Then he smiled. 'Five o'clock. Next to the apples.'

I forced the sheet, duvet cover and pillowcases into the washing machine, added green capsules, started the programme then fetched fresh linen. But I was hopeless at bed-making. It took me ages to persuade the duvet into its sack, and the origami that Mrs Dickson did with the sheet and the corners of the mattress was beyond my comprehension. When I walked back into the kitchen the washing machine was progressing through its routine so I decided to make a start on my next story: about the girl who held apples up to the sun. I thought I might call her Peggy.

In between delirious moments of reliving the events of the previous evening and the night that followed, the writing came easy. By 11:30 I had a rudimentary plot. So I went to the kitchen to find chocolate which I discovered wasn't there. Alfie was asleep on the doormat and the washing machine was still struggling through its programme. The washing didn't take this long when Mrs Dickson did it. I checked the dial. There seemed to be another chunk of washing time left before the drying. Perhaps it was stuck. The doorbell rang. Alfie immediately jumped through the cat flap. I glanced at the clock: 11:38. Perhaps it was Matthew, popping back before taking the new Roald Dahl to lunch. But if it was Matthew he might run into Mrs Parkin, and that would be terrible. I hurried to the door and peered through the peephole. It was Mrs Parkin. Why was she early? I let her in. She waited for me to close the door.

'I'm a little early because …' She paused. 'You have a television?'

'Yes. I …'

'I'm a little early because there are a few things we need to go through.'

'What things?'

'Shall we talk about that over some tea, my dear?'

She indicated the kitchen. I walked ahead of her. It reminded me of a hot and sticky afternoon, being marched along a dark corridor to see Miss Grainger, the headmistress, to explain why I'd emptied a carton of Ribena into Alice Parker's school bag. I felt, just like then, as if I was going to have to justify my actions. Please, Miss Grainger, I don't want to tell you but Alice Parker said my mother was in a loony bin. Alice Parker deserved it.

Mrs Parkin followed me into the kitchen and came to an abrupt halt. 'Are you doing your own washing, Sarah? I thought your cleaner took care of that?'

Please, Miss Grainger … 'Dawn came last week and she didn't change the bed. And I spilled tea. And I want to be able to do my own laundry.' I was aware that this was over-justification. Fortunately, my explanations were interrupted: the washing machine had alighted upon an instruction to spin, which seemed to demand a series of violent collisions with the inside of its cubbyhole beneath the worktop. The noise was deafening.

'Good Lord, does it always do that?' shrieked Mrs Parkin.

I wanted to laugh. 'No, but it should be about to finish,' I yelled.

Mrs Parkin's face contorted with disapproval, but despite the noise she pulled out a chair, sat down and watched me fill the kettle. 'I'll mention this to the ancillary manager. It ought to be checked!' She eased a small packet of chocolate fingers from her bag. 'It's enough to make somebody lose their mind!'

I bit my lip and concentrated on choosing mugs from the cupboard. When I was sure my desire to snigger was under control, I turned and shouted above the washing machine's histrionics. 'I've still got some custard creams from Monday, if you'd prefer.'

Mrs Parkin's face brightened. 'Yes!' she screeched, 'I'll take these to my next client. Waste not, want not!' At that moment, the washing machine moved to a higher pitch. The banging diminished but the machine now sounded like a 747 preparing for take-off. Mrs Parkin jumped up. 'Are you sure this is safe? Good Lord!'

I turned away but not soon enough. Mrs Parkin had noticed. 'Sarah, I don't think this is a laughing matter! I'm surprised your cleaner hasn't reported it!'

I forced myself to be serious. 'It doesn't usually do this.' I hurried to make tea, the washing machine became silent and Mrs Parkin ate a custard cream.

'Now, Sarah,' she began, 'a number of things have arisen in the last week and we need to discuss their implications.' She lifted her mug and extended her upper lip into the tea.

'Things?' I asked.

'It has come to our notice that you have become involved with a *man*.' She paused to gauge my reaction. 'Would you like to explain why you never mentioned this to me during my previous visits?'

I sat down. 'We met in the supermarket and we went for coffee.'

'And then, I gather, you allowed him to come here to your home.'

'His name's Matthew Parry. Dr Gray knows.'

'Sarah, you should take great care when encouraging such arrangements. You're really not ready for this kind of activity. Things might seem to be going swimmingly well, but men will not be satisfied with coming here for a cup of tea.'

'We went to dinner at Gusto in Primrose Hill.'

Mrs Parkin's face contorted with disapproval. 'When did that happen?'

'Last Saturday. And on Sunday he took me to lunch.' Mrs Parkin appeared to have been rendered speechless by these details of my burgeoning social life. I was delighted. 'Then on Monday we had supper at Tony's Bistro.'

'You're seeing this man every day?' Mrs Parkin took a deep lungful of air. 'Sarah, this can only lead to things that you are not yet ready for. However gallant you think this man is, there will be expectations! Dr Williams' assessments have revealed that you are completely innocent regarding the physical relationships between men and women. And he is very concerned that you avoid such complications for the time being.'

'Until I'm ready,' I suggested.

'Yes! Now, since circumstances have brought us to this point prematurely it falls to me to offer you some advice and cautions. So, in anticipation, I have put together a few illustrations to help us understand what might be expected and what it might be best for you to avoid.' She pulled a small folder from her bag. 'If at any point, you do not understand, please ask me to repeat myself.' I feared that if I opened my mouth to speak, hysterical laughter might escape, so I maintained silence, which seemed to satisfy Mrs Parkin. She continued.

'Now, in the clinic it was necessary to explain your monthly cycles to you. Are you completely relaxed now about the significance of these cycles?' I nodded. Mrs Parkin placed the folder down in front of me. The first illustration was an annotated diagram of the female reproductive system, the second a diagram of the male reproductive system. The third illustration was a photo of male genitalia. Mrs Parkin was clearly unsettled by this third illustration. She paused to take a custard cream and a mouthful of tea. 'Now, Sarah, I know this must be quite startling for you. But Dr Williams and I think it's best if you know what to expect.'

I clutched my mug and stared at the privates of this unknown man. 'Mrs Parkin, would you mind if I switch the drying on?'

Mrs Parkin rolled her eyes. 'Yes, all right!' she snapped. 'But, Sarah, these things are not to be escaped.'

I clicked the washing machine to dry and the metal drum started to turn. It was accompanied by rhythmic banging. 'Oh!' I exclaimed. 'It shouldn't do that!'

Mrs Parkin walked over. 'It sounds as if there's something heavy inside. She peered in through the glass door. 'You'd better turn it off. Do you have a linen basket handy?'

I fetched my laundry basket and we stood together waiting for the click that signalled access. Mrs Parkin pulled open the door and began to drag out the tangled mass of wet linen. The first thing I noticed was that the red roses on my duvet cover were now pink. The second thing I noticed was that something heavier than linen was caught up inside the shroud of pink roses. Mrs Parkin bent over and tugged at the duvet cover. After a moment or two she managed to grapple free the cause of the machine's previous distress, although at first sight it was not obvious what it was. Clearly, one doesn't expect to find an iPad embedded in wet laundry. She looked to me for an explanation.

I leapt back horrified. 'Is it all right, Mrs Parkin?'

'I would think not. These things are not constructed to withstand laundry cycles. How on earth did it finish up in there?'

I collapsed onto the nearest chair. 'It must have been muddled up in the duvet cover.'

'Well, Sarah you must be more careful with your things. I think insurance has been arranged for your possessions. We'll ...'

'It's not mine. It's Matthew's!'

'Matthew Parry's?' Mrs Parkin lowered her voice, her uncertainty obvious. 'Has he leant it to you, my dear?'

I folded my arms tight over my stomach. 'No, he was reading a contract when I went back to sleep.' I looked at Mrs Parkin, who was now supporting herself against the refrigerator. Damn her and her picture book! 'After we made love.'

'You've had *sex* with this man? *Sarah*, Dr Williams will be most distressed! You are most certainly not ready for this! You have no idea what dangerous ground you have stumbled upon!'

I forced myself to stay calm. 'I am ready. We were lovers before, in the time I don't remember. Dr Williams can't stop Matthew coming here!'

Mrs Parkin looked horrified. She placed the iPad onto the worktop, went to her bag and pulled out her mobile phone. 'This is totally unacceptable! Has Mr Parry confirmed this previous relationship? What else has he told you?'

'That he's my agent. And we've been lovers for the last two years. But we didn't live together.'

'And has he explained why that was the case?'

'Not really. I think he was in a relationship already, but I don't think he was married. Do you know whether he was married, Mrs Parkin?'

Mrs Parkin was enraged. 'I have no intention of discussing this wretched man's details. Has he mentioned anything else?'

'He said he's been asked not to tell me more.'

'Really?' she snapped. 'Sarah, I have to make a telephone call.'

'Mrs Parkin, it was *me* that seduced *him*.'

Mrs Parkin pursed her lips then disappeared into the lounge. I wandered over and started to flick through the photo folder. There were a few interesting illustrations towards the end, although nothing quite as fleshy as my magazines. I walked over to investigate the iPad, pressed the concave recess the way Matthew had. Nothing. It was all very shiny but whatever pieces of information it had once held behind that black mirror screen were probably lost forever. Washed away in a laundry cycle. I touched the shiny glass. I could see my eyes looking back at me. Black eyes that offered no clue to the things they had seen, to the memories they had facilitated. Memories that had also been washed away. Somewhere on a beach in …

'Right!'

I glanced round. Mrs Parkin was standing behind me, wearing her thin-lipped smile. She sat down, scooped the photo folder back into her bag and took one of her preparatory deep breaths. 'Now, Sarah, Dr Williams has advised me as to how we might proceed. Given our new circumstances. Firstly, we need to discuss protection. I gather Dr

Gray has prescribed contraceptive pills. Have you started taking them?'

'The nurse said start after my next period.'

The patronising smile continued. 'So, in the meantime, we'll need a little back-up.' She pulled two cellophane-wrapped packets from her bag and placed them on the table. 'Now, these are condoms …' My mind began to stray. I imagined Mrs Parkin's bag might be a mystical bag, a portal to another dimension. Of biscuits and condoms and photographs of people having sex … 'Sarah, do try and pay attention! This is for your own good!' Maintaining her smile, Mrs Parkin proceeded to describe, minutely, the application and shortfalls of the condom. I wanted to laugh, not so much at the nature of these male contraceptives, but rather at the thought of Mrs Parkin ever having come into contact with some poor soul's genitalia wearing such a ridiculous object. But I managed to control myself. 'Now, you'll need to use these each time you … and you must insist that Mr Parry agrees to do so. Men can be difficult!' She moved to reassurances. 'There are six here so that should keep you going for a while. And I wouldn't worry about last night. Just once unprotected is not too risky …'

'Three times.'

Mrs Parkin frowned: 'You had relations before last night?'

'No, three times last night.'

Mrs Parkin's mouth puckered. Then she reached into her vast bag and withdrew another, larger, packet from the biscuit and condom dimension.

Episode Twenty-one

Mrs Parkin stayed for another hour during which time she provided a comprehensive opportunity for questions and answers on the complexities of social intercourse and sexual relationships, all of which I attempted to take seriously. One thing I did grasp from Mrs Parkin's counsel was a vague idea of the chasm that existed between the world that I had been observing this last few weeks and the world as it really was. I was grateful that Matthew had taken the decision to protect me from reality. I hoped he wouldn't be too angry when he discovered that I'd ruined his iPad.

Mrs Parkin was pulling her things together when the doorbell rang. The clock said 2:34. I looked at Mrs Parkin.

'You'd better see who it is. I'll just excuse myself before I go.'

I paused to gather myself. The doorbell rang again. I peered through the peephole: Matthew! I let him in.

'Hi, gorgeous. The meeting went well. I left them at it. Thought I'd better come over and stop you worrying about the supermarket. We could go now, if you like.' He stooped to kiss my cheek. 'Did you find my iPad? I think I left it on the bed.'

I threw my arms around him. 'Matthew, I'm so sorry! I boiled it in the washing machine!'

He looked down and met my eyes, took a few moments to consider the information. 'You boiled the iPad?'

'Yes!'

'Why did you do that?'

'I didn't mean to … It was an accident. I washed the sheet and the duvet cover because I didn't want Mrs Dickson to see the marks on them and I must have got your iPad muddled up in them.'

An overly tactful cough interrupted our conversation. Mrs Parkin was standing in the dining area. 'Mr Parry, we haven't met. I'm Jane Parkin, an associate of Dr Williams.'

Matthew detached himself from me. 'No worries,' he whispered. He approached Mrs Parkin and extended his hand. 'I presume that you know I went against advice and orchestrated a reunion with Sarah?'

Mrs Parkin failed to take Matthew's hand. 'Indeed, Mr Parry. I also gather that this reunion has escalated somewhat.'

Matthew lowered his hand: 'As I told Dr Williams, it could have been anybody accosting Sarah. At least my intentions were rooted in a concern for her well-being.'

'Really? I also gather that you assured Dr Williams that this relationship would remain *platonic* for as long as possible. Clearly your self-interest triumphed over your promises.'

I felt the need to redress the situation. 'Matthew did keep his promise!' I felt his arm close around me.

'Calm down, love. Losing your temper never helps.'

Mrs Parkin curled her lip as she spoke. 'Coming from you, Mr Parry, that is complete hypocrisy!'

Matthew squeezed my shoulder. 'Mrs Parkin, I admit I behaved badly, but I was extremely worried about what I thought was bad practice. I've apologised. I was wrong to strike Dr Williams. It was the behaviour of a hooligan.'

I step away from him. 'You *hit* Dr Williams?'

Matthew looked contrite. 'It was more of a slap, really.'

Mrs Parkin straightened her jacket. 'You are fortunate that Dr Williams is choosing not to press charges. As far as I'm concerned it was assault. I would have been more unforgiving.'

'I'm very grateful to him. I've written a formal apology.'

Mrs Parkin closed her eyes in distain then turned her attention towards me. 'Well, Sarah, I shall discuss with Dr Williams whether I can be of any further help to you in these circumstances. He can decide whether I return this Monday coming, if at all. Thank you for your hospitality, my dear.' She went to leave.

I felt a wave of panic pass over me. 'But … Please, Mrs Parkin, I don't think I can carry on without you.'

Mrs Parkin's thin smile made a brief reappearance. 'Let's see what Dr Williams says, shall we, Sarah? If you would prefer it, I'll advise him that we both feel our little chats have been beneficial.' I thanked her and watched the door close behind her.

Matthew folded his arms. 'Stupid, *ugly* cow! I thought you *hated* her.'

'I don't hate her, I just don't like her. And they might send somebody worse.' I stepped close and hugged him. 'I'm really sorry about your iPad. Was there anything important on it?'

'Nothing irreplaceable. Don't worry about it.'

I twiddled with a button on his jacket. 'I spoiled my sheets as well. Did you really hit Dr Williams?'

'Yes! He said something about the credibility of your condition so I slapped him. It was worth it just to see the look on his face.'

'Credibility of my condition? What does that mean?'

'It doesn't mean anything.'

'It must mean something because you hit him.'

'Come on! Let's do the shopping!' He tried to pull me towards the kitchen but I pulled away from him:

'Matthew, why did you hit him?'

'Sarah, for God's sake!' He folded his arms. 'Look, they were supposed to keep me informed. Then the other day you said there were *three* research associates. There were originally two. So I went over to the hospital to find out what was going on, and I discovered that Della Brown had joined their team of *researchers*.'

'Dr Brown?'

'Sarah, she's not *Dr* Brown. She's Detective Sergeant Brown.'

'She said she was a forensic psychologist.'

'Bullshit! She's a fucking cop! Sarah, the police were investigating the possibility that you might be inventing a lost memory to conceal something.'

'Conceal what?'

'I don't … Don't worry about it. Dr Gray's putting a stop to it. I phoned him Tuesday afternoon before I came here.'

'Won't I see Della Brown anymore?'

'Not pretending to be a doctor, you won't.'

I wandered over to the sofa. I've always found thinking comes that much easier when I'm sitting down. I grappled to recall Tuesday's interview. 'She asked me to go to lunch. We went to a sandwich bar because Dr Williams was having an emergency.'

'Yeah, the emergency was me. Della Brown was probably told to get you out of the way in case you ran into me shouting at your psycho-consultant.' He sat down next to me. 'Did you enjoy your lunch?'

'I had a ham sandwich.'

He rolled his eyes. 'Did you eat it?'

'Yes. It was disgusting. But she bought it for me so I had to eat it.'

Matthew leaned back, his face serious. 'Sarah, when she bought you the sandwich, she asked you what you wanted, and you said ham, right?'

'No. She said it was all they had.'

'A sandwich bar with only ham sandwiches?'

I noticed Matthew's eyes turn to anger. 'What's wrong?'

'She was testing you. She'd have known you don't eat ham.'

'Why don't I eat ham?'

Matthew sighed. 'Because you're a vegetarian.'

'I'm a vegetarian?'

'Yes, well a partial one. You don't eat meat. Just fish.'

'And, if I refused the ham, it would prove I could remember that I didn't eat meat?'

'Yes!' He leaned forward into his hands. 'This whole obfuscation ...'

'I can't remember what that means.'

'It means deceiving people. This cop-doctor thing, it's an infringement of your rights. I phoned my brother ...'

'Have you got a brother?'

'Yes, Nick's a barrister. He said they were on very thin ice deceiving you like that. It's probably why Williams is choosing not to press charges. Anyway, now you know about her so it's over. Nick suggested you make a formal complaint. He'll help draft it.'

I mulled that over. Then I smiled. 'You're like my knight in shining armour.'

He laughed. 'Yes, but Sir Lancelot never had to deal with the medical profession.'

'There was Merlin.'

Matthew nodded. Thoughtfully. 'What *do* you remember, Sarah?'

'I'm not pretending!'

'I didn't mean that. It's just difficult to understand how you can remember Merlin and Sir Lancelot. But you can't remember me.'

'I wish I could remember you. But …' I tried to summon up an image I could describe. 'It's like a grey mist and I can't see through it except in some places there are bright holes that I can look through, that lead back to when I was little. And I can see my grandma's garden and my classroom at school. But I'm scared the holes will fill in. And then there'll be nothing left of me. Only what there is now.' I could feel my hands wringing, Matthew holding them steady.

'Hey, Bob Gray's hopeful that your memories are still there, that they'll come back.'

I pulled my hands away. 'What if my mind doesn't want them back?'

'Well, if they don't come back we'll make new memories. About the things we haven't done yet. And, perhaps, if your memories were bad enough for your mind to confiscate them, then it's better you never remember them.'

'But what if it isn't over? What if my mind is going to carry on confiscating, so no memories are safe? Not even our new memories that haven't happened yet. Or my memories from when I was with my grandma.'

'There's no reason why that should happen.'

'But nobody can know, can they?' I clutched at his jacket. 'What happened to me, Matthew? You must know things you're not telling me.'

He was silent for a moment. I could sense he was choosing what to tell, editing the truth down to an unrevealing scrap. He gave a resigned sigh. 'You were unconscious. On the beach. You already know that. They thought you'd fallen overboard and been washed ashore. The coastguard airlifted you to the Devon and Exeter Hospital.'

'Devon and Exeter?'

'Yes. You were found in a place called Beer Cove.'

I shook my head. 'I've never heard of it.'

'You were unconscious for six weeks. I sat by your bedside. Your eyes were open but you weren't aware of anything. Then they transferred you to the National and, just after they moved you there, Geraint Williams suggested my presence might be perpetuating ... they called it a fugue state. So Dr Gray suggested I stayed away for a few days.'

'And did you?'

'Yes, and the following day you sat up and asked for a drink of water. Bob Gray said it was possibly a coincidence but that I'd better make myself absent for a while. Then they discovered the severity of your amnesia and you were moved to Greystone Park Clinic. The police were keen to find out how you finished up where they found you. Bob Gray allowed them two sessions early on, but I don't think you were able to tell them anything. Do you remember the police interviewing you?'

'No, I can't remember anything about those first weeks at Greystone Park.' Again I could sense that Matthew was deliberating over yet another shred of restricted information. 'What are you thinking of not telling me now?'

Another sigh of resignation. 'Two police officers came to interview you. An old guy called DI Broderick, ex-military, I think, and a female officer. Sarah, that was Della Brown.'

'Della Brown interviewed me at Greystone Park?' I paused to consider: that awful woman had already met me by the time Geraint Williams introduced her to me. No wonder she'd looked awkward. In her wrong-size white coat. 'Did Geraint Williams know she'd interviewed me before?'

'Yes. He must have told her you wouldn't recognise her. He probably advised her that she could take advantage of your dynamic memory loss … that's what they've been calling it. Nick said we could argue it was an abuse of the privileged patient-doctor relationship. And accuse him of professional misconduct.' He frowned. 'Although hitting him was far more rewarding. Anyway, the police interviewed you around the middle of February. A month later they brought you here. Just to visit at first. I was warned not to interfere. Williams suggested that seeing me might cause you to relapse. They kept me informed but there didn't seem to be any improvement. Damn it, they had no more idea what was going on in your head than I did! So, first of all I phoned but you never answered, then I started supermarket-stalking you.'

'Which phone?'

Matthew frowned. 'The house phone. Bob Gray gave me your new number but advised me not to call you. So I did. Four times, I think.'

'Only four?'

'Yes. Why?'

I pulled him into the kitchen and opened the tea towel drawer, retrieved a pile of notelets and spread them into a row on the worktop. Matthew prodded four of them out of line. 'That's my mobile. Didn't you recognise it from my card?'

I shook my head. Arranged alongside one another like that, it was clear that most of the remaining scraps of paper bore the same number: 'Do you recognise this number, Matthew?'

'I might!' He pulled out his mobile and checked his contacts. 'I thought so: it's Annabelle. I gave her your new number in a moment of stupidity and asked her not to call.'

'Who's Annabelle?'

'She's your best friend. Annabelle Grant.'

'I have a best friend?'

'Yes. She's a complete liability. Totally incapable of not saying exactly what she's thinking. Ten times worse than you.'

'I don't do that!'

'Yes, you do!' He pinched my waist. 'There's no filtering system.'

'Perhaps I've forgotten how to filter.'

'You've always been like it, although the constant reference to sex shows a much greater lack of propriety than before. At least you used to know when not to talk about that. Which is most of the time. And never mention marks on sheets. Parkin looked as if she was about to die!'

'I didn't realise she was there. Have I always embarrassed you?'

'Always!' He tugged on a strand of my hair. 'Can we please do the shopping?'

*

As I got ready to go to the supermarket I tried to come to terms with this latest avalanche of revelations. I remember wondering how my mind was organising this new information. Hoping it was not too close to the forbidden memories. And I wondered about this best friend, how we had been with one another, about our shared memories that now only this unknown person could access.

'Matthew, how long have I known Annabelle?'

'Since university.'

'Will Dr Gray let me meet her?'

'I'll phone him. This whole isolation thing is falling apart anyway.'

'I won't know how to speak to her.'

'From what I know of Annabelle, I doubt that will make a difference.'

'Do you know her?'

'I do now.' He grimaced. 'And no, I haven't slept with her.'

'I didn't ask that!'

'You were about to. Shall I make tea while you check the plugs twenty times?'

'Have I always done that?'

'You've got worse.'

BEER COVE

It was a grey, blustery day but the sun was just breaking through as Sarah turned in past the dilapidated sign that said TO THE BEACH. She followed the crumbly road downhill until she caught sight of the sea opening out in front of her. None of it was familiar. But then the last time she'd been there, it would have been with Granny Clark twenty-six perhaps twenty-seven years before. Yes, that would have been the last time she'd seen him. Perhaps he had come back and tried to find her. Perhaps someone knew where he was. It was probably one big waste of time but it was worth a try. It's always worth a try. She pulled into an overgrown layby and glanced down at the slim volume on the seat beside her. The first of a series. Her series. Granny Clark had always said she'd be a writer. And now she was. She had been allowed four advanced copies: one for herself; one for Annabelle; one for her mother, although Diana was unlikely to read a children's book; and this one other copy that was lying next to her. To give or to post. Just in case anybody knew where he was.

She re-checked her map. The lane she was looking for ought to have been around there somewhere. She scanned the scrub to her right. Surely that wasn't it. That skinny little path. She needed to ask someone. She stepped out of the car and looked around and spotted a solitary bucket-and-spade shop about two hundred yards down towards the sea. So she refolded the map, eased it into her rucksack along with her book, secured her car and then hurried to enquire.

It was out of season and the sign in the window said CLOSED but there were several bunches of buckets hanging outside and, when she prodded the door, it opened. She stepped inside and waited by the counter. After a few minutes an elderly man emerged from the rear of the shop. 'Excuse me,' she said. 'I'm looking for Headland House. I used to visit it when I was small and I was …'

'Now, there's a name I've not heard for a long time. If I'm remembering correct, that's what they used to call the old house along the cliff path … 'bout a mile. Young man used to live there on his own. Don't know what happened to him.'

'Do you know if anyone's living there now? I was thinking of paying a visit …'

'Oh no, dear, you'll not be getting along that path no more. Part of the old cliff fell away. Almost twenty years back. So the council fenced it off. Put up warnings. It's all grown over by now. And that old house along there have probably fallen into the sea years ago. It were right on the edge.'

Sarah felt a little dispirited.

'Oh well, I'll probably just wander down and look at the sea instead. Thanks for the information.'

She noticed a flash of disappointment in the old man's eyes. She ought to buy something. She took a quick look around and her eyes alighted upon a shelf of tacky souvenirs. One in particular caught her attention: a plastic, water-filled dome inside which was a mermaid sitting on a fishing boat and a banner which read: WELCOME TO BEER COVE. Sarah collected snow globes, the tackier the better, and this one was five-star tacky and to add to its allure a small postcard propped against it read GENUINE ANTIQUE. Sarah made her purchase then went back up to her car and, with only slight trepidation, walked straight past it and veered towards the forbidden path.

For the first four hundred yards or so the track was so dark and overgrown that, more than once, she considered abandoning her quest. Just as she was about to turn back, though, the view opened up. The cliff had fallen away taking the wind-beaten scrub with it on the seaward side. She could see the path ahead, the rusted remains of the old barrier scattered around. She judged that there was still sufficient distance between the path and the cliff edge for it to be safe to continue if she was careful. So she marched on with the sea on one side and an impenetrable mass of tall brambles and gorse on the other.

Eventually, after perhaps another quarter mile of exposed track, the cliff edge moved further away and the path opened out onto high plateau. And in the distance, beyond the plateau, she could just make out the stark grey silhouette of Headland House.

She quickened her pace and soon arrived at the old front door. A plank had been nailed across between the doorposts at the exact level that the doorknob should have been. She tried pushing one of the panels but achieved nothing. Then she remembered the big window that used to be to one side of the door. A mass of hawthorn had grown up to conceal it. She stepped round to investigate and discovered that the tangle of roots had undermined part of the wall so badly that the entire window and the bricks beneath it had fallen in, leaving a gaping hole. She managed to negotiate her way past the hawthorn and broken glass and squeeze herself inside. The downstairs rooms were all derelict and empty. One still housed the remains of a kitchen sink. Nowhere could she see the big table that used to be covered in books and shells and fossils.

Taking her rucksack from her back, she sat down on one of the surviving windowsills. She could see the central staircase looming up towards the top of the house. It looked as if it was about to collapse so she decided against any further exploration. Instead she took out her fourth advanced copy of *The Lost Red Mitten* and wrote 'To Daddy from Sarah' on its title page. Then she closed the slim volume, set it down amongst the rubble and took a last look around before abandoning this long-discarded shell of her childhood and crawling back out into the limp afternoon sun.

Episode Twenty-two

'You haven't taken your pills.'

'I don't want to take them!'

'You have to! They send you straight into deep sleep so you don't dream.'

'Perhaps I'd be able to remember in my dreams.'

'That might be what they're worried about.'

'Are you going to stay?'

'Yes, if you want me to.'

'I do.'

'Good … take your pills.'

*

The first things I saw, when I woke that morning, were Matthew's green eyes. Watching me.

'No dreaming, right?'

'No. What time is it?'

'Five to nine.'

'What!' I sat up and grabbed the alarm clock. 'Mrs Dickson will be here at ten. I'll never be ready!'

Matthew eased the clock from my hand, leaned across me and placed it back on the bedside table. 'Sweetheart, if you spend more than half an hour in the shower you'll dissolve. That gives you at least another half hour to have your cornflakes and clean the fridge.'

I flopped back onto my pillow. 'Aren't you going to work?'

'Yes, I've got a nine o'clock meeting with one of my authors.'

I sat back up. 'You'll never make it. You …' I noticed him grinning at me. 'Very funny! You think I'm daft, don't you?'

'I might do. Come on, I'll make some coffee!'

*

I busied myself with the contents of the salad drawer, collected up the notelets with the telephone numbers and put them in the bin. Matthew drank coffee and watched me. I noticed him smiling.

'She'll be here any minute!'

'I'm drinking my coffee. It's too hot!'

'It's not hot!' I clasped my hands together. 'She'll tell them you were here.'

'They know anyway. And I don't care. And neither should you.'

'Matthew!'

He put down his coffee. 'I'm not hurrying. I'll get indigestion.' I had no choice other than to re-polish the mixer tap and bang things down on the worktop. Matthew responded by folding his arms. 'You obviously don't realise how much I'm used to these infantile tantrums of yours. I'm definitely not hurrying and banging things around is going to get you nowhere.'

'She'll disapprove!'

'Sweetheart, she won't!'

I sagged against the refrigerator. I didn't want Mrs Dickson to be appalled by my recent moral dereliction and Matthew was making me angry and I didn't want that to be happening either. I inhaled hysterically, walked over and pulled his arm around me. The doorbell rang. I became rigid.

He stood up and grabbed my hand. 'Let's see who's there, shall we?'

I allowed myself to be dragged through to the front door, cringing as he opened it.

'Hello, Annie, lovely day isn't it?'

'Hello, Matthew, dear. I wondered when I was going to find you here. Hello, Sarah, I've brought you a nice sponge cake. No balls this time.'

I was confused and irritated, even more irritated. I resisted the temptation to stamp my foot, stepped back and invited Annie Dickson inside. I glared at Matthew. 'You think this is funny, do you? Why didn't you tell me you knew Mrs Dickson? Mrs Dickson, he didn't tell me!'

Annie Dickson patted my arm. 'Don't you worry, dear. Our Matthew likes his silly jokes. He asked me to come and clean for you when you came home. So I could keep an eye on you for him. He was worrying himself into a shadow about you.'

I flounced over and threw myself onto a sofa. Matthew ventured over to sit beside me:

'Don't be angry, Sarah. Annie does the office. And she doubles as tea and coffee maker. And Agony Aunt. And she makes sure the plants don't die.'

I said nothing. I just glared.

'Tuesdays, Wednesdays and Thursday morning,' explained Annie Dickson. 'I'll just go spend a penny. Give you both a chance to have a little argument about Matthew's sense of humour.' She disappeared into the bedroom.

'It wasn't a joke,' Matthew pleaded. 'I just thought not telling you might reduce the fussing time. You can beat me if you like.' He offered me the back of his hand. I pushed it away, jumped up and wafted away into the kitchen. He hurried after me. '*Sarah*, they were arranging for someone to help you around the house. Annie was really happy to do it. They were worried you'd recognise her, but you didn't.'

I spun round, tears pricking my eyes. 'No, Matthew, I didn't recognise her. Or *you*. Or Peggy Lewis. Or the black and white cat. Or anybody else. Like I never happened and my life is just years and years of empty space!'

'Sweetheart, just because you forget things, it doesn't mean you change. You're still the same person.'

'How can I be? I don't know how I used to think about things.' I felt myself start to cry. I tried not to but there were too many tears that had to be wept for that woman I couldn't remember. I wiped my sleeve across my face. 'Matthew, what happened to me? Why can't I recognise the people I used to know!'

He eased me onto a chair, pulled another chair close and sat down beside me.

'I *really* don't know what happened to you. I'd tell you if I did, whatever they say, but I think you're the only person who will ever be able to explain how you came to be lying on that beach miles away from home. It's what everyone, including the police, are hoping you'll remember.'

Mrs Dickson was suddenly beside me offering a box of tissues. 'Don't you upset yourself, Sarah dear. It will all sort itself out, just you wait and see.' She pointed to Matthew's mug. 'Is that your coffee, Matthew? Are you going to drink it?'

'No, it's cold!'

I heard myself choke out laughter. How did he do that? How was he able to make me laugh when I felt so despondent? I dried my eyes. 'Mrs Dickson, I'm so sorry I never recognised you. It must have been awful for you.'

'I was just a bit upset to see you here all on your own, with that foolish woman bothering you like that. They call themselves doctors, but if you ask me, they should never have sent you home on your own. And they should never have kept you away from the people who care about you. Especially Matthew. He broke his heart about it.' She picked up the kettle. 'And you call me Annie, just like everyone else.'

I watched Annie take the tea-making in hand and tried to imagine Matthew in his office, speaking on the phone, miming thank you as Mrs Dickson placed a mug of coffee on his desk. Tried to imagine him breaking his heart. I glanced briefly at his fraught expression then smiled.

'Mrs Dickson … Annie, tell me about Matthew.'

Annie Dickson responded without hesitation. 'He's a lovely boy. But he's a bit too fond of himself. And he drinks too much. I've told him time and again, no good worrying about what you eat if you rot your liver. But you were just pulling him into line nicely, so we're all glad you're together again.' I noticed Matthew rolling his eyes:

'Annie, do you know his girlfriend before me?'

'Sarah, for God's sake! Of course Annie knows her, although mercifully Lucy has not honoured the office with her presence for some time. Annie, why don't you let me make the tea and you can go and get on with whatever it is you do.'

She ignored him. 'Lucy Ashdown was very attractive. Just like a film star. Mr Dickson used to come over all of a bother whenever he saw her …'

Matthew exhaled frustration.

'But she could be a nasty piece of work. No time for the likes of me and Mr Dickson. She treated people like dirt. And she's no friend of yours, Sarah, so you be careful when she's around.'

'OK, Annie, thank you for that excellent summary of my ex-partner.' Matthew positioned himself between me and Annie Dickson: a kind of human barricade against further opinion. 'Sarah, Lucy Ashdown is out of the equation.'

'What does that mean?' I asked, trying to glimpse Mrs Dickson behind Matthew.

'It means she's kicked him out of his house, fleeced him for everything and moved on to some other poor bugger,' said Annie Dickson. I threw my hand over my mouth.

Matthew spun round. 'Annie! Good God, this is ridiculous!'

'I agree with that,' said Mrs Dickson, lifting a large plastic box from her bag. 'Would you like some chocolate cake, Matthew?'

'For your information, Mrs Dickson, and I'm sure you already know this, I was happy for Lucy to occupy my house until she could make other arrangements. And I was only too pleased to buy her out of the company ...'

'It was yours anyway!'

'And I'm sure you'll be very happy working for some other financially ill-advised soft-touch. I'll take my tea in the lounge when you're both ready. And a large piece of cake!' He turned back to me and kissed my cheek. 'Perhaps when you've finished discussing my private life with my cleaning lady, you'll join me for a few minutes before I have to dash off to the office to make some more dreadful decisions.'

I watched him go and waited as Mrs Dickson sliced the chocolate sponge. 'Just a thin piece for me, Annie. Was she really like a film star?'

'She was very glamorous. But nowhere near as pretty as you. Can you pass me the tea plates? Then you'd better go in there and make sure he's all right. I think I might have upset him. But all this messing around with you not knowing things, it can't be good for him either.'

I discovered Matthew slumped on a sofa frowning at the lazy twirls of pink and blue glitter in my LOST snow globe. I took it from his hand and placed it on the coffee table. Then I sat down beside him.

'My publisher obviously thought I was important enough to deserve … what do you call it? Merchandise? Tasteful, isn't it?'

He folded his arms. 'Actually it was me that had them made. For your book launch last summer. There's still a crate of them at my flat. You collect them. They were everywhere in here.'

'What shaky snow globes?'

'Yes, your minders must have packed them away. Hopefully into landfill.'

I tried not to smile. I wanted him to know I was still annoyed with him. 'I'm really angry with you for not telling me things.'

'Sarah, I …'

'When did you move into your flat?'

He sighed. 'Last September.'

'Have I been there?'

'Obviously.'

I traced my finger along his thigh. 'Did we make love there?'

'Sarah, I am not going to discuss our sex life with my cleaning lady in the next room. And yes, we did!'

I leaned against his arm. 'Is it a nice flat?'

'No, it's a shit hole.'

'Doesn't Annie clean it for you?'

'No! Nobody cleans it. It's why it's a shit hole. I'm glad this is amusing you. My life is completely wrecked and you think it's funny.'

The rattle of china announced Annie Dickson's approach. Matthew hurried to relieve her of the tray. 'Thank you, dear,' she said. 'I'll start in the kitchen today.'

Episode Twenty-three

Annie Dickson left well after midday, and not before I had interrogated her further about Lucy Ashdown and Matthew. I tried to continue with my apple stories but by one-thirty I was sick of trying to write while obsessing about Lucy Ashdown. I collapsed onto the sofa, picked up Matthew's *Guardian* and read an article about the Cannes Film Festival. Then I wandered through to pose in front of the bathroom mirror and reaffirm how unlike a film star I looked. For some reason, this realization of inadequacy made me desperate to talk to someone …

'Hello Peggy, I thought we could have some of my chocolate cake.'

'How lovely,' said Miss Lewis. She invited me inside. 'Did you bake it yourself?'

'No, Annie made it.' I handed over the sandwich box.

'The lady that comes on Fridays?'

'Yes. Did you know I knew Matthew from before?'

'Yes, dear, but I knew not to mention. This looks lovely. Shall we have it with some tea?'

She leaned past me to close the door. I waited to be directed whichever way. It would not have been a problem in mine because you stepped into my lounge from the street. But Miss Lewis' house had this small hallway that we were currently standing in, this small receiving area, where you had to make a decision to turn right into the lounge or walk through into the kitchen or alternatively walk straight on up the stairs that were looming directly opposite the front door. To walk into the lounge would have been presumptuous so I waited while Miss Lewis fussed over the latch. Eventually she beckoned me through into the kitchen.

Miss Lewis's kitchen smelled like an old person's kitchen, just like her lounge smelled like an old-person's lounge. It was bright with afternoon sun, which was unfortunately not strong enough to drive away the damp fragrance of cupboard corners and under-sink plumbing. I stood and exchanged meaningless nothings while Miss Lewis made tea and divided the sponge cake on to small china plates. Touching it with her fingers.

'Shall we take this into the dining room and catch some of this nice sunshine?' She said, picking up the tray. 'Would you be a dear and open the door for me?'

I turned and discovered an unexpected door. My kitchen wall had no such door. I turned its brass knob and it opened into a room, less bright than the kitchen, darkly furnished: a table and chairs, a matching sideboard and a long dresser covered in china, special china that looked as if it was never used. Over in the corner there was a grandfather clock with a frozen pendulum and a brass face that declared ten minutes to eleven. I followed Miss Lewis inside. The air was thick with furniture polish and elderly carpet, both competing with the bananas ripening in the fruit bowl in the centre of the table. And there was that unmistakable mousey aroma I remembered from my grandmother's cupboard under the stairs. I moved one of the gargantuan dining chairs, sat down and watched the teapot wobble as Miss Lewis filled the cups, craning my neck round to look at the collection of framed photographs on the sideboard, perhaps a dozen, maybe more, all arranged on a thin velvety cloth that ran the length of the polished surface. A china cup and saucer rattled towards me.

'Alfie was in earlier,' said Miss Lewis, lowering herself into her chair.

'He's at home asleep now. Peggy, how long have we known each other?'

Miss Lewis's eyelashes fluttered above her teacup. 'I brought you some biscuits when you first moved in. So, we've known each other ever since then. You were very kind when my mother died.' She glanced in the direction of the photo frames.

I assumed she was referring to the very old lady framed in silver and black. 'Oh, I'm sorry. I'm glad I was nice to you. When did I move in?'

'Sarah, I'm not sure I should … Didn't they tell you things like that?'

'No. But I don't think knowing that can make any difference. I was just wondering whether I was living here when my first book was published.'

Miss Lewis looked anxious. 'It must be about seven years ago. Perhaps eight. Mother was still able to get around on her own.' She lifted a piece of cake towards me, handed me a small pastry fork. 'She died the year before last, just after her ninety-seventh birthday. You gave her one of your lovely bunches of flowers. She was very fond of you, poor old thing.'

I sipped my tea. 'Was she very ill?'

'No, it was sudden, in her sleep. A lovely way to go, really.'

I suffered a mental image of Peggy Lewis going in to wake her mother that morning, perhaps carrying tea in one of these china cups, finding the old lady cold and dead. Perhaps she dropped the cup, shook her mother's stiff corpse. I experienced a wave of nausea. The smell of the furniture polish was too strong, barely negated by the weak, milky tea. Miss Lewis was watching me, her eyes the only indicator of those sad moments that this conversation must have forced her to remember.

'Peggy, I'm sorry I can't remember that happening. Dr Gray thinks my mind is forcing me to forget.'

'Perhaps your mind knows what's best for you, dear.'

'That's what Matthew said. But you have to know about yourself, don't you?' Miss Lewis helped herself to a small forkful of cake. I waited for her response, watched her help herself to another mouthful. 'You have to know what has already happened in your life,' I insisted. 'They found me on a beach, unconscious. And I need to know why I was there. I can't know properly who I am if I can't remember that.'

Miss Lewis sipped her tea. Her silence seemed to accentuate the smell in the room. Finally, she spoke. 'Sarah, dear, knowing is a very different thing to remembering.' She put down her cup. 'I was less than a year old when my father was killed by a landmine. He left my poor mother widowed with three small girls to look after. Then one night, not long after she learned the sad news, our house was bombed. It was 1941. The London Blitz they called it. Our street was badly hit. My mother carried me to safety in her arms, but my two sisters were crushed in their bed. I know all this happened but I was too young to understand and too young to remember.' She touched her hands together. Their trembling motion looked like suppressed clapping. 'My mother was less fortunate. She never could drive the sound of my sisters' screams from her mind. Every night in her dreams for all of her long life she remembered those two little girls. She remembered waiting for their bodies to be found. And I couldn't share those memories with her. All I could do was stay and listen to her sadness and try to comfort her. So you see, perhaps your mind is doing you a favour.'

I felt horribly selfish. And desperately sad about those things that happened all that time ago. A whole long lifetime ago. But the trouble with time is that it doesn't make things any less terrible, it just erodes away your memories of them, one detail at a time. Or in my case, every detail all at once.

'I'm so sorry, Peggy. I don't remember you telling me that.'

'I never have. Perhaps I shouldn't have mentioned it now. But I can't help thinking that you remembering what happened to you might be worse than you not knowing.'

I picked up my fork. 'I'm sorry about your sisters.'

'Oh, don't you worry about me. Those days are gone. There'll soon be nobody left that can remember them.' She sighed. 'And some futures are just not meant to be. I could never leave my mother to remember alone so I stayed and nursed her until the memories died with her. And now I have my cousins' children, and their children's children.' She smiled at the photographs along the velvet cloth. 'I'm a great-aunt many times over.'

I glanced at the happy framed families. 'I don't think I have anybody, just Matthew. I hope he doesn't get fed up with me being unusual.'

'He won't. You're still who you were. Eat your cake, it's very tasty.'

I stayed with Peggy for almost two hours, listening to stories about Islington after the war: rationing, rag-and-bone men, pea-picking holidays, the coronation and watching the man chopping up live eels to boil before setting them in their own jelly. I mentioned my apple stories and Miss Lewis recalled apple names and recited her sixteen times table the way nobody does anymore. Gradually the smell of furniture polish and musty carpet grew less overwhelming, but I still felt uncomfortable, probably because, next door, this was my bedroom. And some of it was my bathroom, with my toilet over where the grandfather clock was standing. Miss Lewis noticed me staring at its brass face. 'It hasn't worked for years. It always stops just before eleven. Probably a mouse ran up there and got stuck, like in the nursery rhyme.'

I laughed. 'I wish I had enough space for a grandfather clock. Next door this is my bedroom. My dining table's forced into a little nook, under where your stairs are.'

'Well, I'm sure if you decide to stay you could always reconvert the upstairs …' Peggy Lewis looked up and met my eyes. 'Oh dear!'

But I was distracted by the sound of a child's laughter. I glanced through the window into the backyard. It was the same as my backyard: dark, dank, a few unhappy buddleias emerging from the dirt swept up against the back fence. But with no metal staircase leading to an empty upstairs flat. 'Peggy, are there children moving in next door?'

'I don't think so, Sarah. It's being converted into student flats. So we'll all have to get used to a lot of coming and going. Oh, and that reminds me …' Her tone was conspiratorial. She felt in her pocket and pulled out a key. 'They gave me this in case of an emergency. Give it to your Matthew so he doesn't have to wait outside in the rain.'

*

Back in my kitchen, I read Peggy's list of apple names and thought about what she had said about remembering being worse than not knowing. I tried to imagine what my mind might be protecting me from. It must have been something so terrible that I had to be prevented from remembering everything about it. Perhaps I shouldn't try to remember it. Especially here on my own. I glanced over at the collection of tubs and pill boxes, lined up beside the toaster, my own bespoke pharmacy. I hurried over and picked up the tub with 4 written large across it's label, emptied out a capsule and swallowed it ten minutes early.

*

Over supper, Matthew informed me that Bob Gray had okayed my trip to see Annabelle. I was immediately apprehensive about meeting this friend-cum-stranger.

'She's expecting us tomorrow,' he explained. 'It could be dire.'

'Tomorrow!' I was now terrified.

'We can put it off if you don't feel ready.'

'I hate not ready! Will you help me with what to wear?'

'Probably a boiler suit and hard hat.' He laughed at my expression. 'Last time I was there she was welding. She's a sculptress. Works with metal. She's surprisingly talented for a mad person.'

'Does she live with anyone?'

'No. I think the last guy left because he couldn't bear the noise.'

Episode Twenty-four

I sat beside Matthew as he drove the Escort through the weekend congestion, out towards the A3 via Shepherds Bush and Hammersmith. It was unusually warm for the time of year and the pavements were full of foul-tempered shoppers, grizzling children and people who seemed to be leaning against bus stops waiting for the world to end. The overall feeling was one of filth and hatred, an atmosphere that was not improved by Matthew's mood, which degenerated with each inconvenient set of traffic lights and crunched gear. By the time we reached Putney High Street he had taken to winding down the window and yelling at bus drivers, who occasionally deigned to signal their contempt. I tried to concentrate on window-shopping between pedestrians. Then a taxi pulled out and caused Matthew to brake hard and stall the engine. He started up again and pulled away without warning, evoking a horn blast from another taxi:

'These bastards think they own the road!'

'If you dip the clutch when you brake, it doesn't stall like that.'

'If it wasn't such a crap car it wouldn't stall like that!'

'Do you want me to drive? I'm used to it.'

'No, just leave me alone and let me get through this SHIT!'

'There's no need to be so bad tempered.'

'I'm not being bad tempered. I just don't need criticism when I'm driving this heap of rust. You have more than enough money to get yourself a decent car, but you insist upon driving this disgusting wreck!'

'Well, I think you're a terrible driver.'

'Thanks. I'm just trying to make this trip easier for you.'

'What? By getting us both killed? … Lights! CAR!'

'What … fuck!' He slammed on the brake. The Escort jolted to a standstill just short of the bumper of the car in front. Matthew sagged against the steering wheel. We waited in silence for the lights to change. We pulled away and he turned immediately into a convenient petrol station and cut the engine.

'What are you doing?'

'Sarah, if Annabelle upsets you, we leave straightaway, OK?'

'Is that what's been upsetting you?'

He sighed. 'That and the fact that I've received a solicitor's letter warning me to stay away from Geraint Williams' *places of work*, which essentially excludes me from any influence over what that bastard does to you. It was on my desk when I nipped into the office this morning.'

I watched him gripping the steering wheel then looked away through the windscreen, half focussing on a battered litterbin a few feet from us. It was surrounded by more rubbish than it could possibly hold. So much dirt and waste, being carried from one place to another but never really going away. Everything was a mess …

'Matthew, I'm going to tell Dr Gray I'm not going to see them anymore.'

'You can't stop seeing them!'

'No, but I can threaten to, unless you can come with me. Anyway, nothing they do is making the slightest difference. I've not remembered anything.'

'You remembered when …'

'I remembered a feeling, that's all.'

'You should at least tell Dr Gray *that*.'

'OK, I'll tell him that. Then I'll say I'm not coming anymore.'

*

Well over an hour later, Matthew pulled up outside a terrace of houses on the outskirts of an uninspiring little town I had never heard of. He helped me out of my car, handed me the roses that had suffered the journey on the back seat, and escorted me up the short path to my friend's front door. He knocked on one of the glass panels. A shadow approached on the other side and the door scraped open. I did not recognise my friend's face, her voice, her perfume, her house or its clutter. I stepped inside Annabelle's hallway as if for the first time and watched this totally unknown, plumpish, ginger curly-haired woman collapse into an emotional heap in front of me. I stood firm as Matthew coaxed her from her paroxysms of sobbing and led us into her lounge.

'Annabelle, this is not constructive,' he whispered. 'Shall we sit down and try again?' He started to gather up drawings, wire, an adjustable wrench. 'For God's sake, you could have cleared some of this crap away!'

Annabelle wiped her face and collapsed into the space Matthew had managed to clear in the middle of her vast sofa. 'I wanted to show Sarah what I've been working on since …' She looked up at me. I was still clutching the presentation bunch of roses. Once again she disintegrated into sobbing. I wasn't sure how to respond. I tried to empathise with this stranger, who was beginning to look ridiculous, but I simply didn't know enough about her to feel sympathy.

Matthew cleared a space next to the sobbing, sat close and began patting Annabelle's shoulder. I didn't want that to be happening. My disapproval moved me to action. I focussed away from Annabelle's hand which was now resting on Matthew's knee.

'Annabelle, why don't you pretend we've just met and you're telling me about your work?' I bent to pick up a crumpled drawing. 'Let's start with this. What is it?'

Annabelle wiped her sleeve across her face and scrabbled around for a couple of other displaced drawings. Her mannerisms were unfamiliar. 'It's for storing DVDs.' She placed the drawings across Matthew's knees and traced along a few lines with her finger. 'They go in there. It was commissioned by the guy that bought my Tin Man.'

'The Tin Man?' I said. 'Like in *The Wizard of Oz*?'

'Yes, only bigger, with a penis. Do you remember the Tin Man?'

'She remembers things from when she was small,' explained Matthew.

'I remember *The Wizard of Oz*,' I said. 'The Tin Man wanted a heart.' I burrowed deeper into my surviving memories. 'The lion wanted courage and the straw man wanted a brain.' I laughed. 'I could probably do with a new one of those.'

Annabelle chewed her lip and seemed to be about to resume sobbing. I needed to prevent further patting. 'Tell me about how we met. We can start right from the beginning.'

Annabelle threw the drawings over the back of the chair and glanced at Matthew for sanction. He signalled his approval. 'Just about you and Sarah, right? Nothing confusing. I'll put the flowers in water. Is there wine in the fridge?'

Annabelle nodded. Her ginger curls wobbled frantically. Matthew stood up, plucked the roses from my grasp and headed out of the door and through the hallway; I was perturbed at how well he knew his way around Annabelle's house. Around Annabelle. I stepped over and shifted a pair of jeans and sat in the space next to her, not close but close enough that nobody would think of sitting between us.

'Matthew said we met at university.'

'Exeter. We were in Halls next door to each other, in the first year. Then we found a flat.' Tiny tears started to form along her eyelids, waiting for their cue. 'You threw some frozen mince at your window. In Hall. And broke it.'

'What? The window?'

'Yes, you'd decided to be a vegetarian. The mince was OK. I shared it with Mike. Do you remember Mike?'

I shrugged.

'Do you remember the huge hill we had to climb to get to lectures?'

I shook my head. 'Sounds terrible.'

'It was, especially after a night of scrumpy down the pub.'

We chatted. Gradually Annabelle became less tearful. Matthew returned with chardonnay and glasses, cleared an armchair and sat drinking wine and listening to the conversation ramble on: student romances; a holiday in Corfu; me starting teacher training and my brief affair with the headmaster of the school I was sent to for teaching practice, giving up the course and going to work first in a series of offices and then in a florist shop. I felt quite alarmed about the affair with the headmaster. I hoped he wasn't married. I noticed Matthew looking worried. Then Annabelle's mention of her own short-lived marriage really seemed to concern him.

'Why did that fall apart?' I asked.

'Because after we got back from the registry office, we realised we hated each other.'

I laughed. 'Was I ever engaged or anything?'

Matthew interrupted. 'Nothing significant until you met me. Annabelle, I presume you'd like another glass? To go with the other twenty you obviously had before we arrived?'

'I had a couple of shots to calm me down.'

'Really?' He walked over to the cluttered table to refill his and Annabelle's glasses. 'Do you want a top-up, Sarah?'

I shook my head. 'I hope I didn't sleep with too many men before I met Matthew.'

'Why?' asked Annabelle.

'You didn't!' said Matthew.

For some reason that annoyed me. 'How do you know?'

'I just know! Annabelle, did you book a table?'

'Seven-thirty at The Mad Hatter. We can walk, and you said you liked it there.'

I tried to disguise my irritation. 'Have *I* ever been there?'

Annabelle swallowed a mouthful of wine. 'Yes, several times, but then Jeff stopped going there because he hated the chef from when ...'

'Annabelle!' snapped Matthew.

Something was happening. I didn't understand Annabelle and Matthew being suspended like that. Like images captured on a paused video. Not blurred but not right. Slowly disappearing behind the thick grey mist. I tried to call out to them, to come back, but the air was too bitingly cold as it passed down my throat, filling my chest with sharp pains. I wanted to run away but my arms and legs wouldn't move. All I could do was hold my breath and watch the grey mist. It began to sparkle in places. Like fireworks in a cloudy sky. Then all at once it crackled out of existence and became laughter: shrill and unpleasant.

Matthew's voice broke through. 'Sarah, are you alright?'

I turned to try to catch sight of the source of the laughter but outside Annabelle's window there was only empty grass.

'I thought I heard children,' I said. I turned back to Annabelle. 'Have I ever been there?'

'Been where?'

'The Mad Hatter. Have I ever been there?'

'Yes,' said Annabelle.

*

Supper went well enough. Annabelle had clearly benefited from the large mug of black coffee Matthew forced her to drink before leaving and the conversation about our forgotten friendship continued over three courses, wine and coffee. Watching Annabelle consume her rare steak, reconfirmed my commitment never to eat anything that had previously bled warm blood. How dare Della Brown try to trick me that way! By nine-thirty, I had reached saturation. There was a limit to how much of my previous life I could take in a single session. I stifled a yawn.

Annabelle looked distraught. 'Am I talking too much, Sarah?'

Matthew laughed. 'No more than usual. Shall I get the bill? Annabelle, sweetheart, another bucket of wine, or have you had enough?'

'I'm OK, thanks. Are you both at Sarah's now?'

Matthew flashed yet another warning glance, but Annabelle seemed not to notice. She looked straight at me. 'Are you going to sell up and move to Matthew's place?'

'Annabelle!' snapped Matthew. The couple at the next table turned to look. He lowered his voice. 'Do not mention my house, OK?'

I was confused. 'Matthew, I'll drive if you're feeling grumpy.'

'I'm not!' He tried to catch a waiter's eye. 'I just get ratty when people remind me that I own a desirable property in Hampstead, currently occupied by a Gorgon, who's probably defacing my furniture as we speak!'

'She's probably fucking someone in your bed as we speak,' suggested Annabelle.

Matthew sighed. 'Thanks for that, Annabelle.'

'You ought to throw her out and move in there with Sarah. It can't be pleasant in Sarah's place with all those memories.'

Matthew banged down his glass. The couple on the next table stared across with disapproval. 'If you want to use the ladies, go separately.'

'What?' demanded Annabelle.

'I can't risk you saying anything to Sarah that I can't hear.'

'Like what?' I asked.

'I don't know. But I'm sure Annabelle would think of something.'

*

The walk back was almost uneventful. Annabelle rambled on about her projects and about a weekend away with the guy who purchased her Tin Man: 'He wanted to stand Tin Man in his bedroom but his wife said no: one giant hard-on was enough for her.'

'Annabelle,' said Matthew. 'Please spare us the details!'

'Was he married?' I felt uncomfortable.

'Yes, he still is. God, Sarah, have you had a moral rebirth or something?'

'I'm just shocked you can be so casual about committing adultery.'

'Well, you're a fair one to talk!'

'Annabelle,' said Matthew, pulling me to a standstill. 'Will you please shut up about your bloody love life! Nobody wants to know.'

'You are such a miserable bastard these days!'

'And you drink too much!'

'Like you don't!'

I had to intervene. 'Hey, I'm sorry this is difficult. But, please, stop arguing.'

Annabelle folded her arms. 'Sorry. Do you have time to stay for coffee?'

'No,' said Matthew.

'Yes,' I said. 'Of course we do.'

*

Matthew drove back to London, calmer now, after most of his worst fears had been realised and consigned to history. I watched the patches of countryside get taken over by streetlights and thought about Annabelle's strangeness. Matthew's reactions. Perhaps Annabelle had come close to revealing something I was currently forbidden to know. Something Matthew knew. I touched his hand. 'What did Annabelle mean: "all those memories"? Did something terrible happen in my flat? Are the police investigating something that happened there?'

Matthew paused a little too long before he replied. 'No, as far as I know, nothing happened in your flat that might explain why you were missing.'

More half-truths.

We drove on in uneasy silence. As Putney Bridge approached, I felt

Matthew's fingers close around mine. 'What are you thinking about?' he said.

'Annabelle. Did you ever sleep with her?'

Horror flashed across his face. 'No way! I told you.'

I couldn't remember him telling me. 'Would you? Sleep with her?'

'What, if she was the only woman left on earth and I was blind and deaf? No, I wouldn't, I'd find a chimpanzee. Or a ferret.'

I laughed. 'I can't imagine ever knowing her. You'd think I would remember something. It makes me feel I'll never remember anything if I can't remember my best friend.'

Matthew crunched the gears. 'If I had a choice I'd forget her too.'

FRANKFURT

The Frankfurt Book Fair was staggering towards its close. Promises had been made, wallets bulged with newly exchanged business cards. On the J.D. Hillier stand, a few of the more conscientious staff members, recently back from lunch and awaiting farewell drinks at the Frankfurter Hof, were whiling away the time encouraging a group of Beijing trade delegates to take advantage of the numerous freebies that nobody could be bothered to pack up and take home. At the front of the stand, beside a larger than life cardboard cut-out of a small child clutching a single slipper, David Marchant, Hillier's managing director, was directing his attention towards Lucy Ashdown, occasional bedfellow and one half of the Parry & Ashdown Literary Agency. The other half of the agency was not back after lunch. Lucy was casting her eyes around the stands while occasionally smiling encouragingly at whatever Marchant was saying to her. She caught sight of her flamboyant young editor reading his text messages.

'Poppy,' she snapped, 'would you mind locating Sarah and mentioning to her that China is a large market and if she spends any more time signing books the unsigned copies will become collectors' items.'

*

Some of the larger publishers were already vacating their pitches. Trolleys clattered towards the parking access. Their wheels echoed through the last-afternoon emptiness. Sarah didn't like those echoes. Sarah didn't much like the book fair either but she was there because Matthew wanted her there. She was, after all, one of the agency's most noteworthy authors and now, rescued from the wilderness, she was a successful writer. She owed it to Matthew to be there. She wound her way through the literary labyrinth, her hand numb with signing her name. Rounding a last corner, she collided with Poppy.

'God, Poppy, what's the hurry?'

'The Bitch wants you back talking to Chinamen!'

'What?'

'There's a group of Chinese delegates … Oh, shit! They're coming this way!'

The delegates from Beijing were moving towards them. Sarah nudged Poppy to one side and, as they drew near, she pulled her three remaining copies of *The Lost Tabby Cat* from her bag and thrust them at the nearest delegate, eliciting a burst of gratitude. Sarah and Poppy nodded graciously, and hurried back to the stand. Lucy greeted them without a smile.

'That was a major missed opportunity, Sarah!'

Sarah dismissed Lucy's complaint with a wave of her hand. 'Rubbish! I gave them free copies. I'll be essential reading all over Asia by this time next year. Where's Matthew?'

'Where is he ever?' snapped Lucy.

'I don't know. That's why I asked you!' She pulled out her mobile. 'We're supposed to be leaving in half an hour.' She prodded her phone, cancelled and redialed. 'I'm not going to be the one driving in the dark!'

'Sarah, darling, you're wasting your time. He's not answering. I've been trying for the last hour. I need to let him know I'll be travelling back with David. Via Strasbourg.'

Sarah placed her hands on her hips. 'But, Lucy, it's your turn to drive. You said you'd drive on the way back.'

'Well, David insists. He wants to introduce me to the pleasures of the Alsace.'

Sarah glared at Marchant's smug expression. If he hadn't been her publisher she would definitely have kicked him.

'And anyway,' added Lucy, 'you can get Poppy to take a turn at the wheel. He didn't drive on the way here either.'

Poppy nudged a pile of catalogues onto the floor. He bent over to retrieve them. 'Sarah, I saw Matthew with that blonde editor from Parity Press. Asking about …'

Sarah did not wait to hear more. She grabbed her bag and headed straight for the Parity stand, where a dozen or so marketing assistants were helping some South American editors to squeeze a pile of branded T-shirts into their rucksacks. Sarah gathered that Matthew might be in a wine bar downstairs. She headed for the stairs, intent upon hostility.

The ground floor was a chaos of farewells and promises to lunch. Sarah pushed her way through, cursing Lucy Ashdown, Frankfurt and Matthew, but particularly Matthew. How dare he slope off like that! He was a philandering pig! And Lucy was as bad. They were supposed to be a couple but as soon as either of them sniffed an opportunity, everything else went to Hell! She located the temporary bar and stormed inside. She failed to identify Matthew. Typical. She'd phone. She felt in her bag for her mobile. Then in her pocket. Then in her bag again. Her phone wasn't there. Where was it? It was lost. And it was Matthew's fault! She paused to consider her phone, glanced back to check the floor, turned and caught sight of Matthew heading away from her carrying two glasses of wine. She pursued him to his table, determined to ruin his liaison with the Parity blonde, but discovered not the tall and voluptuous recently-hired editorial director but instead a rather severe-looking middle-aged man. Both he and Matthew looked up.

'Sarah, hi! This is Roman Jasinski from Warsaw. We've just come to an agreement over your LOST books, including the three you haven't yet written. Roman, this is Sarah Blake.'

Sarah shook hands. 'I've lost my phone!'

Mr Jasinski's face softened into a smile, then he seemed to realise that this LOST announcement was not one of Sarah's promotional gambits. His expression resumed its severity as he too scanned the path Sarah had just trodden. Sarah rallied, told Mr Jasinski not to worry, then informed Matthew that Lucy was eloping to Strasbourg with David Marchant and they would be one driver down on the way back. And now they were late and they'd be driving fast in the dark! And would probably fall asleep at the wheel and crash. Mr Jasinski looked concerned.

Matthew handed Sarah his glass of wine and assured Mr Jasinski that the phone-losing performance happened at least three times a day and that, as far as the trip back to the UK was concerned, his business partner had already phoned to say that she was taking an alternative route home. He then tried to steer the conversation back to foreign rights. His phone rang. He checked the number and looked puzzled.

'Sarah, you appear to be phoning me ... Hi, Matthew Parry ... Oh hello, Poppy. Have you found Sarah's phone? ... Yes, I'll tell her. Just leave it with one of the others. We'll be back on the stand in about half an hour ... Yes, Poppy, I'll tell her that as well!'

*

With a Polish future secure, Sarah and Matthew wandered back towards the Hillier stand.

'It's getting dark already,' she complained.

'Don't be ridiculous. And besides, I'll do all the driving. It'll be safer.'

'Oh, very funny. You're the one with the points on your licence. Not me or Poppy. And, by the way, what did Poppy want you to tell me *as well?*'

Matthew chewed his lip. 'That he won't be driving back with us either. He's catching a flight this evening.' He attempted to lighten Sarah's mood. 'I think it's something to do with a tall, dark handsome guy with a Porsche and a personal trainer.'

'He never mentioned him to me!'

Episode Twenty-five

On Sunday Matthew suggested we take a trip to the zoo, so that's what we did. And it turned out to be a wonderful day, which was just as well because Monday was terrible. Matthew left early for a meeting. The phone rang soon after. I waited then checked the last incoming number. My mobile rang. The same number flashed across the screen. Steeling myself, I answered it. It was Mrs Parkin confirming today's visit. Mrs Parkin never phoned. I wandered back into the lounge, hating myself for my pathetic telephone hysteria. But I was distracted from self-loathing by an unfamiliar wailing coming from the kitchen, where I found Alfie guarding a tiny, dead mouse, dabbing it so that it seemed to move and then pouncing in order to re-experience the killing. I wasn't sure what to do, so I ran to fetch Peggy who followed me back, armed with rubber gloves. She thanked Alfie profusely then prodded the small carcass into a sandwich bag. 'He brings me one occasionally,' she explained. 'Shall I flush it down the toilet?'

I directed Peggy through into my bathroom and waited outside the door, clenching my fists. Moments later, Peggy reappeared.

'All gone now. On his way to the seaside.' I staggered backwards onto the bed, mumbling words of gratitude. Peggy sat down beside me. 'Dear, dear, Sarah, you mustn't upset yourself about a little mouse.

They're probably having a field day up there in your … in the top flat. I often see Alfie sitting on the stairs waiting for one of them to pop out?' She patted my knee. 'Would you like me to stay for a while, until you feel better?'

'No, I'm fine. Mrs Parkin will be here soon.'

Peggy left and I wandered into the kitchen where Alfie was waiting, triumphant. I allowed him to throw himself against my leg a few times. To believe I was grateful. To believe he had done the right thing. Sometimes thinking you've done the right thing is different from actually doing it, but I was willing to indulge him. I thought about the top flat. The backyard was still in shadow at this time of day and to add to the gloom it was just starting to rain. I leaned across the work surface and looked up at the iron staircase that loomed above the window and imagined a vast, networking community of rodents scurrying around above my head, burrowing their way into the furniture. I watched the rain cascading off the metal steps. I'm not sure how long I was standing there like that but I was suddenly aware that someone was banging on the front door. I ran through to discover Mrs Parkin on the doorstep. She was holding an umbrella over her head. Rain was bouncing in all directions. She came inside, dripping water, walked straight through to the kitchen and propped her umbrella in the sink.

'Is your doorbell not working, Sarah?'

'I'm not sure.' I glanced at the tray down beside the fridge, the teapot not rinsed since breakfast. 'The cat caught a mouse. Miss Lewis flushed it down the toilet.'

Mrs Parkin frowned then removed her wet Burberry and draped it over the back of a chair.

'Filthy day out there!'

She looked around at the aftermath of breakfast with clear disapproval, took out her folder and set it down next to a piece of abandoned toast. 'You'll be pleased to hear that, for the time being, the doctors have agreed that I continue to visit twice a week.'

I was both irritated and relieved. I filled the kettle. Mrs Parkin started to collect up breakfast things and carry them over to the sink.

'I'll do that, Mrs Parkin!' I flicked the kettle switch then started to load the dishwasher. 'Matthew says breakfast is the most important meal of the day.'

'Really?' said Mrs Parkin. She pulled out a chair and checked through her notes. 'Ah yes, let's get this out of the way before I forget!'

I turned. Mrs Parkin was pulling a multipack of condom boxes out of her bag. She placed them on the table and tore a slip of paper from the cellophane wrap. 'Take this repeat prescription to the hospital pharmacy if supplies run low. You'll need to use them for another month at least. Preferably after that as well, to guard against HIV. Have you started taking the contraceptive pills?'

'I haven't had my period yet.'

'Good Lord, Sarah, are you late?'

'No. What does HIV mean?'

Mrs Parkin looked stern. 'It's something that we don't need to be worrying about.' She burrowed again into her bag and pulled out a packet of chocolate digestives, which she placed next to the condoms. I found their proximity unsettling so I wandered over and picked up the multipack:

'I'll just go and put these away,' I whispered.

'Yes,' said Mrs Parkin, her thin lipstick lips almost breaking into a smile, 'not the most appropriate thing to have on the table if Miss

Lewis decides to pop back!' It was almost a joke, but not a very humorous one. I forced a smile then hurried to the bedroom and crammed the multipack into the back of my lingerie drawer, alongside the three other unopened packets. When I walked back into the kitchen Mrs Parkin was already munching a chocolate digestive. I made tea, wiped the table and took a deep breath.

'Mrs Parkin, I'm really pleased that you'll carry on coming to see me but I'm beginning to think that my sessions with Dr Williams and Dr Gray are a waste of everyone's time and ...'

'Has Mr Parry told you to say this?'

'No!' I continued to wipe away non-existent crumbs. I could feel Mrs Parkin watching me:

'Sarah, you may not be fully aware of the contribution your physicians are making to your recovery, but I do assure you that to abandon their treatment plan, at this *particular* time, would be ill-advised. It is due to their excellent counsel that you now find yourself able to lead this comparatively normal existence, but, as I have said before, this is a false confidence.'

I listened patiently but I was determined to declare my intention. I poured the tea and handed Mrs Parkin her mug.

'Matthew has been warned to stay away from Dr Williams' places of work.'

'Hardly surprising given the circumstances!'

'I want Matthew to attend my appointments with me.'

'Dr Williams will not permit such a thing.'

'Well, in that case, I'll phone and cancel my visits.'

Mrs Parkin's face twisted into a spiteful smile. She helped herself to another biscuit. 'Are you so fully competent with your phone that you now feel able to do that, Sarah?'

I stared at her: 'If I have to, I will. The alternative would be for me not to turn up and let Dr Williams work it out for *himself*.'

Mrs Parkin swallowed. 'My dear, have you any idea of the investment that has already been made towards your recovery, in both time and money? You cannot simply turn away from such commitment on the part of others, not just Dr Williams and Dr Gray, but also Drs Mustafa and Clegg.'

'And Dr Brown?'

Mrs Parkin narrowed her eyes. 'It would seem that Mr Parry has been corrupting your opinions. He is utterly unqualified to advise you regarding medical practice.'

'Medical practice? Della Brown is a cop!'

Mrs Parkin winced. 'She is a police detective.'

'She was introduced to me as a research associate. I was allowed to assume that she was a doctor. And you have encouraged that lie.'

For a brief moment Mrs Parkin's jaw wobbled: 'Your situation has demanded … has benefitted from a few harmless untruths.'

'She thinks I'm pretending not to remember. Is that what *you* think, Mrs Parkin?'

Mrs Parkin paused to consider her defence. 'Did Mr Parry put these ideas into your head?'

'She bought me a ham sandwich!'

'What on earth are you talking about, Sarah?'

'Della Brown took me to lunch when Matthew was having the row with Dr Williams …'

'When he was assaulting Dr Williams!'

'And we went to a sandwich bar and she bought me a ham sandwich to trick me because she knew I didn't eat meat.'

Mrs Parkin leaned back in her chair, her expression derisory: 'Sarah, how did you discover that Della Brown is a detective?'

'Matthew told me!'

'And what makes you think you don't eat meat?'

'Matthew told me that too.' I could hear confusion creeping into my voice.

Mrs Parkin narrowed her eyes: 'And what else has Mr Parry told you?'

I tried to stay calm. But I could feel my hands shaking, hot tea spilling onto my fingers.

Mrs Parkin hurried over to take the mug away from me, shunted me towards a chair and pressured me to sit down. 'Sarah, there's absolutely no point in getting yourself worked up like this. Dr Williams and I have feared that Mr Parry would try and manipulate things for his own benefit.'

I forced myself to think through the burgeoning doubt. 'I threw a packet of mince at my window!'

Mrs Parkin stepped back. 'What?'

'When I was at university, I decided to become a vegetarian and I threw a packet of frozen mince at my window and broke it.'

'Have you just remembered that?'

'No, Annabelle told me.'

'Annabelle? Annabelle Grant? When did you see her? Has she visited you? You should have told me straight away!'

'Matthew drove me to see her on Saturday. And yesterday we went to the zoo.'

'The zoo!'

'Yes, but there were no elephants.'

Mrs Parkin leaned past me to retrieve her folder. 'Mr Parry had no right to undertake these excursions without advising the doctors of his intention.'

'He told Dr Gray.'

'Well, there's absolutely no mention of his doing so in your notes. Did you stay away overnight? Ms Grant lives towards Portsmouth, doesn't she?'

'No, we came home.'

Mrs Parkin continued to scrutinise her folder. 'Did Ms Grant tell you anything else?'

I particularly remembered the Tin Man with a penis but I chose not to mention it. 'She said I worked in a flower shop.'

Mrs Parkin cleared her throat. 'Anything else? What you did after the flower shop?'

'Do you know what I did afterwards, Mrs Parkin?'

'Sarah! Where was Mr Parry when you were being told all this?'

'He was listening. He wouldn't let Annabelle be on her own with me, in case she accidentally said something that upset me.'

'Yes, I can imagine. This is all disastrous! I need to make a telephone call, so if you don't mind, I'll go into the lounge. Then we'll need to discuss this entire pickle that you've got yourself into with Mr Parry. If you ask me, Dr Gray should never have risked exposing you to his interference!'

Episode Twenty-six

I went to the bathroom while Mrs Parkin was making her phone call. Matthew's wash bag was on the floor, propped up against the shower door. I picked it up and smelled the mix of aftershave, toothpaste, shampoo, deodorant. It smelled safe and I liked it being there. I put it on the shelf above the bath and turned to check myself in the mirror, combed my hair. When, finally, I stepped into the bedroom I discovered Mrs Parkin standing beside my bed, glaring at Matthew's leather holdall, open on the floor. His red scarf had fallen down beside it. I went to pick it up but thought better of it.

'Does Mr Parry intend to move in here with you?'

'He goes back to his flat every day to collect clothes and things. In Crouch End. He's got a house in Hampstead but his girlfriend's living there at the moment.'

Mrs Parkin folded her arms.

'It was only partly my fault they're not together.' I noticed Mrs Parkin's rear view reflected in the wardrobe mirror. It could have been the reversed rear view of any number of people. On the other hand, the front of Mrs Parkin was quite unique. The face could never belong to anyone else. I watched its unfriendliness turn to concern.

'Sarah, you must not believe everything this man tells you. And have you considered that there might be certain things that he would prefer you not to remember?'

I was angry on Matthew's behalf. 'Matthew does want me to remember. He's upset that I've forgotten our time together.'

Mrs Parkin shook her head. 'My dear, you have a lot to learn about people. At times I think you must have always been as gullible as this.' She cast a last disapproving glance at the leather holdall. 'We need to discuss Dr Williams' contingency plan.' She turned and left the room. Before following her, I stooped to pick up Matthew's scarf and folded it flat on my pillow. Then I braced myself for whatever was to follow, knowing that before all this I would have known what *contingency plan* meant.

Mrs Parkin had taken it upon herself to put the kettle on. I walked over to organise mugs but she snapped at me to sit down. 'We have a lot to discuss. Dr Williams has recommended ...'

'Mrs Parkin, I'm not sure what *contingency plan* means.'

She gave me a look of exasperation. 'It's a back-up plan if circumstances change. Now, sit down and focus. I'll do the tea!'

I sat down. Mrs Parkin took mugs from the cupboard. 'Dr Williams has recommended that you return urgently to Greystone Park for reassessment, initially Thursday to Saturday this week. Dr Gray is in agreement.'

'He wants me to go back to the clinic?'

'You'll have your own room and en-suite.'

'What about Matthew?'

'I'm sure Dr Gray will allow visitors.'

'But will he be able to stay?'

'Clearly not!'

'In that case, I'm not doing it! I'm not going back into hospital without him!'

'It is not a hospital. It's a private clinic.'

'I don't care what it's called, I'm not going!'

'You have agreed to this treatment.'

'I'll cancel my agreement.'

Mrs Parkin paused to pour. 'Sarah, I'm afraid that we can insist upon re-admittance, whether you agree to it or not.'

'How can you insist?'

She took a deep breath. 'The Mental Health Act 1983 provides for the detention of patients if two or more doctors consider incarceration … hospitalisation necessary to the patient, for the purposes of assessment or treatment. It is sometimes referred to as sectioning.' She handed me a mug.

'What does all that mean? What's the point of explaining things to me with words I don't understand? What does *incarceration* mean?'

'It means that it would be better for you if you agree to come to the clinic and stay for the recommended period. Under Section Two of the Act, you may be forced to do so and then kept under assessment for up to twenty-eight days. So clearly, the voluntary visit is your best option.'

'No! You can't make me!' I banged down my mug and tea slopped on to the table: 'Matthew won't let you!'

'Mr Parry is not in a position to overrule medical professionals.'

I caught my breath. Uninvited thoughts began to invade my mind: footprints in the wet sand, seagulls screeching, the scream of brakes, a child laughing. My head was becoming heavy with the weight of sounds and images. Too heavy.

A crash brought me to my senses. My cheek was against the wet surface of the table. I pushed myself up, caught sight of my mug smashed on the floor. Tea was everywhere, cold across my face, down my legs, splashed across Mrs Parkin's shoes.

'Sarah!' snapped Mrs Parkin. 'There's absolutely no point in behaving like this. It's for your own good.' She looked down at her feet. 'My goodness, look at this mess! We'd better get it cleaned up. Where do you keep your paper towels these days?' She pulled open a cupboard and froze. Slowly she turned. I watched her looming there, perfectly framed by cereal, her face revealing a trace of bewilderment, a trace of panic. I watched her walk over and pick up her tea and stand drinking it, staring at the multitude of cornflake boxes. Finally, she spoke.

'You've collected these since arriving home. What, eight weeks, is it? Why have you done this, Sarah? This is not normal behaviour. Does Mr Parry know about this?'

I nodded. Felt myself start to snigger.

'Yet he saw fit not to mention this behaviour to anyone?'

'He said if we eat them every day, they'll be gone by Christmas.'

Mrs Parkin was clearly appalled by this response. 'This is no laughing matter, Sarah! If you ask me, I think the pair of you should be sectioned.'

'Good! Then Matthew would be able to stay at the clinic with me.'

Mrs Parkin gasped. 'Sarah, I sometimes think you are treating this whole situation far too flippantly, but then I remind myself that most of your adult experience is compromised and that I am talking to an irresponsible child. Of course, this behaviour …' she indicated the cereal cupboard, '… is absolute confirmation that you need to be reassessed straightaway. I will have to make a full report of what I've seen today. Now, go and change out of those trousers and I'll mop up.'

When I stepped back into the kitchen, Mrs Parkin was tipping broken china into the bin.

I took a deep breath. 'Was that mine?'

'Beg pardon?'

'The mug. If it belongs to the landlord, I ought to replace it.'

'I wouldn't worry about that right now. There are plenty of mugs to be getting on with.'

'Is any of the furniture mine?'

'The furniture?'

'In this flat. I hope the sofas are mine.'

Mrs Parkin rolled her eyes. 'Sarah, let's not discuss the furniture right now. I assure you it will all be sorted out in due course.' She walked over to wash her hands.

'Is the landlord leaving the upstairs flat empty because of me? Are both flats being paid for out of the funds?'

'Not now, Sarah! Right now we need to discuss your stay at the clinic.'

'OK. I'll want Matthew to drive me there. And visit me. And drive me home.' I checked the chair for tea and sat down.

'I'm sure that will be acceptable. And I'm glad that you seem to be coming to terms with your stay. Now, can we discuss …?'

'I'm *not* coming to terms with it, but it seems to me that I have no choice. And I'm not like an irresponsible child. I've just forgotten how to react in certain situations. But I haven't forgotten about being responsible. And Matthew is helping me more than anyone and I don't think it can be in the least *constructive* for me to be away from him. And he did phone Dr Gray about visiting Annabelle. He told me so. And I believe him.'

Mrs Parkin shook her head. 'Well, we'll have to work around Mr Parry then, won't we? It's your choice. And so long as you agree to this voluntary stay, it will remain your choice.'

Episode Twenty-seven

When Mrs Parkin finally left, after what seemed like hours, I took a moment to arrange my thoughts: three days was definitely better than twenty-eight days, but I couldn't bear to think of being apart from Matthew for even that long. I decided to take my mind off my return to the clinic by choosing the sketching things I would take with me. I remembered a large pencil tin in my desk drawer, located it straightaway and started to fill it with coloured pencils. I poked around in the depths of the pencil pot for the metal sharpener I knew was there, tipped its contents onto my desk, picked out the sharpener then loaded everything back into the pot. Drawing pins, paper clips, buttons. I paused over a key, tried it in the front door. But it wasn't a key to the front door. I returned it to the pot, rechecked the tin. Now this first preparation had been undertaken, I felt a little more relaxed about my no-choice stay at the clinic. By the time Matthew phoned mid-afternoon, I was able not to mention it. So after an awkward conversation involving many pauses, a conversation which proved to me that I *was* able to filter what I did and didn't say, he asked me if I would drive over to the supermarket and choose fish for supper because he was stuck in a meeting. He reminded me to check sell-by-dates. My concerns over the clinic were instantly displaced by the burden of choosing an evening meal and affirming dates beyond which fish became deadly.

*

Footsteps approached and passed by. None of them belonged to Matthew. Finally, I saw him walk past the window and veer towards the door. I had opened it before he was able to insert Peggy's key. He stepped inside.

'Hello, crazy person. Have you been waiting for me? Did you make it to the supermarket?'

'I bought salmon and chilli prawns.'

'Sounds great!' He pushed the door closed with his elbow and stooped to kiss me.

'I checked the dates. They probably won't kill us.'

'Well done!' He threw his bag against my desk.

'And I've got to go back to the clinic for reassessment.'

He stared at me. 'What? Who decided you needed reassessment?'

'Mrs Parkin said the doctors. But I think it was mostly Dr Williams.'

'Bob Gray never mentioned anything about it. I phoned him this morning to tell him the trip to Annabelle's went OK. Tell them you won't go.'

'I can't. They'll section me.'

'What? Who told you that?'

'Mrs Parkin.'

'Right!' He pulled out his phone. 'Let's see what Bob Gray has to say about this reassessment!'

I listened from the kitchen and, from what I could hear, Matthew raised his voice only twice, when he said, 'This has been badly handled' and 'He sees her as nothing more than a lab rat.' But mostly he said 'yes' and 'no' quietly, and 'I don't want to be restricted to visiting hours' very quietly indeed. When he joined me in the kitchen he was smiling but I knew he was upset. His green eyes always revealed more about his thoughts than his expression ever did.

'How's dinner progressing?' he asked.

'I've put the oven on. What did Dr Gray say?'

'He said don't worry. It will be mostly interviews. I don't think this reassessment was his decision. I got the impression he'd only just found out about it. I didn't want to mention the sectioning over the phone, but he did reassure me he'll have the final word with anything they choose to do to you. We'll check you in Thursday morning and bring you home Saturday afternoon. And, if you want, I can be there all the time.'

'*All* the time?'

'Yes, although I don't think they do doubles in clinics. And he said no need to attend your appointment with Williams this week. But he'd like us both to nip over for a chat on Wednesday.' His face broke into a smile this time reflected in his eyes. 'So, why don't you come into the office tomorrow? They can't wait to see you.'

'Will Annie be there?'

'Of course she will. She brings flapjacks in on Tuesdays.'

*

After supper I decided to visit my wardrobe and chose something to wear to meet a group of strangers I had known for four years. I left Matthew grovelling under my desk trying to untangle cables and locate a free socket for the CD player. He had decided not to re-watch any more of his favourite movies, since they were invariably better the first time around. The cursing drifted through to the bedroom.

'You'd think they would have sorted this out for you. This is a fire hazard!'

I walked back into the lounge. 'Shall I wear a skirt?'

Matthew turned to answer and banged his head on the underside of the desk drawer.

'Ouch! You can wear whatever you want. There's a disconnected router under here. They obviously don't want you to be in contact with cyberspace.'

I went back to sorting through my clothes. Finally, after further cursing, Matthew called to ask what music I wanted to listen to. I called back, 'You choose, I've lost my memory, remember?'

Moments later, I stepped out of my room to demonstrate my outfit and found Matthew kneeling next to the CD box holding my hidden cache of pornography.

'Oh,' I said, 'I forgot about those!'

His expression was a mixture of amusement and disbelief. 'What in God's name … Are these part of Mrs P's rehabilitation programme?' He carried the magazines over to the table.

'I bought them so I didn't make a fool of myself when we made love.'

He thumbed through a few pages. 'I've been wondering where all the innovation has been coming from.' He snorted. 'Good God!'

'*Matthew*, is this all right?'

'What?' He glanced up. 'Hey, you look gorgeous! Have you read these?'

'Mostly. *Matthew*, is this all right for tomorrow?'

'Yes! I already *said* yes. Although you ought to wear shoes as well.'

I rolled my eyes with exasperation then nudged a magazine towards him.

'Turn to page forty-six, and put some music on.'

At a table just inside the door, a woman was sitting alone, checking her mobile. She looked up as her senior colleague stepped into the room, slapped a file onto the table then heaved himself into the seat opposite her.

'Della?'

'Mike, thanks for making time. How's prostitution?'

He pushed the file towards her. 'Awaiting your contribution.'

She laughed. 'Any time now. Royston's pulling the plug on the Hornsey case. And Robert Gray's making moves to obstruct any further questioning of Sarah Blake, on the basis that it might tip the stupid bitch completely over the edge.'

'What about Williams? I thought you'd managed to …'

'There was an incident involving Matthew Parry. He's back on the scene. Prancing around like some kind of demented knight in shining armour. If Sarah Blake actually has lost her memory, the situation might well have been compromised by now. She's possibly been told about Jeff Blake.'

'And Arachne Dawson?'

'Who knows. Either way, the situation's become more difficult.'

'What about the mother?'

'Still drifting with the fairies. I've contacted Robert Gray to arrange another interview.'

'From what I saw, I wouldn't bother.'

'You're probably right. I'm also going to request a controlled interview with Sarah Blake in the presence of a physician and counsellor. I might get away with it. I've just had a call from Shoumi Mustafa. Apparently she's being pulled back into Greystone for reassessment over the next few days. So I might try and kill two birds with one stone.'

'Sounds familiar.'

'Yeah. Or I might just nip round and pay her a visit. Catch her when she's on her own. And I'll take another stab at Abercrombie. Check whether Parry's alibi is still holding up. Someone knows something and I've got until the end of the week to find out what it is.' She indicated the file in front of her. 'So, Mike, this is the story so far, is it?'

'Yep. The third body's confirmed. The network seems to be bigger than we thought. So, something for you to get your teeth into, Sergeant Brown. Some good old-fashioned pimps and gangsters. A fuck load easier to deal with than a bunch of hysterical lunatics. Fancy a beer?'

Episode Twenty-eight

I woke with the breaking light. I could hear the town birds organising their day, issuing instructions to avoid the black and white cat. I moved closer to Matthew so I could feel his breathing. I wanted to ask him more about the people at the office. I was nervous about meeting them. But it would have been wrong to wake him. He must have been so tired with all the worry I had caused him, was still causing him. And something else was bothering me ...

'Are you watching me?' His eyes were still closed.

I slid my arm across his chest. 'Yes.'

He opened his eyes. 'Are you worried about coming into the office?'

'A bit.'

'Don't be. It'll be OK.'

I wriggled closer and my lips tingled as they contacted the light stubble along the bottom of his jaw. Then suddenly I remembered what was bothering me.

'Matthew, why would Della Brown think I'd lie about losing my memory? What does she think I'm trying to hide?'

He was suddenly wide awake. 'I don't know, Sarah. I don't know what she thinks.'

*

The offices of Parry & Ashdown Literary Agency were situated in a 1990s-renovated office block, just east of Tottenham Court Road. Matthew suggested we took a cab there because parking was near to impossible and extortionate. So, after a tedious half hour in traffic, the cabbie deposited us outside the agency offices just before ten thirty, accepted a generous tip and disappeared behind a massive construction site. I stared up at a lone workman many feet above us.

'How can he work up there? I'd be scared that high up.'

'Well, I hope you're all right on the inside. Because the agency's on the top floor.'

I clung to Matthew's arm, in through the foyer, past a man behind a desk, and into the lift. I was terrified. The situation did not improve when I stepped into the brightly-illuminated and deserted reception of Parry & Ashdown Literary Agency.

'Typical,' complained Matthew. 'Mandy's probably having a fag on the fire escape.' He pointed to the ladies' bathroom. 'Do you …?'

I nodded and headed for the door, more steps away than I would have preferred. But I made it inside and came to rest against a bank of washbasins, steel bowls perched on top of a marble bench, invisible plumbing, gleaming taps reflected in the mirror that furnished the entire wall behind them, a mirror so large that I couldn't fail to see myself, dressed up for the day, holding onto the cold marble. Cubicle doors were lined up behind me. I pulled my hands away, checked my hair, smoothed the collar of my jacket. Felt better. Felt almost able to go back outside. Then, as I was straightening my skirt, a woman, perhaps in her mid-thirties, stunning, stepped out of one of the cubicles, walked over to the basin next to me and began washing her hands. I inhaled her perfume: it was expensive, intoxicating, the kind of perfume that could make a heart beat faster. And she was so tall, her brown hair so long and sleek. The heels on her black shoes were even higher than my patent impossible-to-walk-in ones, and she was dressed in a vivid red outfit that perfectly matched the colour of her lips and nails. She met my eyes in the mirror suddenly, as if she hadn't noticed me before that moment:

'Well, hello there!'

I was horrified. 'Hello, I'm just visiting. With Matthew Parry. I'm an author.'

'Really? An author? How exciting!'

I felt very small. 'I'm sorry, I don't remember people. Have we met before?'

The woman laughed. 'Once or twice!' She walked over to dry her hands. 'I hear that you and dear Matthew are now an item.'

I felt very awkward.

'Actually, I'm just nipping in to see him myself. We could go together. Do you remember the way?'

'No. But he said he'd be waiting outside.'

'Matthew? Waiting outside a ladies' toilet? Well I never!' She turned sideways, considered her reflection, smoothed her hair, opened her bag and took out a lipstick, touched up the crimson layer, glanced at my reflection beside hers and smiled.

I smiled back. 'That's a wonderful colour.' I looked at my own reflection, the subtle hue applied to my lips. 'I'd be too scared to wear anything as bright as that. But it looks fantastic on you!'

The woman laughed. 'You really are something, aren't you? Absolutely *unreal!*'

I saw my own expression snap to confusion.

The tall woman proffered her hand by way of invitation. 'Come on, Sarah, sweetheart, let's go find your man, shall we?' She strode towards the door and pulled it open for me to step through, then followed me.

Matthew *was* waiting. He froze.

'Lucy, what the fuck are you doing here? I've signed all the papers!'

'I just thought I'd pop in to drop a few things off. I see you've brought Holly Hobbie in with you. How sweet!'

I hurried over to stand close to Matthew. He put his arm across my back, much to the amusement of his previous mistress. She gave him an unpleasant little smile.

'How unbelievably lovely. Matthew Parry, the nice guy.' She transferred her unpleasant smile to me. 'Well, aren't you going to introduce me to my *most recent* replacement? She doesn't seem to have the slightest idea who I am.'

I replied as confidently as I could. 'You're Lucy Ashdown.' I glanced up at Matthew. 'I'll wait downstairs if you want. I don't mind.'

'Don't be silly, Sarah. Everything's fine.'

Lucy Ashdown laughed out loud: 'I can't believe it! Matthew the Bastard has a heart.'

'Will, you shut up!' snapped Matthew.

Lucy Ashdown stepped nearer, assessing me from top to bottom. 'She really doesn't remember any of it, does she? Any of the squalid truth? How it all happened?'

I felt Matthew's confidence fail him. When he spoke, it was with atypical resignation.

'Lucy, please, don't say anything. It's not her fault.'

'You know that do you? It's all officially fine now, is it?'

I had no idea what they were talking about.

'No, it's not fine! Look, Luce, I'll give you whatever you want. Just leave her alone.'

'Matthew, darling, I know this must come as a complete shock to you, but you really don't have anything left that I'm interested in.' She was suddenly distracted. 'Ah, Poppy, my sweet, still loitering in doorways?'

Matthew turned and sighed. 'Poppy, mate, don't get involved!'

'You can't stop me!' With a flurry, the young man swept over to me, disconnected me from Matthew and threw his arms around me. 'Don't worry, gorgeous girl, I'll protect you from the vicious cow!'

I instantly adored him, his dark brown eyes highlighted by just a flash of taupe shadow against his olive-brown skin, his striking features, the thin line of beard outlining his jaw and bisecting his chin, his petite exuberance.

Matthew recovered his wits. 'Poppy, would you take Sarah through to meet the others. Please. Let me deal with this.'

'I want to stay!' I insisted over Poppy's shoulder.

Lucy Ashdown clapped her hands. 'Look, Matthew, here come some more of the woodentops. Rallying to your defence.'

A stout woman in her late thirties hurried over to stand beside Matthew; she was flanked by a lanky young man, wearing a beard and ponytail; and, beside him, Annie Dickson.

'Hello, Lucy, my dear,' said Mrs Dickson, 'lovely to see you again.'

'Hello, Annie, how's the menopause?'

Perhaps it was some kind of energy that I was absorbing from Poppy, or, more than likely, it was just the way I was, but I felt something rise within me. I stepped forward.

'Just around the corner for you, you bitch!' I snapped.

There was silence. Then once again Lucy Ashdown laughed.

'Well, done Sarah, oh writer of books for the young and innocent! That's a response that even I would have been proud of. Anything else to say?'

'Yes, I have got something else to say. Whether you're interested or not, I'm sure Matthew hopes that you'll find proper happiness one day. And I think the best way you can do that is to go and find someone not interested in a meaningful relationship.' I stopped speaking and waited to die.

Lucy Ashdown continued to smile as her manicured fingers flicked open her bag.

'Actually, Sarah, I anticipated your good advice and have done exactly that. I've just called in to return these.' She pulled out a set of keys and tossed them at Matthew. 'House, car, garden shed, summerhouse. You'll need to change the bed. And there haven't been any dishwasher tablets for a few weeks. Oh yes, and the cleaner walked out in a huff, so everything's a bit of a mess. Perhaps you have a spare week, Annie. So, it's cheerio, everyone. Thank you for the generous settlement, *Matthew*. And best of luck in the economic downturn.'

Poppy hurried to call the lift.

Lucy followed him over. 'Thank you, Poppy darling!' The lift doors opened. She stepped inside and took a last look at Matthew. 'You two deserve each other,' she said. Then the doors closed.

Matthew sighed. 'I presume my office isn't empty. So I can't go in there and cry?'

The stout woman clasped her hands together. 'Shall I tell them to get out?'

'No, Mandy. Why weren't you on the desk to warn me she was here?'

'We were using your phone, so she wouldn't hear us. We were

trying to warn you she was in her old office. We weren't expecting you as early as this. You said after eleven.'

'Of all the days she could have chosen to come in!' Matthew put his arm around me. 'Are you all right?'

I took a deep breath, probably my first for several minutes. 'I'm fine,' I said, not at all sure that I was.

'You were fantastic,' said the lanky young man. He held out his hand. 'I'm Ed … IT. We know each other.'

I shook hands and tried to sound calm. 'Ed, Mandy, Poppy, Annie. Is that right?'

'Yes,' said Poppy. 'But you like me best.' He patted Matthew's arm. 'I'll go tell the others they can come out from under your desk. And, cheer up, soldier, you've got your house back. And your car. And Sarah.'

Episode Twenty-nine

The offices were crammed with desks, filing cabinets, books and papers, computers, printers, gym bags, bicycles and apprehensive, reintroduced people. All of the latter were gathered in Matthew's office, chatting nervously and watching me eat one of Annie's flapjacks. Their interest in my every move was making me uncomfortable and I worried that if I choked one of them might suffer a heart attack. 'I'm fine,' I said to no one in particular. There was instant silence, which made things worse.

Annie came to the rescue. 'Good gracious, she's only lost her memory! It's still the same old Sarah, writing her stories to help pay your rent.'

'Thank you, Annie,' said Matthew.

'We're all shell-shocked after the harridan,' explained a pixie-ish woman, who might have been Jenny or Kate, I couldn't remember which.

Poppy pointed an accusing finger. 'You were hiding in here.'

'Well, she's always hated me the most.'

Ed interrupted the bickering. 'We're a bit worried about saying the wrong things. And we're all worried about you, Matt. You look exhausted.'

There were mumbles of agreement. I turned to look at Matthew, in the chair beside me. He was being unusually quiet. What things had he told them not to say? What exactly were the wrong things to say? I observed the earnest faces around me.

'It's all right if we talk about now,' I said, 'because now is the same for all of us.' There was silence. More crushing than the previous silence. I tried again. 'Matthew said you liked my apple story.'

'Hillier loved it!' said Poppy.

Matthew perked up instantly. 'Have they got back to you?'

'I showed them the text. They wanted to know how many there will be. So I said at least six. I would have said ten but I didn't know if there were that many kinds of apple.'

'There are loads more than that,' laughed Debbie the redhead.

'True,' said Matthew. 'But Poppy's world is a very simple one. Look, guys, I'll buy lunch. Mandy, order some takeaway. But do you think you could give me and Sarah a while on our own? And somebody needs to give me a rundown on the rest of the week. I'll need someone to fill in for me Thursday and Friday.'

I'd asked him not to tell them about the clinic.

'Have you remembered Charlie Baxter tomorrow afternoon?' said Poppy.

'I should be back but you'd better stand by just in case. Do the tour. Now, why don't you all go and pretend to do something?'

I watched them file out, apart from Poppy, who lingered until the others had gone then hurried to stand beside me. 'We did try and warn you. Anyway, she was a hag beside you, sweetie.'

'A very glamorous hag,' I said, with a familiarity that was unfamiliar.

He leaned over and kissed my cheek. That's because she's had the stumps of her horns filed down again. Would you prefer Chinese or Thai?'

*

As soon as we were alone, Matthew seemed to deflate. 'Sarah, I'm so sorry. I assumed she'd never set foot in here again.'

I stroked his hand. 'Is she always that nasty? Was it because of me?'

'No, she's always like that. I used to find it attractive.'

'I could practice being a bitch. If you think it's attractive.'

He smiled. 'Actually, you didn't do too badly just then.'

'She called me Holly Hobbie! I had a Holly Hobbie lunchbox. She had a big head and stubby feet.'

'Not at all like you, then?'

'You can live in your house now.'

'Sounds like she's trashed it.'

'I'll help you mend it. What did she mean by "the squalid truth"?'

'She was just being a cow. It didn't mean anything.'

'What have you told them not to say?'

'Just things you have to remember yourself.'

I searched his eyes and saw far too many secrets. Too many half-truths. 'Lucy's older than me, right?'

'She's forty-five. So the menopause comment probably struck home.'

'God, she didn't look as old as *that*! She is stunning!'

He heaved a sigh. 'You know, right now, I could do with being unconscious.'

'Matthew, it doesn't help.

*

230

Over lunch, Matthew gradually relaxed. I listened to him taking part in the banter. He was clearly well-liked by everyone, easy-going with their eccentricities, but there was also respect towards him. I felt excited to have been chosen by him, above that glamorous older woman with her expensive perfume and her practised sophistication. I had felt like a schoolgirl beside her: naïve, clumsy, about as sophisticated as Holly Hobbie. Poppy leaned across to touch my hand.

'Would you like my last prawn cracker? Only very small animals have died in its manufacture.'

I shook my head and laughed. 'You know, I didn't even know I was a veggie until Matthew told me.'

People stopped eating. The previous awkward silence resurfaced. Poppy closed his hand around mine. 'We're so sorry about what happened to you.'

'Poppy!' snapped Matthew. 'We don't know what happened to Sarah!'

Poppy held on to my hand. 'We just want her to know we care.'

'She knows. So please, just be as normal as possible. She's OK! She can't remember a single horrible thing I said to her.'

I looked at him. 'Did you say horrible things to me?'

'I said you couldn't cook.'

'I can't cook.'

'See, you haven't forgotten how not to do that.'

'And another thing you've remembered is how not to spell properly,' said Poppy. 'So I still feel needed.'

Matthew got to his feet. 'Why don't you guys clear up while I show Sarah the library?'

'Is that part of the tour?' I asked.

'It is the tour,' said Poppy.

*

'Vampires, wizards, broken homes, bullies, fairies and princes in disguise.' Matthew demonstrated the many books that the agency had been in some way involved with bringing before the public. 'Pet dragons, anthropomorphic rodents, pubescent angst, the promise of underage sex. It's all here, waiting to fill young heads with expectations. That lot over there are non-fiction and school texts: usual stuff: dinosaurs, Romans, kings and queens, saving the planet. Some schools can still afford to buy books. Ed handles the electronic stuff.' He pointed across the room. 'And that's your section.'

I walked over to investigate: there were many copies of each of my LOST books, arranged across several shelves.

'Why are there so many?'

'Different translations. Signed copies. How's your signature?'

'OK. If I don't think about it.' I read along the spines, running my finger from book to book until it came to a premature halt just before the end of a row. '*The Lost Christmas Tree*? I haven't got a copy of this.'

'We launched it last December. It was a sell-out.'

'How the hell can you lose a Christmas tree?'

'Read it and find out.'

I eased out a copy and as I did so my attention was drawn to a large framed photograph set in the recess next to my shelves. I recognised Matthew straightaway, smiling, his green eyes free of the secrets that currently discoloured them. He was standing beside a woman, attractive, also smiling. She was holding a book up to the camera: *The Lost Tabby Cat*. It was one of my books. And I was holding it. 'That's me!'

'It was your book launch. At the London Review Bookshop.'

'But I look fantastic!' I scrutinised my previous self. 'I'm wearing nail varnish!'

'Poppy did it. You spent the rest of the week picking it off!'

I looked down at myself in disgust. 'How can you still want me? I'm too thin!'

'Well, that's easily remedied!' Annie Dickson was standing in the doorway. 'I don't mean to interrupt …'

'What is it, Annie?' Matthew put his arm around me.

Annie stepped inside and closed the door behind her. 'I'm just off now, but I was wondering whether, what with everything, you might like me and Mr Dickson to go over to Hampstead and check your house for you. Make sure she's turned the taps off, not left anything on the stove. It'd be nice trip out for Mr Dickson.'

Matthew appeared to be caught off guard. 'Annie, I …'

'I don't mean to interfere.'

'No, Annie, that would be wonderful. But … God knows what state she's left it in!'

'Don't you worry, dear. Me and Mr Dickson will nip over later. We know the way.'

'Phone me straightaway if there's anything wrong. The keys are on my desk. Thank you so much.' I felt him becoming less tense.

Mrs Dickson went to leave: 'Oh yes, Sarah, are you not home this Friday?'

I put my hand to my mouth. 'Oh, I forgot to mention!'

'Not to worry, dear. But I'll need a key if nobody's going to be there.'

Episode Thirty

The taxi took a different route back and all the way I clutched *The Lost Christmas Tree* and tried not to think of Lucy Ashdown. Matthew was subdued and clearly also grappling with thoughts of this other woman.

'How long were you and Lucy together?' I whispered, when I could stand it no longer.

'On and off for over ten years. It started on and became increasingly off. We didn't live together most of the time. She had a place in Kensington but she sold it last year and she's been hanging out in Hampstead ever since. It was always an open relationship. Have you got everything? We're almost there.'

'Yes. What kind of open relationship?'

'The kind that involved other people.'

As soon as we were home, I hurried through to examine myself in the long mirror. It was a disaster. To come anywhere near to competing with Lucy Ashdown I would need a new body and lessons in choosing the right clothes and … I saw Matthew's reflection appear behind me, felt his arm around my waist, his cheek against mine.

'I could have made it work with Lucy. But I loved you.'

'I've ruined you. She's taken all your money.'

'Not all of it. Just the bit I'd set aside for our first holiday together. And I had to re-mortgage. And sell my golf clubs ... and my grand piano.'

'Do you play the piano?'

'No, but I was enjoying the look on your face.' He started to laugh. 'We'll manage as long as you get on and write your books. With the central heating off.'

I turned to face him. 'What did Lucy do before the agency?'

'She shopped ... I can't remember. Some kind of liaison for a fashion house in Paris. She speaks fluent French. And Italian.'

This latest information did not help my feelings of inadequacy. I wriggled away from him. 'What's she going to do now?'

'More shopping.'

I sat on the bed. 'You must have been my age when you met her.'

'Thirty-five and devastatingly handsome.' He laughed. 'Are you jealous about who I was with before we met?'

'You'd be jealous if I'd had someone else.'

He sat down beside me. 'Probably. Sarah, I chose to be with you.'

'But you weren't with me. You were in your flat and I was here.'

'And that was then and this is now.' He closed his palm over my knee. 'And right now I'm contemplating ...'

'Did you used to cook for Lucy?'

He rolled his eyes. 'Sometimes. She was about as good at preparing food as you are.' He stroked his hand up my thigh. 'We ate out a lot.'

'Did she know about you and me?' I resolved to wear a skirt more often.

'Yes. She'd never cared in the past but with you she did. Now, can we think about something else?'

*

I cleared away after supper and sang along with the music …

'You remember the words!'

Matthew was holding a CD case. Keane: *Hopes and Fears*. I took the case and read the titles. 'Somewhere Only We Know'. That was the song I'd been singing.

'Matthew, I'm not pretending to have no memories.'

'God, I wasn't suggesting that! It's just … perhaps music might help you remember.' All at once Matthew's mobile sounded like an angry duck. 'Shit, that's Annie! … Hello, Annie, what's up? … Good Lord, really? A note? … No, better not. I'm in the office tomorrow afternoon. Just leave it on my desk … Good Lord … Really? Look, Annie, thanks a million. You did check for booby traps, did you? Bombs? Mustard gas? … Really? … Thanks again, Annie … Bye.' I folded my arms and waited.

'It was fine,' he explained. 'Three bottles of Clicquot in the fridge. Car not wrapped round the gatepost. Grass cut. She must have hired a clean-up team.'

'Will you move there right away?' The thought of him going away made my chest hurt.

'Not until you're ready to come with me. There's a garden. Alfie will love it.'

I didn't know how to live anywhere that wasn't my flat. 'What about Miss Lewis?'

'Well, I'd rather she didn't come and live with us.'

'No! I mean she'll miss Alfie.'

'Shall we worry about that when it happens?'

We carried on sorting through the CD box but Matthew's thoughts were clearly elsewhere. Eventually, he stopped.

'I ought to phone her.'

'Who?' I knew who he meant.

'Lucy. I shouldn't let things end like this.'

I forced myself to stay calm. 'Like what?'

'Lucy redeeming herself and me not acknowledging it. Do you mind if I make a quick call?'

Yes, I did mind. 'I don't care what you do.' I carried the CDs to the sofa and sat facing away from him, as he moved to the cramped dining area. I breathed quietly, and listened:

'Lucy, hi, it's me. Look, Annie's been over to the house … no, not yet. I just wanted to say thanks. You didn't have to do that.' He chatted, said a few things about the agency, mentioned a project Lucy was working on in New York. I hated to hear him being nice to her and I was devastated when he said, 'You were looking good today' and promised to buy her supper next time he was in Manhattan. 'OK, Luce,' he concluded, 'take care … Of course I will. Bye.'

I continued to not look at the CDs. Matthew sat down beside me and eased one from my grasp.

'I'm sorry, I had to make that call.'

'When are you going to Manhattan?'

'I'm not going to Manhattan.'

'Did you think she looked good today?'

'For a child of Satan, she looked bloody fantastic! Sarah, those are the things people say. The people they're speaking to expect to hear them.'

I sighed. 'I've forgotten how to behave, haven't I?'

He stroked my cheek. Then he laughed. 'I can't say I notice the difference!' He caught my fist as it arced towards him. 'Hey, will you come and share my house with me?'

I smiled. 'I might.'

Episode Thirty-one

We arrived at the Regent's Park rooms with time to spare and had to wait while Bob Gray dealt with his previous patient. Denise brought refreshments and that came close to improving things, so I resigned myself to sipping coffee and ignoring Matthew's relentless wisecracking. Eventually Denise showed us into a consulting room, waved us towards a long Chesterfield then left, closing the door behind her. After a few moments Bob Gray appeared.

'Hello, Sarah, Matthew, I thought we'd meet in here today. I call this my lounge. Matthew stood up and shook hands. I remained seated. 'And how have you been, Sarah?'

I moved slightly away from Matthew. 'I've been fine.'

'Excellent,' said Dr Gray. 'Now, before we go any further, I don't want you worrying yourself about the next few days. There'll be nothing very different from what you're used to. A few cognitive tests.' He sat down in the armchair near to me. 'And I think that after such a rigorous assessment, if all's well, we can consider reducing your hospital consultations to once a fortnight.' He looked from me to Matthew. 'Give you more time to get to know each other again.'

'We've pretty much got that covered,' said Matthew. I looked at my lap.

'Jolly good! And how are *you*, Matthew. I realise how difficult this has been for you.'

'I have apologised …'

'Matthew,' interrupted Dr Gray, 'that whole episode with Detective Brown was regrettable.' He looked straight at me. 'Matthew has told me about the performance in the cafeteria. She had no right to encourage you to leave the hospital.' He looked back at Matthew. 'I gather Geraint has received a solicitor's note.'

'It was a shot across the bow,' said Matthew. 'I took advice regarding Sarah's rights. It will go no further.'

Bob Gray nodded. He sat back and lowered his spectacles to the end of his nose. 'Now, Sarah, do you have any concerns about your stay at the clinic?'

'Mrs Parkin said I'd be sectioned if I didn't agree to be admitted.'

Dr Gray's smile disappeared. When he spoke it was with barely concealed anger. 'Matthew did not tell me that. Sarah, that is most certainly NOT the case. I shall …'

I clasped my hands together. 'Please don't say anything to her!'

'Right! Well, perhaps we should see about discontinuing home visits.'

I felt empowered. 'Dr Grey, I'd like Matthew to attend some of the sessions during my stay at Greystone.'

'I'm sure that will be possible. In fact, I look forward to Matthew's input.'

Denise brought fresh coffee and Matthew asked Bob Gray about the purpose of these new investigations. He asked lots of questions and I got the impression there had been previous conversations. Conversations I knew nothing about. I listened in silence. Matthew's interrogation of my physician was making me increasingly uneasy, until Dr Gray, obviously aware of my discomfort, assured me that, in cases such as this, he was very happy for a patient to have an accompanying advocate.

'Are there cases such as this?' I asked.

'That is an insightful question. And I'll try to give you a satisfactory answer.' He chose his words carefully. 'It became clear to us that yours was an unusual condition, firstly when you remained in a state of compromised consciousness, yet demonstrated no neurological damage, and secondly when we discovered your severe memory loss. We presumed that the circumstances under which you were found were implicated in your condition but, having ruled out any physical cause, we were forced to conclude that you were suffering some form of dissociation.' He paused to take a mouthful of coffee. 'Patients suffering dissociative or fugue states often demonstrate wandering. That might be the simple explanation as to why you were found where you were. Essentially, your memories have become curtailed due to some trauma that dislocated you from normal life, and your unconscious mind has chosen to deprive you of anything that might lead you to recalling the circumstances involved. Sarah, this is an involuntary process. And, whatever Detective Brown might have implied by her trickery, yours is an unequivocal case of memory repression.'

He glanced at Matthew. 'Memory repression is regarded by some practitioners as not a true amnesia, although … and may the Lord protect us from yet another reclassification of dissociative disorders, Sarah does have dissociative amnesia.'

I let my hand stray towards Matthew's, not at all confident about Dr Gray's explanations. He sensed my confusion. 'Your memories are deeply hidden. Early attempts at hypnosis proved unproductive. But we believe the memories are still there.'

'There have been similar cases, haven't there?' said Matthew. 'I'm sure I've read about amnesia after psychological trauma.'

'It's interesting that you should phrase your statement in that way. Indeed, a corpus of case histories has been built up, involving psychogenic memory loss, but the majority of them exist within the pages of fiction. Retrograde amnesia following psychological shock has often been used as a plot device. Sam Clegg has compiled an extensive list. But actual documented cases are few and far between in the real world. Their authenticity has often been challenged. In fact, the whole idea of memory repression is controversial. So, Sarah, your condition is of enormous interest to clinicians and researchers alike.'

He pulled out a handkerchief and proceeded to clean his spectacles. 'One thing we are all trying to ascertain is the dynamic nature of your condition. Do you have anything to report?'

I shook my head. 'I haven't been able to recall anything.' I felt the colour rise in my cheeks. 'But I knew I'd made love to Matthew before. I knew it wasn't for the first time.'

Dr Gray smiled. 'I must admit, the sensory and emotional aspects of memory... is a bit of a minefield. Is there anything else?'

'Well, things I do automatically are OK. And now I can write sentences not just words.'

Dr Gray explained that my procedural memory, concerned with skills, was unaffected by my condition as was much of my semantic memory that dealt with language.

'Goodness,' I said. 'How many kinds of memory are there?'

Bob Gray laughed. 'That depends upon who's drawing the diagram. In your case we're interested in that part of your memory that stores your own personal record. But we'll need to tell Sam and

Shoumi about the sentences. They'll be interviewing over the next few days.'

'Will Dr Williams be interviewing me?'

'He'll attend some sessions. His interest will be in preparing for any further MRI investigations.'

'Will Matthew be able to attend the MRI appointments with me?'

'I think it might be advisable for Matthew to avoid the National for the time being. But Greystone Park is my territory. Obviously, there might be instances where a session requires isolation from surrounding influences but, other than that, if you want Matthew there, then he will be welcome.'

CAMBERFORD TERRACE, REGENT'S PARK

Clouds were gathering over the Park, casting their shadows over one of the largest collections of displaced animals in the United Kingdom and spreading gloom inside the well-appointed consulting rooms of Robert Gray, MD, MRCPsych., FRCPsych., and his colleague, Geraint Williams, BSc., PhD., MRCPsych., MClinPsychol..

'Geraint, I can understand that this last few days have been distressing for you, but this is a situation that might well have been avoided if you had taken my advice. It's regrettable that things have been allowed to get so badly out of hand.' Bob Gray indicated the chair on the opposite side of his desk. 'Please, *do* sit down, *Geraint*!'

Geraint Williams remained standing. 'I never imagined I would find myself exposed to physical violence in this way. And now to be threatened with litigation!'

Bob Gray raised his hands. 'No, no, surely you're not letting that distract you, Geraint, you of all people. You've practised all those years in the United States where litigation is the normal state of affairs. I'm sure this is not your first encounter with the legal profession. And, besides, Matthew Parry has no intention of encouraging further action. I spoke with them both this morning, about last week's crisis and about the mendacious presence of Detective Brown. Mr Parry has assured me that he has only sought to be Sarah's advocate during these stressful circumstances. His discovery that the police were still regarding Sarah with suspicion, and that we, her physicians, appeared to be complicit, was more than he could accommodate.'

He opened the file in front of him and turned a few pages. 'I've received a copy of his formal apology to you. It obviously remains your choice as to how *you* proceed, but I advise you that the accusation of duplicity would not be easy to dismiss. And such an accusation would not be good for any of us.'

Geraint Williams said nothing.

'And I'd also like to assure you that I hold myself at least partly responsible for endorsing the unnatural separation of these two people.'

'Neither of whom can be proven guiltless,' interrupted Dr Williams.

Bob Gray considered this observation for a long moment. Then he leaned back into his chair. He spoke slowly, authoritatively. 'Culpability is not our immediate concern here, Geraint. Sarah Blake is a patient under our care. Our primary aim is to assist her in a full recovery, after such a terrible sequence of tragedies.'

Again he indicated for his younger colleague to take a seat and this time he watched him do so. 'This is a singular case, particularly if we consider the possibility of earlier manifestations of the same repressive strategy, but we must be cautious. Some observers might regard Sarah's isolation as being geared more towards obtaining research results than as a successful therapy.' He watched Geraint Williams' eyes narrow. 'Obviously, any research findings will be important, but they are not as important as the well-being of Sarah herself.'

'Bob, I do hope I am not being accused of being unethical here!'

'Good Lord, no, Geraint, not unethical. But we may have *all* allowed our enthusiasms to run away with us. As I said, I hold myself *equally* responsible for Sarah's isolation; an isolation which, in retrospect, was doomed from the start.'

'*In retrospect*, it might have been kinder if she had remained at the clinic and not been released into a world she was incapable of comprehending, prey to all manner of advances.'

'Indeed, it's fortunate that it was Mr Parry who approached her. Otherwise we might have been dealing with a worse crisis. And how long would you have recommended her internment? Do you still believe that such extreme isolation might assist her recovery? As you know, Geraint, that was not and still is not my view. Indeed, what we all must do now is be more determined to stabilise Sarah's condition and help her recover her past. At your suggestion, she is returning for reassessment. I have made myself available for the entire period, during which I intend to inform her of her circumstances up to the time of the catastrophic event.'

Geraint Williams eyes widened with surprise. '*All* her circumstances?'

'As much as is unequivocally known.'

'Do you imagine that she will be able to retain this information?'

'The next three days will answer that question.'

'And what do you intend to tell her about her mother?'

Bob Gray sighed. 'One step at a time, Geraint. A life revealed episodically.' He tapped his fingers together: 'Is Mrs Dawson well?'

'She appears to be stable. And as barking mad as everyone else along the corridor of the insane.' Geraint Williams straightened his waistcoat. 'I gather Sam Clegg intends to mind-map Mrs Dawson's interminable reminiscences with regard to dynamic psychonarrative, whatever that might mean.' He paused to check his watch. 'Incidentally, Bob, if you remember, I have a US colleague arriving this evening for two weeks. It was my intention to brief her on Sarah Blake and, perhaps, invite her to observe an MRI session.'

'Well, let's see what can be arranged, shall we? Perhaps you would let me have a copy of your brief.'

'Of course.' Geraint Williams' shoulders straightened. 'Will Mrs

Blake be accompanied over the next three days? During the interviews?'

'From what I gathered earlier, I doubt whether we'll get to interview her alone. Not only do we appear to have squandered a certain amount of her trust, which is unfortunate, but also the presence of Mr Parry seems to encourage her to take a more proactive role in her dialogues. Certainly those with myself.' Bob Gray leaned forward in his chair. 'So, are we agreed that the time is now right for Sarah Blake to recover her past and that we have to be more aggressive in assisting that recovery?'

Geraint Williams' expression was unfriendly. 'It would seem from my observations that any recovery of episodic memory becomes more unlikely as the weeks pass. And my major concern remains: I am not convinced that Matthew Parry's motives are as selfless as you suggest, an opinion which I share with Detective Brown.'

He got to his feet. 'And it is also my opinion that concerns for Sarah Blake should include a caution regarding those individuals who might prefer her not to recover and for the events of *that* day to remain a mystery.'

Episode Thirty-two

I watched Matthew's taxi disappear in the direction of Bloomsbury then secured the front door, but as I did so I noticed a small card lying on the doormat. It was the same size as the Parry & Ashdown card Matthew had given me, but this card had **Det. Sgt. Della Brown** written across its middle. I turned it over and read a brief note on the reverse: *12.45pm – called round to return personal items.* I remember staring at the spidery writing for a few panic-stricken moments, wondering what I was supposed to do about this failed visit, then hurrying through to the kitchen and throwing the card in the bin. As if that would make the situation go away.

I was too tired to eat lunch. I needed to organise my thoughts, but this morning's conversation was still careering through my brain. And now I was alone and the walls of my bedroom were threatening to close in on me. I moved over to lie face down on Matthew's pillow and tried to recapture the smell of his hair but nothing could stop the frantic activity in my brain. I needed to articulate my concerns, but there was no one there. I needed talk to the black and white cat.

Alfie's platter was licked clean but he was not there. I looked for him on the wall, on the flat roof of the garden shed. He was nowhere. I made toast, sat at the kitchen table and watched the second hand on the wall clock tread its slow path, slower with every step. Why was that cat never there when I needed it? I searched again from the window, along the wall and the flat roof. I leant across the worktop to see into my backyard and caught sight of a mass of black and white fur, high above the window, between the metal steps that led to the flat above.

Out in the yard I made my way alongside the staircase until I could see Alfie perched two steps from the top, basking in the limp sunshine. I called his name. He observed me from his superior position. It was clear he had no intention of moving. I called again. Alfie yawned then nestled down to go back to sleep. I considered being cross. My eyes strayed from the black and white fur, across the big metal landing, to the upstairs door, a very wide door, painted black, directly above my kitchen. Next to it was a long window. Above my bedroom window. I turned to check the alleyway then placed my foot on the bottom step, heavily so that it made a clanging noise, which reverberated through the entire metal staircase. It was a noise that seemed vaguely familiar. Could I remember it? Perhaps I used to hear the person that lived upstairs coming and going past my windows. I took another step. Alfie raised his head. Inconvenienced.

'Would you like some tuna, Alfie?'

Alfie got to his feet and stretched, but instead of walking down towards me he padded up the remaining two steps, across the metal landing and in through a flap in the black door. I caught my breath. My cat had been going into the top flat! What if he'd been taking dead mice in there or, worse, what if he had been using the upstairs flat as a toilet? The whole staircase clanged as I ran up. I pushed the black door. Pointless. I knelt down and pushed open the flap, but it was too dark inside to make anything out. I leaned over the banister and tried to see between the slits in the window blind, but it was impossible. What could I do? Matthew was in his meeting. So I ran back down the clanging staircase and through the side alley to fetch Peggy.

Peggy was out. I went back to the flat to check that Alfie had not nipped back in while I was ringing Peggy's doorbell. Perhaps to check out the offer of tuna. He wasn't there. I looked in the lounge and the bedroom just in case he had decided to break *all* the rules. Then I went back up the metal staircase and sat on the top step, opening the flap from time to time and making come-here-cat noises. Slowly, the sun disappeared behind a bank of cloud and the metal grew cold beneath me.

After a while, I pulled myself up and walked over to the rail that ran along the edge of the metal platform. From here, I could see down into Peggy's yard, and back over towards the rear of the Indian restaurant where several builders were working on the new fence. I tried to wobble the handrail but it was rigid. In fact the whole staircase and platform were extremely solid. And there was some kind of pulley system beside the black door. I took a step towards it and felt my toe jar against a low ridge. I glanced down. My shoe was resting against the edge of a large central plate, a flat square section, which was slightly proud of the metal surround. It occurred to me that I was standing on some kind of lifting device. Oh God, perhaps the previous tenant had needed a wheelchair and this was ... I glanced over towards the side alley and imagined a wizened old man navigating his way round past my window ... No, why on earth would someone in a wheelchair have an upstairs flat? A few drops of rain began to fall, so I retried the door then went downstairs, secured myself in the kitchen and made tea.

I felt terrible about what Alfie might have been doing up there. Perhaps he was responsible for those upstairs noises. There were no noises now. He was probably asleep somewhere. I carried my tea through to my desk and tried not to imagine my landlord discovering his ruined furniture. I caught sight of my pencil tin and remembered my visit to the clinic. This was now less of a worry than my trespassing cat. Absentmindedly I pulled the pencil pot towards me to double-check for things I might need and, as I did so, I remembered the key. I fished it out and looked at it lying in my palm. It occurred to me that the person upstairs might have given me a key, in case of an emergency, just like Peggy had been given a key. I closed my fingers and went back up to the black door.

I felt breathless. I wasn't sure I should do something as bold as go into an unoccupied flat. Actually, I told myself, this might not be the correct key. I wiggled it into the keyhole. At first it seemed not to fit, then all at once it clicked into position and turned. The door creaked open and, after a brief episode of uncertainty, I stepped inside.

It was dark in there and it smelt of mice and chips. The light switch just inside the door failed to turn on any lights but after a few moments my eyes adjusted to the shadows. Alfie was nowhere to be seen, but what could be seen was downright peculiar. I pushed the door wide open and the light illuminated what I had already guessed from the shadows. I was standing in a huge kitchen. It must have occupied the entire area of my downstairs flat. The floor was covered in white tiles, as big as paving stones. Most of the long wall to my left was lined with deep metal shelves, stacked high with plates and bowls, steel saucepans, pots and trays, with a space set aside for two tall, tiered trolleys with wheels, the kind that spin in all directions. The other long wall, my bedroom and lounge walls, was occupied by ovens and long worktops that stretched above things that must have been refrigerators, freezers, dishwashers. The surfaces were covered in kitchen appliances, more pots and pans. A central workstation ran the length of the room, its top piled high with cardboard boxes; there were more boxes and some large packing crates on the floor. I fetched one of the smaller boxes and propped the black door open, just in case it slammed shut. Then I returned to the workstation, tested the strength of a crate and sat down. Over in the far corner, above my front door, there were stacks of skinny chairs piled high in front of the shelves, loads of them, all painted gold, like the chairs one might expect to see around a banqueting table in a fairy-tale castle. A few additional chairs were randomly placed against the worktop that ran along under the window above the backyard. Alfie was asleep on one of them. I wandered over to open the blind.

'What is this place?' I asked my sleeping cat. A brief burst of purring acknowledged my presence. 'How could anybody live here? There's no bed and there's no ...' I scanned the room. There was another door, above where my sink unit must be on the floor below. It opened into a small washroom with a sink and another door that opened into a toilet. There were mouse droppings everywhere. Above the sink there was a grubby mirror, still clean enough to reveal the apprehension on my face.

I went back into the kitchen, secured the cloakroom door and returned to my crate. I tried to think. Perhaps this room was something to do with the Indian restaurant. But there was no smell of spices and curry. Just the mice and chips. And, if the restaurant had depended upon this back-up kitchen, how the hell would it be managing without it? There had to be some other explanation. I noticed some frames, paintings most likely, stacked tightly between two of the packing crates. I investigated, eased out a tall steel frame. It was a print of a strange stylish couple, draped in gold. He was bearing down on her, holding her head in his hands, kissing her, almost crushing her. Her toes were curled in ecstasy, her eyes closed, one of her arms was around his neck, preventing his leaving. I imagined his pastel green eyes, imagined this couple on the wall above my bed. There was no way that these lovers should be left in this barren kitchen, so I carried the print over to the door and propped it ready to be stolen.

The stack of frames was much easier to negotiate now that the golden couple had been removed. There were two abstract paintings, mostly dull blues and purples. I pushed them to one side and slid out a light wooden frame that held a fairy print: *The Fairies have their Tiff with the Birds* by Arthur Rackham. Number 20/250. It was lovely. What a shame that this twentieth print had been consigned to a darkened kitchen, when the other 249 identical copies were probably hanging somewhere, appreciated every day. I decided to take that as well, carried it over to the golden couple then returned to the diminishing stack of frames: a fat woman eating a cream cake; an old menu, flattened under glass; two smaller frames alongside one another, squashed down between some larger prints. I lifted one of them, ill-prepared for what I was about to see. It was a framed photograph, horribly familiar, a smaller copy of the one I had so recently seen, hanging in the library of Parry & Ashdown Literary Agency. Here I was again, holding a copy of *The Lost Tabby Cat*, Matthew at my side.

My stomach churned. I glanced around at the worktops, my sleeping cat, the stacked chairs, the black door, the landing outside. How could this be here? I tried to think rationally. OK, this top flat, this weird top flat that was given over entirely to the preparation of food, it was owned by the same person who owned my flat. They had probably arranged for it to remain empty. And since they were paying for it, from the funds that Mrs Parkin occasionally referred to, then there was every reason why they would be allowed to store my clutter up here. Alfie undoubtedly felt at home here surrounded by the smells he had been used to downstairs. I began to feel calmer. I glanced over at the two prints I was intending to steal. They were probably already mine. I had been looting my own possessions. But surely I hadn't chosen those abstracts. If they were mine, they could go straight to the charity shop. I looked down at the photograph, touched the glass just by Matthew's smile, then walked over and stood this latest acquisition against my two reclaimed prints. I wondered if Matthew knew my things were up here? Why would he not have told me?

I was quite excited to see what the other frame might reveal. Perhaps another photo of Matthew and me. Perhaps one with Annabelle, taken in Corfu. I lifted the frame, looked at the photograph and at first did not know either of the two people. Then I recognised the woman. Recognised my younger features, blissfully happy. Remembered an emotion, not a whole emotion, just a trace. Remembered a place and a time. And in that moment of remembering my new, fragile world collapsed around me.

*

'Sarah! Sarah, are you up there? The back door's open!'

Matthew?

I could hear him running up the staircase. The metal platform outside was now wet with rain. He stood in the doorway, his long,

253

dark shadow falling across the darkening room. Then he saw me sitting on the floor, my back against one of the packing crates.

'Sweetheart, what are you doing up here?' he said, kneeling down beside me. He put his hand on my shoulder but I shrugged it away. I needed him not to be touching me.

I felt him touching my hand, moving it slowly, cautiously. 'What have you got there? Let me have a look. Sarah, they only put all this up here to get it out of your way.' Then he recognised the framed photo on my lap. 'Oh God, Sarah! Come on, let me have it. Sarah, let's go downstairs and talk about it, shall we?' He tried to ease the frame away from me but I wrenched it back. Again, he went to touch my shoulder but I leaned away from him and held the frame close against my legs, wiped the glass with my sleeve, traced my fingers across my earlier face, across the face of the forgotten man beside me, down his arm that was close beside mine, until my fingers came to rest upon my younger hands clasped tightly around the pink and white roses and the tumbling ribbons of my unremembered bridal bouquet.

FRANKFURT

Wet and humourless, the urban sprawl of Frankfurt gave way to the river plain of the German Rhineland. Matthew drove. Sarah watched the cars coming towards her at an unreasonable speed. No one should want to drive that fast! She turned to check that her shoulder bag was down behind the seat where it had been ten minutes earlier. Yes it was, although her complimentary copy of *Breaking Dawn* had slithered out onto the floor. She'd never be able to reach it without undoing her seatbelt. Not advisable at this speed. Besides, she ought to talk to Matthew now that he was faced with most of the driving. Hopefully *all* of the driving.

She noticed her shopping crammed onto the back seat, squashed to one side by Lucy's far more numerous designer acquisitions. That bitch had a real cheek, sloping off with David the Wearisome like that and expecting them to transport all of her bags of extravagance home. She glanced at Matthew. She ought to say something to him, in case he started to fall asleep and crashed the car. She couldn't bear to die in a road crash in Germany. That would be too complicated. Jeff would have to fly over and identify her mangled body and …

Matthew broke her reverie: 'You OK?'

'Yes, what time is it?'

'Twenty past four.'

'German time?'

'Yes, we're in Germany, remember?'

'When will we be in France?'

'In about an hour.'

'Good. I prefer France. I'll drive if you want.'

'You don't like driving on the wrong side of the road.'

'But I will if you're tired.'

'Well, thank you, but I'm fine.'

What time will we get there?'

'Hopefully just before nine. I've booked supper.'

'How many for? There should have been four of us until the others abandoned!'

'I booked for two. I phoned before we left and cancelled Poppy's room. While you were forcing your crates of Christmas trimmings into the car.'

'You get nicer Christmas decorations here. Are you grumpy because of my shopping?'

'No, I'm delighted it's been such a fulfilling trip for you.'

She frowned. 'Are you cross that Lucy's gone off with David?'

'No, not at all.'

Sarah watched him watch the road and was suddenly overwhelmed by the need to offer an opinion. 'I don't understand you two. Don't you mind if she goes off with other guys?'

He glanced at her then smirked at the road ahead. 'No.'

Sarah disapproved of his answer so she resumed silence. She listened to the repetitive sound of the wheels thudding along the Autobahn, the sound of the wiper blades screeching across the not-wet-enough windscreen. 'Doesn't *she* mind?'

'Mind what?'

'Mind you sleeping with other women.'

'Not usually.'

Sarah continued to watch him. 'You are cross about something, aren't you?'

'I'm not. I'm just stressed.'

'Is it because Poppy decided to fly home early and it's just the two of us driving back?'

'No!'

'What then?'

'Nothing!'

'You can't be stressed about nothing!' She caught sight of a heron perched on a fence, grey and wet, with nothing better to do than watch the cars go by before retiring to his swamp for the night. She could write a story about that: Wolfgang the Heron … 'We should have left earlier. Then we'd be nearly there by now.'

'Sarah, your powers of logic astound me. And if we hadn't had to go back to the stand and look for your laptop we *would* have left earlier.'

Sarah chose not to defend herself and, instead, took out her mobile and checked for missed calls. There was a text from Annabelle reminding her about the theatre next Thursday. Nothing else. She decided to ring home, then she rang Jeff's mobile and left a voice message: 'Sarah here. We're just leaving Germany. I'll text when we get to the hotel. It will probably be late.'

Matthew spoke without taking his eyes off the road. 'No luck?'

'He's probably with a client.'

Matthew nodded. 'When's the last time you spoke to him?'

'Why?'

'I was just wondering whether he phoned to ask how your interview went.'

'He's not interested in my *success*.'

'Well, he ought to be. If you ask me, he's jealous.'

'Don't be stupid. He thinks I write crap!'

'Nice. Put some music on.'

'No, you put it on.' She located Coldplay and pressed play.

After ten minutes or so, Matthew turned off the music. 'We could do with a filling station. There's not been one for ages.'

'Oh God, are we going to run out of petrol?'

'Not yet. Just keep your eyes open. We should have filled up before we left but I was keen to get away.'

The next thirty-three kilometers were accompanied by Sarah's attempts to use the satnav on her phone to find a service station. Eventually a large road sign saved her further anguish.

'It says services in fifteen kilometres,' said Matthew. 'That's less than ten miles.'

'Have we got enough petrol to get there?'

'Yes.'

'Can we get some sandwiches as well? I'll start to feel sick if I don't eat something soon. I've never been able to travel far on an empty stomach.'

'Yes, I remember.'

While Matthew was inside paying for the fuel, his mobile vibrated. Sarah pulled it out of the drinks well to see who was calling. It was Poppy. She answered.

'Hi, Poppy, it's Sarah … He'll be back in a minute. Where are you? … He's paying for petrol. What's up? Why didn't you say goodbye? I looked for you.' She caught sight of Matthew hurrying back through the rain. 'Here he comes now. Speak to you later.' She handed the phone over as Matthew threw himself into the car. 'Poppy wants to speak to you.'

He handed her a wet plastic bag and took the phone. 'Hi, Poppy … Yes … Oh …' His expression became weirdly furtive. 'OK … no, I don't think that will be a problem … yeah, obviously I will … OK, see you in Blighty, safe flight … bye.'

Sarah waited for an explanation. Matthew pulled away. 'His flight's been cancelled. He won't be able to leave before tomorrow morning.'

'When did he tell you he'd decided to fly home?'

'This afternoon.'

'He never mentioned it when I was with him. He just left without saying goodbye.'

Matthew changed the subject. 'Can you phone the hotel and say we'll be arriving after nine but we'll still want supper. The number's in my contacts under Chagny.'

Sarah investigated his contacts page, found the number of the chateau and frowned.

'There's no signal.'

'Well, keep trying. Have a sandwich. In case you start feeling sick.'

She investigated the contents of the plastic bag, helped herself to a cheese sandwich, took a bite and grimaced. 'Yuck, I hate this smoked stuff. It tastes like dustbin scrapings!'

'Well, I'm sorry, your majesty, but bland cheddar is not a popular dairy product along the Rhine. Just eat and try not to think about it.'

Sarah finished her sandwich then poked around in the bag for something else. She helped herself to a bar of chocolate. Matthew handed her his phone. 'See if there's a signal yet.'

'Yes, there is.' She had a short schoolgirl French conversation which did not go well due to the large lump of chocolate she had in her mouth. She put the mobile back into the drinks well. 'We can arrive at any time. Our rooms are assured but she is afraid zat zere is no 'ot food after 'arf past ten. I hate Europe. Do you want a bit of chocolate? It's disgusting.'

Sarah abandoned the bar of chocolate then slept. So Matthew was able to drive dangerously fast. Soon he had left Germany behind and was heading at breakneck speed through Burgundy. Suddenly, his phone vibrated against its plastic surround. Sarah opened her eyes.

He glanced down. 'It's Lucy! Don't answer it!'

The vibration stopped. Sarah's mobile rang. 'It's Lucy,' she said. 'I'd better answer in case something's wrong. She never rings me.' Matthew groaned. Sarah ignored him. 'Hello, Lucy … He's driving … no, it didn't ring. He probably needs to charge it … no, I didn't know that.' She looked at Matthew who was concentrating on not looking back at her. 'Really? Do you know why? … Yes, I'll get him to ring when we get there … Thanks for calling. Bye.'

She rang off and glared at Matthew. 'That was Lucy. Nothing in particular. She just thought it was important that I knew that as soon as you found out she was going to Strasbourg with David, you phoned Poppy and bribed him to fly home. So you and I would be travelling back alone together.'

Episode Thirty-three

'You knew I was married. How could you not tell me? How long did you think it would be before I found out? When we became lovers, was I still married? Am I ... I can almost remember. Am I still married?'

'No, you're not. Let's go downstairs.'

He tried to put his arm around me but I pushed him away as hard as I could. I pulled myself to my feet, clutching my wedding, my husband, my past, against my chest, my mind brimming over with half-formed memories, with hate and fear and hopelessness, emotions that seemed to be unattached to anything. Just there.

'Why am I not still married?'

He stood up and looked around at my piled-up possessions. 'Sarah, love, we can't have this conversation up here, surrounded by all this.'

'These are my things!'

'They thought you'd be confused by them.'

'Confused? They've been hidden up here, and you knew. When we were together you knew these things were up here above our heads.'

'I did what they told me was best for you.'

He tried to touch my shoulder but I moved away. I wanted to hurt him. Really hurt him. Because I knew that somehow he was to blame, that he alone was responsible for the hate and fear and hopelessness.

So I closed my hand into a fist and struck out at him. I aimed for his pale eyes but he was too tall, and the blow fell low. The impact pushed me off balance, forcing me to stumble towards him and grab at his sleeve to save myself. I lost my hold on the photo frame, felt it sliding away from me, heard it crash down to the tiled floor. Matthew moved to pull me clear as the sound of shattering glass echoed off the metal shelves, the empty pots and pans.

The room was silent. My head was filled with betrayal and anger, and a desperate desire to run away. But I also felt an intense need to stay in the arms of this person who had allowed me to live this lie. A suffocating tightness was growing in my chest and that odious child was laughing at me. My legs were becoming too weak to support me. I needed to touch the ground.

'Sarah, mind the glass!'

I felt myself lifted.

'Are you all right? Speak to me! Can you hear me?'

Yes, I could hear him.

'Sarah, can you hear me?'

'Yes.'

'Thank God. We need to go downstairs.'

I looked around me. I had no idea where I was. I was sitting on a golden chair. Matthew was sitting on another golden chair, close to me, so close our legs were touching. He was holding my hands. His face was smeared red.

'Sarah, love, we're upstairs, remember? Above your flat. Do you know what's happening? You came up here and found these things.'

I pulled a hand free and touched his face, moved my fingers down his cheek. He turned to kiss my hand then eased it away and I gasped at the blood smeared across my fingers.

'I bit my lip. It's nothing. Try and remember. What were you doing up here?'

I grappled with my memories. 'I found a key.'

'A key?'

'I had to find Alfie. In case he was bringing animals in here.'

'Alfie was coming in here?'

'Yes.'

'Great. They didn't bloody think of that, did they! How long have you been up here?'

'I don't know.' I glanced beyond Matthew's shoulder, to the broken glass and the fat woman eating a cream cake. 'How did you bite your lip? Did I do it?'

'It was an accident. I'm fine.'

I looked again at the glass. 'It's a picture of me and ... Was I married?' He said nothing. I studied the concern in his eyes. 'Did I hit you with that?'

'What?' He turned to look at the debris across the floor. 'No, of course not. You just ... punched me. I deserved it. I ought to punch myself for letting them talk me into this.'

'I'm so sorry. I hurt my wrist.'

'Let me see.' He turned as Alfie walked in through the open door, a large moribund rodent twitching between his teeth. 'Oh God, that's all we need! Listen, we should go downstairs ...' But he was interrupted by the sound of small bones splintering in Alfie's jaws. 'Thanks, Alfie,' said Matthew. 'That's *really* made my day.'

I left Matthew excavating my wedding from the glass and carried Alfie downstairs away from his secret lair. Moments later Matthew came into the kitchen and put the photograph on the table, then went to the bathroom to repair his face. I followed him, reluctant to be on my own in the same room as that image of the person I had once been. And the man I had married. I sat on the side of the bath and watched him observing his lip in the mirror.

'I'm sorry, Matthew.'

'No worries, I think it suits me. But I'd better try and disguise the damage before tomorrow. They'll wonder what we get up to if I walk in looking like this. And we'd better order in some food. Then we'll talk. OK?'

Despite being only a two-minute walk away, the Indian takeaway was to take thirty minutes to be delivered, so I improvised Matthew an ice pack with a tea towel and a bag of frozen peas then went to the lounge to avoid the photo and any conversation that might relate to it. Matthew followed me, carrying the photo and sat down beside me. I avoided his eyes.

'You knew I was married and you never told me. I'm not married now, am I?'

'No, you're not. Sarah, they warned me that telling you might make things worse.'

I glanced at the photo. 'What's his name?'

'Jeff Blake.'

Blake. Not Clark. Mrs Parkin had lied about why I didn't share my grandmother's surname. Lies. Not harmless untruths.

'Where is he now? Why am I not still married? Or have you got to tell me more lies because it's not *best* for me to know?'

'I haven't lied, it's just not been the whole truth.' He sighed. 'Jeff died.'

'He *died*?'

'He fell down a flight of stairs and broke his neck. He died six weeks later of an infection. He never regained consciousness.'

'Oh my God! Was I sad? Am I sad?' I remembered my conversation with Peggy: knowing is not the same as remembering. 'Were we still married when he died?'

'Yes, but you were going to leave him.'

'To be with you?'

He pulled the ice pack away from his mouth. 'Yes.'

I leant forward and looked at the photograph. Shook my head. 'I was married to him and I don't recognise him.'

I knelt down on the floor to take a closer look at this man who had been my husband. He was tall, but not as tall as Matthew, and he had a nice smile. I couldn't make out the colour of his eyes but they were probably brown because his hair was dark brown and curly. You could tell it was curly even though it was cut short for his wedding day. I studied his face, his hand with its new gold ring. What can you know from a photograph? A new husband and wife, both smiling at the camera, believing they would always be together, me and this person who was now so utterly gone not only from my life but also from my memories.

'When was this? When did I get married?'

'It was before we met. Almost eight years ago.'

I tried to imagine speaking to this person, this husband, tried to imagine making love to him, deceiving him, deciding to leave him to be with Matthew. 'Did he know about us?'

Matthew put the ice pack on the floor.

'Yes, but he was with someone else. He was pretty much always with somebody else. You just used to ignore it and concentrate on your writing. But things changed and you decided to leave him.'

I tried to imagine the conversations, perhaps seven years after this smiling day: shouting, saying it was all over, that the promises were all broken.

'And we lived here? Me and Jeff Blake?' I paused to digest this new information. 'Is that why you didn't live here with me?'

'Yes. This was Jeff's house. He owned it before you were married.'

I looked at him: 'This house belonged to my *husband*?'

'Yes.'

'All of it? Even that huge kitchen upstairs?' I looked up at the ceiling. 'Matthew, why *is* there a giant kitchen upstairs?'

He pulled me up onto the sofa. 'Jeff ran his catering business up there.'

'Catering?'

'Yes. Amazing Days Catering. Weddings, luxury garden parties.'

'But why was the kitchen upstairs? Why wasn't it downstairs?'

'It was like that when he bought it. Something to do with kosher food preparation. He got it cheap for that reason. He had the whole elevator and stairs re-constructed. You used to be able to drive in through the back of the Indian restaurant. He had an agreement with them over access, but he was always in dispute over dustbins. Anyway, they're fencing it all off now. I think Jeff was planning to move to larger premises and convert this into bedsits. I'm not sure.'

'Was it those metal stairs that broke his neck?'

'No, not those stairs.' He took hold of my hand. 'Jeff used to buy flowers from the florist where you were working. Then you went to work for him.'

'I worked for a florist? You could have told me that.'

'Didn't Annabelle …'

But I'd turned my attention towards the big cupboard. 'There are loads of vases …'

'You used to practice new ideas. Whenever I came to see how the writing was going, you'd be messing around with flowers. I used to moan at you to get on with your writing. And you used to throw twigs at me.' He winced and touched his lip.

I picked up the ice pack and held it to his mouth. I needed to be angry with him for deceiving me, but I was too tired to be angry. 'Did we ever make love here? When I was … When Jeff Blake lived here?'

'No. Never here!'

I looked back at the photo. It was difficult to believe that this man's life was extinguished just through falling downstairs. However badly he had treated our marriage, he didn't deserve to be dead. It was very sad. But the sadness wasn't there. Like when you listened to the news: 100 people killed in a landslide; 400 dead in a plane crash. You know it's sad, but you can't really feel sadness like if Matthew died or Alfie or even Mrs Parkin the liar, because those people you know. And, right then, with his image staring back at me, I didn't know Jeff Blake. His life held no meaning for me.

*

After supper I cleared away and tried to imagine this man I'd been married to, bound to, in a marriage that had become unloved by both of us. Tried to imagine what I lacked that had made him always need to be with someone else. I tried to imagine my husband with these other women, ridiculing me behind my back: I can't stand her but she does the flowers. In between writing drivel for children. Other people's children. I half turned. It wasn't laughter. Not this time. It was a kind of snorting, like laughter escaping through childish fingers: don't tell Sarah, she'll cry. I felt Matthew's arms around my waist.

'We need to get you ready for tomorrow. Have you packed anything?'

'Not really. Mathew, did Jeff Blake have an affair with Annabelle?'

He stepped away. 'As far as I know he made a couple of moves and she told him to go to hell. Which in Annabelle's case is an enormous declaration of loyalty to you. She pretty much hated him.'

'Did she tell me?'

'I'm not sure. You can ask her. She's driving up on Saturday evening. For takeaway. And Poppy's coming over with some cover designs.'

'What if they don't let me come home?' I lifted the kettle and winced.

'It's not a prison, Sarah. If you don't like it we can leave. Is your wrist hurting?'

'A bit.' I looked at his swollen lip. 'I'm sorry I punched you.'

'Sometimes it helps.'

*

Matthew lounged on the bed alongside my suitcase, watching me put things in then take them out to rearrange them. I glanced up. 'When I left Jeff Blake, was I going to move into your flat with you?'

'Yes, until Lucy moved from Hampstead.'

'But, when he died, I stayed here in his house?'

'Sarah, it's your house now. Jeff never made a will. So everything's yours.'

'This is my house?'

'Yes.'

'Including the giant kitchen? And the sofas?'

'Yes, all of it! House, money, everything!'

'That's the *funds* that Mrs Parkin always refers to?'

'Yes.'

I resumed packing, uneasy now about this unexpected burden of ownership. I didn't want to own an enormous kitchen and stacks of golden chairs, although …

'The golden picture of people kissing. I'd like that down here.'

'The Klimt? That used to hang there.' He pointed to the wall beyond my bedside table. 'I'll bring it down at the weekend.'

'Where did the fairies hang?'

'If you mean the Rackham, it hung over the dining table. Jeff despised it.'

'Why did they put my pictures upstairs?'

'I don't know. I wasn't involved. I was shocked to see how empty it was.'

'There's a picture of you and me.'

'At the book launch? It used to stand on your desk.' He sighed. 'Sarah, I'm so sorry.'

I ignored his apology. I wasn't ready to forgive him. Not for a long time. I closed my case. 'Will you drive?'

'Of course I will. We'll take my car.'

'What car?'

'The one Lucy's been borrowing. Poppy drove me over to collect it this afternoon. It's parked outside the Indian. They said they'd keep an eye on it. It'll probably have no wheels by the morning. I'll have to get the van moved so I can park it inside.'

'What van?'

'The Amazing Days van, which you also own. It's in Jeff's lock-up.'

'I don't want a van.'

'Well give it to Annabelle so she can carry her monstrosities around in it.'

I carried my wedding photo into the kitchen, took my pills then sat beside Matthew while he helped himself to a nightcap of red wine. I pulled the photo towards me. Marvelled at my enormous white dress. Maybe it was hidden up there above my head, along with the clutter. And perhaps some of Jeff Blake's things: clothes, books, toy trains, report cards.

'Matthew, are Jeff Blake's things up there as well or did I get rid of them?'

'I don't know what's up there.' He started to work the cork back into the bottle.

'Did he have any family?'

'His parents live in Newcastle. He didn't have much to do with them. There'd been some kind of family row.'

'But they must have come to his funeral.' Matthew said nothing. I pushed the photograph away. I needed to concentrate, to sort something out in my mind, a question half formed. But every time I almost realised it, that laughter drove my thoughts away. I knew it wasn't real.

'Matthew, sometimes I imagine I can hear a child laughing. A horrible child that hates me. It's been ever since I woke up in the clinic. I know it's just in my head. It's not often but today there's been lots of it. It stops me concentrating. Like just then, I was trying to ask you something and I couldn't think what it was.'

'Sarah, that's an important thing to tell Bob Gray. Have you mentioned it to him? Or Geraint Williams?'

'No, I don't think so. They'll think I'm crazy.'

'Sweetheart, you need to mention it. Was the thing you wanted to ask me about Jeff?'

'No, I think it was about you.' I stood up and carried the wedding photo over to the tea towel drawer. I slipped it inside and, as the drawer closed, I remembered the question, the confusion that came before the laughter. 'I was confused because you said we never made love in this house and I wondered why, because I would have been here on my own after Jeff Blake died. Why weren't you here with me? Why did you carry on living in your flat?'

Matthew sighed. 'It's complicated.'

'How complicated?' I watched his colour draining away.

'There wasn't time for us to be together.'

'Why? When did Jeff Blake die?' He failed to answer. 'Matthew, *when* did my husband break his neck?'

'The day you went missing.'

The words rumbled around in my brain, refusing to make any sense, refusing to accommodate things I had already been told. I had been found unconscious on a beach. I had no idea how I got there, in fact, no memories of my adult life, my marriage, my husband. And now there was an additional coincidence of time that linked my disappearance and Jeff Blake's accident.

'Matthew, where were you when I disappeared?'

'Looking for you. I've no idea why you were where they found you. You'd never mentioned that place to me.'

'What place?'

'Beer Cove.'

'Beer Cove?' I shook my head. 'I've never heard of it. Is that where they found me?'

Matthew frowned. 'Yes.'

I tried to fathom an explanation. There's always an explanation. Something that explains something else. But now the medication was starting to take effect, something alien was disrupting my consciousness, forcing me into an unnatural sleep. And in its wake something else, not at all alien, was scavenging my tiredness for quarry of its own. All around me things were beginning to coalesce into too many questions, too many lies, into breaking glass and splintering bones. I could feel the floor beneath my feet, no longer firm enough to support me. I tried to tread lighter, softly to stop myself falling through into nowhere.

'Matthew, the roses are for my mother.'

I caught hold of a chair. Felt a hand on my arm.

'No, not yet ... I need to tell grandma what happened.'

But the night was all around me. And tomorrow there would be palaces beneath the sea, and witches spinning promises that could never be broken.

BURGUNDY

'I just wanted to talk to you in private.'

'About what? Something you didn't want Poppy to hear?'

'No. Can we just get there, Sarah? Then I'll explain.'

She looked out at the darkening sky. 'At least it's stopped raining. How far away are we?'

'About ten minutes.'

She looked at him. 'What time is it?'

'Just after half past eight.'

'That's not possible. How have you got here as quickly as that?'

'I drove like shit when you were asleep.'

'We could have died.'

'Well, we didn't, did we? And we're in time for dinner. Did Lucy say anything else?'

Sarah scanned down her phone for messages. No messages, no missed calls. 'She said I ought to realise that you'll probably try and make a move on me. Where would she get an idea like that from?' He was silent. 'Because if there was even the slightest possibility of that, it would be the complete end of our friendship. And our professional relationship.'

Matthew looked horrified. 'Why, for God's sake?'

'Because ... Are you watching the road? Because you've got no right to assume you can change our relationship without discussing it with me first.'

'Has it occurred to you that might not be what I had in mind?'

'Was it what you had in mind?'

He said nothing, indicated and pulled off the main road.

'And has it occurred to you that Lucy might have been winding you up?'

'Matthew?'

He kept his eyes on the road ahead. 'Look, I know you're attracted to me. You told Poppy.'

'I said you were attractive. That doesn't mean I want to commit adultery with you.'

'Adultery?'

'Yes, that's what they call it when you're married and you fuck other people.'

'For God's sake, Sarah! You know that's exactly what Jeff is doing as we speak!'

'Well, that's my problem. It's got nothing to do with you.' She switched off her phone. 'You realise this has already ruined our being able to work together. I'll finish my LOST series then I'll find a new agent.'

'What? That's insane! If I've compromised our friendship, then I'm sorry, but don't do that. God, Sarah, that's really overreacting. And besides, we haven't done anything. You can't kill a man for thinking! How was I to know you'd be the only bloody woman in the world who doesn't want to sleep with me?'

'Prick!'

They drove on in silence. After five minutes or so Matthew slowed down. 'The turning's coming up any minute. It's easy to miss it.'

Sarah leaned forward and scanned for road signs. 'There it is!'

He pulled off the road into the driveway of their chateau for the night. Sarah peered through the windscreen. The sight of the two magically illuminated pointed towers, the raised terrace, the baronial doors took her breath away.

'It's beautiful,' she said before she could stop herself. 'I can't believe it!'

'I thought you'd like it. I thought it would remind you of one of those fairytale castles you dream about.'

Sarah tumbled back to reality. 'And you thought I'd be a certainty when I saw it?'

'Can we give up on that one, Sarah? I've admitted my mistake.'

'Have you brought many other women here to fuck?'

'I've been here three times with Lucy and once with Poppy. And I didn't fuck him. We just drank a lot of excellent wine.' He pulled up outside the main entrance. 'Sarah, I'm sorry if I've offended you. It's a great place. The food's amazing. Shall we call a truce and you can punish me when we get back to London?' He cut the engine. 'I'll get the bags. Don't forget your phone.'

Matthew was changed and waiting when Sarah walked into the dining room. A bottle of crémant was already open on the table. She looked around at the paneled walls, the ornate lighting, the numerous French people, some elegantly Parisian, some well-dressed local, all of them united in having enough money to pay for such privileged dining. The manager escorted her to her seat and beckoned a waiter to fill her glass.

'Cheers,' said Matthew, when they were alone. 'You've changed. That's the dress you wore to the reception. I've still got a very vivid mental image of Marcus Harrington groping you in it.'

They clinked glasses, sipped bubbles and discussed the à la carte. They chose mostly the same and ordered a bottle of Chassagne Montrachet. Sarah toyed with a minute bread roll and watched Matthew squirm. He checked nobody was in hearing range and leant towards her. 'I'm sorry if I've offended you. Please don't leave the agency. I'll make it up to you.'

'How?'

'I don't know. I'll eat dirt.'

'What if Poppy's plane crashes because you bribed him so you could get me alone?'

'I don't think that's likely to happen.'

'But you can't know, can you? I phoned to wish him a safe journey and tell him I'd never confide in him again. He said he was sorry he took the bribe. How much did you offer him?'

Matthew sighed. 'All expenses, first class, a considerable autumn bonus and a new laptop when I get back. OK? I'm sorry. How many more times would you like me to apologise?'

A waitress interrupted with a small plate of canapés, which she laboured to describe in English: minute cheese soufflés, tiny morsels of asparagus on rye, mini prawn pastries. Sarah's mood improved. 'Did you tell them we were vegetarians?'

'Yes.'

'You've obviously thought of everything, haven't you? Apart from the possibility that I'm not interested in becoming your latest conquest. Are you surprised Lucy shopped you? I thought she didn't care if you screwed other women.'

'She doesn't usually. It's just you I'm not allowed to sleep with.'

Sarah was incensed. 'Why aren't you allowed to sleep with me?'

'Keep your voice down!'

'Why aren't you allowed to sleep with me?' she whispered.

'Because it's only all right if things stay casual.'

'Well, why should that be any different with …' She paused as her entrée was served, glanced over and met Matthew's green eyes looking back at her. She waited for the waiter to walk away. 'Why me?'

He sipped crémant and watched her. Sarah's intention was to demand an answer calmly but her senses succumbed to the proximity of the Château-smoked salmon. She spoke with her mouth full.

'I'm that special, am I?'

'Lucy seems to think so. Bon appetit.'

He ate slowly; Sarah did not. 'God, that salmon was fantastic!'

He smiled. 'Would you like the rest of mine?'

'Don't you want it?'

'Not as much as you obviously do.'

'OK!' She glanced around to check that none of the other diners would be appalled by her lack of etiquette, then manoeuvred Matthew's salmon onto her plate. She was determined not to let his inappropriate intentions spoil her dining experience, and indeed the lime sorbet proved to be superb, the baked *raie* unbelievable and the selection of cheeses surprisingly next. However, as she drained her third glass of Montrachet, she began to fester about Lucy Ashdown's prejudices regarding her mistresshood. Then dessert arrived, a Grand Marnier crème brulée for Sarah and a plate of perfect strawberries for Matthew. Sarah eased off a piece of the burnt sugar toping and popped it into her mouth.

'My diet starts tomorrow.'

Matthew laughed. 'That might be too late.'

She scooped up a mouthful of the baked cream. 'Why, won't you fancy me any more if I'm fat? I presume you did fancy me, or isn't that a prerequisite with people like you?'

She glanced up. He forced a smile. 'Would you like a strawberry?'

Sarah shook her head. 'That was rude of me. I'm sorry.'

He shrugged. 'I probably deserved it.'

She returned to appreciating the brulée. 'Would you like some?'

'No, you eat it.' He looked around him. A single couple were left on the far side of the room. 'I think we've driven everyone away. Can you manage coffee after that? There are heaters on the terrace. We could go out there and look at the stars. It's quite a clear night now.

So Sarah scraped up the last of her dessert, pulled on her pashmina and agreed to coffee on the terrace. Then she agreed to a glass of champagne on the terrace and sat quietly alongside her agent, watched the stars and allowed herself to fall in love with Burgundy. Perhaps it was the silence that caused her, shamelessly, to make such a surprising statement.

'I've often imagined what it would be like making love to you.'

Matthew was caught off guard. He spoke with apprehension; or alternatively it might have been anticipation. 'And does what you imagine usually go well?'

She looked at him through a mild alcoholic haze. 'It gets better every time.' She picked up her glass, sipped the bubbles and failed to regret what she had just said.

He said nothing. He did nothing. He just looked. Not frowning, not smiling, just looking.

Sarah was unable to bear it. 'I don't want to go home.'

Still he said nothing.

'Jeff probably doesn't even care when I'm getting back and ...' His silence was making her feel stupid. 'I'm sorry, I'm a bit ...'

She watched him take her glass and place it on the table, felt his arm around her, his kiss so much more real than imagining can ever be.

He placed his hand over hers. 'I booked a room for tomorrow evening. Before we left Frankfurt. I confirmed it when we checked in.'

She detached herself from his arm. She was instantly sober. Or almost sober.

'You confirmed a room for an extra night after I'd said I wouldn't sleep with you? Did you assume I was that much of a pushover?'

'No.' He paused. 'I just thought that if you decide you wanted to stay, there might not have been a room available. And I didn't want you to be disappointed.'

His eyes looked so damn sincere! Sarah paused to consider the situation, then to reconsider the situation. She finally decided not to re-check her phone for messages but instead, to go with her instincts. 'And do you think I'll be disappointed, Matthew?'

He picked up his glass and smirked at the champagne bubbles. Unstoppable. 'Not a chance in Hell, gorgeous. Not a chance in Hell.'

Episode Thirty-four

I knelt on the floor of the lounge reorganising my case at the last-minute, removing a pencil tin I no longer needed. Matthew emerged from the bedroom, car keys in hand.

'Sarah, what are you doing? There's no time for that! I'm just going to fetch the car. If the wheels are missing we'll take yours. Be ready in four minutes, OK?' The front door closed behind him. I hurried into the kitchen to check everything was turned off. I wouldn't touch anything. I'd just look. Things seemed to be OK. There were biscuits for Alfie. Peggy was going to feed him while we were away. The front door opened.

'Are you ready? I'll take your case. And I'll close up behind you.'

I grabbed my bag. Outside I was confronted by a very noisy car. Matthew opened the door. Upwards.

'Why's the door like that?'

'It's supposed to be like that.'

'Did you *want* a red car?'

'They're usually red. Mind your head when you get in.'

He waited for me to bend myself inside before carefully closing the door. I had managed to fasten my seatbelt by the time he climbed in beside me. I pointed to a small golden heart stuck on the dashboard. 'That's nice.'

'You put it there, to remind me not to go too fast.'

'Have I been in here before?'

'Several times. And you were wearing that same look of disapproval every time.'

'There are only two seats.'

'How many do you want to sit in?'

*

It was a sunny morning, with a sky that was fresh and blue, still teetering on the threshold of summer. I sat quiet and watched Matthew driving his shiny red car, fast and low and far away from the chaos of people and buildings that were too high and too close together. Far away from the chaos of freedom: back to ordered captivity. I watched the spaces between the concrete grow wider, out along the road that led to Wales. I knew that journey well, and I knew, when I saw the sign to Windsor, that we would soon be there. We pulled off the motorway. Matthew tried to chat about my apple stories but I felt too worried to do anything other than watch the road ahead. I felt Matthew touch my hand.

'Are you OK?'

'Yes.'

'You're not worrying about the next few days, are you? We'll be home before you know it. And then we can go visit our place in Hampstead. And if by this afternoon you're not happy there, we'll leave. And go to Gusto for supper, OK?'

I allowed myself to smile for the first time since leaving Islington. 'They won't keep me there longer, will they?'

'No.' He indicated off the dual carriageway. 'Shall we stop somewhere? We don't have to be there for over half an hour.'

I shook my head. 'We could have left later.'

'I was worried we'd get caught in traffic.'

Silence. 'Matthew, I'm sorry.'

He flashed me a glance. 'What?'

'Before all this I probably was a person you'd want to be with. And share your house and car with …'

'Matthew Parry shares his car with no one ever again!'

'Matthew, listen! If, after this next few days, if it's clear that I'm never going to be that person again, I don't want you to waste your life with me.'

'Sarah, don't …'

'Please! I won't let it happen to you. I … What are you doing?'

He pulled up on the side of the road, uncomfortably close to the hedgerow but not touching, cut the engine and put the hazard lights on. 'Matthew, this is dangerous!'

'So is driving and listening to you talking rubbish.'

'It's not rubbish. This is still my life and I can decide whether …'

'Are you still angry with me?'

'Yes … no!' I ought to have been angry, but the whole hopeless situation was somehow dulling the anger. 'Matthew, I know you loved me but I'm not that person anymore and I don't think I ever will be again.' I had meant to say this all unemotionally, but there I was *crying*.

'Sarah, don't say such stupid things.' He unfastened his seat belt and took my hand. 'It's my decision as well and, if you want me, I stay. I spent too long waiting for you to be free of that bastard to give up on you now.'

'What bast…?'

'Oh shit!' Matthew's attention was suddenly on the road ahead. 'Here come the cops!'

A patrol car was pulling in just ahead of us. Matthew refastened his seat belt and lowered the window ready for confrontation. A policeman was ambling towards us putting on his hat. His partner seemed to be marooned, his door too close to the hedgerow to open. I scrabbled in my bag for a tissue.

'Everything all right, sir?'

'Yes, officer. We've just had a bit of bad news and my partner's a little upset. I pulled in for a couple of minutes to make sure she was OK.'

The officer leaned low to look at me then his head disappeared from view. 'Bit dangerous stopping here,' he said. 'Some of the bikers use this bit of road as a speed track. If one of them comes round the corner and sees this parked here, he might go a bit unnecessary.'

'I'm sorry. I'll move. Sarah's fine now.'

'OK, sir. Hope things sort themselves out. They usually do, one way or another.' He stepped away and looked along the road. 'Don't get a lot of opportunity to talk to someone in one of these. Very nice. You be careful when you pull away.' He touched the peak of his hat and walked off, back to his car.

Matthew closed the window. 'We'd better get going.' He pulled away behind the patrol car. 'And I don't want to hear another word about wasted lives. This is my life and I choose it with you, whatever happens over the next few days.'

*

The Greystone Park drive was long and lined with rhododendrons and chestnut trees. Matthew parked his car and carried our bags into reception, where the only evidence of the building's purpose was a slight smell of disinfectant wafting in from beyond the carpeted lounge. Passers-by, straying in from the manicured grounds, might have imagined that they had stumbled upon a tucked-away country-house hotel dedicated to an ascetic lifestyle. It was the way wealthy addicts and celebrity alcoholics expected to be dealt with. Celebrities not at all like me.

A woman wearing navy blue and pearls greeted us, called for our bags to be taken to our rooms and then escorted us to wait in the seating area overlooking the golf course.

Matthew walked over to appreciate the view. 'Should have bought my clubs.'

I smiled at the back of his head. 'I thought you sold them to pay off Lucy.'

He turned. 'You've remembered that have you? Actually, that *was* a fib. I've still got them. But I never play.'

'Why?'

'Hate being beaten. Even you can hit the ball further than me and you're a girl.'

I laughed. It might have been hysteria, but then again, it might have been really funny.

'Was your house OK when you went to collect your car?'

'Yes, not a toy boy in sight.'

I rolled my eyes. 'I remember the food's OK. Although, don't have the scrambled eggs.'

We glanced round as another woman in navy blue and pearls approached and introduced herself. Her lapel badge read 'LYNNE BARR: ATTENDANT' and that is who and what she declared herself to be. She escorted us into the lift and up to the third floor, where we stepped out into a corridor I recognised from over two months ago. However, the suite we were taken to was an immense improvement on my previous room. I was now clearly worthy of two bedrooms, each en-suite, and a small, bright lounge with a seating area, a dining table and chairs, potted plants, numerous objets d'art, a bowl of perfect fruit and no TV.

'My God,' said Matthew, as soon as we were alone. 'This is nicer than your flat. Although it would benefit from a kitchen.'

I turned away from the laughter I knew wasn't there and caught sight of the tray: tea, coffee, hot chocolate and gingerbread men. 'Matthew, they've thought of everything!'

He was investigating the contents of the small minibar in the corner. 'Evian, coke, apple juice. *Almost* everything!'

Our bags had all been placed in the main bedroom, although the bed was not even big enough for occasional sharing. The bed in the adjoining room was smaller. 'Looks like Mrs Parkin was in charge of beds,' said Matthew. 'Why don't you unpack? I'll pour.'

Ten minutes later there was a knock at the door. Matthew opened it. Bob Gray came in and shook his hand.

'Hello, Sarah, Matthew. I hope you're pleased with your rooms. They're the best we have. Usually reserved for royalty … foreign of course.' He looked at Matthew and then looked more closely, pulling his spectacles to the end of his nose.

'I walked into a door,' said Matthew, covering his lip.

Dr Gray seemed satisfied with that.

'Now, Sarah, we have a whole programme of things for you to take part in. Sam has put together some exciting cognitive tests.' He lowered himself into a chair. 'First session is one thirty. Mrs Barr will collect you. Just myself and Sam to start with. Drs Williams and Mustafa will join us later, together with a guest practitioner from the United States.'

He helped himself to a gingerbread man and asked me if I had any questions. I asked whether the other doctors were aware that Matthew was attending the sessions. Bob Gray glanced at Matthew.

'As I said before, I am very happy for Matthew to observe, although fisticuffs will be strictly forbidden.'

Matthew folded his arms.

'Lunch begins at noon. I've arranged for a vegetarian selection to be served in here, but if you'd prefer to mingle in the restaurant, just let reception know. I gather there's pistachio soufflé or banana cheesecake for pudding today: always a difficult choice, so I advised them to bring double helpings of both.' He checked his watch. 'Now, you have a good half hour before lunch, and it's a lovely day for a stroll in the grounds. Sarah knows the way. If you need anything, just call reception.'

Sarah was maintaining her most intransigent frown. 'But, Poppy,' she insisted, 'Jenny Berry *has* to visit Raggedy Lyme to save it from disaster!'

'*Sarah*, Raggedy Lyme was made up by Jenny's grandma. It's not real.'

'What makes you say that? I've never at any point suggested that Raggedy Lyme is not real.' She slapped her file shut. 'And, anyway, what is *real*?'

'Pretty much the frustration that Poppy's wearing on his face at this very moment,' said Matthew. He turned to his exasperated editor. 'Poppy, mate, Raggedy Lyme is real inside Sarah's head. And if she wants to take her small protagonist there, to save the place that helps pay your gym membership, then I'm sure she'll find a way.' He glanced back at Sarah. 'But, you'll never do it in thirty-two illustrated pages.'

'I don't intend to. I'll finish my LOST series and then I'll start on Grandma's apple stories. And then I'm going to bring Jenny Berry back for a full-length adventure of twenty-five thousand words.'

'Full-length adventure?' said Poppy.

'Apple stories?' said Matthew.

Sarah folded her arms with satisfaction. 'Yes and yes. And you're both gaping.'

'I never gape,' said Matthew. He got to his feet. 'Take me to lunch, madwoman, and pitch your idea to me. And I can look uncompromising and professional while considering your proposal. And we can pretend, *for a tiny while*, that I actually make the decisions around here.'

She laughed. 'OK. You coming too, Poppy?'

'No, Poppy's tidying his desk for the rest of the day.'

Sarah looked from Matthew to Poppy then back to Matthew. 'What?'

Poppy snatched up his things and headed for the door, pausing briefly to turn to Sarah. 'The philandering pig just wants to get you on your own again. But this time there are no perks in it for me. He's just pulling rank!' The door closed behind him.

Sarah refolded her arms and waited. Matthew ran his fingers through his hair. 'Sarah, we had two days of unforgettable passion, which I am unable to be calm about, yet for the last two weeks you have behaved as if nothing happened.'

She continued to say nothing.

'And, I have to say, I'm feeling crushed by your casual disregard for my emotional turmoil. I'm exhausted with trying to read where I stand with you! We need to talk about where you want us to go from here, yet ever since we've been back, you've avoided being on your own with me.'

Silence.

'Did those two days mean nothing to you? Sarah, will you *please* say something?'

'Where shall we go for lunch?'

Episode Thirty-five

Our walk had left us both feeling strangely elated and very hungry, so it was fortunate that, no sooner had we arrived back in our rooms, than lunch arrived. Matthew was impressed with the food and, during our meal, I managed a rare moment of relaxation. However, by the time we were on to coffee I was becoming anxious, and when Mrs Barr called in to escort us to the first session, I was feeling very ill at ease. Matthew stayed close beside me as we were led down to the second floor. With every set of double doors we passed, the atmosphere progressed from hotel to hospital corridor. The penultimate turn took us past numbered doors with the names of their inmates displayed in steel frames, presumably those whose stay was likely to be longer than two days. I felt that this might have been the corridor where I was first kept. The final double doors opened into a waiting area surrounded by consulting rooms. Dr Gray ushered us inside one of them and Sam Clegg rose to greet us.

We settled into a semi-circle of bucket chairs, stylish grey leather, myself between Drs Gray and Clegg, and separated from Matthew by the younger man. I was still feeling apprehensive, although Sam Clegg's relaxed friendliness did a lot to calm me and I felt even calmer when Bob Gray sat back and asked him to start the session.

Sam briefly declared his interest in my forgotten time then smiled. 'Sarah, you're an accomplished storyteller and when you write you do so according to some very basic rules that have been obvious to storytellers since time began. Aristotle ... Do you remember Aristotle?'

'Maybe.'

'OK, Aristotle said that every good story has to have a plot with a beginning, a middle and an end and, if you take one of those things away, the story's no longer complete and your storyteller's mind tells you something's wrong.'

I was intrigued.

'OK. Now, let's try a couple of tests. They're very simple. Even Dr Gray managed them first time.'

'I was having one of my better days,' said Bob Gray.

Matthew caught my eye and smiled.

Sam Clegg took three sheets from his folder and handed them to me. They were nicely-drawn cartoons, black, red and white. 'Sarah, these three drawings tell a story. I'd like you to place them in the order you think they happened. Take your time.'

I took no time at all. 'This is the first: the boy sees a jar of sweets on the shelf but he can't reach it.' I handed him the cartoon. 'And this is the second. He's climbing up on a stool to reach the jar. And this is the third. The jar's broken on the floor.'

'Excellent,' said Sam. 'Your mind can immediately see the logical sequence, which occurred in a forward direction in time. But those events are also linked *causally*: one thing causes another. So, it's clear that the boy climbed on the stool to reach the shelf *because* he wanted the sweets, and the jar is smashed *because* the boy was balancing precariously and nudged it onto the floor.' He collected the sheets and put them to one side. 'Your mind has interpreted those drawings in respect of temporality *and* causality.' He took out another three cartoons. 'Now, in what order do you think *these* events happened?'

'Ah, now this one confused me,' said Bob Gray.

I took the sheets. The three cartoons showed the same boy, at least it appeared to be the same boy because his hair was spiky and he was wearing the same red and black striped jumper. In one of the cartoons he was eating a large apple. The two other cartoons showed the boy rubbing his stomach, in one he was smiling, in the other his expression was wretched. I looked at Sam Clegg and smiled. I handed him the picture of the boy eating the apple. 'This is the middle one. But both the others could come first or last. There are two possible stories. He could be miserable because he's hungry so he eats the apple and feels better. Or he might start off seeing the apple then eat it and get stomach ache.'

'Anything else?' asked Sam Clegg.

'Well, this looks like the same boy that knocked the sweets off the shelf, so he might be the kind of naughty boy that would climb a fence and steal a sour apple.'

'A perfect response!' said Sam. 'It demonstrates the ability to construct alternative scenarios. And your observation about the previous, or subsequent, escapade with the sweet jar, shows tacit knowledge, the ability to apply previously-acquired information to a new situation. And you've also demonstrated an open mind in that you offered your interpretation as a suggestion not an assumption.'

'If only suggesting and not assuming was a more widespread ability,' said Dr Gray.

Sam Clegg gathered up his papers and placed them back in his folder. 'So, Sarah, you've demonstrated that your mind works perfectly.' He sat back and folded his arms.

'But my mind doesn't work perfectly, does it?'

'Yes, it does. The part of your mind that deals with the logic of your internal narrative is fully competent and it's with that knowledge that we must consider your lost memories.'

Bob Gray cleared his throat. 'Sarah, our lives are made up of many events. And we remember those events in sequence rather like a story. And all of those events influence the way we interpret new situations. We perceive and remember within the context of past experience. Now, your unconscious mind, for what it sees as your own protection, is denying you access to an event in your recent past, although it wants you to be able to function. But if something is missing, an episode or a context, then you'd know that wasn't right.'

Sam was unable to contain himself. 'Your mind has to take away what comes before and after so that you're not experiencing a story with a hole in it. But taking out *that* primary sequence creates a problem because *that* sequence is part of a larger sequence. Sarah, your unconscious mind has committed itself to a continuum of repression until anything that relates to the forbidden event has been expunged. But the process of repression can lead to confusion. For instance, some of the reasons why you regard things in certain ways might have been edited out as a result of the repression, so you're left thinking things without knowing why you think them.'

'Like not feeling right about asparagus?'

'Possibly, although you just might not like asparagus.'

'Like loathing orange shoes?'

Sam Clegg looked at me. 'Do they make orange shoes?'

'I found some in my wardrobe but I gave them away.'

'Well,' he said, 'loathing orange shoes might well be an example of what we're talking about. There might be a forgotten event in your past which caused you to hate orange shoes. You see, if you take away memories, then other things related to them become stranded. Orange shoes are not that critical so it's all right if the reasons for your attitude towards them are missing. But some things that are more critical will stick out a mile if their associated experiences are expunged, so the mind solves the problem by getting rid of them too. And, we believe that's the situation you find yourself in. Having committed you to forgetting a particular episode, the clean-up operation has had to be far-reaching, to the extent that much of your past has become involved. Sarah, a large tract of your time and experience has been removed in an attempt by your unconscious mind to protect you. Right back to the safety of childhood.'

I glanced at Matthew. 'Dr Clegg, sometimes I can't remember what a word means, like when Matthew said *obfuscation*, and when Mrs Parkin said *HIV* and *incarceration*. I must have known those words once because they sounded familiar but I couldn't remember what they meant. Have I forgotten words back to my childhood, just like I've forgotten events? Because I think my language is more mature than a child's.'

'Quite so,' said Dr Gray. 'As I mentioned before, your personal experiences and your language abilities are organised in different parts of your brain, although we must tell Dr Mustafa about your forgotten words. Perhaps they are also victims of your mind's clean-up operation. And tell me, Sarah, why exactly was Jane Parkin mentioning *incarceration*?'

I didn't answer. Matthew replied for me. 'It was when she was warning Sarah that she would be sectioned if she refused to come for assessment voluntarily.'

'Good God, that's a bit steep!' exclaimed Sam.

'She has been reassigned.' said Bob Gray quietly.

Mrs Parkin reassigned? I had to bite my lip to prevent myself smiling with satisfaction.

Dr Gray referred to his notes. 'Now, Sarah, let's assess the situation. You returned home eight weeks ago and have been managing well but, as far as you're aware, you have recovered no details of your past,' he looked up at me, 'despite re-establishing your relationship with Matthew, and your friendships with Miss Grant and your work colleagues? Is that correct?'

'Yes. Nothing jogs my memories. Although some smells seem strangely familiar.'

Dr Gray made a brief note. 'That's very interesting. Fragrances can be very evocative. Sam, has Geraint considered olfactory stimuli during MRI?'

'I'm not sure. We should mention it.'

There was a rap at the door. Sam Clegg got up to open it and Mrs Barr carried in a tray. The room filled with the rich burnt aroma of fresh coffee.

'Now there's a fragrance that's always welcome,' Dr Gray said.

We drank coffee and discussed my LOST stories. Sam Clegg asked me whether I could remember writing them. I confessed that I had now read them so often that I was not sure whether I was remembering them from before or after whatever happened.

'That is the problem,' explained Dr Gray. 'New memories can influence or even substitute original memories. That was the rationale behind our returning you to a comparatively minimalist environment. So that we could judge any improvement in your condition uninfluenced by the clutter of your previous life.'

'Dr Gray,' interrupted Matthew, 'that suggests that the way Sarah was planted back into her home, deprived of the trappings of her past, was geared more towards your investigation of her condition than to her recovery. We don't wish to seem ungrateful, but when I first inveigled myself back into her life, Sarah was living like a prisoner in her own home, being visited only by that unpleasant witch!'

'Matthew!'

Dr Gray touched my arm. 'It's OK, let Matthew speak. As it turns out, his support has been invaluable. In retrospect it was a mistake to distance you entirely from your friends. But, please understand, we were concerned that sudden reminders of people and things your mind had chosen for you to forget ... We were concerned that such exposure might cause further collapse, possibly psychosis. Luckily, that worry seems to have been unfounded.' He turned to Matthew. 'We are all treading new ground here, and I do assure you that the intended outcome is Sarah's recovery.'

I knew how Matthew would respond.

'Dr Gray, I don't doubt that you and Dr Clegg have Sarah's interest at heart, but I have to say that others in your team seem more driven by their investigation of her brain than by the welfare of the person who owns it.'

I sighed.

'Point taken, Matthew. I understand your concerns. For some of my colleagues, indeed for some in the wider research community, Sarah's situation is very interesting. Ultimately, however, I am the person overseeing her case and I assure you I am also in charge of reining in any practice which I see as intrusive. I will decide upon Sarah's treatment and I will do so in Sarah's, and only Sarah's, best interest.'

Matthew nodded. 'Thank you. We both needed to hear that.'

'Indeed. Now, shall we take ten minutes before the others arrive? And, Matthew, let me do the sparring. I'm an old hand.'

Episode Thirty-six

As we were walking back, Matthew asked me why Mrs Parkin had mentioned HIV. I told him about the condoms. 'She said we ought to use them even after I start taking the pill because of HIV.'

He pulled me to a halt. 'Are you not taking the pill?'

'Not yet. I have to wait until after my period.'

'Right! And when should that be?'

'This week, I think.'

We walked on.

'Sarah, when Bob Gray was asking you about things from the past not jogging your memory, why didn't you mention Jeff?'

'Who's …? Dawn!'

A young woman was walking towards us. I recognised her though she looked different today in black heels and a tight grey skirt.

'Hello, Sarah,' she said. 'How are you?'

'I'm fine. Do you clean here as well?' She'd never have been able to vacuum in that outfit.

Dawn laughed. She extended her hand towards Matthew. 'I'm Dawn Hayley, Geraint Williams' assistant. I stepped in the other week when Sarah's cleaner was indisposed, so that she wouldn't be confused by a change in routine.' She smiled at me. 'Although I don't think I proved to be a very good charlady, did I?'

'No!' I realised that was probably a rude response. 'But thanks.'

'You're welcome. Perhaps we'll run into each other over the next couple of days.'

Dawn went on her way.

'Williams got her to clean your flat when Annie wasn't well?'.

'Yes.'

'Right! I hate that bastard!'

The arc of seats was fully occupied when Matthew and I walked back into the consulting room. During our absence, the group had expanded to include Professor Isabel Bluet, an expensively-dressed yet relaxed middle-aged woman, who was sitting beside Dr Gray. Shoumi Mustafa was squashed into the chair between Professor Bluet and Geraint Williams, his smile even more sycophantic than usual. Williams himself was looking smug. Sam Clegg was sitting in a corner tapping away at his laptop. He glanced up at Matthew and rolled his eyes. A chair had been placed centrally in front of the arc of buckets, a kind of amphitheatre awaiting my performance. No bucket had been set for Matthew, so he escorted me to my seat and then went over to sit beside Sam. I noticed Bob Gray look over at them and raise his eyebrows.

Geraint Williams took up a position between me and his colleagues and proceeded to outline my case report, unnecessarily since his audience each had a copy complete with imaging sheets. I felt very small, as small as an amoeba about to be poked with a pin. I listened to details of my weeks of unconsciousness, the discovery of my amnesia, numerous clinical investigations, my rehabilitation into my home and the wealth of tests to which I had been subject since this relocation. Williams mainly addressed Professor Bluet, rarely looking at anyone else. His expression made me nauseous. He concluded his presentation with details of my reactions to visual stimuli during MRI. He lifted up a composite of three photographs.

'This series of prior contacts, designated Series 1, was shown to Sarah – British notation I'm afraid – on 06/03 of this year, before her return home, and on 03/04, two weeks after relocation. There was no haemodynamic response on either occasion. However, since these sessions, it has come to light that M. Parry, who was included in **Series 1** and who is with us today ...' He indicated Matthew. '... has re-established contact with the patient and has facilitated her further contact with the other Series 1 individuals: A. Grant and A. Abercrombie.'

I looked at Matthew. His face was tense with anger.

Geraint Williams was still talking. 'I anticipate that subsequent sessions will provide positive responses with all Series 1 individuals. So no pulling the wool over our eyes there!' The remark elicited constrained laughter from Professor Bluet and, particularly, from Shoumi Mustafa.

I heard myself interrupt: 'If you'd shown me a photograph of my grandmother you would have got a positive response with that!'

Dr Williams straightened his waistcoat. 'Ah yes, we did not include an image of the paternal ...'

'Dr Gray had a photograph of my *paternal* grandmother,' I said, annoyed at Granny Clark's exclusion.

'Thank you, Sarah!' Again, he pulled at the bottom of his waistcoat. 'We did not include an image of the paternal grandmother since she died several years ago.'

'It would have provided an excellent experimental control!'

Geraint Williams turned to Sam Clegg, his face barely disguising his irritation. 'Thank you, Sam. I do assure you that we are fully satisfied with our experimental paradigms.'

He turned back to his guest. 'Indeed, our control images can be seen in the composite marked Series 2, which includes images of Dr Gray and, of course, myself.'

More constrained laughter. I exchanged a brief look of triumph with Sam Clegg.

'Now, let us come on to the three prior contacts in Series 3. The patient was thrice exposed to this series on 06/03, 03/04, and during an additional session two weeks ago. I will refer to these three individuals according to the initials DD, JB or AD printed below each photograph alongside each of their relationships to the patient. On each occasion, with a first exposure to the three images, the patient demonstrated no recognition. However, a second presentation was, on each occasion, characterized by intense and erratic brain activity, with a third presentation invariably demonstrating no recognition and a return to negative response.'

I had absolutely no idea what any of this meant.

Professor Bluet moved to interject. 'Geraint, has the patient been exposed to the Series 3 images other than during imaging?'

Williams was clearly pleased by this question. 'Indeed, Isabel, she was given two opportunities to view the images under ordinary circumstances, and demonstrated a complete lack of recognition on both occasions.' His face was bright with confidence. 'In fact, I am quite certain I will be able to demonstrate this lack of recognition right now.' He turned to look at me, unsmiling. 'I am going to ask Ms Blake to observe JB, and I am inclined to believe that once again she will demonstrate no recognition.' He stepped forward and held a single photograph in front of me and asked me if I recognised the person. I shook my head.

'Sarah, are you telling me that you have never seen this person or any image of this person before?' His face was triumphant.

I looked again at the photograph. I so wanted to prove him wrong, spoil his pompous performance, but the person in the photograph was a complete stranger. I felt a hand on my shoulder, looked up and met Matthew's frantic green eyes.

'Mr Parry, would you mind returning to your seat,' said Dr Williams.

Matthew looked at Geraint Williams then snatched the photograph he was holding and held it forward so that I could reconsider. 'Sarah,' he said. 'This is Jeff.'

'Jeff who?' I replied.

Episode Thirty-seven

Geraint Williams stepped back, all at once willing to relinquish centre stage. Matthew knelt down and held the photograph across my lap.

'Sarah, do you really not recognise this person from yesterday? It's from the same photograph.'

'What photograph?'

'The photograph from the upstairs flat!'

'What upstairs flat?' I was beginning to feel frightened. 'Do you mean the flat above my flat?'

Matthew let the image slip from his hand. He lifted my fingers to his mouth so that I could feel the slight swelling around the wound. 'Sarah, how did my lip get cut?'

'You told Dr Gray you walked into a door.'

'Do you remember that happening?'

I pulled my hand away. 'No!'

'That's because it's not what happened. Tell me what happened.'

'I don't know what happened.'

'Sarah, you were there!'

'I was there?'

'Yes, in the upstairs flat. You found the paintings and the photographs.'

I turned my head, distracted by something, some sound, over by the door. But when I looked there was nothing, just a plain wooden door. Matthew looked round too. 'What's wrong?'

'It's the laughing.' I tugged at his sleeve. 'It's not there, is it? But I can hear it!'

'Sarah, would you like to take a break?' Bob Gray asked.

But Geraint Williams turned his back on him, unstoppable, buoyant with success.

'Isabel, this is a *perfect* demonstration of the process I was describing earlier. We are witnessing the aura, a sound that heralds unconscious activity and an episode of repression. Following factual input, the patient frequently complained of hearing laughter, and was subsequently unable to recall both the information provided and the aura itself.'

'Well, she recalls it now!' said Matthew. He disengaged me from his sleeve and stood up. 'Dr Clegg, Sam, would you Google "Klimt Kiss Images".'

I fought to calm myself as I watched Sam hand over his laptop.

'That's the one,' said Matthew. 'Thanks.' He held the laptop steady so that I could see the screen. 'Sarah, look at this. Try and remember.'

I looked at the image: a strange, stylish couple, draped in gold; he was bearing down on her, holding her head in his hands, kissing her, almost crushing her. Her toes were curled in ecstasy, her eyes closed, one of her arms was around his neck, preventing his leaving. The laughter in my head was continuous but I found that if I concentrated on the screen, kept re-seeing it, I was able to prevent the laughter from coming closer. I touched the image, ran my finger along the man's dark, curly hair, littered with leaves and petals, along his sculptured brow. Imagined his green eyes open while mine were closed. I looked up, reached up to touch Matthew's cheek.

'I hit you, didn't I?'

'Ha!' Geraint Williams said. 'What irony!'

Matthew ignored him. 'It's OK, Sarah. Don't upset yourself.'

I watched him hand over the laptop, carry his chair over to sit facing me. Nobody tried to stop him. They seemed satisfied to let the scene unfold. By now the laughter was tearing at my thoughts. And I was very frightened. Frightened that I'd hit Matthew. Was it something to do with the golden man? Perhaps the stranger in the photograph? I looked at the photo on the floor.

'Who is he?'

'Your husband,' exclaimed Geraint Williams.

I remember holding my breath for far too long, looking at Matthew for some kind of explanation, an immediate explanation, that would allow me to start breathing again. He was glaring at Dr Williams. He looked back at me, a trace of hatred still in his eyes.

'Sarah, it's OK …'

I breathed.

'… You were married to this man. For nearly eight years. His name was Jeff Blake and he had a bad fall and he died. But before that happened you were going to leave him to be with me.'

I listened to the words, just discernible above the laughter, but I couldn't make them mean anything. Matthew looked past Geraint Williams and spoke directly to Bob Gray.

'Sarah found a key to the flat upstairs. Yesterday afternoon. Apparently, her cat had been going in there. She found her wedding photo. I had to explain. I told her about Jeff Blake.'

He looked back to me. 'I told you about Jeff falling and breaking his neck, never regaining consciousness. I told you it happened the day you disappeared. We talked about him over supper.'

I grappled to recapture memories of the previous evening. 'We had Indian takeaway.'

'Yes! Sarah, try and remember the flat upstairs. You went inside to look for Alfie.'

And, suddenly, I remembered a black and white cat, *my* black and white cat, asleep on a gilded chair. 'It was like a giant's kitchen. With huge pots and pans. And mice. The door was open and it was raining.'

'That's right. Is the laughter still there?'

'Yes, but it's not getting any closer.'

'Sarah, can you remember finding your wedding photograph?' Matthew picked the photo from the floor. 'You and this man? Your dress? Your flowers? The glass broken on the floor?'

There was an uneasy silence as the room waited for my response. I tried to remember: dress, flowers … and all at once an image came into my head. 'Pink and white roses.'

Geraint Williams interrupted. 'This is recollection of a secondary image, remembering the photograph rather than the original reality. This is exactly why we exclude reported experiences. What the patient comes to remember is not the original event but rather a secondary phenomenon.'

'She's remembering!' snapped Matthew. 'Isn't that enough?'

Geraint Williams' eyes narrowed. 'Filling Mrs Blake's mind with new images will undoubtedly reduce the possibility of her recalling *actual* events. But then, Mr Parry, I have never been convinced that you wish for Sarah to recall the events of the day in question.'

'I don't want her future to be destroyed by nightmares from her past. Sarah was confused and distressed. I told her what she needed to know.'

I watched Geraint Williams turn towards Isabel Bluet, his arm stretched towards me, anticipating my reaction to his next question:

'And, while you were imparting all this information, Mr Parry, did you make any mention of Sarah's younger sister, Arachne, who died the day that Sarah's husband's neck was broken, the same day that Sarah disappeared?'

The laughter was all around me, filling my head until there was no room left for anything else. I lifted my hands to protect my eyes and felt my hair fall unrestrained to mask my forgetting. Nobody must know.

*

'Sarah? Sarah, *can you hear me?*'

I felt my hands being eased away from my eyes. Matthew was holding me steady in my chair. Dr Gray was beside me, his fingers pressed into my wrist. Professor Bluet was watching, still seated; she seemed impressed by the floor show. I had clearly lived up to expectations. Beside her, Shoumi Mustafa had actually paused his notetaking; his mouth was gaping slightly. Geraint Williams and Sam Clegg were standing just to my left.

'I'm sorry,' I said. 'I felt dizzy.'

'Would you like to lie down?' said Dr Gray. The door opened and Mrs Barr hurried in with a glass of water, which she handed to me.

Geraint Williams took a step towards me. 'Sarah, what is the last thing you remember me saying?'

But before I could even consider my answer, Bob Gray addressed the room. 'I think that's enough for today. Sarah is obviously exhausted.'

'Bob, it would be constructive to allow her to confirm ...'

'Geraint!' Bob Gray's tone was more authoritative than I had come to expect. 'This really has been wonderfully informative but I think that right now Sarah needs to rest. We will reconvene here briefly in half an hour. Professor Bluet is most welcome to join us.'

'Bob, with respect ...'

'Geraint, she is *exhausted*.'

I sipped my water and watched Geraint Williams over the rim of the glass. After a moment he straightened his waistcoat and turned to his guest. 'Isabel, the tea urn summons!' Without casting another glance in my direction, he gathered his files and strode towards the door, and led his contingent away. Sam waited for Mrs Barr to close the door behind her then moved to one of the vacated buckets. The air settled and I asked would somebody please explain what just happened. Bob Gray asked me about the dizziness.

'The noises suddenly got worse. I told you about the laughter, didn't I? Did I faint?'

'Not exactly.' Bob Gray tapped his fingers together for a moment, then he regarded Matthew over the top of his glasses. 'Matthew, give me a moment, would you?' Matthew surrendered his chair. 'Sarah,' said Bob Gray, 'if anything upsets you tell me straightaway. All right? Now, do you remember what we were talking about?'

I placed the glass on the floor. 'I think so. Dr Williams showed me a photo of a man I didn't recognise. He said it was my husband. Jeff Blake. Matthew said we were married for eight years but he died. He told me about the upstairs flat and finding the wedding photo and he showed me the picture of the golden man. And I started to remember a giant kitchen. And my bouquet. But then the noises became too loud. I know they're not real.'

'So, despite the noises, you can remember discovering the photo of Jeff Blake?'

'I can remember what Matthew told me before I felt dizzy and I think that made me remember being in the upstairs flat and finding the photo. But it's difficult to know whether I'm remembering what I was told, or what actually happened.'

'Well, don't worry too much about that for now.' He turned to Sam. 'Sam, I can't be certain, but I think that what we're dealing with here are degrees of separation, the distance from the event through a tiered system of recall. Perhaps it allows Sarah to negotiate around the repression.' He turned to reassure me. 'This is all very good.'

'But, Dr Gray, I'm forgetting new things.'

'Only very specific things, Sarah. Do you remember anything else?'

I tried to recall some of the more significant moments in Geraint William's malign performance.

'Dr Williams accused Matthew of not wanting me to remember. And Matthew said he didn't want my future destroyed by nightmares from my past.' I glanced up at Matthew; he smiled to reassure me but his eyes betrayed anxiety. 'I'm sorry, I can't remember. What happened?'

There was an awkward pause. At last Sam broke the silence. 'Bob, someone will tell her if we don't. But, what about taking advantage of the degrees of separation? Tell Sarah what was said to her, rather than the thing itself.'

Bob Gray frowned. 'You might have a point there, Sam. And I suppose the worst that can happen is that it will elicit the same response. But at least we'll be prepared.' He placed his hands on his knees and his blue eyes looked straight at me. 'Are you ready, Sarah?'

'Can Matthew tell me?'

Bob Gray got to his feet. 'Matthew?'

Matthew sat down opposite me and just held my hands for a moment. I wasn't sure whether it was my hands that were trembling or his but when he spoke he sounded calm.

'Sarah, when you had the scans, Dr Williams singled out three people for his Series 3. One of those people, JB, was Jeff Blake. Do you remember that?'

'I don't remember being shown pictures of him during the scans.'

'But you do remember the photo Dr Williams showed you today?'

'Yes.' I tried not to panic. 'Matthew, I'm forgetting new things.'

'Only *some* new things. Now, if the noises start again, try to ignore them. Dr Williams thinks they're your mind forcing you to forget.' He took a deep breath. 'A second person in Dr Williams' Series 3 was AD and that was the person he mentioned here today just before you became dizzy. He stood right here…' Matthew inclined his head to the side. '… and said that you had a younger sister, called Arachne, and he told you that she died that same day your husband fell and broke his neck. The day you disappeared.'

Of course, the laughter began but this time I told myself to ignore the noises. I could hear myself repeating that instruction. Time after time. And slowly, imperceptibly at first, the laughter subsided and the crashing of waves became my own breathing. Matthew was still holding my hands. I searched his eyes.

'Yesterday, when you told me about Jeff Blake, did you tell me about a sister then?'

Bob Gray interrupted. 'We advised Matthew that the information might elicit …'

'The kind of reaction we all just witnessed,' said Matthew.'

'Yes. But, Sarah, can you recall what Matthew just told you?'

'Yes, I think so. He said that Dr Williams told me I had a sister who died. But I don't think I believe him. I don't really believe I had a sister who died.'

'Do you think this denial is a coping device?' interrupted Sam.

'Possibly.' Bob Gray folded his arms. 'Sarah's mind is so many steps ahead of us, I'm at a loss as to where to go from here. But we seemed to have moved on. How do you feel, Sarah?'

'I don't know how I feel. Dr Gray, how did the sister die?'

Bob Gray paused before answering. 'She fell into the path of a lorry. But I don't want you to concern yourself with remembering that at the moment. I think you've had enough for one day.' He checked his watch. 'You both need to slip away before the others come back. And, Sarah, this evening, I'd like you to keep reminding yourself what you've been told today. Keep it fresh in your mind. Reinforce the progress we've made and don't worry about anything else. If I'm needed, I can be here in half an hour. Sam is in residence.'

I chewed my lip, uneasy about something. Then a question tumbled into my mind.

'Dr Gray, who was the *third* person in Dr Williams' Series 3?'

Bob Gray frowned: 'I think, Sarah, that for the time being, this person would be an unimportant complication. Let's concentrate on remembering the husband and sister for now, shall we?'

ISLINGTON

Jeff threw down his phone. 'What do you mean you can't do that Friday? I gave you plenty of warning. You've known about this wedding for months.'

'I can't help it. They're giving me a prize. We only found out about it this morning. Everyone at the agency is really excited. I can't not turn up.'

'Everybody? You mean fucking pretty boy and his tart, right? This is an important wedding, Sarah. There's no letting me down on this one.'

'Well, I'm sorry. I'll do the flowers the night before. But you'll have to get someone else to do the photography. I'll ask Annabelle. She did *our* photos. Some of them were really …'

'Don't talk crap! These people are the very people I need to get in with. I'm not having that fat slut cavorting around, flashing her tits at anybody in trousers. Tell pretty boy to collect your prize for you. God, what will it be? A pair of silver-plated kiddie boots? But then, I suppose that's the nearest you'll ever get to those.'

Sarah caught her breath. 'The consultant said there isn't any reason why I can't get pregnant. He said the next step is for you to be tested. Before we can start IVF.'

'Here we go again! I'm not doing anything of the bloody kind. There's nothing wrong with me.'

'No, I'm sure a thousand women can attest to that. And yet, strangely, none of them seem to get pregnant either, do they? *Do they?* Annabelle warned me not to get involved with you.'

'But you did! And part of the deal was that you did weddings.'

His phone beeped with an incoming message and Sarah watched a familiar smirk spread across his face.

'Well, *Casanova*, this time you're going to have to find someone else!' She grabbed her satchel. 'There's fresh coffee downstairs if you want any. I'll be back after lunch.'

She was heading for the stairs when she felt Jeff's hand close around her arm.

'Hey, let go of me! Jeff, you're hurting me!'

*

Matthew looked up as his door swung open. 'Hi, madwoman, Hillier have just phoned and ...' he paused. 'What happened to you?'

'I walked into a door. We fought. The door won.'

He stood up to take a closer look. 'When did that happen?'

'Just as I was leaving to come here.'

He stepped over to his phone and pressed a single digit. 'Poppy, Sarah's arrived. Bring the chardonnay.' He put down the phone. 'Are you OK? How can you cut your lip on a door? Has Jeff seen what you've done?'

'No, he wasn't there.'

Episode Thirty-eight

The corridor leading back was the same corridor we had walked along less than four hours earlier but this time each set of swing doors took us further away from the hospital atmosphere and from the likelihood of running into Geraint Williams. As we took the lift up to the third floor, I registered Matthew's agitation.

'Did they tell you I was still losing memories?'

'They said your mind was refusing to let you remember.'

'About my husband? And a sister who died the day I disappeared?'

'Yes.'

'It's a never-ending list of things you haven't told me, isn't it?'

'Sarah, love, I've tried to do and say what they told me was best for you.'

'Which at no point included throwing an apple at me.'

'I …'

'It's OK. I almost forgive you.'

Tea and menus were waiting in our suite. By the time the cheery attendant came to clear away, we had decided upon Thai prawns, Portabella ratatouille and pineapple brulée. Our order was hurried away and I stretched out on the sofa to try to fix in my mind what I had been told about a husband and sister, both deceased. Matthew wandered around turning on lamps and fruitlessly searching the minibar.

'I'd give anything for a gin and tonic.'

'Annie said you drink too much!'

He arched an eyebrow. 'Well remembered!' He went to the window to check on his car.

'Is it still there?'

'I'm just pleased to have it back. And I'm pleased to have you back. I have got you back, haven't I?'

'Maybe. Was it expensive?'

'What?'

'Your car. Was it expensive?'

'Yes, Lucy bought it for my fortieth birthday.'

I sat up. 'My God!'

He started to laugh. 'I'm *always* attracted to wealthy women. Apart from you. You're my folly!'

I laughed too. 'Did she really buy you the car?'

'Yes. And she provided most of the money to set up the agency. I just provided the good looks.'

I lay back 'What was she called?'

'Who?'

'The sister. What was she called?'

'We told you.'

'Perhaps it's one of the *specific things* I'm not allowed to remember. Remind me!'

'I'm not sure … God, I wish Bob Gray had given me a session on how to handle this.'

'I don't think he knows how to handle it.'

'Now I really need a gin and tonic.'

'Matthew, come and sit down! Tell me her name!'

'Let's wait until after supper.'

'*Matthew*, now!'

'Oh God, all right.' He sat down. 'This is exactly what Williams said: "Did you mention her younger sister, *Arachne*, who died the same day her husband fell and broke his neck." The same day you disappeared.'

I stared at him: 'Are many people called Arachne?'

'Probably not. In Greek mythology she was changed into a spider. How do you feel?'

'I don't feel anything. Apart from afraid that my mind's about to empty out completely. But no, I don't feel anything. No noises, no laughing.'

'You remember about the laughing, do you?'

'Yes, of course. And I remember what I've been told. About a husband and a sister who died the day I disappeared. But I can't feel anything because I don't remember it happening. And I don't really *believe* it. It might all be lies.'

'I wouldn't lie to you.'

'You pretended not to know me.'

'Sarah, I …'

I touched my finger across his lips. 'I'm glad you did what you did. I couldn't have survived any longer on my own. And, besides, the sex has been spectacular!'

Matthew frowned.

I frowned back. 'What?'

'That sounded like you. From before. Every day, but especially today, you sound more like you from before.'

'So there *is* a difference?'

'No, the sex was always spectacular! Are you still remembering?'

'Yes. Do you think the bed's big enough for two?'

Matthew sighed. 'Sarah, I am now worried that you've gone mad!'

'I haven't. It's just that the food won't be here for at least another hour.'

'Sarah, stop thinking about sex! Tell me the name of the sister.'

I tried to remember. 'It was an odd name, wasn't it? I watched his frown deepen. 'She was changed into a spider. But I can't remember… yes I can: Arachne. Why was she changed into a spider?'

'She pissed off a goddess! So you *have* remembered?'

'It seems.' I tugged at his shirt. 'It's a really big shower.'

*

Getting dressed for dinner seemed to be an odd thing to do in a clinic, but we did it anyway, although Matthew said that acknowledging the occasion was intensifying his need for alcohol. I continued to remind myself about my husband and sister until, at precisely seven o'clock, our banquet was wheeled in complete with fine china and crystal. Matthew thanked the porters, watched them leave then sat and stared miserably at the jug of water. He fished out two slices of lemon.

'Why do they always …? What are you smiling at?'

'The first time we went to Tony's bistro you ordered no lemon for me and I was too stupid to realise you already knew I didn't like it.'

'Clearly I'd never make a successful liar.'

'Really?'

The prawns and the ratatouille were delicious but by dessert I was sick of remembering. I repeated yet again: 'Jeff Blake, Arachne …' I threw down my spoon. 'This is ridiculous!'

Matthew glanced up from his brulée. 'What's ridiculous?'

'Saying these things like they mean nothing. I ought to feel sad. And, anyway, how could all those things happen on the same day?' I turned towards a distant rumbling. 'Two accidents and me disappearing …'

I fought to ignore it. But it was drawing closer. I could feel that cold, grey mist rising up all around me, engulfing me, turning my feet to ice. And through it, beyond it, a darker shadow. I opened my mouth wide and tried to shout but I had no breath to shout with. Then all at once the mist began to disperse. I could feel Matthew shaking me. And it was gone.

He pulled his chair round next to mine. 'Why did that just happen? What started it?'

'I don't know.' I gripped his sleeve. 'It was suffocating me.'

'Sarah, you know it's not real. Tell me what you've been remembering.'

'I've been remembering a husband who died. Jeff Blake.'

'Who else?'

I couldn't remember anybody else. I shook my head.

'Sarah, what was the name of the woman who was turned into a spider?'

'A spider?'

'*Sarah*, try to remember our conversation! I told you her name.'

I could feel his frustration. I didn't want to be doing this to him. Then a cold shock rippled through me: these new things I was forgetting … I choked back the panic.

'What's wrong? Is it starting again?'

'I've forgotten you!'

'What do you mean? You haven't forgotten me.'

I was barely able to turn the fear into words. 'I've forgotten things you said. That means I've forgotten you when you said them. My mind has stolen my time with you.'

'Sarah, no! The time's not stolen. It's just out of reach because of the information that's in it. Come on, let's start again. We told you you had a sister who died. Concentrate.'

'A sister?' I tried to think of a sister.

'Yes, we told you she died the same day Jeff had the accident.' He ran his hands through his hair. 'Sarah, tell me about Jeff Blake. What happened to him?'

I didn't know. I closed my eyes and searched inside the darkness: Jeff Blake. He was alive and then he was dead and something happened in between. Earlier that evening I had known what it was. I had to pull that memory back. My own memory that was being hidden from me by my own mind. I rummaged through the hopeless jumble of thoughts, traces of the evening so far. Lucy. Matthew's car. The shower. I opened my eyes.

'He fell, didn't he?'

'Yes. He broke his neck and later he died. No one knows how it happened.'

'But you said the husband had the accident the same day the sister died.'

'Yes, the day you disappeared.'

'Did the sister fall as well?'

'No!'

I went to ask *how*, then, could those things all happen the same day, but before I could even formulate the sentence I heard the laughter approaching:

'It's what I mustn't know! What my mind keeps erasing every time

I get close to it. I mustn't remember *how they died*.' Ignore the noises.
'Did they die in the same place?'

'Pretty much.'

Ignore the noises. 'Where?'

'At your mother's house. In Hornsey.'

Episode Thirty-nine

'But my mother's dead. How can she have a house?'

'She isn't dead. She's in an institution. With severe dementia.'

'But they told me she was dead.'

'No, apparently they let you assume it. They didn't warn me about it. Your mother's well but she needs constant care because of the dementia. Do you remember what that is?'

'Of course I do! But isn't dementia something really old people get?'

'Diana's not that old.'

'Is that my mother's name?'

'Yes, Diana Dawson.'

'Dawson?'

'She remarried. Diana has a long history of alcohol abuse, which was why you went to live with your grandma. She was Geraint Williams' third person, DD. She was there that day. Then she was taken into care. She hasn't been able to tell anybody what happened.'

'Where did you say my mother's house was?'

'In Hornsey.'

I shook my head and tried to absorb this new information but as I embraced non-orphanhood, an unpleasant possibility presented itself.

'Was I at my mother's house that day?'

'Sarah, *that's* what nobody knows. The last time anybody remembers seeing you was that morning. Two days later you were unconscious on a beach and no-one knows how you came to be there or if anyone else was involved.'

I tried to concentrate. Then something occurred to me, something really bad.

'Matthew, you said the police suspected I hadn't really lost my memory. Do they think I was there that day? Do they think I did something terrible and … ?'

There was a sharp rap on the door, which instantly swung open. Sam Clegg stepped in flanked by two porters. He looked different: his suit trousers and starched white coat had been abandoned for jeans and a sweatshirt; in fact he looked like a completely normal human being. He set his laptop case down and asked if we were receiving visitors.

Matthew leapt up. 'Sarah, are we receiving visitors?'

I said yes, we were. Perhaps this would be an opportunity to stop worrying about the things I couldn't remember. The things I might have done.

The table was cleared, the porters left and our young psychologist unzipped his laptop bag and pulled out a large packet of crisps and a bottle of Merlot.

'Here, Matthew,' he said, 'I thought you might appreciate this.'

'Sam, you might just have saved my sanity.'

'You're welcome.' He sat across from me and smiled. 'How's the recall?'

'I'm forgetting new things.'

'We know. We'll make it right.'

We chatted easily. I watched them enjoying their wine and tried to force my most recent fears from my mind. Matthew asked Sam a couple of questions about his research and edged around asking his opinion of Geraint Williams. I was nowhere near as tactful.

'I don't know how you can work with that bastard Williams,' I declared. 'And Shoumi Mustafa's a creep!'

Sam laughed. 'Well observed, Sarah! But Geraint is an accomplished surgeon and he's rumoured to be a good clinical researcher. He did time at Caltech a few years back. The drug companies love him and that brings bags of money our way, so Bob tolerates him, despite the fact that he's an arsehole. And Bob's your physician so he'll always be the one making the decisions. Between you and me, he was absolutely furious about Della Brown.'

'Me too!' said Matthew. 'Would you get it in the neck if Bob knew you were here?'

'No, I asked him if it was OK, and he said yes, but no discussing what an arsehole Geraint is because it's unprofessional. But, I'm research staff, so I can be as unprofessional as I like.'

Matthew laughed. I was relieved to see him relax. I, on the other hand, while the conversation rambled on, was mulling over the fact that my mother was still alive in an institution somewhere, and the possibility that the police suspected that I'd been involved in something terrible. But I seemed to have forgotten exactly what that terrible thing might have been. With all the excitement of Sam's visit, the memories had ceased to stay fresh in my mind. I needed to ask them to remind me what I was supposed to remember.

'Sweetheart, are you OK?' They were both staring at me.

'I'm fine.' I looked at Sam. 'Matthew told me my mother's still alive.'

'I said that Diana has been in an institution since the incident with Jeff and Arachne.'

Jeff and Arachne. It occurred to me that it might help if those names were written down.

'Sam, would it be cheating if we wrote those names down?'

Sam stretched over and grabbed his notebook. 'There's no cheating, Sarah. We're making this up as we go along.' He pulled out a page and handed it to me along with his pen, then watched me write down the two names, helped me to spell Arachne. 'I should have thought of physical processing … and taking advantage of visual memory.'

Another kind of memory. I placed the piece of paper on the table and felt instantly relieved of some of the burden of remembering. 'Perhaps if I could see photos?'

Sam took a quick mouthful of wine before responding. 'Geraint is of the opinion that photographs corrupt memories rather than enhance them. And I'm inclined to agree with him up to a point. We often remember photographs of people rather than the people themselves. Nevertheless, it is Bob's intention to show you photos tomorrow.'

'Will Geraint Williams be there?' asked Matthew.

'Not first thing. He'll be showing Isabel around. Exhibiting his most interesting patients. Then he'll be allowing some drug rep to take them all to lunch. So it's just the four of us until two-thirty.'

I felt a wave of relief pass over me. I looked again at the two names on the paper 'When did you first become interested in memories, Sam? Or don't you remember?'

He laughed. 'Actually, I do remember. It was shortly after I fell out of a tree. It was an old apple tree covered in mistletoe. A slight variation on Mr Newton's iconic moment. But still significant.'

'Are you going to enlighten us?' asked Matthew.

Sam took another swig of Merlot. 'I was twelve. I'd built this dodgy tree house with my brother. And we were sitting in it arguing about whose idea it had been. So I jumped up and declared that I'd been planning to build it since before he was born. Which was unlikely since I was only two years older than him. And I fell off the edge of the platform. Broke my leg in three places. Had to have a rod stuck through my femur.' He acknowledged our groans of sympathy. 'Then, a few weeks after the surgery, it started to dawn on me that there was a whole stretch of the previous year I couldn't remember: about six weeks, that just happened to include my birthday. My parents had given me a mountain bike, but I couldn't remember getting it. And I'd been taken to Alton Towers for my birthday treat and all I could remember were disconnected fragments of the day: things I'd remembered since. It wasn't investigated because I didn't tell anyone, but it was the beginning of my interest in forgetting.'

'Did the memories come back?' I asked.

'No. They were gone. In retrospect, it must have been the anaesthesia. Small foci inside my brain must have suffered hypoxia, low oxygen, and just burned out. If it hadn't have involved my birthday memories I would never have noticed. We forget things all the time. That's the normal state of affairs. But memories about my birthday, about things I would have chosen to remember, they ought to have been there.'

'Do you think my memories have burned out?'

'No, I don't. But you need to gain access to them.' He pulled open the bag of crisps, offered them across the table then helped himself to a handful. 'You know, Matthew, I think it was great the way you got back with Sarah. The whole isolation idea was ridiculous. Bob was willing to go along with it for a while. But he insisted on Sarah's return home. I think he knew at that point the isolation would be impossible.' He looked at me. 'So, you discovered the things in the upstairs flat?'

'Matthew was going to let me carry on not knowing.'

'Sarah, I …'

'Did you punch him?'

'Yes!'

'It wasn't his fault, you know. He argued your case the whole time.'

'He hit Dr Williams!'

'I was there. It was the best moment of my entire career.' He topped up their glasses. 'So, how's the memory refreshing at the moment?'

'I don't know.' I picked up the piece of paper. 'Everything to do with these two people drains straight out of my head as soon as I know it. And now I've been told my mother's alive, and I can't remember her. Sam, the photos Dr Gray gave me, of my birthday, in one of them, my granny and I are smiling at the person taking the picture. I remember that day but however much I try I can't remember who the third person was. I would remember my mother, wouldn't I?'

Sam looked thoughtful. 'It is possible that person might not have been significant enough to be remembered from all those years ago. Nobody remembers everybody. But, alternatively, from what's been learned from interviewing you, it might be that this third person was significant enough for you to *forget*. This process of repression, it might be a unique facility your mind has perfected over the years to conceal unpleasant memories.'

Matthew sat forward. 'You think Sarah's done this before?'

'Bob thinks so.'

'He thinks I've deliberately forgotten my mother?'

'Sarah, none of it's *deliberate*. It seems your unconscious mind can operate independent of your volition, of your will. A coping mechanism that arose in childhood.'

'But I'm smiling at her in the photo. If it's her. Why would I need to forget my mother?'

'You probably felt abandoned every time she went away. Children don't always understand their parent's actions. Occasionally they blame themselves. Sometimes she would have stayed away for several months.'

'Alice Parker said my mother was in a loony bin.'

Matthew's wine glass stopped half way to his lips. 'Sarah, love, who's Alice Parker?'

'She was a girl in school. We hated each other.'

'From what I've gathered,' said Sam, 'there were frequent periods of institutionalisation. It was during rehab that she met John Dawson.'

Matthew lifted the sheet of paper from my lap and pointed to one of the names. 'He was her father. Arachne Dawson. AD. She was your *half*-sister. That's right, isn't it, Sam?'

I watched Sam nod his head. I remember thinking how strange it was that everybody knew more about my life than I did. Sam Clegg seemed to know more than anyone.

'Sam, how did you find out all these things about me?'

'Medical records, social services.'

'And this was all done without me knowing?' I could feel myself becoming angry.

'Not maliciously,' said Sam. 'And tomorrow, if you're happy to see it, Bob is going to show you the data I accumulated.'

'The story of my life that everybody knows except me? Will it be illustrated?'

'Illustrated?'

'Yes, Dr Clegg, I've got a whole fucking cupboard full of camera equipment and no photos! Will the story of my life include my photographs?'

Matthew moved to put his arm around me. 'Hey, Sarah, everyone's trying to help.'

'Well, perhaps I can't be helped.' I shrugged him away. 'Perhaps my *unique* mind is going to carry on burning out my brain until there's nothing left. Have either of you any idea what it's like being told about your life by other people?'

'Sarah,' said Sam, 'I know this must be awful for you. And tomorrow there *will* be photos. As I said, Geraint believes photos corrupt memories, but to an extent they can also evoke them. And then those memories might access other memories: like stepping stones back to when you yourself can remember.'

'Back to things the police are interested in? That happened in *that* place.'

'In Hornsey?' said Sam. I had forgotten that name. Sam leant forward, his tone quietly conspiratorial. 'Sarah, we want you to recover your memories so you can come to terms with them and move on. There's a chance we might be able to help you remember your life by taking you back over it, like rewinding a videotape that's got a glitch in it. Do you remember videotapes?'

'Yes, of course!'

'Well, if you remember, the best thing to do when a videotape got a kink in it was to wind it back to the beginning then forward to the piece you wanted to watch. It's only a theory but it might work. And then it will be up to you what you tell people.'

'What I tell people?' I searched Sam Clegg's eyes: friendly, brown, truthful. I scanned those brown eyes for any sign of meaning that was different to the one I now feared. 'And it will be up to me what I *don't* tell people, right, Sam? Do you think there are things I'd want to conceal?' I pointed to the two names. 'About what happened to those two people? And my mind's helping me by not letting me know either?'

'No, Sarah. I think your mind is protecting you from things that are too hurtful to remember. Perhaps related to the circumstances in which you were found. What happened to those two people could well be some tragic coincidence.'

I looked down at my hands, clasped together, like a criminal begging for forgiveness. Like Sarah Blake begging for a future not destroyed by nightmares from her past.

'How huge can a coincidence be, Sam? Two people's lives ended and I disappeared. Perhaps the thing my mind is protecting me from is the truth.' I reached over for the phone. 'I'll call down for some tea.'

'Let me do that!' Matthew eased the phone from my hand.

I snatched it back. 'For God's sake, I can make a telephone call!'

Sam got to his feet. 'I'm sorry. I didn't mean to upset you.'

I sighed. 'I know. I'm just terrified about what I might have done.'

'There's no suggestion that you did anything,' Matthew said.

'You can't know that.'

*

Tea arrived. Matthew convinced me to sit and enjoy it and we chatted more about Geraint Williams. Sam was only too pleased to provide detailed criticism, and I was heartened by every negative appraisal.

Eventually, the conversation turned to football, so I left them discussing transfer fees and wandered off to fetch my pills. I found my room in semi-darkness, illuminated by a cold, unnatural light coming in from outside. I went over to the window to close the blind and was forced to shade my eyes. The grounds outside were deathly still, uniformly illuminated by a vast number of intense, blue-white lights, hidden in the shrubbery so that they cast their shadows upwards into the empty sky. A single golf buggy had been left outside to suffer the damp night air. I could see headlights passing in the distance, their drivers oblivious to the anguish trapped at great cost within this fine institution, every one of them blissfully unaware of the personal crises that were unravelling just a few hundred yards away from their uncomplicated lives. I envied their distance, because, for all its manicured gardens and excellent cuisine, this was not a place of happiness. I turned as the door half opened.

'Can we come in?' said Matthew, manoeuvring one end of a mattress into the room.

Sam appeared, supporting the other end. 'Matthew's scared to sleep on his own,' he said.

Episode Forty

Hoping that sleep would come quickly, I got into bed, placed the paper with the two names under my pillow and lay there watching Matthew arranging his pillows against the spindle legs of the bedside table. Eventually he resigned himself to discomfort, kissed me, turned off the light and crawled into his makeshift bed. I hung my arm over the side, so that it rested against his cheek. 'This is just another inconvenience I'm causing you.'

'Nonsense, woman, I've never been more comfortable in my life. And I can see under the furniture from here so that's a bonus I wasn't expecting. Go to sleep.'

I watched the darkness and listened to Matthew's quiet breathing and the whirring of the minibar in the next room. I shifted around on the mattress. It was too hard and it was getting harder. I tried to ignore it and waited for sleep to come. After perhaps twenty minutes of rigid expectation, I realised something had gone wrong. Why did this have to be the one night that the pills failed to work? Probably all the thoughts racing through my head had united and launched a counterattack on the chemical invasion that usually allowed me to sleep. I was wide-awake. And I had spent so long drifting to sleep in a pharmaceutical blur that I could no longer remember how to fall asleep unassisted. I had forgotten how impossible it is to go to sleep deliberately, how the more you try to sleep the more unlikely it becomes. And the more your thoughts and fears catch hold of your failure. I needed to instruct my mind to let me sleep. But my mind had a mind of its own. Like an internal parasite. This was why I was in this state, and why Matthew was on a mattress on the floor.

I stared at the ceiling, my eyes now adjusted to the light flowing in from around the edges of the blind. I could pick out the furniture, the bathroom door. I wondered if Matthew was still awake. It would be ridiculous for us to both be lying there unable to sleep. But I was too close to see him where he lay. I moved to the edge of the concrete mattress so I could see over. Quietly, so that the bed wouldn't creak.

'Are you all right?' he whispered. He sat up. 'Can't you sleep?'

'No.' I reached out and touched his shoulder. 'I can't stop thinking about what Sam said: about only telling people what I want them to know. You said the police thought I might be pretending. Why would they think that if there wasn't something to hide?'

He reached up and turned on the bedside lamp. 'Did you take both your pills?'

'Yes, but they're not working. Matthew, was I at my mother's house that day?'

He sat up on his knees. 'Sarah, it's important you remember for yourself.'

'I need you to start the memory. Like Sam said: one memory leading to another. You have to tell me if you know. You might think you're protecting me, but you can't protect me from the truth. It's my choice, Matthew.'

He settled himself back against the pillows and the bedside table, as if he needed to secure himself. He held my gaze. 'You phoned me that afternoon to say you were going over to your mother's place to tell Arachne you were leaving Jeff. And that, if anything happened to Diana, she could find you with me.'

I took a moment to digest the gravity of what he had said. But I was confused. 'Did Arachne live with my mother?'

'Yes.'

'And was Jeff Blake also there that day?'

'I argued with you not to go there until I got back. I'd been in Birmingham the previous evening at a book launch. I was on my way back when you called. I went straight to your flat but you weren't there and you weren't answering your phone. When I got to your mother's place the police were already there. Two days later they found you. Nobody knows what happened that day. The police checked your phone records. I told them you phoned me about sales of your book. Nobody knows you intended to go over there. I've not told anyone.'

'And did I go there?'

'Sarah, all anybody knows is that on that day your husband was critically injured, your sister died and you went missing. Jeff died six weeks later of an infection. The police have provisionally concluded that Jeff's fall was an accident and that Arachne ran out of the house for help and fell into the path of a lorry. She died instantly. They believe there might be suspicious circumstances simply because the circumstances remain unexplained. Nobody saw you there. Nobody knows how you came to be lying on a beach over a hundred miles away. The police can only assume that the circumstances of your disappearance are an additional mystery that may be unrelated to the events at your mother's. Like Sam said, an unfortunate coincidence. Sarah, I truly don't know what happened that day and there's nobody left that can explain it. Apart from you.'

I stared at Matthew and he stared back, expressionless, probably because no expression could be adequate. I lay back on my pillows and waited for the laughter. It didn't come. Perhaps the pills were achieving something after all.

'Matthew, if the police knew I intended to go there, do you imagine they'd still think it was all an unfortunate coincidence?'

'Possibly not. It's important they don't find out.'

He crawled up to sit on the edge of my bed and rested his hand lightly across my chest. I could feel my stomach churning beneath his touch, my lips tingling as the blood failed to reach them. He had not told me all he knew, I was sure of that.

'Do you want me to remember, Matthew?'

'I want us to be happy.'

'And you think that if I remember, I'll remember something that will make that impossible? Do you know if I was there? Matthew, *tell me*!'

He shook his head. In resignation rather than denial. 'The police let me through the cordon. They were hoping I'd be able to throw light on what had happened. The clean-up team were there. Diana had been taken away. I told them I was looking for you. That I was worried because you'd been feeling unwell and you were not answering your phone. I left after about an hour and started to walk back to Crouch End.' He paused. 'Your car was parked in the next street.'

I pushed myself up. 'My car was in the next street?'

'It was unlocked. The key was in the usual place, under the mat. There was a box of books on the passenger seat. Your suitcase was in the boot. Your bag was under the driver's seat. I got in and drove to my flat and unloaded your things then I drove to Islington and parked your car round past the Indian takeaway. It was towed away a couple of days later. I told the police the builders had been parking in your place and you often had to park away from the house. I said you'd been staying with me. I had to give them your things. But I destroyed your phone.'

He waited for me to react. Eventually I did. 'So you lied to the police? Is that because you thought I'd done something awful?'

'No! I don't believe you'd hurt anyone ever. But I think it's best if the police never find out you were there. And, Sarah, just remember I love you, whatever happened that day.'

I crawled over and hugged him. He didn't deserve all this. It was as if he was being punished for caring about me. He'd been guarding these lies alone, and I couldn't even be sure I'd remember any of it by the time the morning came. And now, finally, the pills were taking effect.

I sat up and shook away the tiredness. 'We need to sleep. Will you set the alarm for eight? I'll phone first thing and tell Dr Gray we'll be there at ten. Then, if I've forgotten everything you've just told me, promise me you'll tell me again, Matthew. I'm going to work out what to do about all this, I really am!'

Episode Forty-one

I opened my eyes to see Matthew sitting on the edge of my bed, dressed and ready for another day. 'Get out this side,' he said. 'There's a mattress on the other one.'

'I remember!'

'What do you remember?' He held my dressing gown ready.

'That you were scared to sleep on your own! Did you manage to sleep?'

'After a fashion. It's twenty past eight. I've phoned Sam to say we'll be there at ten.'

I stepped out of bed. 'I said I'd do that!'

'You remember saying that?'

'Yes. We were talking until late and we were upset, so I said set the alarm for eight and I'd phone Dr Gray.'

'Do you remember what we were upset about?'

'About my husband, Jeff Blake. And a sister. Her name was ... I can't remember. I've only just woken up. Something to do with a spider.' I took a few steps towards the bathroom then paused, returned to my pillow, felt beneath it for a slip of paper and read it aloud: 'Arachne.' I folded the paper into my dressing-gown pocket. 'I've made up my mind, Matthew. Today things have to change.'

*

I picked at my breakfast and tried to piece together fragments from the previous evening's conversations: about a husband falling and a half-sister, my half-sister, running into the path of a lorry. I could remember the very clear image I had constructed when Matthew told me that. I watched him poking at his plate. 'I told you to avoid the eggs.'

'Yes, but I didn't think anyone could scramble eggs as badly as this.'

'She was called Arachne. She died. And so did Jeff Blake. But my mother is still alive and in an institution for people with dementia.'

'Sarah, that's a lot to have remembered!'

'But I can only remember being told those things. I can't remember them being real. And I can't make myself have any feelings about them.'

'But it's an enormous improvement. Last night you were forgetting those things straightaway. Every time you tried to remember there were noises, forcing you to forget.'

'They're still there, but I'm keeping them away. When I was in the shower, watching the water drain away, I started to think about those noises, the laughter and the waves. There's also the sound of waves. And I realised that I've just been letting them creep up on me and wash my memories away, letting my memories be sucked away and drowned. So I've decided to be prepared. To stay ahead of the waves. And if I do that, then I'll be able to sort out what to do about everything else.'

He half frowned, half smiled. 'That sounded so much like the Sarah you used to be.'

'But I still can't remember from before.'

'Who cares about before? Now is enough.'

I pushed my plate to one side. 'Last night, I remember we were upset. About something you told me. But I've forgotten what it was. I must have been falling asleep. It was about my car.'

As I spoke the words I could hear the laughter approaching.

'Damn it!' I grabbed my fork and poked it hard into my palm and winced at the self-inflicted pain.

Matthew leapt up. 'Sarah, what in God's name!'

I looked up at him, amazed. 'My car was parked in the street next to my mother's. You lied to the police. You moved my car.' I looked at the four small puncture wounds in my palm, two barely through the superficial layer of skin, one filling slowly with watery ooze, and one actually bleeding. 'Oh God, I must have been there when it all happened. And my mind is forcing me to forget. I have to remember! I have to know what I did.'

'You didn't do anything.' He grabbed a napkin and held it against my palm. 'Hold that there. I've got a first aid kit in the car.'

'Matthew, this is a medical institution. They'll have a plaster. Sit down for a minute.' I watched him return to his seat. 'Don't you see, I've remembered!'

'Sarah, that is not an ideal way of retrieving your memories! What are you going to do, carry a fork around with you and stab yourself in the supermarket if you can't remember what you came in for?'

'No. But don't you see? I've remembered what you told me. And that means that however tired I was, and however much my mind is working to make me forget, those memories are still there. And that probably means all my memories are there, not burned away like Sam's. I have to find a way of getting them back.'

'Not with a fork!'

'No, but somehow I have to remember what happened at my mother's house, because I really need to know I did nothing wrong. And you need to know that too.' I pulled the napkin away from my palm and frowned. 'This hurts like hell!' I scrutinised my hand.

'Matthew, where's my wedding ring?'

'Hyde Park.'

'What?'

'Are you cross because I brought sandwiches away with me?'

'No, I think it's perfectly reasonable to go to a classy reception and leave with a pile of food wrapped in a napkin.'

'The waitress said they'd go to waste if I didn't take them. And I knew we were going to be walking back through the park.'

'We're only walking back through the park because you wanted to feed those sandwiches to the ducks. This is out of our way.'

'But we've not got to be at Hillier's for ages. And Poppy said the rose garden's spectacular at the moment. And you know how much I like roses.' She linked her arm through his. 'I'll go on my own if you're going to be grumpy.'

'I'm not grumpy!'

'Is it because you're moving out of your house so Lucy can live there?'

'No, I'm quite looking forward to moving from my desirable mansion in Hampstead to a tenement in Crouch End.'

'It won't be for long.' She hugged his arm. 'And we'll be able to spend clandestine afternoons there, won't we?'

'Yes, we will.' His face broke into a smile. 'Look, madwoman, ducks ahead.'

Still hugging his arm, Sarah pulled Matthew towards the edge of the lake and started to unwrap her stash of sandwiches, an activity which caused an immediate migration of ducks out of the water and towards them.

'Sweetheart, I think they're about to stampede!'

She threw a handful of sandwiches way past the birds and they immediately turned and splashed and quacked back into the muddy water. 'It's not possible to stampede if you've only got two flat feet.'

He smirked. 'Do ducks eat prawns?'

'Looks like it.' Sarah threw another handful as far into the water as she could. And then another. 'Oh!'

'What?'

'My ring.' She watched the thick gold band arc through the sunlight and land with a plop several yards from the bank.

'What, your wedding ring?'

'Yes, it just flew off my finger. What shall I do?'

Matthew observed the dispersing ducks and the still water beyond: 'We could Google FROGMEN …'

'Matthew, this is not a laughing matter!'

'No, it's the fates seriously telling you to leave Jeff and move in with me.'

'Don't say that! We're all right as we are.'

'No, we're not. I hate that you're still with him.'

'He'll go insane if he finds out I've lost my ring.'

'Sarah, love, he won't even notice.'

He lifted her hand and kissed her ringless fingers. 'Marry me and I'll buy you a new ring. And we'll superglue it to your finger.' He pulled her towards the path. 'Come on, let's nip over to the Dorchester for a glass of cold fizz.'

'Roses first. Does the Dorchester do milkshakes?'

'Sweetheart, your sophistication never fails to astound me!'

Episode Forty-two

Bob Gray was still in his shirtsleeves when we stepped into the waiting area. The door to his consulting room was open and we could see him perched on the corner of his desk, chatting on the phone, laughing at some private joke or other. He caught sight of us and held up his hand in recognition. Sam appeared in the doorway.

'Hi, Bob's just on the phone to his daughter.'

'Hi, Sam, we're a bit early ...'

I pre-empted Matthew's explanation. 'I thought someone might fetch me a plaster.'

Sam grimaced at the napkin wrapped around my palm. 'Oh, is it bad? I'll fetch a nurse.' He disappeared through a door on the opposite side of the waiting area.

Dr Gray put the phone down, buttoned his waistcoat and put on his jacket. He frowned at the napkin. 'What's the problem?'

'I cut my hand. Sam's fetching help.'

Today Dr Gray's seats were arranged in two arcs of four, placed opposite each other at some distance, the coffee table between them. I could see that he intended for things to proceed differently after lunch. He indicated two seats towards the middle. We were joined immediately by Sam and a young nurse carrying a small first aid kit. I unwound the napkin and offered her my wound.

'Good gracious,' exclaimed Bob Gray, 'how on earth did that happen?'

'Fork!' explained Matthew.

I rolled my eyes and, while the nurse sanitised my hand, explained to Dr Gray that this was not so much self-harming but rather a counterattack on my subconscious. Without revealing what I had forced myself to remember, I explained that at breakfast I had been unable to recall things I had been told the night before, and I could hear the laughter drawing closer as I tried to recapture them. So I had launched my surprise attack, and the memories just tumbled into my thoughts. 'The best form of defence is attack, Dr Gray!'

Bob Gray nodded sagely. 'Well, my dear, well done for contriving this strategy but this stabbing process would seem to be a rather violent affront upon your psyche. I do congratulate you. However, I would rather we find a more acceptable means of controlling this anarchic mind of yours.'

'Dr Gray, I'm tired of being a victim!'

Bob Gray's eyebrows arched above the rims of his spectacles. 'Yes, I can ...' He noticed that I was pulling my hand away from the nurse's attempt at applying a bandage. 'Is something wrong?'

'No, but I don't want miles of bandage wrapped round my hand. It will look worse than it is. If Dr Williams suspects I've been damaging myself, he'll have me sectioned.'

Sam snorted. Bob Gray frowned. 'Now, Sarah, that is not a realistic concern.' He looked at the nurse who was clearly not certain how to proceed. 'Do we have a plaster, nurse? Perhaps if you could ...'

Bob Gray waited for the nurse to apply the plaster and leave then took the seat beside me and asked Sam if he had anything new to contribute. Sam sat down beside Matthew. 'No, I'd just like to ask Matthew if he secretly cloned Sarah in the night and left the original up on the third floor.'

'This *is* the original,' said Matthew.

Sam smiled at me. 'You're different. What happened?'

'She had an epiphany in the shower,' said Matthew.

Again Sam snorted. It was left to Bob Gray to pull the session back to serious. But his blue eyes betrayed amusement. He asked me to summarise, so I explained that I had discovered I could retain new memories by re-remembering them and being ready to pounce when the forgetting tried to happen. 'Dr Gray, I think too much time elapsed while I was unconscious and my memories were hidden before I could re-remember them.'

'And how do you feel about that?' he asked.

'It's like there are two separate minds living in my brain and battling for custody of my memories. Do you think I have a split personality?'

'My goodness, where on earth did you get an idea like that?'

'Mrs Parkin said Dr Williams was interested in schizophrenia, so I looked it up.'

'No, no, Sarah. We are not treating you for anything that could possibly be referred to as schizophrenia. Our focus is your memory loss. And we are all anticipating the complete recovery of your memories and of your normal life.'

'Assuming that those two things are compatible,' I said.

Dr Gray paused to glance over at Sam. 'Sarah, all things can be dealt with and dealing with things is ultimately preferable to denying them.' He placed his hands on his knees. 'Matthew, I think we are all aware of Sarah's new determination. Would you like to mention any recent changes you have noticed in her general mode of expression?'

'What does that mean?' I demanded.

Matthew placed a reassuring hand on my arm. 'Since yesterday, but particularly this morning, I told you that you were sounding more like you. Dr Gray's clearly noticed it.'

'Can you notice it yourself, Sarah?' asked Bob Gray. 'Do you feel more able to think things, or more able to find the words to express what you're thinking?'

I considered the question. 'I don't think I feel either of those things. I suppose I just feel more confident. But, I presume that's what words do, they give you confidence.'

'Absolutely! Where would we be without our words! Sam, any comments?'

Sam looked up from note-taking. 'I did notice a change last night but I wasn't sure whether it was the informal circumstances. But this is great, Sarah.'

I folded my arms. 'Are you all implying that I've spent the last several weeks sounding like a complete cretin?'

Sam laughed. 'Not exactly, it's just there's such a marked change of authority. You said you were fed up with being a victim. I think that realization is influencing the way you express yourself, how you interact with others. You're more in control, Sarah.'

'But I still can't remember from before.'

'But you are coping with your life as it is now,' explained Bob Gray. 'Remembering how to make decisions, how to interact with people, that's all built up over long years of experience. You lost much of that experience along with your memories. You became a stranger in your own world and over these last few weeks you've been striving to get back to where you were before. It probably involved reaching some kind of psychological critical mass.'

'But, without my past, how can I be a whole person?'

'All in good time, Sarah. Now that we have you back as a fully-functional person … and I realise how much we need to thank you for that, Matthew … Now we can start to worry about retrieving your past. But, let's not be too desperate. We can do without most of the past. Most of it we are *all* free to forget.'

The phrase unnerved me. I looked into Dr Gray's quiet, blue eyes and tried to decipher any hidden implication behind that statement.

'Dr Gray, terrible things happened and I need to know I did nothing wrong before I can reclaim my life.'

'I fully understand that. The improvement in your ability to retain new information is a significant step in that direction. But right now we need to understand the way in which this strategy of your unconscious mind has affected you. So, if it's OK with you, I'm going to ask Matthew to tell me about the Sarah he has known over the last three weeks compared to the Sarah he knew before. It will give us a clearer picture of the disorder your unconscious mind has levelled upon you. Is that OK with you?'

I nodded my approval, so Bob Gray turned to Matthew. 'Matthew, enough of the festering silence. Tell us about Sarah. Then and now. You can edit out the more embarrassing details.'

Matthew sat back and folded his arms. 'It's all pretty embarrassing. But here goes. From day one: I was in my office …'

Episode Forty-three

I listened to Matthew's abridged account of our relationship both professional and personal, everything from our first chaotic meeting up to but not including the events of the previous December. A past I was now able to know only through his recollections. I listened to him describe our slow reunion since that supermarket morning. Dr Gray thanked him then asked me if I could single out a moment of pure, unbridled happiness in those last three weeks. I closed my eyes and relived the days one at a time.

'On Primrose Hill. Our first kiss.' I opened my eyes and smiled. 'Our second first kiss.'

'And there would have been a first first kiss that would have also made you happy?'

'Yes. Possibly terrified, but undoubtedly happy.'

'So your mind has …'

'Stolen that moment as some wretched by-product of expunging my memories.'

'I suppose if we were military men we might call that collateral damage,' said Bob Gray. He opened the folder on his lap. 'Now, Sam has recently interviewed your friend Annabelle …'

'And you survived?' mumbled Matthew.

'It was a telephone interview,' said Sam. He pulled his chair round. 'Sarah, from what Annabelle told me and a few other sources, I've been able to construct a reasonably thorough timeline for you. But before we look at that I'd like you to show me how *you* see the period from when you woke in the hospital compared with your time living with your grandmother. But, in particular, I'd like you to show us how you see the period from the time you left your grandmother to the time you woke up in the hospital.'

I looked at Sam's earnest brown eyes then slowly I shook my head. 'I don't see the years between, Sam. If I try to think further back than the clinic, my memories take me straight back to my grandma. But they're fuzzy memories because they're so long ago. And I know I ought to remember things. But I don't.'

'You're aware that things are missing?'

'Yes. Is that important?'

'It's another indication of the competence of your mental processing. In some cases of memory loss, the patient attempts to reconcile missing events by inventing something to bridge the gap. It's a kind of strategy for making the best of available information. And the patient believes these alternative narratives are true. They're tantamount to false memories. It's called confabulation. But your brain is not resorting to it. Your mind is erasing your time, but you're not being fazed by it into patching things together to deny what it's up to.'

'Should that make me feel good about myself?'

'Yes, I think it should,' said Sam. 'I think that you have a very competent mind, despite your memory dysfunction. And, right now, I'd like to investigate a particular component of your declarative memory, which we refer to as your autobiographical memory. It determines how you've stored details of time and place, along your *personal* timeline. Is that OK?' He frowned at my compromised hand. 'You're right handed, yes?'

'Yes!'

'Just as well. Your counteroffensive might have ruined this entire experiment.' He handed me a felt tip and a long strip of card, perhaps a metre wide and six inches high, with a bold black line running along its centre. He waited as I balanced it across my lap. 'OK, this is your timeline. At the moment it's empty. So would you start by writing your date of birth on the far left of the line and NOW on the far right?'

I did as I was asked.

'OK, starting backwards from NOW, I'd like you to mark along the last stretch of the line anything you can remember since waking up in hospital. Try to label everything in the correct order.' He watched me carrying out his instruction. Then he asked me to start on the far left and note down my earliest memories. I shifted the card then paused.

'Dr Gray gave me photos of my birthday. That's a new memory isn't it?'

'Yes. But you did say the photos evoked actual memories, so include them.'

So I marked down my seventh birthday, the Ribena incident, my granny going into hospital. I paused again: 'I remember a little rag doll, but I had her for a long time.' Sam suggested I mark her down where it seemed most appropriate. So I did. I looked up.

'I've no idea what happened to that doll. She was called Raggedy.'

'Raggedy?' said Matthew.

'Yes! And we had a cat, but it wasn't always the same one. Unless it was a magical cat that changed colour. I could put the cats down in the order I remember them.'

'That would be fantastic, Sarah!'

When I'd finished locating my memories, Sam asked me to focus on the middle section of my timeline.

'You'll notice that, not only is that middle section empty, it is also disproportionately short.'

'Does that tell you anything?'

'Yes, it does! Essentially, there are two things to consider when we think back over our lives. One is the long stretch of time that has passed and the other is the events that fit into it. Your mind has been working to expunge those events. And, metaphorically speaking, if there are no events in time to maintain its integrity, then it shrinks away.'

'But if my memories come back, will there be time left for them to fit back into?'

'Sarah, nothing is actually disappearing. This is just a representation of the way your mind is diminishing your time. But, if you're going to confront this mind of yours, it's essential you realise what it's denying you. It might help you refine your own *conscious* strategies.'

'Do you think that's possible?'

'Yes! You already have successful strategies. Apart from the fork counteroffensive, which we do not recommend. You believe you can outmanoeuvre the repression by pre-empting it. And you're also re-remembering. We all have implicit, procedural memory, which deals with everyday skills. It involves repetition. You're managing to mimic that repetitive process against attempts by your mind to wipe the slate clean.'

I looked from Sam to Dr Gray and felt inclined to complain. 'You've all known that my mind was still *wiping my slate clean* but you never told me.'

Bob Gray regarded me over his spectacles. 'We find ourselves here not up against a static retrograde amnesia, which would be difficult enough. We are instead confronting a more dynamic, on-going repression. Right now things are improving and new information is being retained. That's more than we hoped for a few weeks ago, I have to say. And we don't want anything to confuse these improvements. We are your physicians. We are not so much concerned with your past; we are concerned with helping you remember it. Do you want to remember your lost time, Sarah?'

'Yes, I do.'

'Then we must go back to the beginning.' He handed me a folder. 'This is your story up to about a year ago. Let's take a look at it. Then when you're ready we'll try moving closer to the moment things went astray.'

I opened the folder and smiled at the first page. A single photo. A new child, fresh into the world, ready to embrace a life unchosen. In her tiny plastic crib, fingers splayed with the horror of new light and noise and smells, the little girl lay learning her life. New things had to be dealt with and dealt with straightaway. But more than anything she would have to remember so much. I couldn't remember back then, nobody can, but I could imagine the feeling of isolation. And I could feel some inexplicable sadness. Perhaps because I knew that that small girl would one day be sitting in this room with a past so terrible that to remember it was incompatible with any happiness she had ever known. I breathed a sigh.

'Where did you get this from, Sam?'

'From your photo albums. It's a copy. We've put all the originals back as they were.'

I mustered a smile and turned the page: a baby in her mother's arms; a toddler with her mother paddling in the sea; a tiny girl stumbling towards a man's outstretched arms.

'Is that my father? What was he called?'

Sam answered. 'Jack Clark. He and your mother separated when you were two years old, but he visited several times when you were at your grandmother's, for possibly another three years. According to Annabelle, you tried to trace him when you were in college. She thinks he emigrated to Australia. We're trying to check.'

'Sam, where did my parents live when they were together?'

'You were born in Wimbledon. The 1981 census lists both your parents as living there in April of that year. On the night of the 1991 census your mother was living in the house in Hornsey with you and your half-sister.'

'Do you remember the name Hornsey?' interrupted Matthew.

'I think Sam mentioned it last night.' There was an exchange of glances.

Sam continued. 'Your stepfather, John Dawson, had left by this time. He and your mother separated just after you went to live with her following your grandmother's death.'

'Did they blame me for him leaving.'

Dr Gray held up his hand. 'According to Miss Grant, you were, quite wrongly, accused of contributing to the breakdown of this second marriage by both your mother and your half-sister. You were never close to either of them. It's far more likely that the marriage fell apart due to alcohol abuse. Your mother and Dawson were both addicted to alcohol. Dawson was twice arrested for driving under the influence of alcohol and barbiturates. It was while driving under such influence that he caused the accident which took his life.' He looked at me. 'It seems that it was at this point that your mother resumed her excessive drinking.'

Sam indicated the folder. 'The next pages illustrate the years with your grandmother in Kent, near Margate. There are several seaside images. Two of your father. There are others in your collection around this time. One of them shows a rock face in the background. It's a bit of a long shot but we're trying to determine whether it could have been taken by the cliffs at Beer Cove.'

'Where?'

'It's where you were found,' said Sam.

I shook my head and turned the pages, looked at scenes, vaguely familiar. I pointed to a garden photo. 'It's Raggedy and the ginger cat!'

'I thought you'd like that one!' said Sam.

My school report at age seven spoke of the creative imagination of a child whose writing would be improved if she concentrated more on her spelling. I laughed.

'Grandma said one day computers would do my spelling for me. What did Granny Clark die of?'

'Pancreatic cancer,' said Sam. 'Quite suddenly.'

'I hope my memories of her are safe. I'll keep remembering them just to be sure. Do you know how often my mother visited when I was at my grandma's?'

'It seems she came down a few times. In the most recent of the Margate shots, she has the new baby with her.'

I found the photo. Studied myself, standing beside my mother, slightly apart, looking up at her. The mother I couldn't remember, smiling down at the new baby in her arms. I looked at myself, probably eight years old; at the woman, thin and pale but still recognisable as the mother of the elder daughter that had been me. But now the baby in her arms was the half-sister, asleep, protected, whereas I had been sent away. Her baby fingers were just distinguishable against the mother's bare arm. Touching as I was untouched. Included as I was excluded. I felt a deep pang of rejection echo across the forgotten years. My eyes became uncontrollably fixed upon the tiny fingers. And then the tiny fingers began to move, closed tight against soft skin and pulled the mother's arm further away from the untouched girl. When the laughter came, it came from within the mother's arms. I gasped.

'She's laughing at me!'

Sam pulled the folder away. Slowly I relaxed. 'I'm sorry, I forgot to be ready.'

'Is the laughter there now?' said Sam.

I shook my head. 'It's a long way away. It was the sister. My mother holding her. Arachne. I remember her name. Why? I can't remember anything about either of them.'

'But you clearly did,' said Bob Gray. 'And they are clearly at the heart of your anxieties. Your husband maybe not so much. But then husbands and wives come and go and you can get over them. Fathers and mothers and sisters can break a child's heart forever.' He clasped his hands together. 'Now, it's almost lunchtime, so why don't we …?'

'But Dr Gray, what about the rest of the folder?'

'Perhaps tomorrow, Sarah. The next section details the years you lived with your mother and sister.

Episode Forty-four

Geraint Williams's contingent filed into the consulting room. I watched a brief flicker of irritation in his eyes as he directed Professor Bluet to her seat.

'Bob,' he said. 'I hope you don't mind: I've invited Andrew Booker to observe today.'

He indicated a youngish man who looked as if he had just emerged, newly-suited, from his Bond Street tailor; even Geraint Williams looked shoddy beside him.

'Andrew, let me introduce Robert Gray, our senior clinician and Dr Samuel Clegg, our research psychologist, seconded from Manchester University. This is Dr Andrew Booker from Dubrais Pharmaceuticals.'

Bob Gray got to his feet and offered his hand. 'Dr Booker, welcome. Geraint, we had better ask Ms Blake if she is happy to continue with these interviews in front of such a large gathering. Particularly, in the light of yesterday's turn of events.' He turned towards me. 'Sarah? I know you're feeling quite exhausted after this morning's session.'

I enjoyed a brief and quite malicious satisfaction at the look of surprise on Geraint Williams' face as I offered Andrew Booker my hand.

'I hope I prove to be sufficiently interesting to justify your time, Dr Booker. This is my partner, Matthew Parry.' I watched Matthew and Andrew Booker shake hands. Aesthetically it was very pleasing; psychologically it was more pleasing than that.

When everybody was seated, Bob Gray opened the session. He gave a brief summary of my new strategies then asked me if I would confirm these developments in my own words. I tried not to feel too exhilarated by the significant narrowing of Geraint Williams' eyes as I addressed my audience, although his clear annoyance provided me with the precise burst of confidence I needed. I described how I was able to confront the threatened removal of my new memories by pre-empting the aura.

'Are you hearing the laughter all the time, Sarah?' asked Isabel Bluet.

'No, Professor Bluet, but I know it's there. I think it has something to do with my sister and mother. I have no memory of them and it seems my mind doesn't want me to ever remember them.'

Geraint Williams barely waited for me to finish speaking. 'I am hoping to …' He paused, clearly dissatisfied with the way in which Shoumi Mustafa was wobbling in an attempt to comment. '… I will be hoping to demonstrate any changes in the pattern of recall during this coming Tuesday's MRI session. The scans …'

'Dr Williams, I'm sorry to interrupt, but I won't be able to attend this Tuesday. I have a prior engagement with my editor to discuss my latest series of children's books.'

All attention in the room was directed at me. Geraint Williams broke the silence. 'Sarah, this is an expensive procedure. We were fortunate to acquire a slot at short notice.'

'Well, I'm very sorry, but I really am not able to make alternative arrangements. My editor has already been forced to make changes to accommodate these days at the clinic. I was unaware that another scan was planned. And I assumed that, following these extended sessions, next week's scheduled interview would be unnecessary.'

Geraint Williams frowned at Shoumi Mustafa, whose increased fidgeting was now accompanied by an obsequious waving of his hand. 'Shoumi, in a second, please! Sarah, we have reached a critical stage in our assessment. If this observation is not made, and made urgently, there is every possibility that something significant will be overlooked, and this might have repercussions in the future.'

I glanced at Bob Gray. His eyebrows appeared above the rims of his spectacles. He had clearly decided to allow me to handle this disagreement. I turned back to Geraint Williams. 'Dr Williams, I am really grateful for everybody's concern, but I hope that on this occasion you'll allow me to take responsibility. You must realise that my writing is very important to my future. I think Dr Mustafa wants to contribute.'

'In a moment, Shoumi!' exclaimed Dr Williams. He turned to Bob Gray. 'Bob, I must question Ms Blake's competence with regard to the management of her own ill-defined psychosis. Patients with dissociative disorders often exaggerate their own abilities.'

'Geraint, I fully agree with you regarding the spectrum of competence within the group of disorders we refer to as dissociative.' He softened his tone. 'And I am very aware that, in Sarah's case, we are treading unmapped territory. But I do assure you that, after these most recent sessions, I have no doubts about her ability to make decisions, or about the importance of Sarah continuing to maintain her professional life.'

Geraint Williams grasped the bottom of his waistcoat. 'Bob, with respect …'

His protest was interrupted by my most convincing sneeze. I touched my fingers over my nose. 'I'm so sorry!' I glanced across at the folder on Sam's lap. 'Does anyone know whether I suffer from hay fever?'

Dr Gray smiled. 'I'm sure that will be somewhere in our notes.' He handed me a box of tissues. 'Compliments of the house. Now, where were we? Ah, yes, will our guests still be available next Tuesday week?'

Isabel Bluet said that she would be; Dr Booker said that he was fully booked, but he would follow my case with great interest.

'Excellent!' said Bob Gray. 'Geraint, could we possibly reorganise the scan?'

Dr Williams paused for a brief moment: 'Quite so, Bob. I will have my assistant co-ordinate with all concerned.'

'Excellent! Now, perhaps we ought to ask Shoumi what he wants to say.'

I noticed Sam pinching his nose.

Shoumi Mustafa sat forward. 'It's Ms Blake's language. Her presentation is completely changed!'

'Would you like to elaborate, Shoumi?' said Geraint Williams, once again grasping the ascendancy. He addressed his guests. 'As you know, Shoumi is investigating the relationship between memory and language. Shoumi, please, your comments.'

Shoumi Mustafa proceeded to address Dr Williams and his guests, ignoring everyone else. He detailed my immature speech patterns from previous tapes and interviews, my diminished vocabulary, inability to suggest synonyms, specifically regarding certain thematically-linked or emotive-content words. He stressed my previous tendency to rely upon simple single-clause sentences, with the occasional compound rather than complex constructions, whereas today I had demonstrated a command of subordination and multiple embedding within complex sentences. I was clearly more relaxed with sentence modality which indicated greater confidence with both assertion and interrogation. This increased confidence was also obvious, today, in my lexical choices, my use of extended noun phrases and the tone and the controlled meter of my discourse.

Professor Bluet waited for a pause and asked if Dr Mustafa might give examples of these changes, since her understanding of psycholinguistics was quite basic. I listened to Shoumi Mustafa detail my changing discourse and marvelled at the extent to which this zealous man had recorded my utterances. I noticed Geraint Williams' fixed smile disappear. Five minutes into the presentation, he interrupted. 'Shoumi, I'm sure that by now everyone has a very clear picture of the patient's altered speech patterns. I wonder if we might determine whether there have been any other changes in her capacity to recall. I speak of course not of instruction since the catastrophic incident, but rather of anything from before. Has anything arisen in the previous session, Bob?'

Bob Gray turned to me: 'Sarah, would you like to mention memories that have been evoked by reminders of *any* kind?'

I noticed a slight sparkle in his eyes. I looked at Dr Mustafa. 'Since *the incident*, my ability to write trailed behind my ability to read. But, recently, I've been able to write …'

'And other than the writing skills?' interrupted Geraint Williams. 'Any changes in your capacity to recall anything from before the catastrophic incident?

As best I could, I mimicked the insincerity of his smile. 'I remember making love, not any actual occasion, but I was certain I already knew the emotional intensity. And I knew I had experienced those moments with Matthew. I knew it was with him.'

There was a brief silence. Geraint Williams' expression changed from scorn to surprise. Dr Mustafa's pen was still. Dr Booker shuffled in his chair. Then Professor Bluet spoke. 'Those feelings run deep, Sarah. The sensory memory snaps up those sensations and passes them on for encoding and storage. And it seems that, however they are stored long term, the mind finds ways of clinging on to them.' She leaned forward in her chair. 'Are you saying that when Matthew introduced himself, in a shopping mall, I believe, you did not recognise him? Yet when you were intimate, you were able to recognise your intimacy? And am I correct in assuming that still no memory of your previous relationship has returned?'

'Yes, I …'

'We are still trying to assess the repercussions of Mr Parry's supermarket stunt,' interrupted Geraint Williams. 'He risked sending Ms Blake into crisis both then and at every stage of his reintroduction into her life, not least of all on the occasion of sexual intercourse.'

'Occasions,' I said. 'Dr Williams, I assure you, I was very proactive in re-establishing my relationship with Matthew. Looking back on our meeting, I think that somehow I anticipated the intimacy from before.'

Professor Bluet laughed. 'Sarah, I'd be delighted to read your account of these experiences.' She glanced up at Geraint Williams. 'If that's OK by you, Geraint? I have a small group investigating these exact areas of emotional priming.' She turned to Bob Gray. 'We're interested in the role of emotion and sensation in memory processing, the haptic and tactile components. But other members of the faculty would be interested in Sarah's language recovery. We believe that some words are learned tagged with episodic components. Shoumi, have you considered lexical tagging?'

'Isabel,' interrupted Geraint Williams, 'Shoumi will be presenting his findings in tomorrow's seminar …'

'I'd be pleased to write about my sensory memories, Professor Bluet,' I said before Dr Williams could say more. 'If that's OK with my physicians.'

*

As soon as we were safely ensconced in our lounge, I eased the plaster from my palm and assessed the damage.

'Is it OK?' Matthew asked.

'I'll live.' I watched him wander over to the window to check his car. 'I wish I'd seen you punch Geraint Williams.'

He turned and folded his arms. 'It was a modest slap. Nothing as devastating as your lack of doctor-patient subordination this afternoon. Have you actually arranged a meeting with Poppy next Tuesday?'

'No.'

*

Once again Sam arrived as supper was being cleared. Tonight his laptop bag concealed four cans of Heineken.

'Dr Clegg,' said Matthew: 'I hope this isn't compromising your professional distance.'

'Definitely not.' He turned to me and laughed. 'Loved the bit about emotional memory. That definitely got Issy Bluet going.'

I threw myself onto the sofa. 'So, Sam, exactly what gets *you* going?'

'Sam,' said Matthew, 'this is almost the original Sarah you see before you. As tactful as a category five hurricane.'

Sam smiled at me. 'Girlfriend in Manchester. She didn't want to come here. I didn't want to stay there. So not much action at the moment.'

Time passed. We discussed possible strategies, some ludicrous, for defeating my unconscious antagonist. And I tried to embrace them all. 'But, Sam,' I said, 'I'm worried there will always be an impasse and that my mind will never let me remember that day. I'm terrified about how I might have been involved. How I finished up where they found me. And I'm scared that if I try to remember too much, I'll wake up one morning and my head will be completely empty.'

'I don't think the empty head is likely,' said Sam. He set his glass down and watched me for a moment. 'Sarah, when I mentioned Beer Cove today, had you really never heard that name? Do you not remember anybody mentioning it to you previously?'

I shook my head.

'I've mentioned it. Twice.'

I looked at Matthew. 'What?'

'It's obviously towards the top of the list of things you mustn't remember. To start off with you were also blocking any mention of Hornsey, but you seem to be able to remember that now.'

'It's where my mother lived. Where it all happened.'

'But you don't remember any previous mention of Beer Cove?' said Sam.

'I remember you mentioning it this afternoon. But not before today.'

'That suggests it's a significant location. It's not far from where you were at uni. I asked Annabelle but she said she'd never heard of it.

'Can either of you imagine what it's like, having to wage this internal war all the time? It tires me out to think that it's going to be forever, that each time I lose concentration, I'll start to regress. It's like being eaten away from the inside. I've got to think of a way of beating it.' I got to my feet. 'I'll fetch my pills.' But as I wandered towards my room a thought suddenly occurred to me. I turned and looked at Sam: 'Matthew said these pills send me into deep sleep. But maybe when I'm asleep, I can't fight the forgetting.'

'You think the repression operates when you're asleep?' asked Sam.

I wandered back and sat down. 'Perhaps when I'm not fully conscious I can't challenge the repression. Which is why I'd forgotten so much to start off with. Perhaps each evening when I take my pills I'm handing the advantage to my subconscious.'

'It's important you sleep,' said Matthew.

'But it's not normal sleep, is it? And I didn't take the pills the night I wrote my story. Or the first night you stayed. I've got no idea what the daytime pills even are.'

'They're antidepressants and an antipsychotic,' said Sam.

'Well, I'm not depressed and I don't want to be taking pills.'

Sam frowned. 'Bob's reviewing your medication tomorrow with a view to reducing the sedatives. But, it's unlikely he'll recommend discontinuing any of your other drugs just yet.'

'Well, I'm not taking my pills tonight. This is a war I have to win!'

'But no more forks, right?' said Sam.

Episode Forty-five

'Can we go home now, Daddy? I'm cold. And the tide is here.'

'There's plenty of time, Sarah! I just need to break this big piece of shale open. Because inside I'm going to find you the biggest fossil you've ever seen.'

'But I don't want any more fossils.'

'Just wait 'til you see this one!'

'Daddy, the tide's in my shoes! And Raggedy's frightened.'

'Well, take her up the steps.'

'Will you come too?'

'Yes. Hurry, it's up to your knees.'

'Daddy, the steps are very slippery.'

'Go further up. That's right. Wait at the top.'

'Hurry up, Daddy! That big wave will be over your shoulders!'

'No! Raggedy, come back, don't leave me!

'Daddy, I dropped Raggedy and she's run away.

'Daddy, I can't see you anymore.

'Daddy, is that you?'

'Give me your hand and I'll pull you up.

'Daddy, your fingers are too wet. I can't hold you tight enough.

'Daddy, come back

*

'Sarah, wake up, it's just a dream!'

Matthew was leaning over me. I grabbed his sleeve. 'My rag doll ran away. And the sea was washing my father away and it was trying to pull me down with him. I can't remember any more.'

'That's normal. Everyone forgets dreams when they wake up. How do you feel?'

I let go of his sleeve. 'OK, I think.' I sat up and peered down beside the bed. 'Where's the mattress?'

'I put it back. Tonight we sleep in a proper bed.'

I lay back on my pillows. 'Matthew, when we move to Hampstead, can we buy a new bed? I don't really want to sleep in the bed you slept in with Lucy.'

'I don't particularly want to sleep in the bed I slept in with Lucy either. And I haven't much enjoyed sleeping in the bed you shared with …' He paused.

'With Jeff Blake. See, I remember.'

'Yes, well, that's something I'd eventually like you to forget.'

I watched him walk over to open the blinds, imagined being with him forever. I hoped forever might happen. I couldn't feel it was a certainty. I thought about all those forgotten years with Jeff Blake. Living beneath that giant kitchen. Just the two of us. Almost eight years and just the two of us.

'Matthew, do you think me and Jeff Blake couldn't have babies? Because I'd like us …' But suddenly pain was ripping through me. I pulled my knees up against its intensity and fell willingly into forgetfulness.

When I opened my eyes, Bob Gray was sitting on the bed beside me. Matthew was standing next to him, his face full of concern. Sam was at the end of the bed, arms folded.

'Welcome back,' said Dr Gray. 'Do you remember where you are?'

I looked around me. 'I'm at the clinic. It's Saturday. I'm going home later. I had a half-sister, called Arachne, my mother is alive and I used to be married. And I remember where they found me. Beer Cove. And I had a really bad pain. Here.' I touched my groin.

'Is it still there?' asked Dr Gray.

'No, not at all. How long was I unconscious?'

'Less than ten minutes,' said Matthew. 'These guys move fast.'

'Do you remember what was happening when the pain started?' said Bob Gray.

I shook my head. 'I remembered something too close, didn't I? It's like I said: there are things that my mind will never let me remember. And it's willing to rip me apart and make me unconscious if I try.' I placed my hands over my face. 'I've achieved nothing!'

'Now you know that's not true, Sarah,' insisted Bob Gray. 'You're managing to retain new information. And that's something you were not able to do just a few days ago. You've made enormous progress. And you'll carry on doing so. But we have to remember none of it is going to be easy. So, why don't you rest for a while and we'll wait downstairs for you?'

He went to stand, but I caught his sleeve.

'We were talking.' I looked up at Matthew. 'Do you know what it was that did this to me as soon as I mentioned it?'

'I think there were a number of things that ...'

'Exacerbated the collapse,' said Sam.

*

I watched my blood fill first one tube then another. I always worried that, if the nurse fainted and let go, my blood would gush out onto the floor until I was completely empty. I knew that was a stupid thing to think but knowing the foolishness of one's thoughts never stops them from happening. I was relieved when the bloodletting was over and further haemorrhaging was being prevented by a blob of cotton wool and a strip of transparent tape.

'We probably won't get any joy with that lot until Monday,' said Bob Gray. 'So we'll review your drug regime by the time we see you next Wednesday. We'll do an entire profile. Check your ...'

'Human?' suggested Sarah.

Dr Gray peered over his glasses. 'That will not be necessary, Sarah.' He glanced at Matthew. 'Are you all right, Matthew? You're very pale.'

'I'm not that keen on the blood thing.'

I rolled my eyes. 'Do you want to go outside for a bit?'

'No, I'm OK.'

Dr Gray indicated the arc of chairs. 'Just the four of us today. There's a research seminar that takes precedence.'

I glanced at Sam. 'Don't you need to go to it?'

'God, no. I've got proper things to do.'

Bob Gray took his place beside me. 'Now,' he began, 'I had scheduled a session of hypnosis, but Sam and I have discussed what could possibly be gained by it at the moment. The two previous sessions were unproductive and my feeling is that it would achieve nothing. I think that, now you have demonstrated that you can overcome much of the dynamic component of the amnesia, our time would be better spent trying to determine the more recent focus of this unconscious repression. We think that the best way of helping you remember your past will be to actively investigate it rather than simply present it to you in a linear sequence.'

I felt a wave of apprehension pass down my chest and settle in my stomach. 'How?' I asked trying to sound more engaged than hysterical.

'By constructing a three-dimensional map of everything we know and then trying to fill in the gaps. To determine whether there is a sequence that links the events at your mother's house with your being found two days later on the south coast. It's undoubtedly what lies in the gaps that your mind is determined to deny you access to.'

'Do you think that's wise?' asked Matthew. 'You've seen how this affects her.'

'We'll take this very slowly.'

'I'm really not happy,' he snapped.

'Matthew, I need to know.' I looked at Dr Gray, holding his gaze for a few moments. 'The things I tell you, are they in confidence?'

'Of course.'

'Will Dr Williams be entitled to listen to this recording?'

'You'd prefer that not to be the case?'

Matthew got to his feet. 'Sarah, please!'

'Matthew, sit down! I can't do this on my own.' He sat down.

Bob Gray asked Sam to stop the recording and delete the session so far. Sam did as instructed then asked me if I would prefer him to leave. I insisted he stay. I folded my arms about my stomach to control the dual sensations of nausea and panic and the room became filled with expectation, silent apart from the distant sound of voices, perhaps coming from outside, perhaps approaching from within.

'Dr Gray, I truly have no recollection of the events of that day or of the two days I was missing. But Matthew does. He told me something the night before last and I've remembered him telling me. And it's something that might suggest a link between what happened at my mother's house and my disappearance. Matthew hasn't shared this information with anyone else, because he's trying to protect me. But it's not a burden I want him to bear. I'd be grateful if this remains confidential. Can I depend upon that?'

'Yes, Sarah,' said Dr Gray.

'Of course,' said Sam.

I touched Matthew's pale hand. 'I need to say this.'

'Sarah, you don't!'

But I knew I did. 'That day ...'

*

'So we must assume, from what Matthew told you, that your intention was to visit your mother's house that afternoon, and that your car being parked nearby would suggest you did just that. And that when you went missing it would likely have been following this visit. Are you hearing the aura at the moment?'

'Not really. Dr Gray, I'm terrified I might have done something awful and it's that thing that my mind is forcing me to forget.'

'And the police have not been informed of these facts?'

'No.' I frowned at Matthew's persistent pallor. 'Matthew, are you still feeling woozy?'

He looked up and forced a smile.

I noticed Bob Gray glance over at Sam before walking over to refer to a folder, open on his desk. He seemed suddenly to arrive at a decision.

'Sarah, I think I *would* like to try a session of deep relaxation. If these new details are pertinent, we might be able to use them ...'

'What does that mean?' snapped Matthew.

'It means that, following hypnotic induction, we might be able to use this new information to lever our way into …'

'Like a crowbar!'

I was surprised at Matthew's anger. But Bob Gray remained calm. 'No, as a means of focussing in, away from peripheral awareness, to allow Sarah to investigate her own dissociative state.'

'There's controversy over the use of hypnosis in the recovery of repressed memories, because of the fear that false memories will be recalled. Sarah has imagined things about that day and it might be that those imagined memories seem like real memories.'

Bob Gray frowned. 'Well researched, Matthew. The answer to any such confusion would be corroboration.' He turned to me, his voice still calm. 'Sarah, would you be willing for me to attempt to access your memories via this new information.'

'Will Matthew be able to stay?'

'I'm afraid not. To achieve a hypnotic state we have to reduce all awareness of surroundings. We'll ask Matthew to take a walk in the gardens.' He glanced at Matthew. 'The air might do him good.'

'I don't need air. But I'll wait outside, if that's what you want.'

'I'll be all right,' I assured him. 'It probably won't work.'

Dr Gray walked over and opened the door. 'Matthew, I'll call you back in when we're ready.'

Matthew turned as he left the room, his face pale and drawn. 'Sarah, now is enough.'

Sam stayed where he was, with Matthew's empty chair still between us. Bob Gray returned to sit beside me. 'Now, Sarah, tell me again what you know about that day.'

'Are you going to hypnotise me?'

'Not for the moment. Just start by telling me again what you believe happened.'

'And this is still not being recorded?'

'No.'

So I repeated the picture I had of my involvement that day, all the while wondering what Matthew was doing outside. Sam seemed to be writing notes throughout, so as soon as I'd finished, I asked him if what I had just said was consistent with my previous version.

'Spot on,' he said. But he looked troubled.

Bob Gray leaned forward in his chair and inhaled deeply. 'Sarah, you realise that we have no way of confirming these facts and that your knowledge of them depends entirely upon information gained from Matthew alone?'

'What do you mean?'

'I mean that, given your current state of memory loss, you have no way of knowing whether any of it is true.'

'Are you suggesting Matthew would lie?'

I watched Dr Gray return to his desk to fetch the open folder. Sam shuffled awkwardly in his chair. Bob Gray walked back towards me, reading, his glasses balanced on the end of his nose.

'I've just this morning been copied a report regarding Della Brown's investigation of the events of last December. She states that you were convincingly ignorant not only of the events of the afternoon in question and of the circumstances which caused you to finish up where you were found, but also of your entire adult life to the extent that you have been rendered socially inept.' He regarded me above his glasses. 'I wouldn't pay any attention to that last comment. However, she cautions that the involvement both of yourself and Matthew Parry on the day in question remains unresolved.' He sat down beside me. 'She has requested a further interview with you, in the presence of Dr Williams or myself. Specifically, to discuss Matthew.'

'Do they suspect that Matthew moved my car?'

'How do you know that Matthew moved your car, Sarah? In fact, how do you know your car was parked anywhere near your mother's house? That you made that call?'

'Matthew told me.'

The police questioned Matthew about his whereabouts earlier that day and throughout the afternoon. They were keen to know when he had last seen Jeff Blake.'

'Why?'

'Because your husband's business partner, Alex Harris, told them that Matthew had argued with Jeff Blake two days earlier and had struck him several times.'

'Matthew hit my husband?'

'According to Mr Harris, Matthew confronted Jeff over his persistent affairs. And it got out of hand.'

'Has Matthew spoken to you about it?'

'No. It has no bearing on your treatment.'

I looked down at my lap. 'You said we were going to try a session of hypnosis. Was that so that you could accuse Matthew behind his back?'

'We needed to speak to you in private, Sarah. We are your physicians, but we are concerned not only about your medical recovery, we are also concerned about your safety.'

'My *safety*?'

'We must consider the possibility that Matthew has not been telling the truth. That you did not make that call and that your car was not parked where he said it was. And that perhaps Matthew has his own reasons for wanting you to believe you were at your mother's house when the incident occurred.'

'Why would he want that?'

'To hide the fact that he was there himself.'

Episode Forty-six

So few words, yet they were enough to empty my life all over again. I closed my eyes. I could hear Bob Gray's voice retreating into the distance, laughter further away than that. The cry of the gulls rising above the waves, lulling me to sleep. For a hundred years if necessary until everything about that day was far away and long forgotten. Even Matthew ... I opened my eyes.

'I want Matthew back in here now!'

Bob Gray was still beside me. 'Sarah, we have had to tell you these things.'

'I know that, Dr Gray. I'm grateful for your candour but, since what you've just suggested bears such relevance to Matthew, I feel he should be here to defend himself.' I got to my feet. 'Either that or I will have to leave!'

'Sarah,' began Dr Gray, 'we are concerned with ...'

'Matthew has not lied to me!'

'He deceived you in order to re-establish your relationship.'

'He hasn't lied to me *since*.'

'You cannot know that, Sarah. Matthew has no proven alibi for much of the day in question. A colleague, Mr Abercrombie, has stated that he joined him in Birmingham, and was with him until the late afternoon, but the police have not been able to substantiate this.'

'Poppy? You think Poppy lied as well?'

Sam shifted in his chair. 'Sarah, if it's any consolation, I don't believe Matthew has lied, but we would not be behaving responsibly if we didn't tell you these things.'

'Have you been suspecting Matthew all this time? When you spent the evenings with us? Talked to us about falling out of trees. And about helping me get my memories back?'

'No, of course not. We're on your side, Sarah.'

'I want Matthew back in here, now!'

Without further comment, Bob Gray went out into the waiting area. Matthew followed him back into the room. He still looked pale. I hurried over to him. He put his arm around me, tried to make eye contact with Sam.

'Is somebody going to tell me what happened?'

Bob Gray started to explain. 'We decided against hypnosis. In fact, that was not the reason we asked you to leave the room. We needed to speak to Sarah in private. To inform her of the various concerns that the police ... indeed, that we as Sarah's physicians ...'

'The police?' Matthew exclaimed.

I held my hand up to Dr Gray then pulled Matthew over to the far side of room and sat down next to him. 'Apparently, the police suspect us both. You have no alibi for that day, other than one Poppy gave you, which hasn't been confirmed. Because of this, Dr Gray felt it necessary to advise me that you might be inventing the story about my phone call and moving my car. To create a smokescreen, so that no one would think you were involved in what happened inside my mother's house.'

'But I wasn't involved.'

'Apparently, you fought with Jeff two days earlier.'

Matthew caught his breath: 'I … He found out about us. He was abusive on the phone. So I went over to reason with him. Outside his lock-up. He called you a slut, so …'

'So you hit him? Do you often hit people, Matthew?'

'No, I don't.' He sighed. 'Just your husband and your neurologist. I told you the truth, Sarah. I was travelling back from Birmingham when you called. It had all happened by the time I got to your mother's house. I found your car and moved it. It's all true.'

'You told the police you were with Poppy. Was Poppy at the book launch?' Matthew looked over at Dr Gray, pushed his hand through his hair. I leant away from him in disbelief. 'So Poppy lied about being with you!'

'Poppy was *supposed* to come with us. But he called off and spent the two days grizzling in bed about some guy from Brazil who was two-timing him straight. He told the police he was with me so they'd stop pestering me when I was busy worrying about you.'

'*Us?*' I said.

'What?'

'You said "Poppy was supposed to come with *us*." Who's us?'

Matthew wouldn't look at me. 'Lucy was there.'

I stood up. 'You were in Birmingham with Lucy? Did I know?'

Matthew still avoided meeting my eyes. I stamped my foot. He cringed. 'No. I knew you'd be upset. We drove up together. … She had to go, damn it! She commissioned the bloody book. The author brought her children along to meet her.'

'And you both stayed overnight? Did you sleep with her?'

Again he pushed his fingers through his hair. 'The hotels were packed. It was just before Christmas. We knew we were splitting up, so I ... we ...'

'So it was a farewell fuck, was it?'

Sam snorted. Matthew flashed him a look of desperation. Bob Gray made an attempt at breaking the tension. 'Sam, would you mind popping outside for some coffee?' He cleared his throat. 'Matthew, it seems that you might have an alibi after all ...'

'Not really. Lucy left early. Around nine. I checked out about an hour later and went for a walk. I needed to do some thinking. I didn't catch a train until the afternoon. But I've no way of proving that. So Poppy lied for me.'

Bob Gray frowned at his young colleague. 'Sam, coffee? And would you please take care to close the door behind you?'

I watched Sam hurry out, then stomped over and took his seat. Bob Gray regarded me with caution.

'Well, we have at least managed to clear up a few things.'

I pointed across the room. 'He's an oversexed pig!'

Matthew flinched. Bob Gray attempted to restore calm. 'I'm sure ...'

Matthew interrupted. 'You did not decide to leave Jeff until that afternoon. Up to that point, despite my repeated attempts to convince you to do so, you were against ending your marriage.'

'You said you asked me not to go over and tell my sister about leaving Jeff. Is that because you'd changed your mind about wanting to be with me after a night with Lucy? And probably an evening and afternoon. Did you actually go to the launch?'

Matthew gave a frustrated sigh. 'I wanted you to wait for me to go with you, Sarah ... Jeff had been violent towards you in the past.'

'Is that true, Matthew?' said Bob Gray.

'Yes.' He tried again to reason with me. 'I'd been with Lucy for years. You wouldn't leave Jeff. I'd been living in that disgusting flat for weeks. And you never once stayed over in case Jeff suspected you. It didn't seem that wrong to spend a night with Lucy.'

The door opened and Sam stepped back in and assessed the atmosphere. 'Coffee's on its way.' He sat down next to Matthew, pulled a stethoscope from his pocket unnecessarily and fiddled with it.

Matthew looked across at him. 'Could I borrow that to strangle myself?'

'Self-garrotting isn't permitted in the consulting rooms,' whispered Sam. He dared to address me. 'Did it get worse?'

'How much worse do you think it can get, Dr Clegg?'

Bob Gray attempted to calm the situation. 'Sarah, do you feel able to proceed with our mapping exercise or are you too exhausted? We could reconvene this coming Wednesday. Back here if that's possible.' He adjusted his spectacles. 'Perhaps you'd like to decide after lunch.' He glanced up as the door opened. 'Ah, Lynn, thank you. Just set it down there.'

As Mrs Barr withdrew and the door closed behind her, I could feel Matthew's eyes on me but I resisted the temptation to look at him and, instead, accepted the cup Dr Gray was offering me. I sipped my coffee and, for a few moments, let the silence declare my supremacy. Then I spoke:

'Dr Gray … I've learned enough over the last two days to realise that I really need to know how I was involved on that day. But I think I'd like to wait a while before we try digging any deeper. I want to be sure that the things I've been told so far are secure. So if it's OK with you, I'd like to go home right now.'

At last I allowed myself to look across the room. Matthew was indeed watching me, his face still ashen, his pale eyes almost completely colourless. I felt the need to pull him back before he disappeared altogether.

'And I think Matthew has had more than enough blood and gore for one day.'

'Arachne, is that you? Are you OK? You sound a bit breathless … Of course I'm not criticising you. Look, I've got a couple of book signings next week, so I'll be away for two nights. If Diana needs me while I'm away, will you phone me? I'll text you the hotel numbers as well. Just in case there's no signal … Arachne? Arachne, are you there? … What do you mean, she's in hospital?' Sarah put her hand to her mouth to stifle a gasp. 'When did that happen? Why didn't you let me know? … Has she got her mobile with her? … What do you mean: she's lost it? … No, I'm not accusing you of anything … I'll ring later … Bye.'

Matthew touched her arm. 'Diana's in hospital?'

'She fell over. She's sprained her wrist. But they're keeping her in for observation.'

'When did she fall over?'

'The day before yesterday. I'm going to drive over and see her.'

'I'll come with you. We'll take a cab. Sarah, love, don't worry.'

'What about your lunch meeting?'

'I'll ring Poppy and explain. He can handle it on his own. Sarah, calm down.'

'But why are they keeping her in?'

'They've probably noticed how dippy she is. And they're probably drying her out before sending her home. She'll be OK. Just sit down for a minute and breathe.'

She allowed him to manoeuvre her towards the edge of the bed. Watched him gathering up her scattered clothing. Reloading the things that had fallen out of her bag.

'I'm worried that she's being left on her on her own for too long. I knew something like this would happen. I've said I'd go and sit with her. But Arachne doesn't want me in the house.' She threw herself back onto the crumpled duvet. 'And how can she have lost her phone? She never leaves her room. I bet Arachne's hidden it so I can't call her.'

Episode Forty-seven

I must have fallen asleep immediately we pulled onto the motorway. I woke in stationary traffic just by Madame Tussaud's. Matthew glanced across at me and smiled. I smiled back. It felt good, waking from a normal sleep, happy to forget those small, crazy moments of dreamtime as they faded into reality, leaving behind only the slightest trace of a thought. About a sister and …

The traffic moved briefly. 'Are you OK?'

'Yes. But it's weird.'

'What's weird?' He looked slightly panicked.

'Trying to fit everything together. It's like trying to organise a story you've been told in the wrong order but there doesn't seem to be any reason why one thing follows another.' I watched him gripping the steering wheel, edging himself towards yet another declaration of contrition and pre-empted it. 'Matthew, why was Jeff at my mother's house? Did he go there often?'

Matthew's knuckles turned white. 'Apparently.'

'But Dr Gray said I wasn't close to my mother?'

'You only went there when it was necessary.'

I watched the taxis edge past my window. And slotted yet another piece of the puzzle into place. 'And my sister still lived with my mother? Was Jeff going there to see Arachne?'

Matthew kept his eyes fixed on the road ahead. 'Let's talk about it when we're home, shall we? This traffic's terrible and most of the cab drivers in London seem to be aiming for me.'

'Well, you shouldn't drive such a ridiculous car, should you?' I saw his jaw tighten. 'I'm sorry, I didn't mean it. It's a lovely car.' I patted his hand. 'So, my husband was having an affair with my sister? Did I know about it?'

'I don't think so. You always ignored Jeff's philandering. But, I think you would have reacted if you'd known about him and Arachne.'

'Did *you* know about it?'

'I found out just before I left for Birmingham. It's why we had our "encounter". He had the cheek to criticise you and me and meanwhile he was ... He didn't try to deny it. ... I didn't go there with the intention of punching him. It just happened. And I didn't tell you about it because I didn't want to upset you before I went away. I wasn't thinking straight.'

'Did Jeff confront me after you hit him?'

Matthew sighed. 'As far as you knew he was in Nottingham. I let you carry on believing it. I don't think he went back to the flat again before what happened.'

'Because he was with Arachne?'

'Yes. I was going to try and resolve things when I got back. I shouldn't have left you not knowing. In fact, I shouldn't have gone to the launch at all; Lucy could have handled it.'

I watched him negotiate the traffic. All the time, more half-truths. More half-lies. I tried to imagine my forgotten husband and sister together, tried to picture the man beside me in that wedding photo caressing ... but, of course, no picture came. 'I don't know what Arachne looked like! We never got to that page in the folder, did we? I never saw photos of her as an adult. Or a recent one of my mother.'

'They'll probably show you them on Wednesday. Neither of them looked anything like you. You obviously took after your father.'

We pulled into Farlington Close. I was surprised to see that the builder's skip had disappeared. I glanced up at the top window and remembered the giant kitchen, the boxes and crates. The deceit.

'Good God,' I exclaimed, 'you can park in the visitors' place. You'll be able to watch your car through the window all night. You can sleep in the lounge and keep an eye on it.'

Matthew reversed into the parking bay. 'Am I banned from sleeping with you then?'

'I haven't decided.'

*

Alfie popped in through the cat flap as I made tea.

'Hi, puss, how've you been? I've had a great time, learning about myself. My parents abandoned me, my mother was an alcoholic and now she's gaga in an institution. My husband was screwing my sister, who must have hated me, and I had no idea about it until ...' I banged down the teapot. 'Until ...'

'OK, cases in the bedroom. Hello, Alfie. We could do with a late lunch. I'm starving. Then I'd better nip over to Sainsbury's and get some wine for ...' He stopped. 'What's up?'

I could barely speak through the panic. 'Do you think, that day, I went round to my mother's house, thinking I'd just see my mother and sister, and ... and instead of that I found Jeff and Arachne

382

together? Is that why you tried to persuade me not to go, because you knew Jeff wasn't in Nottingham and you knew I'd discover them ... and do something terrible?'

'Sarah, you didn't do anything terrible.' He put his arm around me. 'And, anyway, your mother would have been there, doddering around in the kitchen, bad-mouthing you probably, talking to the wallpaper. You would have been more concerned with protecting her. Don't think things like that.'

I sagged against him. 'I don't think I can wait until next Wednesday. I have to know what happened *now*! We should have stayed.'

'But nobody knows what happened.' He stretched over to pick up a mug then manoeuvred me into a chair. 'Sit down and drink this. Poppy and Annabelle are coming over tonight so let's try and have a normal evening.'

I shook my head. 'I've got to see that folder. Maybe I'll remember something if I see photos of my sister. Sam gave you his mobile number, didn't he? Phone and ask him to bring it over?'

'Sarah, I can't ask him to do that. He probably wouldn't be allowed to do it anyway.'

'Give me the number then. I'll ask him.'

'No, wait!' Matthew pulled out a chair and sat down beside me. 'Let's calm down.'

'I can't calm down! Does Dr Gray know about Jeff and Arachne?'

'Yes, I told him. But he would have realised anyway, along with everyone else.'

'Why along with everyone else? God, what else can there be?'

I watched as Matthew struggled with indecision before deciding that the truth was the easiest option.

'Because when Arachne ran into the road outside your mother's house, she was practically naked. And Jeff was lying at the bottom of the stairs *completely* naked.'

'My mother was in the house and they were …'

'The police found her watching the television and eating rice pudding out of a tin. With Jeff still lying at the bottom of the stairs.'

I stared into my lap, trying to arrange the jumble in my head. Disconnected thoughts that had to be organised into the right order.

'When I phoned to say I was going over to my mother's, you said you were on your way back. Were you with Lucy?'

'No, I told you, I caught a train.' He arched an eyebrow. 'Lucy drove there. We were supposed to be driving back together. But I told her I wanted to do some reading on the train. Actually, I wanted to be on my own. To get my head straight.'

'What time did I phone?'

'About four o'clock. I was less than an hour from Euston. I caught a cab straight here, then I got the cabbie to drive me over to Hornsey. I got there around six.'

'And when did Arachne get run over?'

'Just before five. Sarah, why are you asking?'

'Because, it's clear that I did drive over to my mother's, probably straight after talking to you. So I would have got there at around four-thirty and there's not much time between four-thirty and five, is there? There's only just enough time for me to have arrived to speak to my sister and discover her with Jeff and …'

'Sarah, love, if you did discover Jeff with your sister, you'd probably have left straightaway. Before anything happened.'

'Even though my mother was there? And why did I leave my car? And why was I found on a beach two days later with no memory?'

384

'Sam said that often with psychological trauma, patients wander and find themselves in places not knowing how they got there.'

'Psychological trauma? Do you think just discovering that my sister and husband were having an affair would be enough to do that to me, considering that I was not close to my sister and was leaving my husband and had been sleeping with you for over a year?'

Matthew failed to answer.

'Don't you think it would take more than that to drive me into that state? Like pushing my husband downstairs and breaking his neck and chasing my sister outside into the path of a lorry?' I walked over to the sink and emptied my cup. 'Give me Sam's mobile. I need to know this stuff or I'm going to go properly mad.'

'I don't think this is the right thing to do.'

'Why? Because you're scared I might not be innocent? I need to know the truth because anything else is as good as a lie.'

Sarah managed to find a parking place directly outside her mother's house.

'OK, Diana,' she announced. 'We've got you home. We'll come inside and have a cup of tea with you, shall we?'

Her mother shook her head. 'Has Arachne got enough milk?'

Sarah looked at Matthew and rolled her eyes. 'Will you go and check Arachne's there. You'd better ring the bell. She doesn't like me just turning up and going inside.'

Matthew sighed and got out of the car, stepped up to the door, rang the bell and waited. He rang again, knocked hard then turned and signalled that it was hopeless. He walked back to the car. 'What now?'

'She's gone to get some milk.'

Sarah turned to look at her mother. 'I'd better go in and see where she's got to. You stay here with Matthew. All right?' She checked it was safe then stepped out onto the road just as the front door opened to reveal her sister barefoot and swathed in a bathrobe.

'You woke her up,' said Diana.

'Mum, it's two o'clock in the afternoon.'

As soon as they were inside, Arachne disappeared upstairs, leaving Sarah to manoeuvre her mother into her chair in the lounge. Straightaway, Diana grabbed the remote control and started waving it at the television.

'Her wrist seems much better,' laughed Matthew. 'Her bag's at the bottom of the stairs.'

'Thanks. I'll go and make tea. The kitchen's probably a tip. Do you want a cup?'

'No thanks, I don't think my tetanus jabs are up to date.'

'OK. Stay here and watch Diana, will you?' Sarah stepped into the hallway and called up the stairs to ask Arachne if she wanted tea. She waited for a reply which was not forthcoming then disappeared into the kitchen.

Matthew wandered over and asked Diana if she wanted him to find her a movie.

She handed over the remote. 'Is Arachne bringing biscuits?'

'She's upstairs getting dressed. Sarah's making you some tea.'

'And biscuits?'

'Probably. What about *Mamma Mia!*? You like that, don't you?'

Diana's face cracked into a wide grin. Matthew handed back the remote then walked over to clear a space on the sofa, but as he was shifting a pile of clothes he caught sight of something down beside one of the cushions. It looked like a credit card. He eased it out and sure enough it was just that. The signature was illegible. He turned it over and read the name printed along the bottom, frowned, glanced up at the ceiling and slid the card into his pocket just as Sarah stepped back into the room. He watched her set the tray down, and hand her mother a mug of tea and a packet of biscuits.

'Is Arachne still not down?'

He shrugged.

'I'd better go up and see what she's doing. I can't leave Diana down here on her own.'

She turned to leave the room but Matthew caught her arm.

'Sarah, wait. She's … she'll think you're interfering. You know what she's like. There's no hurry. Sit down and drink your tea.'

'It's for Arachne, in case she wants it. I don't fancy any. I feel a bit nauseous. And I think the milk's about to turn. I'll take it up to her.'

'No, don't! I mean … I think that's her now.'

Moments later Sarah's sister stepped into the room wearing a T-shirt and knickers. 'You can go now,' she said.

Matthew walked away and looked out of the window. Sarah stared at her sister.

'Social Services are coming over later this afternoon to check Diana's OK. Assess whether or not she needs to have any handrails fitted. Things like that. Arachne, you ought to be properly dressed when they arrive. If you want me to stay until …'

'I'll get dressed. Close the door behind you.'

'Sarah, let's go,' said Matthew. 'Diana will be fine.'

Sarah glanced at her mother who was busy watching the TV and dunking custard creams into her tea. She wandered over and kissed her grey hair before heading for the front door.

Matthew followed her but just as he was passing the hall table he paused to glance up the stairs, took Jeff Blake's credit card from his pocket and put it down next to the telephone. Then he hurried outside to stop Sarah getting into the driver's seat:

'Sarah, love, let me drive.'

'I'm OK.'

'No, you're not. Let's go over to my flat and talk about it, shall we? Come on, don't cry.'

'Matthew, I've never done anything to make Arachne hate me like that.'

'I know. She's not right in the head. Let's see what Social Services say about it.'

He put his arm around her, walked her round and helped her into the passenger seat. Then he climbed in beside her but, before fastening his seat belt he leant across and kissed her.

'I'll make you pancakes for lunch, OK?'

She smiled and kissed him back. As they pulled away, they both failed utterly to notice the tall figure glaring down at them from the upstairs window.

Episode Forty-eight

'Right, Poppy and Annabelle will get here around six. Sam said he'd try and make it by seven. Will you be alright for an hour or so while I go to Sainsbury's? And I'd better nip over and collect a couple of things from my flat. You can come with me if you want.'

I shook my head. I didn't want to be on my own but I didn't want to be among people either.

'Will you get something to go with the takeaway? Does Poppy eat ice cream?'

Matthew hurried over and put his arm around me. 'Sarah, it's going to be OK. Try not to worry. Clean the fridge or something. That always makes you feel better.'

I watched his car drive away, watched it disappear, red into grey. The fridge. Yes, I would clean the fridge. And I'd talk to Alfie. Talk to the fridge if necessary. Anything to pass the time until the four o'clock pills. I hurried to the kitchen. For once Alfie was there when I needed him. I dared to stroke his ear, washed up the two mugs and fetched a clean tea towel. The photo of Jeff Blake looked up at me from the tea towel drawer. I pushed it closed and pulled open the fridge. Even I could see that it didn't need to be cleaned. So I turned my attention to the freezer. I should throw away some of those frozen burgers and sausages that Mrs Parkin had put there ready for when I came home. Make room for the ice cream. Why had Mrs Parkin filled my freezer with burgers and sausages? Didn't she know I didn't eat those things? The middle drawer was full of them, all frozen into one huge dead lump, untouched for eight, no, nine weeks. I prodded the top packet free and then the one next to it, placing them both next to the sink. The doorbell rang. Had Matthew forgotten something? Misplaced his key?

I pulled open the front door. Matthew was not there. Della Brown was. On my doorstep, a black carrier bag nestled in her arms. And behind her, her silver-grey car was parked in the visitor parking space.

'Good afternoon, Mrs Blake. I thought I'd take the opportunity to call round and return a few things you might have been missing?' She edged forward.

I fought to stay calm. Imagined Matthew returning, having actually forgotten something, finding his parking space occupied, uncurling himself from his shiny red car to hurl abuse at the sight of this woman, inadvertently revealing the truth. I was frightened, no, I was terrified. Then, amidst the panic, I fell upon a strategy.

'Dr Brown ... Oh, sorry, I mean Inspector Brown. I mean ... You're a policeman, aren't you? I mean a policewoman.' I clenched my hands together in apology. Took a step back. 'Would you like to come in? How did you know where I live?'

Della Brown came in and dropped the carrier bag onto the coffee table. I watched her detective eyes assess the room, coming to rest upon my Raggedy Lyme snow globe standing alone on the mantelpiece. Her scorn was visible. She turned to me.

'I did call round last Wednesday but there was no reply. I popped one of my cards through your letterbox.'

I made a display of turning to look at the doormat.

'I usually go to see Dr Gray on Wednesdays. And Dr Williams on Tuesdays. Perhaps my cleaning lady found it.'

'Well, not to worry. So, how have you been, Sarah?'

'Oh, I'm feeling much happier. I've just been back to the clinic for assessment and they sorted out my medication. Dr Gray was very pleased with me. He said I only have to visit the hospital once a fortnight now. So that gives me more time to do my writing. I'm writing apple stories at the moment. The ones I used to make up with my grandma.' I fiddled with my cuff. 'I remember we went to lunch together, didn't we? Would you like me to make you a cup of tea? I've got chocolate biscuits.'

Della Brown's eyes widened. She glanced at her watch. 'I ought to be going. I just wanted to make sure you got these things back.' She indicated the plastic carrier bag.

I stepped over and looked inside.

'Your husband's things.'

I glanced up. 'My husband? Oh yes, I had a husband. Jeff Blake. But they told me he fell downstairs and then after that he died of an infection. In the hospital. When I was unconscious. He had a van but I'm going to give it to my friend.' I picked up the bag. 'I can make coffee as well. If you like. The kettle's in the kitchen.' I started to walk towards the kitchen. I could feel my heart pounding in my ears but I was reasonably certain that it wasn't obvious on the outside. I could hear Della Brown's footsteps following me. I headed straight for the kitchen table and tipped the contents of the bag onto its surface. Alfie was asleep on his chair. He raised his head at the commotion, so that his pink nose appeared above the far edge of the table.

'Oh, a cat!' exclaimed Della Brown.

'Yes. Miss Lewis said he's mine. He's called Alfie. Do you like cats, Dr Brown?'

'Not particularly.' She walked over to stand by the sink.

I poked at the items spread out before me: a wallet, keys, an organiser, two mobile phones, an electric razor, a polythene bag containing some loose change. I could feel Della Brown watching me so I made a particular display of peering into the empty bag.

'There are a few bulkier things that you might like to collect from the station ... the police station,' said Detective Brown. 'Business papers, his clothes, toiletries, and a few other personal effects recovered from your mother's house.'

I concentrated on arranging the objects into a row then picked up the two phones.

'I have my own mobile, so I'll probably give these to a charity shop.' I looked up at Della Brown: 'I could ask my boyfriend to help me collect the things from the police station. But I don't really want any more papers. And I think all the other things from my mother's house are being sold to help pay for her to be looked after. She's in a clinic now. Because she has ...er, I can't remember what it's called. But I don't think she'll be able to go back to her house ever.'

'Do you remember your mother's house, Sarah? The one in Hornsey?'

'Not really.'

'I believe your mother lived there with your sister, Arachne. Do you remember your sister? Did they tell you what happened to her?'

'I think she was run over. I'm sorry, I can't remember anything from before I woke up in the hospital. My memory's not right.' I picked up the electric razor, wandered over and threw it in the recycling bin. Della Brown followed me with her eyes and as she did so her attention fell upon the two packets of beef burgers lying next to the sink. She leant forward and rubbed her finger along the layer of frost to reveal their contents: 'Beef burgers?'

'I'm just thawing them out. I haven't had my lunch yet. But there's plenty there if you'd like to stay for something to eat.'

She smirked. Then she slotted a packet of cigarettes and a thin lighter out of her pocket. 'I've already eaten. Do you mind if I smoke?' She was already removing a cigarette and placing it in her mouth.

Did people still do that in other people's houses? I shook my head. 'No, I don't mind. I think I've seen an ash tray in one of the cupboards.' I took a deep breath, headed over and pulled a tall door open wide: 'Oh no, this is the cereal cupboard. It must be somewhere else. Perhaps they put it away.'

I paused then turned as I closed the door. Della Brown was staring at me, her lighter frozen in the air awaiting the opportunity to ignite. She recovered, lit her cigarette and inhaled a lungful of fumes.

'Not to worry. I'll use the sink.' Another smirk. 'You eat cornflakes, then?'

'They're really good for you.'

'I'm sure they are. Did your husband, Jeff Blake used to smoke?'

'I've no idea. I've got a photo of him if you'd like to see it. I fussed around opening drawers and finally pulled out a pile of tea towels with my wedding photo resting on top. I placed the pile on the work surface and handed her the photo. 'That's me and my husband. Jeff Blake. Shall I make the tea now?'

Detective Brown flicked her ash into the sink then took a step back. 'No, I had better be getting back.' She handed me the photo.

'Oh, all right. It's been nice to see you again. Thank you for bringing these things.'

Della Brown took a last critical look around her then walked through to open the front door. 'Thank goodness it's not raining!' she said as she stepped outside. 'Bye, Sarah. Enjoy your lunch.'

I stood on the step and watched her get into her silver-grey car, holding her cigarette in her mouth as she fastened her seatbelt and drove away.

Episode Forty-nine

I heard the front door close and Matthew walk through into the kitchen. I ran through and found him standing beside Alfie staring at the things on the table. 'Where'd all this come from?' He looked worried. 'Are you OK? What's wrong? What happened?'

I sobbed out a jumbled account of Detective Brown's visit while Matthew made toast and forced me to sit and eat it. He tried to reassure me that I was worrying unnecessarily, that she probably *was* just returning Jeff's things. My head wobbled hysterically. 'She thinks I murdered Jeff. I know she does.'

'Nobody murdered Jeff. If she thought you were guilty of anything she would have had you arrested.'

Arrested. That word spiked through me, made me feel like a criminal, a proper criminal that has to leave home and go and live in a jail. I looked around my kitchen at the everyday things that I would have to leave behind me. 'If I go to prison, you'll ...'

'Sarah, stop! This is ridiculous. Jeff fell down stairs. It was an accident. Nobody would ever be able to say otherwise.'

'Except me. If I remember. If, after this evening, I remember.'

'We can still cancel the others, if you're not up for it.'

I shook my head. 'I need to know the truth, Matthew.'

I paced up and down as six o'clock drew nearer.

'Have you told Anabelle and Poppy everything?'

'Mostly. Obviously, I haven't told them about the phone call and moving your car. Sarah, calm down.'

The doorbell rang. My stomach took a dive. Matthew hurried through to relieve Poppy of a vast bunch of red roses so that he was free to embrace me unencumbered by foliage. Momentarily forgetful of my fears, I pulled him into the lounge and waited for his reaction to my stripped-down home. He looked around.

'Darling, where *is* everything?'

'Deadly, isn't it? They piled everything upstairs, so I could bring it down at my leisure. Apart from the husband. He's permanently gone.'

Poppy threw his hand across his mouth. 'Are you sad about that?'

'Don't know. I need to know what happened before I can decide *what* I feel about it.'

'Matthew said we have to help you remember.'

I took a deep breath. 'Well, thank you for still coming. And Poppy, I'm sorry you had to lie to the police about being with Matthew.'

The bell sounded again. Matthew pulled open the door and Annabelle strode in and smirked at the flowers he was clutching.

'Those for me, Matthew?' She hugged me and noticed Poppy. 'Hello, Poppy. Do you remember me?'

'Annabelle, darling, how could I ever forget you?'

'True, true!' She turned her attention back to me. 'Matthew said we're going to brainstorm. So I brought supplies.' She delved into her bag and pulled out a giant packet of chocolate buttons and a small foil-wrapped package, tied with a yellow ribbon; she handed them to me. 'No expense spared!'

I puzzled over the yellow bow. 'What's this?'

'Skunk.'

'For God's sake,' said Matthew. 'Annabelle, can't you grow up! We don't need any of that crap to add to our problems!'

'Speak for yourself, gorgeous,' said Poppy.

I lifted the small package to my nose, sniffed it and recoiled slightly, before passing it to Poppy. I nudged Matthew's arm. 'Shall I put those in water or do you want to do it?'

He handed me the roses. 'I doubt Sam will approve of people rotting their brains with that stuff.'

'Who's Sam?' said Annabelle. 'Is he the guy who phoned me? Is he married?'

'Is he gay?' asked Poppy.

Matthew rolled his eyes. 'He's a research psychologist. And yes, he did phone you, he's not married and he's definitely not gay. He's coming over to make sure things go smoothly. Poppy, there's wine in the fridge.'

We settled in the lounge, drinking chardonnay, chatting awkwardly and avoiding the matter at hand. They watched me kneeling at the coffee table, arranging my roses. Cutting and snipping. The activity was calming.

'At least they give the place a bit of colour,' said Annabelle. 'It's like a mausoleum in here. Did they throw all your stuff away?'

'They stacked it upstairs,' explained Poppy.

'What, in Jeff's kitchen?' Annabelle caught her breath. 'I can mention Jeff, can I?'

'Sarah's all right about it,' said Poppy, 'but any mention of him makes me nauseous.'

I carried my flowers over to my desk and prodded a single leaf towards perfection. 'Shall we go up and collect some of my things? You can warn me if anything's likely to make me mental.'

So the Klimt, the fairies and the fat woman with a cream cake, a large cardboard box containing my collection of snow globes, the photo of me and Matthew, and a bin bag full of red and green cushions were hauled downstairs and reinstated. And I felt strangely OK about it. In fact, it was with a thrill of excitement that I started to unwrap the snow globes: a wrong-coloured Tower of London, a crinoline princess inappropriately dressed for a snowstorm, an old, scratched Snow White and her faded dwarfs.

'They used to stand on the bookcase and all along the mantelpiece,' said Matthew. 'Jeff hated them. Poppy, help Sarah arrange them. And make sure none of them are leaking. That stuff inside is probably toxic.'

Poppy plucked out a watery Bambi. 'These are really naff, Sarah.'

*

At seven-twenty, a large box of Indian takeaway and Sam's cab arrived together. Matthew attempted introductions. Annabelle nudged him aside.

'Hi, I'm Annabelle, we spoke on the phone. You look nothing like I imagined you.'

Sam laughed. 'Is that a good or a bad thing?'

'In Annabelle's case, it's meaningless,' said Poppy.

Over supper, Matthew tried to lighten the deepening anxiety that was overtaking our guests. By dessert I had joined in the reassurances.

'It's OK, guys, if I start to freak, Sam's probably brought something along that will calm me down.'

'Absolutely! I go everywhere with a pocket full of happiness. And a mallet.'

'Well, if they fail,' suggested Annabelle, 'there's always the skunk.'

Sam's spoonful of frozen yoghurt came to a halt. 'Skunk?'

Matthew sighed. 'Sam, not only have we asked you to pilfer medical documents and come here, risking your entire career, but just to add to the nightmare, Sarah's *insane* friend has brought illegal shit with her.'

'Chocolate buttons aren't illegal!' protested Annabelle through a mouthful of yoghurt.

Matthew put his head into his hands. I looked at Sam begging support. He lowered his spoon. 'Matthew, mate, you need to calm down. Bob knows I'm here. We discussed contingencies. And, yes, he did give me permission to bring some emergency supplies. But nothing quite as interesting as skunk.'

Matthew bristled at his response. 'Well, if we hear a truncheon rapping on the window, we'll bundle you out the back door, shall we?'

'I'd argue I was using it therapeutically.'

'Do you prescribe it for lunatics?' asked Annabelle.

Sam laughed. 'We do use cannabis occasionally, but nothing as strong and random as skunk. But it's a bit of a double-edged sword. It can help, but it can also induce psychosis.'

'That's probably what happened to Annabelle,' said Matthew.

Things were cleared away, glasses replenished, crisps and chocolate buttons were poured into bowls. I rearranged cushions in an attempt to create a relaxed atmosphere then sat down beside Matthew with my fists clenched in my lap. I felt his arm around me and felt worse.

'We don't have to do this now,' I whispered. 'We could wait until Wednesday.'

Sam sat down on the coffee table opposite me, the folder in his hands. 'Do you want to wait until Wednesday?'

I wanted to say yes, leave it, but I could see Annabelle and Poppy, together on the smaller sofa, their faces deliberately relaxed, their eyes betraying anxieties.

'No, I'm OK. Let's get on with it.' So Sam handed me the folder. I turned the first few pages and revisited my years on the Kent coast, the years before my unremembered relocation to the emotional turmoil of my mother's house in Hornsey. I passed the folder to Annabelle and Poppy so they'd feel included. Annabelle contributed by remembering things I'd told her over the years, childhood memories, including a muddled memory about fossils.

'Fossils?'

'Yes, you remembered collecting fossils. On a beach, I think.'

'Are there fossils on the beach in Margate?' asked Poppy.

Sam shook his head. 'Do you remember that, Sarah?'

'I'm not sure. Annabelle, when was I talking about?'

'When you were small. I remember you telling me you found fossils and in the evening you looked at stars through a telescope.'

'Hang on a sec!' Sam took out his notepad and flicked through the pages. 'Sarah, do you remember, two weeks ago I asked you to introduce a character into a remembered day. You imagined a crazy astronomer. Is that just a coincidence?'

'I remember you asking me to do that. But I thought I was inventing an imaginary person. I don't remember anything about an astronomer from when I was little. Or fossils.'

Sam nodded. The pages turned. I arrived at the photo of my mother with the new baby. I remembered the possessive fingers, but this time the laughter failed to approach. I hoped this meant I was winning by degree, achieving small incursions into my own life, undertaken so gradually that my mind was failing to notice. I touched the photo and felt nothing, turned the page: school photos; then one of a girl, who I recognised as me. I was pushing a toddler along in a stroller. She had a mass of blonde curls pulled into bunches.

'Is that Arachne?'

'It says *Sarah and Arachne 1992*,' said Sam. 'Are you OK?'

'Almost.' I glanced over at Annabelle and Poppy and smiled.

The next page had a studio photograph of me, perhaps fourteen years old, seated, my blonde sister beside me. We were holding hands. I shook my head, surprised that I felt nothing. The opposite page had several sheets attached.

'They detail periods of foster care,' Sam explained, 'when Diana was institutionalised. You and Arachne were placed together until you were seventeen. Then Arachne was placed alone while you remained at home with visits from a social worker. I'd guess that this enforced separation exacerbated the rift between you and your sister. Annabelle remembers you telling her about it.'

'That's terrible,' I said.

'It wasn't your fault,' said Sam. 'In fact, you deferred your place at university for two years to look after Arachne when Diana suffered a serious relapse, rather than have her taken into care again.'

'She didn't seem to have been grateful for that,' said Matthew.

'There were other underlying issues,' said Sam. 'We've accessed Arachne's medical files.' He paused. 'Actually, we already had her files.'

I looked up from the photo: 'How come?'

'Because Arachne was Geraint's patient long before all this happened.'

Episode Fifty

Matthew sat forward: 'Nobody told me that!'

'It would have been a breach of patient confidentiality.' Sam's brief show of professional detachment seemed incongruous against his jeans and sweatshirt. 'It would have been confidential.'

'What even after she died?'

Sam ignored Matthew's jibe and turned to me.

'You agreed to an interview. Last August. With Geraint.'

'I met Geraint Williams before?' I could feel myself gaping.

'It was an attempt at family therapy. Yourself and Arachne in the presence of Geraint and an observing counsellor.' He forced a smile. 'Not Mrs Parkin! It ended in chaos. Arachne had to be restrained. Geraint concluded that her accusations were delusional.'

'What accusations?'

She accused you of physically abusing her during childhood. She was close to being sectioned on that occasion but, since her outrage was directed specifically at you, Geraint proposed that, if you avoided contact, sectioning might not be necessary.'

'Sarah, you didn't tell me any of this at the time,' said Matthew.

'Perhaps I didn't want you to know. But, Sam, Arachne was living with my mother. Was he suggesting I should avoid contact with her as well?'

'I think, with the rapid decline in Diana's mental state, some kind of institutionalisation was on the agenda. So avoiding contact with your sister would not have been that much of a problem.'

I looked down at the photo: 'So did Geraint Williams take an interest in me because of Arachne?'

'Yes. It was his decision to move you to the National then, when they discovered your persistent memory loss, he handed the case over to Bob, although he asked if he could use you in his MRI trials. Are you OK about this, Sarah?'

'Not really. Why was Arachne his patient?'

'Paranoid schizophrenia. Functional. There'd been two unconvincing suicide attempts. On both occasions she phoned you to tell you what she'd done. Her focus of anxiety was always resentment of you. She was jealous of your normal life.'

'My normal life? Abandoned by my alcoholic mother, married to a serial adulterer?'

'The most recent interview suggested she was controlling the resentment.'

'Perhaps that's because she was screwing my husband!' I sighed at Sam's expression. 'Matthew told me. Do you think she was doing that to spite me? Or do you think they were actually attracted to each other?'

'I don't know,' said Sam. 'Jeff doesn't figure in Arachne's case notes. It might have been vindictive.' He glanced at Matthew. 'Matthew thinks, in Jeff's case, it had a lot to do with the fact that Arachne was due to inherit Diana's estate.'

I turned to Matthew and wondered at these conversations that had been going on in my absence. Secrets and lies. Things untold. I looked back at the image of my sister, perhaps five years old, her time just beginning. There was nothing there that might reveal the seeds of psychosis, suicide attempts, hatred of the sister who was holding her hand.

'Does any of this ring any bells?' asked Sam.

I stroked my sister's blonde curls. 'Nothing. No bells. No memories. Just years and years filled with nothing. Perhaps my memories really are gone.'

'What about the laughter, is it there at the moment?'

'It's a long way away. I don't even know whether I'm hearing it or imagining it, although I suppose I'm imagining it either way. But I think that every time I learn things about the past, I'm able to retain a little more. Like I'm burrowing into forbidden territory, one step at a time.'

'Do you think the laughter stems from a particular incident?'

'I don't know, Sam. I'm scared to analyse it in case I invite it in. I think it's to do with my mother and sister ridiculing me. Or perhaps just me believing they were ridiculing me.' I turned the page to reveal photos of college. 'Annabelle, it's you with long hair.'

Annabelle hurried to kneel at my feet. 'You used to trim it for me, remember?'

I shook my head. More pages turned. Holiday snaps. Hot beaches, Annabelle beside me on a rocky outcrop. Surrounded by blue sky. People I didn't recognise. Then flowers, tables set for some kind of grand function, and the first appearance of Jeff Blake. We looked happy in the photographs taken together, especially on our wedding day. How could things have gone so badly wrong? I studied the faces. I could barely recognise my own features let alone anyone else's. I touched Annabelle's shoulder. 'Weren't you there?'

'I was taking the photos, so I didn't get to be in them. Usually you did the photography but obviously that day you were being the bride.'

'I took photos at weddings? And I did the flowers?'

'Yes, until about three years ago, when your books really took off. Then Jeff brought Alex into the company.' She pointed to a group photo, to a pale young woman standing to one side, slightly out of focus. 'That's Arachne.'

I lifted the folder closer. 'Are you sure?' I nudged it towards Matthew: 'Do you think that's Arachne?' He nodded and I felt an awful wave of regret ripple through me. About a sister I no longer had. I scanned the other photos. 'Where's my mother?'

'She was in hospital recovering after a minor stroke,' said Sam. 'Two weeks earlier. The next page has photos taken at your mother's sixtieth birthday party.'

I turned the page and tried to make out various people in the crowd: Annabelle, a person I assumed was Jeff Blake. I wasn't absolutely certain. I picked up a white folder, embossed, the kind of folder that usually holds a print of a wedding. I went to open it, but Sam stopped my hand. 'It was taken that evening: you, your sister and mother.'

'Just the three of us?' I whispered. I opened the folder, recognising myself smiling, radiant, just the way I had looked on the library wall at the agency. My sister was standing beside me. Her features clear, her skin pale, the curls in her long blonde hair styled away. Physically we had nothing in common. But what we did have in common was sitting in front of us. Our mother. We each had a hand on her shoulder; hers were lying in her lap, limp and bony, like the rest of her. She looked wasted. Her dress, smart as it was, seemed nothing more than a drape, politely concealing a naked skeleton; her eyes sunken into grey sockets, one half of her face falling away, sliding down under the influence of gravity so that the smile on one side was reversed on the other.

I looked at my hand on my mother's shoulder, my left hand, touching the mother I could not remember. I looked at my mother's head. Was it a stroke, some kind of paralysis, that was causing her to lean that way, or was she deliberately leaning away from my touch, leaning towards her younger daughter. After all these years, did Diana Dawson still blame me for the loss of her drunken husband? And Arachne, my sister, her pale blue eyes were not really directed towards the camera, but rather down at the head leaning towards her, smiling at that thin, lifeless hair. A shared resentment binding them.

I fought hard not to hear the laughter that was rising out of that joint portrait of a mother, her daughter and the person they both blamed. I tried to hold the image in my head, but the more I concentrated, the louder the noises became, until all I could hear was the shrieks of the gulls circling overhead, screaming for me to let go before the memory could be made, before the image could be tagged, processed, stored for future reference, because that subconscious thing that claimed ownership of my thoughts was tearing that image from me. Denying me the right to remember. I had to let go.

Sam pulled the photograph away.

'What's happening?' said Annabelle.

'Is it the noises,' Poppy whispered.

I forced myself to recover. Pointed to the folder. 'Show me again, Sam.'

'Are you sure? Can you recall where we got to?'

'My mother's party, then that photo.' I shook my head. 'I'm sorry, I can't remember.'

'Can you really not remember?' said Annabelle.

I felt Poppy's hand on my arm. 'I'm sorry if this is upsetting you both. You don't have to stay. Really.'

'God, Sarah,' exclaimed Annabelle. 'What kind of friend do you think I am? You've spent whole nights with me while I puked into the toilet. The least I can do is be with you while you lose your mind.'

'Annabelle!' snapped Matthew. 'Sarah is not losing her mind.'

I touched Annabelle's shoulder. 'We must have had great times.'

'Too right, and you need to remember them!'

'And you need to remember all our lunches,' said Poppy, 'with me trying to edit your manuscripts and you refusing to change anything including the wrong spellings.'

I longed to share those memories. 'Sam, please show me the photo.'

Sam handed over the folder. I studied it. The noises began. I closed my eyes and let them fade, looked again. And again.

'It's my mother. Every time I look, the face has nothing in it. And then I start to see a drooping mouth and the noise becomes so loud I have to close my eyes. And when I open them it's an empty face again.'

'The same every time?' asked Sam.

'I think each time I can see a little more.'

'During the MRI scans, you were shown images of your mother from way back into your childhood. But you never recognised them. It might be that your mother is the core of your anxieties, your original reason to forget.'

Matthew cleared his throat. 'Have you spoken to her lately, Sam?'

What? I looked at Sam and waited for an explanation.

He took the folder and put it on the coffee table. 'Diana's been at Greystone Park since the beginning of March. Bob had her transferred there.'

I stared at him in disbelief. 'She was there? When I was there? When were any of you thinking of telling me that?'

'Bob wasn't sure you were ready.'

I couldn't believe what I was hearing. All these people still deciding what I was ready to know. Knowing things about my life and calculating when they might deign to inform me, Sarah Blake, whose actual life it was. I stood up and strode over to my desk.

'You let me roam around in that bloody clinic and all the while my own mother was there and you never told me because you'd decided I wasn't *ready*? Well, I'd like to announce that I'm completely pissed off with all of you! I'm sick of being drip-fed snippets about my life so I'm going to stand here and wait and you're all going to tell me everything you know and if it means I wake up tomorrow like a brainless jelly then so be it!'

'I don't know anything,' said Poppy. 'I'm just here to be with you.'

'Thank you, Poppy. Annabelle?'

'I'm also here to be with you. But I feel guilty about not telling you about Jeff.'

'For God's sake! What didn't you tell me about Jeff?'

Annabelle picked up Sam's glass and gulped down a large mouthful of his wine. 'It was last November. I'd been staying at the Royal Crescent in Bath with this guy I was doing some work for. I was waiting while he checked out. Suddenly Jeff came walking into reception. I got ready to say hello, but then your sister came trotting in behind him. Bold as brass. I don't think they saw me. But I never told you and I've been worrying that if I had you might not have gone to your mother's house that day and ...'

'Did Matthew say that's what happened?'

'No. I'm just worried that ... Sarah, I'm sorry I never told you. I should have confronted that cheating bastard then and there, but I was with a client ... I'm so sorry.'

'And I'm sorry I never told you about Jeff and Arachne,' said Matthew. 'And about my confrontation with Jeff. Sarah, come and sit down. Please.'

'I'm staying here.' I folded my arms. 'And I'm waiting.' The silence was marked. 'So there is something else, is there?' I pulled the chair out from under my desk and sat down, facing them. Whatever this something else was, it was clearly something they all knew. Part of their conspiracy of silence. I saw Sam glance at Matthew. Watched Matthew give his silent consent. Sam walked over to stand beside me:

'There *is* something else and it's likely to upset you. But you need to know.'

ISLINGTON

'Matthew?'

'Yes.'

'Where are you?'

'I'm on the train coming back. Is something wrong?'

'When will you get here?'

'I don't know. I'm about an hour away from Euston. Has something happened?'

'I need to speak to you.'

'About what? Sarah, what's wrong?'

'Matthew, I'm pregnant. I went to see the doctor this morning and … I'm pregnant. And I don't know what to do … Matthew are you still there? *Matthew*?'

'Yes, of course I'm still here. But the signal's useless and I've got hardly any battery left. Sarah, did you just say you're pregnant?'

'Yes. I can't stay here. Jeff will go mad if he finds out.'

'Did you forget to take your pill or something?'

'No. Matthew, can I come and stay in your flat with you?'

'Of course you can. I've been asking you to do exactly that ever since I moved there.'

'But what about me being pregnant?'

'I'll get a bigger bed.'

'Matthew, be serious! I don't know who the father is.'

'It doesn't matter who the father is. Look, I'll come straight to your flat as soon as I get back. Wait for me there. Then we'll sort out what to do.'

'I've packed some things. I'll leave a note for when Jeff gets back from Nottingham. And I'd better go over and tell Arachne that I'm moving in with you so she'll know where I am if anything happens to Diana.'

'What? No, wait, Sarah, don't do that! Wait until I get back … Shit, I think my phone's about to die. Sarah, I'll get to you by about six. Sarah, do NOT go over to Hornsey until I can go with you, OK? … Sarah? Sarah, are you there?'

Episode Fifty-one

'Miscarriage?'

'You must have been lying there for some time, possibly since the early hours of the morning. Fortunately you'd avoided being covered by the tide but, nevertheless, you were suffering from exposure and significant blood loss. There were concerns that your coma was due to brain damage following hypovolemic shock. Following haemorrhage. Initial scans suggested that was not the case but, when they discovered your severe memory loss, concerns were reawakened.'

I looked at Matthew. 'I was pregnant? Did you know?'

'You told me when you phoned that afternoon. The doctor had confirmed it that morning. I wouldn't have gone away but I never knew you suspected it.'

'Whose baby was it?'

'You said you didn't know.'

Sam touched my arm. It was a very practiced touch. Do they teach doctors how to do that as part of their training? I'm sorry there's no hope. Best put your things in order. Would you like to speak to the hospital chaplain? Would you like me to tell your husband, wife, son, daughter? I pulled my arm away. Sam tried a different approach.

'Sarah, it's not clear at what point over those two days you started

to miscarry, or whether it was due to anything that may have happened to you. There was a lot of bruising and your arm was broken. There didn't seem to be any permanent damage. And there's a chance it might have been a doomed pregnancy from the start. There's no way of knowing, unless you can tell us what happened.'

All at once I needed to be alone. But people were touching me, saying words that were meaningless, all their sense corrupted by the sounds in my own mind gnawing away inside my head, determined that I must never remember. I needed to get as far away as possible from the people and the words. Then further away even than that.

'Sarah, what are you doing? Poppy, hold the door!'

'I've got something in my bag.'

'Sarah, love, you can't go outside!'

'Sarah, it's Annabelle. It's OK. God, what's happening to her eyes?'

'Nystagmus.'

'What?'

'This will calm her down. Hold her still …'

'No!' My voice rang clear above the chaos. 'I don't need it!'

'It's just a mild sedative, Sarah.'

'I don't need it, Sam! Please, you're both hurting me.'

I felt Annabelle and Matthew slacken their hold.

'Please, something inside my head told me to run away. But I'm not going to.'

I felt Annabelle let go of my arm, Matthew's arm close around me. He walked me over to the sofa and sat down beside me. Asked Annabelle to fetch more wine. I was trembling.

Sam resumed his previous position. 'Well done, Sarah. How did you snap out of it like that?'

'I suddenly saw myself. I mean I *really* saw myself. From about where

I am now. With you all trying to stop me running outside. It was like time had split into two and, in the time I was in, I could see myself, with my arms flailing around. And I thought how useless it was, behaving like that. With you all trying to help and me hitting out at you. I could actually see myself doing that. So I made myself stop and then I was over there in the different time and you were holding me.'

'That happened to me once, after a tab.' Annabelle was standing behind the sofa, clutching a bottle of Australian chardonnay.

'It sounds like depersonalisation.' He glanced up at Annabelle. 'Sarah, you're trembling. You ought to let me give you something. Just a pill.'

'I don't want pills. I want to remember.'

'Do you think you remembered something then?'

'I don't think so. It was just that you said I was pregnant and I didn't know who the father was and I remember thinking if it was Matthew's baby, then I wanted it back and if it was Jeff's then it was gone and he was gone and I didn't want either of them back. But how can you feel those two completely different things about the same baby and how can you feel that about a baby anyway? And then I thought perhaps it would have been better if I'd been a doomed pregnancy. All those thoughts flooded into my head at the same time as the laughing and the waves. I just wanted to run away.' I could feel tears running down my face. Matthew's arm around me trying to steady me. Poppy was still barricading my exit. 'I'm so sorry, Poppy.'

Poppy edged away from the door. 'Darling,' he said, 'no need to apologise. I haven't had so much fun for years! But you should let Sam give you his pills, sweetie.'

'They really will help, Sarah,' said Sam. 'If you carry on shaking like this you'll make yourself sick.'

'Will they put me to sleep?'

'No. They'll just calm you down. 'But Sarah … Bob suggested you take your evening medication tonight. He said it would be all right to take it with the sedative.'

Take them, Sarah,' whispered Matthew. So I took the pills.

And slowly things around me became calm and my hands became still. Then the weird tiredness came. I fought against it, scared to sleep, scared about what I might remember, what I might forget. I listened to their conversation without really paying attention to what they were saying. Then I heard Sam say, 'Sarah needs to sleep.'

I felt a wave of panic, not a running-out-the-door panic but rather a scared-to-let-go panic. I forced myself to speak.

'Sam, what if my mind is determined that I can't know these things you've told me?' The words might have been coming out slurred. 'What if every time I get too close to remembering that day my subconscious erases another whole slice of my mind? Perhaps this time it will erase everything I've ever known.'

'But I thought your subconscious was your mind,' interrupted Annabelle.

'It is,' said Sam. 'And Sarah, that hasn't been the nature of the repression. So far you've forgotten specific information but your early memories have remained intact. I …'

'Sarah, what are you doing?' said Matthew, catching hold of me as I tried to stand.

'I want to look in the big mirror.' I pulled myself upright and started to stagger towards my bedroom, with Matthew half helping, half trying to get me to return to the sofa. The others followed. They watched me pull open my wardrobe door, watched me watching my reflection looking back at me. 'Where is it, Sam?' I said.

'Where's what?'

I peered deep into my own eyes. 'My subconscious.' Now my speech was definitely slurred. 'I presume it's in my head. I mean, if you cut off my arms and legs, it's still there isn't it?' I poked my reflected forehead and staggered backwards. 'Stuffed in with all my memories, and dreams. And the stories I haven't written. Where is it, Sam?'

'Well, it isn't actually anywhere. It's just a concept, a term. More of a lay term really. Freud didn't ... It's actually your unconscious mind, and that's everything that goes on in your mind that you're not consciously aware of. But, ultimately, it's just chemical pathways and transmitted messages in different tissues in your brain. I admit it's poorly defined ...'

'So this ... poorly defined concept ... this part of my mind, which isn't anywhere, is doing this to me and nobody knows how?' Over my reflected shoulder I could see Sam frowning. 'Just pathways inside my brain. And all my memories just a bag of chemicals.' I swayed closer to my reflection. 'Sam, my pupils are holes into my head, aren't they?'

'What? No, they're holes that let light fall onto ... Why? What are you thinking of?'

I felt Matthew grab my arm. I pulled away from him and caught hold of the wardrobe door to prevent myself falling inside. 'I'm getting as close to my non-existent subconscious as I can. So I can tell it to fuck off and leave me alone.'

And that's what I did. Then I let everyone escort me back to the sofa and make me a mug of hot chocolate.

*

417

It's strange the things you remember. And right now I can clearly remember sitting there, at the end of that strange evening, half awake and dunking chocolate digestives into milky hot chocolate, thinking of Mrs Parkin who, among other things, had disapproved of dunking. Somehow that simple indulgence made me believe that everything was going to resolve. Or perhaps it was just the combination of the sedative and my evening medication that was making me believe that.

I watched Sam packing his Sarah Blake folder back into his bag. 'I'm really grateful to you all. But … I'd better go to sleep now,' I said.

'If you like, I'll stay over and doze on the sofa,' said Sam. 'I'm not back in the office until Monday.'

'I'll make breakfast,' said Poppy.

'I'll help,' said Annabelle. 'It's too late to go home now.'

'It's only eleven-thirty,' protested Matthew. 'And where will you all sleep?'

We left them in the lounge negotiating blankets. Matthew manoeuvred me to sit on the edge of the bed. 'Are you OK?'

'I'm scared. In case everything's gone by the morning.'

'We'll tell you it all again.'

'No. I mean *everything*. Right back to that …that tiny baby in the crib. Knowing nothing. With all this waiting to happen.'

He sat down beside me. 'Come on, love. Sam said that wouldn't happen. And we really have told you as much as we know, and you've been able to hold on to it.'

'Yes … I know the things you've told me. But I don't remember them … being real. And there are other things that nobody can tell me. Because nobody knows them. My private thoughts. I can't remember those things either. Even if I didn't do anything wrong.

Perhaps ... Perhaps I wanted them to die. And my mind is protecting me from the shame. Perhaps that's the choice. An empty head, or a life ... a lifetime of guilt or shame.'

'Come on, let's stop worrying about all that now. You're falling asleep.'

I sagged forward and allowed him to undress me but as he eased my jumper over my head, my eyes fell upon the flat of my abdomen. I imagined it once nurturing a tiny doomed existence. Through all the haze, I could almost recapture a memory of this small other, living inside me, utterly dependent upon me.

'Matthew, I'm sad. About the baby. Not knowing whose father ... who the father was. Would you still want me?'

'It was your baby. And, Sarah, listen to me. I'll always want you.'

*

Sleep came soon. Deep and empty and without time. Then the emptiness came to an end and time started. I was awake but my eyes were still closed. I tried to open them but I had no control over my eyelids. I tried to lift my hand, my arm. But I had no control over them either. Then came the smells. Smells from before. Jasmine. Ginger. Roses and violets. A sour apple stolen from Farmer Joe's orchard. The smell of the sea in summer. The oldness of shale split open. A creature long gone, exposed to the air after millions of years of containment. The cold odourless smell of leaving and absence and nobody caring. My smells. Being taken from me. One by one.

What was this? Had I died? Was I breathing? I tried to sit up. But my arms and legs and back and front had forgotten how to do that.

Then came the sounds: the soft hum of the lights, the distant laughter of a child. Please, not that child. Not *that* child. I could feel my body start to vibrate. I could feel myself becoming higher, suspended, then falling, upright, feet first, with no hope of saving myself. I had to make it stop.

Stop!

Was that my voice? Where did it come from? Not out of me, surely. If only I could open my eyes. I needed to see. But I listened instead. Listened to the laughter. Louder now. Closer. Then came the mist. My eyes were still closed but I could see it. Grey mist painted on the inside of my eyelids. But impossibly far away. I watched. And as I watched, the grey mist moved closer and things emerged from its depths. And all I could do was witness them appear one by one, then sparkle and disappear like fireworks in a cloudy sky. First my Raggedy doll. Then Rackham's fairies, clawing and scratching each other; my books, their spines bent backwards, their pages sucked into the swirling mist. Then came the people. Their faces were empty. But I knew who they were: Grandma Clark, Jeff Blake, Arachne, Sam, Poppy, Annabelle. Matthew. Sparkling out of existence one at a time. My people and my things being taken from me. Soon there would be nothing left of me.

Now it was almost upon me. Dense, cold, shapeless. This mind within my mind was finally making itself known to me. My strength was draining away, my chest collapsing, caving inwards as this grey otherness closed in on me, stealing my past, my present, my future. If I failed to act now I would be over and done with. A husk. A remnant. But I was so very tired of fighting it. It would be so much easier just to let this miserable, doomed life be over.

'Sarah, wake up. It's just a dream.'

I opened my eyes. But nothing changed. The greyness was all over me, crushing me. And all the while, the laughter, coming from deep inside this thing that, without ever seeking my sanction, was claiming ownership of my thoughts. I needed to run away. But now the waves were sucking the sand from under me, pulling me down, filling my throat with sea water instead of air. And I was too exhausted to care. Too exhausted to …

'Look, here comes Grandma with our ice creams.'

'I'll give you half this apple if you read my book because … Your eyes are a very strange colour, aren't they?'

Too exhausted to …

'It's about a place called Raggedy Lyme where there's wasted time.'

Too exhausted … Wasted time?

My time? Wasted? My time. Taken from me. Lost. I want it back.

I search for the words that I need. So many words to choose from and it's taking me too much time to find them. I need to … but now the laughter is gnawing, consuming me …

Stop!

Was that my voice? Yes, it was.

Silence. I stare deep into the grey mist and I fight it. I begin to see a starlit sky rising high above the dark outline of a chateau in Burgundy. I smell the fresh night air and the promise of a new beginning. Taste a kiss so much more real than imagining can ever be. Time, if there is time, comes to a halt. And in that no-time, my thoughts crystallise and become my own. My life becomes my own. And I know that whatever might happen in it, however bad these things might be, they all happen to me. And it's my right to remember them. I will not let some ill-defined bag of chemicals carry on stealing my life from me. Because whatever this mind within my mind might be, the one thing it has failed to realise is that if I end then it ends too. Because without me it is nothing.

Silence. The grey mist thinned and receded. The air around me became clear and sweet. And bitter with the things I knew I had to remember.

*

I woke alone. As my eyes opened, they focussed upon a strange, stylish couple, draped in gold. He was kissing her, almost crushing her. Her toes were curled in ecstasy, her eyes closed, one of her arms was around his neck, preventing his leaving. I turned away from them, stepped out of bed and pulled on my dressing gown. I glanced out through the half-open curtains at the backyard, at the fence that concealed much of the sky. But I could see that the sky was blue and that summer was here at last. I opened my bedroom door and stepped into the cramped dining area, heard someone moving around in the kitchen, checked the belt of my dressing gown and went to investigate.

*

Matthew looked up.

'Sarah! We let you sleep. You had a bad night. Your pulse was all over the place. Sam was worried it was a reaction to the drugs. Are you OK?' The back door burst open and Annabelle, Sam and Poppy hurried inside and came to a silent halt alongside one another; a thick aroma of putrefying herbs followed them in. They watched me and waited. Matthew came towards me.

'Sarah?'

I looked straight into his pale eyes. 'It was a Red Delicious.'

'What?'

'The apple I put on your desk.' I pulled out a chair and sat down. 'It was a Red Delicious. From Borough Market. I went there that morning. Specially.'

Sam hurried over to stand beside me, lifted my hand and felt my wrist. 'Is this something that happened?'

'Yes, it is. Is that all you've remembered, Sarah?'

'No, I've remembered everything.' I took a deep breath. 'But it's not the same. I can see myself almost as somebody else. Someone I've just met but I know her whole life because I've seen it not lived it. I can remember what she did and thought. Way back. And I can understand why she did things and why she thought things but as if I was sharing the thoughts with the person who was having them. I can remember not remembering and being told things one at a time. My things. And I can remember that day. Seeing inside my mind but not being inside my mind. Like an observer. And it's terrible. Annabelle, Poppy, you might not want to hear this.'

We relocated to the lounge. I drank a mouthful of tea. Then another. I felt strangely calm.

'I went to my mother's house, like I said I would. I parked in the next street. I was only going inside for a few minutes so I left all my things in the car. I went round the back, in case Diana came to the door and escaped into the street. The back door was unlocked ...'

The kitchen's a mess.

'Hello, is anybody there? It's Sarah. Mum, are you there?' I'm walking through into the hallway, picking one of Diana's slippers off the filthy, wooden floor, carrying it into the lounge. The television is on but there's no sound. I carry the slipper back into the hall. Check the dining room. The table's covered in dirty plates and saucepans, opened cans, spoons congealed in half-eaten food, empty bottles, mostly gin. A loaf of bread has spilled a few curled, grey slices onto the floor.

I look down at the slipper in my hand: where is she? What if she's gone walking and Arachne's out looking for her? She should have phoned me. No, don't panic. Arachne would have phoned me. Arachne's probably slipped out to get something and forgotten to check the back door before leaving. Mum's probably upstairs asleep. I'll phone Arachne.

I'm feeling in my pocket for my mobile. Damn, I left it in the car. I'll check upstairs before I start worrying. I hurry upstairs. The exertion excites a wave of nausea. I pause on the landing to catch my breath. Diana's room is straight ahead of me. The door is ajar. Another wave of nausea this time accompanied by panic. I rush in. Diana is slumped on her bed, breathing, asleep in her clothes. She sleeps a lot lately. I think Arachne has been feeding her pills, more than she needs. I touch her arm to wake her but she doesn't stir.

'Mum?'

I can hear noises coming from the next room. Arachne's room.

I leave Diana sleeping and walk along the corridor to investigate. Arachne's door is closed. I step inside without knocking. Arachne and

Jeff are in bed … Well, they're *on* the bed. She's on top of him. Across him. He's supposed to be in Nottingham. But he's not. He's here, underneath Arachne. She's naked. Apart from my jacket. She's wearing my red leather jacket, the one I bought for the winter launch. Matthew helped me choose it. Jeff is gripping its matt sleeves, pulling her down onto him. I'm standing at the bottom of the bed, holding a slipper. Looking at them. They're covered in sweat. Arachne's arse looks huge spread out across my husband like that. She's turning her head. She's seen me. Her face is smeared with lipstick, bright red, all across her cheek and her chin. I can see Jeff's face beyond her thigh. Looking back at me. He pushes Arachne off and tries to pull the sheet over himself but she pulls it away so I can see. Her lipstick is all over … all over … She looks at me and laughs. Like a mad person. Ridiculing me. The same laughter I used to hear when I was in my room crying over my memories of my granny. And my father going away. And about my mother not wanting me. The laughter is making me queasy. I want to lie down.

But Arachne is coming towards me. Laughing. Throwing her head backwards and forwards. She looks insane. She's shouting at me.

'Why are you here? Why don't you fuck off! Jeff can't bear you because you're boring and frigid.'

I need to leave, but now Jeff's getting off the bed. He shouts my name: 'Sarah!'

He grabs his underpants and holds them over his dick. I can still see the red smears either side. Arachne is still screaming for me to get out. I'm backing towards the door but now something is in the way, stopping me from going any further. It's my mother. My sister yells at Diana to get out. I don't know what to do. I can't leave my mother exposed to this. I have to stop it happening. I think I'm crying. Yes, I'm crying.

'Arachne, let me phone and get Mum taken somewhere. Until things settle down. Just let me make that call. I'll wait downstairs with her and then I'll go, and you don't ever have to see me again.'

But they're pointing at me. Shouting at me. Arachne is accusing me of spying on her. Jeff says he knows my slut friend told me she saw them together but it wouldn't make any difference because I'll get nothing. Because of me and Matthew. I don't know what he's talking about and I don't want this to be happening in front of my mother so I put my arm around her and lead her out on to the landing.

Now Arachne is clutching at the doorframe, yelling at me. 'You won't get any of her money. It's all mine. She never wanted you. You're just a waste of time!'

Diana is mumbling to herself, pulling her slipper away from me. I need to get her away, to calm everything down.

'Arachne, I don't want anyone's money, it's all yours, and as soon as I'm sure Mum is safe, I'm leaving. I'm going to be with Matthew.'

Suddenly Jeff is crazy. He pushes past Arachne and stands right in front of me, still holding his underpants, calling me a whore. Diana is shouting senseless words, smacking the slipper against his shoulder. Jeff throws his pants on the floor, snatches the slipper from Diana's grasp and throws it at the wall. He's grabbed hold of my arm, he's pulling me away from Diana. She has to catch hold of the banister to stop herself falling over.

'Jeff, I …' He throws me hard against the wall. My arm cracks. A terrible pain shoots across my hips and all I can think of is the baby. I hear myself shout: 'Please, Jeff, I'm pregnant!'

He grabs my hair.

'Jeff, I'm scared for the baby … your baby!'

He sneers at me. 'My baby? You stupid bitch!' He slaps my face. 'You've had no idea, have you?' He's pulling me down onto the floor. 'I had the snip way before I ever ran into you and your pathetic, bloody daydreams. So it's all *his*!'

And now he's kicking me in the stomach and I know the baby is going to die. Matthew's baby's going to die. And I'm so very sorry I've let them both down, like I've let everyone down. The kicking's stopped and I'm rolling over onto my back and looking up at him. He's getting ready to kick me again. But suddenly a slipper bounces off the side of his head. Diana is looming behind him, with her bony arms and her hands, grabbing him, pulling him back. And she's yelling ... this time proper words. Words I can understand.

'Don't you hurt my Sarah! Don't you touch her!'

Her yellow fingers are digging into his bare flesh, pulling him away from me. He turns to push her away. Grabs her shoulder. I don't want him to hurt her. Please don't hurt her. He's heavy but she has managed to swing herself round. She wails like an animal. I try to get up, to protect her, but I don't need to. She's pushed him. He's lost his footing. He's stumbling backwards, grabbing the air, scrabbling to save himself. He's snatching at the stair rail. His fingers grip it, but his hand is slippery with sweat and slime. He's losing his hold. He's falling. Something, his leg, I think, hits the edge of a stair and I hear a bone crack, clear above his yelling. He's crashing down the whole of the staircase, slowly, one step at a time. Each impact echoes as his skeleton breaks. I'm holding my breath. I know I am. Then he hits the hall floor. And everything is quiet.

Diana is leaning over the banister mumbling to herself ... just swear words, I think. And Arachne is flat against the wall on the landing as if somebody has stuck her to it. I pull myself up. The pain is still there, as if he is still kicking me. But I manage to crawl to the top of the stairs. I can't put any weight on my arm. Jeff is lying on his front. His head is on the hall floor but his neck is twisted completely round. One of his arms is folded underneath him, his legs are stretched up the stairs. One of them is bent the wrong way. Arachne screams. I use the stair rail to pull myself up and now I'm moving downstairs. Slowly, in case Jeff moves. I'm stepping over his legs on to the hall floor. He is breathing. We have to call an ambulance. But I can see Diana feeling her way down towards me. There are terrible pains in my back but I'm managing to help my mother down past Jeff's legs, leading her into the lounge, sitting her down, handing her the TV controller.

I've shut the door and I'm going back to Jeff.

There's another scream and Arachne is bending over Jeff. She's still wearing my red jacket. She's moaning and wailing. I have to phone for help.

'Arachne, I have to phone …'

'You've killed him!'

She launches herself at me. The pain rips through me, right up to my throat. I feel myself falling. I catch hold of the stair post to stop myself landing on top of Jeff. Blood is coming out of his mouth. Arachne is screaming.

'You've killed him!'

'Arachne, no … we need an ambulance.'

But she isn't listening to me. And now she's running to the door. I pull myself away from Jeff. I don't want to fall on him and hurt him.

Arachne's pulled open the front door.

'Arachne, stop!'

She's on the pavement outside. She's running towards the road. I'm

right behind her. I can't stop her. I see her stumble forward and …
There's a screech of brakes and a flash of red and my sister is gone.
And where she was there are just big double wheels still moving,
slower and slower. Then a crash of metal and breaking glass. And now
everything's still. But Arachne's gone and I can't see where she is.

It was all my fault. I need to tell Grandma what happened.

But I don't think Grandma's there anymore.

Perhaps Daddy will help.

Episode Fifty-two

The room was silent. I felt Matthew's arm tighten around me. I wanted to tell him how very sorry I was. But not then. Not there. With other people hearing. I glanced over at Poppy and Annabelle huddled beside one another. Watching me.

'I'm sorry you all had to hear that.'

Still nobody spoke. Sam got to his feet. 'Do you need anything, Sarah?'

'I'm OK. There isn't much more to tell. I can't remember anything after the lorry hit the car, just bits and pieces that might not be real, but I must have wandered off straightaway because you said nobody reported seeing me and there must have been people on the scene very quickly. I've got a few disconnected memories of headlights coming towards me. And walking with pain in my back and down my legs.'

'You would probably have gone into immediate shock,' said Sam. 'The wandering is a survival strategy. A flight away from an unmanageable situation. But it was a big distance to have covered in the state you must have been in.'

Matthew rubbed his eyes. 'I don't understand why no one reported seeing you walking around like that for two days.'

'People don't like to get involved,' said Poppy. 'They'd rather die than help somebody in trouble.'

'And you left your bag in the car, so you wouldn't have had any money on you.'

Annabelle looked at Matthew and chewed her lip. 'Perhaps someone gave her a lift. We used to hitch to the coast all the time when we were at uni. Truckers will pick up anybody, no questions asked. But I've no idea why Sarah finished up in that cove place.'

'It could have been anywhere,' said Sam. 'But Sarah, you must have found somewhere to shelter. It was bitterly cold those two nights. Below zero. You must have managed to get yourself under cover.'

They watched me get to my feet and walk over to the bookcase.

'Where they found me wasn't just *anywhere*.' I pulled out my old, battered dictionary and carried it back to the sofa. 'This was my granny's dictionary. This and a copy of *Andersen's Fairy Tales* are all I have left of her. Two books and the stories we used to invent.'

I flicked through the thin pages to find a black and white postcard and handed it to Sam.

'After my father left Diana, he moved south to be near the sea. Granny Clark used to take me to visit him, not often, but perhaps half a dozen times. We used to go on a train to a place called Raggedy Lyme.'

'Where the LOST things hide?' said Poppy.

'Yes. It was actually Lyme Regis.' I smiled. 'My father had a lonely old house, high on the cliffs above Beer Cove. It had big windows overlooking the sea. And a telescope upstairs, so he could look out towards the horizon and watch the stars. I used to stand on a stool and watch the moon move across the night and he'd tell me the names of the constellations. He told me there were some stars that you could only see on the other side of the world. Like the stars of the Southern Cross. And one day he was going to go and see them and write and tell me what they were like. During the daytime we used to go to a beach and find fossils. Then one day Grandma said we were not going to see him for a long time because he'd gone across the sea to the southern stars.'

I closed the old dictionary and put it on the floor. 'He wrote me letters but then suddenly Granny Clark was gone and I was living with Diana and the letters stopped. Diana said he must have forgotten me. I tried to trace him when I first went to college, but there was no record of him after he left for Australia. I've taken a couple of trips to Beer Cove, over the years, the last time just after my first book was published. I suppose I thought that somehow he might know that I'd become someone worthwhile. That I'd earned his return. But the house was boarded up and nobody remembered him. I think the things that happened at my mother's wiped everything out, took me back to those times with my father. I might have gone to his house on the cliffs. Perhaps I thought he was still there and he'd want to help me.'

'Sarah, love, we'll try and trace him.'

I shook my head. 'If he'd cared about me, he would have taken me with him. He never attempted to contact me after my grandmother died. If he did I never found out about it. And he shouldn't have gone so far away from her. She was broken-hearted. People never consider how going in search of their dreams is sometimes a selfish thing to do. People are horrible.'

'You're not,' said Poppy. 'You're my favourite, kindest person. Equal with Matthew and Michael Jackson.'

I smiled. 'So, I think that's it. Every last disgusting moment of it.

432

At least it's all the moments I can remember. And, now it's all back in my head, I can't help thinking that my mind really was doing me a favour by hiding it from me. And I'm scared that if the police ever find out I was there and that Jeff was thrown downstairs, they'll suspect that what I've just told you is my version of something far worse.' I tugged at Matthew's sleeve. 'I think I'd better get dressed. And, Sam, would you tell Bob I've got a load of my memories back and could he please think of a way of helping me forget them. One that doesn't involve forgetting the four of you. Or Alfie.'

*

We ordered in pizza. And as we ate, I listened to Annabelle quizzing Sam about a recent drug experience that left her seeing purple, Sam assuring her that enduring psycho-emotional conversion was not that uncommon and had she considered sticking to something more reliable like sparkling wine.

Matthew folded his arms in disgust. 'You shouldn't indulge her, Sam!'

'He's not indulging me. And I like the weird stuff. Especially when I'm welding. It was Sarah who hated it.'

'What?' snapped Matthew.

'Sarah had a thing about time turning orange. She's a complete lightweight.'

Matthew put his head in his hands. 'Sam, please give Annabelle something to stop her talking?'

*

Poppy left late afternoon, clutching two boxes of cornflakes, delighted that I'd cancelled my hospital appointment in order to spend Tuesday with him, bickering about grammar. Annabelle hugged him goodbye then offered to drive Sam back to Swiss Cottage, but first she needed to spend a while upstairs, sifting through Jeff's kitchenware; she thought she might be gestating an installation involving saucepan lids.

Sam watched her go then turned to me. 'She's quite unique, isn't she?'

So, while Annabelle crashed around upstairs, Sam and Matthew sat with me at the kitchen table enjoying a post-lunch glass of rosé. Eventually, Sam went to collect his things. He returned carrying one of my snow scenes.

Matthew laughed. 'Thinking of starting a collection, Sam?'

Sam handed me the water-filled globe. 'I noticed this when I was leering through the window at Matthew's car. You'd think somebody might have noticed it when they were packing things away, wouldn't you?'

I held the tacky object up for Matthew to see. It featured a mermaid and a fishing boat and a banner which read: WELCOME TO BEER COVE. I shook it to disturb a shower of silver snow then set it down on the windowsill.

Episode Fifty-three

Of all the things I loved about Matthew I loved his pastel green eyes the most. And the scent of his hair, the way he smiled, the things he said, the sound of his breathing when he was asleep, the fact that he cared about children's books. In fact, I loved everything about him but really, more than anything else, I loved that he was lying there beside me, after everyone had left and now the house was still. I loved those quiet end-of-the-day moments. I still do.

'Matthew?'

He rolled over to face me. 'Mm?'

'Thank you.'

'It was a good one, wasn't it?'

'Not that, idiot! I mean thank you for not letting me be alone through all this ...'

'Hey, come on, Sarah. No tears.'

'Matthew, I have to cry.'

He sat up. 'Sam said to talk about it. He said it would help.'

I wiped my eyes and tried to organise my feelings into words but my head was too full of repeating scenes, of lies and guilt and disappointment that words could never adequately describe.

'I'm sad about how Jeff let me carry on taking the pill all that time.'

I fought back the useless tears. 'And I didn't even know it was your baby.'

'We'll try again. They don't think the miscarriage caused any permanent damage. We'll make sure. Then there'll be no stopping us.'

I took a slow breath. 'I can't believe I wasted all those years with him. Living with his lies. I know I was stupid to marry him. And stay with him. But I wanted to belong to someone. It was all right to begin with but …'

'Sarah, it was never all right. And he really did want you to belong to him. Just him. He treated you like a piece of property.'

'Perhaps that's what Arachne found attractive about him. I'm so sad about Arachne. However much she hated me, she was still my sister. I'd prefer her and Jeff to be alive and together and just leave me to be with you. And I can't help wondering what kind of person she might have been if she'd just had an ordinary family.'

'It's all over, Sarah. There's no point in dwelling over things like that.'

'But she never had a life. It was terrible, seeing …' My throat was aching with trying to control the tremor in my voice. 'She disappeared under those huge wheels. I can't forget the noises. The brakes screeching. And the crash. Every time I close my eyes, she's there, painted on the inside of my eyelids, accusing me.' I threw my hand over my face. Felt Matthew lifting it away.

'Sarah, love, we'll talk to Bob on Wednesday. I don't think you'll ever forget those things … Not again anyway, but he can help you come to terms with them.'

I placed my finger across his lips. 'Matthew, I know Sam has to tell Dr Gray. But I don't want anyone else to know what I've remembered. Once people discover I was there, it comes down to believing my version of what happened.' I watched furrows of confusion deepen across his brow. 'How do you know I've not lied? To all of you.'

'I trust you.'

'I've lied to you in the past.'

'No, you … When have you lied to me?'

'I've lied about finishing my final draft when I haven't even started it.'

He threw his head back and laughed. 'Sarah, I trust you.'

'But what about all the people who won't trust me? Della Brown suspects me. And she's in cahoots with Geraint Williams. He's not going to lose interest, is he? Even if nobody tells him I've remembered, that scanner will tell him. They don't hang murderers anymore, do they?'

'Sarah, you didn't do anything.'

'That hasn't always stopped people being hanged.'

'Look, we'll speak to Sam about it. Before Wednesday. OK? And I'll go over and collect those other things from the police station. Whatever they are. I'll take the Escort. Brazen it out. Guilty people never walk into the mouth of Hell.'

I tried to smile. 'I really like Sam.'

'Me too. Let's hope he made it back to Swiss Cottage. Annabelle had that look in her eye. He should never have asked her about her welding.' He stroked my hair away from my forehead. 'You ought to try and get some sleep.'

'I can't sleep. My head's too crazy with memories, the new ones and the old ones, all jostling around, trying to arrange themselves into the right order.'

'Well, I hope the ones about me come out on top.' He briefly held my gaze. 'You do actually remember me, right?'

'Yes.' I twiddled with his hair. 'I remember trying hard not to be in love with you.'

'Why?'

'Because losing somebody you love is terrible. Maybe that's what my mind was doing. What it's always tried to do: make me forget people I loved so I wouldn't be sad when they went away. Like my father went away.' I let my hands slide up and around the back of his neck. 'I can remember lusting over you before we were lovers.'

'In Frankfurt?'

'No, two weeks ago. With my primary school brain and my porno mags. It must have been like being seduced by Holly Hobbie. And you actually said no to sex, which is *unbelievable*.'

'I even surprised myself.'

I let my hands fall back onto my pillow. 'I've been thinking: when they found me, how did they know it was me? Because I didn't have my wallet or driving licence with me.'

'Well, Miss Hobbie, you had a credit card receipt in your jeans pocket and they managed to decipher it and contacted me.'

'It was *your* credit card receipt?'

'Yeah, for those black patent shoes. The ones that you can't walk in.'

'Did *you* buy them?'

'Yes. For the book launch. You accused me of trying to turn you into a sex object. Or a human version of Lucy. So I gave you the receipt and told you to exchange them for a pair of slippers with bobbles on. Remember?'

I briefly panicked that I'd forgotten something I ought to know. That it was all starting again? Then, suddenly, I recalled that argument and started to laugh.

'I wasn't really going to take them back. I was going to practise walking in them and surprise you by wearing them when you least expected it.'

'Well, you certainly managed to do that. I don't think I'll ever be able to look at them again without seeing you naked.'

'I was wearing knickers.'

'Oh yes, so you were. Aren't you tired?'

'No, not really.' I traced my finger across his chest. 'I don't want to take much with me when we move to Hampstead. Just the Klimt and the fairies. And Alfie. Jeff's parents can have everything else.'

'Perhaps we can leave your disgusting car here as well. You can buy a new one with the money from the TV series.' He smiled at my confusion. 'In all the excitement we forgot to tell you. Poppy's negotiating a Jenny Berry episode deal.' He tugged a strand of my hair. 'They want you to write more.'

I studied his eyes for a moment. Then I laughed. 'You know, that was the best half apple anyone ever invested!'

Episode Fifty-four

Most days are just days. But some days are all about change; and the day back at Greystone Park was going to be one of those. What I could not possibly have known was how many changes that day had in store for me.

Sam, I knew, had already discussed my recovered memories with Dr Gray, but nevertheless they both listened intently as, once again, I sat beside Matthew and detailed the events of that December afternoon. This second time of telling was nowhere near as difficult as the first, perhaps because the first time I was telling myself as well as the others and this time I already knew every last detail. Bob Gray let me finish and the room was silent for a while before he offered any comment. Eventually, he leaned away from his desk and peered at me over the top of his spectacles.

'Well, Sarah, you have remembered many terrible things, things that you needed to remember, and now your next challenge will be to allow yourself to forget. Time will assist you in that, but also please be assured that we are here to help you however and whenever you need us.'

'I know that Dr Gray.'

'And in the meantime, my dear, I must congratulate you on your courage and determination. Well done!'

'I had a lot of help. Dr Gray, I'm very grateful to you and Sam for guiding me through these last few weeks. And for giving me my life back. I'm even grateful to Dr Williams and Mrs Parkin because, somehow, disliking them as much as I did galvanised my determination.'

'I'll probably not pass that on to them,' laughed Bob Gray.

I felt Matthew's hand close over mine.

'Bob, how much of this do you have to pass on? I suppose Sarah's recollections all become part of the case report, do they? And then the police can seek access?'

Bob Gray's face became serious. 'What's worrying you, Matthew?'

I answered. 'We're worried that if I tell the police what I've just told you, they might not believe I'm telling the truth.'

'If Sarah even admits she was there,' said Matthew, 'and that Jeff was pushed downstairs, won't that encourage even more suspicion? Will you be obliged to reveal what we've just told you? The problem is that Della Brown called round and …'

'Sam informed me of that.' Bob Gray turned to study his laptop. 'Actually, just this morning, I received an email from Detective Brown regarding the Hornsey incident. Presumably composed following her most recent visit to your home. She has recommended that, "now that Mr Parry's whereabouts are established" – apparently bank records have now confirmed that you purchased a train ticket at 14.47 on the day in question – she has recommended that any investigation of "the involvement of Ms Blake or any other as yet unidentified individuals should be suspended until significant changes occur in Ms Blake's ability to recall the circumstances leading up to her being found unconscious." She has recommended that a request be placed "on file" that such changes be reported by any "current or future physicians".'

441

'What does "on file" mean?' I asked.

'It means we have a lot of files,' said Sam.

'What if they find out that I've remembered and they haven't been told?'

'Sarah,' said Bob Gray, 'as far as the police are concerned, your sister died as the result of being hit by a lorry. The driver reported that she ran out of nowhere. He saw her in his headlights only at the last minute. Jeff Blake died only indirectly from a broken neck. Although he did not regain complete consciousness, his condition was stable. It was an unfortunate hospital-acquired infection that took his life. So even if foul play was suspected they would not easily be able to level a charge of manslaughter against anyone, since the fall did not kill him.'

I was not that convinced and my frown obviously demonstrated as much. Bob Gray resorted to specifics.

'Sarah, there is no point in anyone knowing that your mother's attempts to protect you inadvertently contributed to your husband's calamity, since due to her extreme diminished responsibility, she cannot be charged with anything. And, as far as any investigation is concerned, nothing can be gained by any further intrusion into your life. I am perfectly able to advise all concerned that, despite some recovery, you appear to have an intractable memory loss, which *is* true regarding the period surrounding your being found unconscious. And, considering the physical circumstances in which you were found, this memory loss might *possibly* be due ...' He glanced at Sam. '... to some minute foci of hypoxia which have erased whole sectors of your past. The unpleasant details you have remembered need go no further than these four walls.'

I tried to smile but I still found it impossible. 'Dr Gray, even if the police have decided not to investigate further, I'm scared these memories will make me crazy. That I'll start to suspect they're false memories and I really did do something terrible.'

'We will make sure you do not think those things, Sarah.'

'But you can go mad thinking that if you behaved differently ...'

'My dear, the past is made up of all the time anybody has ever had. And that time could have been made up of many things, until it occurred, but once it has happened it cannot be changed. Your past is immutable. But what we can do is to change how you think about it.'

'But what about regret and guilt? Will you be able to help me deal with those things at the same time as allowing everyone to assume I haven't remembered?'

'Yes, we will. And Sarah, Sam and I will allow you a tiny smidgeon of regret, but none of us in this room will allow you to feel guilt.' Bob Gray pulled his laptop closer and checked the screen. 'I'm recommending that we remain available for future consultation, that we carry out routine checks, and that, as far as any further research is concerned, this case is on hold.'

'Can you do that?' I asked.

'Sarah, my dear, I am the boss around here. Ask Sam if you don't believe me. And when I say an investigation of one of my patients is on hold, or indeed, completely terminated, that is the way it is.'

'But what about Dr Williams? He'll still want to investigate my dynamic memory loss. Those scans are like lie detectors. He'll know I'm concealing things.'

Dr Gray tapped his keyboard then smiled. 'There will be no further scans for the time being because, although they are relatively non-invasive, we prefer to err on the side of caution.' He looked directly at me. 'You are in the very early stages of pregnancy, Sarah, suspected last weekend and confirmed in the bloods taken when you arrived this morning. So, once again, well done! Both of you! Matthew, do try to breathe.'

Things calmed over cappuccinos. Eventually, Bob Gray leaned back and linked his fingers across his waistcoat. 'Is there anything else we can help you with?'

I wiped my lips, just in case they were covered in chocolate powder, then stepped over to retrieve a bunch of pink roses. 'I'd like to see my mother, please?'

'Certainly, my dear. Sam, would you do the honours?'

Sam led Matthew and me through the double doors, into the stretch of corridor where the rooms had permanent nameplates. He stopped at a door marked 'Diana Dawson', a door that I had walked past repeatedly without noticing it. He knocked, turned a lock and stepped inside. 'How are you today, Mrs Dawson? I've brought you some visitors.'

Diana looked well. She had gained weight during the weeks of luxury care and there was more colour in her cheeks than I could remember. She was sitting in a cosy chair beside her bed, dressed in a pale green cotton frock and matching canvas shoes. Around her neck hung the string of pearls, which I had purchased with the first royalties from my LOST series. Matthew hovered just inside the door.

I walked over and sat on the edge of the bed beside my mother. I handed her the roses. 'Hello, Diana. I remembered you liked roses, I said. 'Shall I ask somebody to put them in water for you?'

Diana handed them back. 'In a vase! In the kitchen cupboard.' She flapped her hand to indicate the corridor outside. 'Arachne bought me flowers when I was married.'

'That's lovely,' I said. I put the roses down on the bed. 'What a lovely room. And you've got a nice big television.'

'Sky Movies!'

'Yes! You like the movies, don't you?' I smiled. 'I love your necklace.'

'My daughter bought it for me.'

'Arachne?'

'No, my other daughter. Sarah. She's going to be a writer when she grows up. She's living with her grandma at the moment because the builders are mending the roof. Do you know her?'

'Yes, I know Sarah quite well,' I said.

Diana was clearly delighted. She began to get up. Sam hurried over.

'What do you want, Diana? Shall I get a nurse? Do you need the bathroom?'

Diana tapped Sam's arm. 'No, silly boy, I want to get something. From over there!'

Sam stood back and grimaced as my decrepit mother shuffled over towards the television. All three of us watched her bend down to retrieve something from behind the chest of drawers.

'What have you got there, Diana?' asked Sam.

'Go away, silly boy,' she snapped. Sam looked at Matthew and rolled his eyes.

Diana carried a small, battered package back to her chair and eased herself down. Her bony fingers prodded the brown paper into some kind of order. Then she looked at me.

'Will you give this to Sarah when you see her.' She handed me the parcel. 'But no peeping!' She glanced at Matthew and gave a dismissive wave of her hand. 'You neither!'

I accepted the package and stowed it in my bag, which seemed to satisfy my mother. Encouraged by this exchange, I continued my efforts to communicate, but Diana started to tell me about a seamstress who was making her bridesmaids' dresses. I could sense Matthew's desire to leave, so I kissed my mother on the cheek and got to my feet. Straightaway, Diana's sinewy arm reached over for the TV remote.

'Goodbye, Diana. Take care.' I smiled, but Diana was pre-occupied so I followed Matthew and Sam into the corridor, but before closing the door I paused to snatch a look at the back of my mother's head. Diana was shaking the remote at the TV screen and mumbling aggressively, quite oblivious to her departing visitors.

'Goodbye, Mum,' I whispered. I pulled the door, but just before it clicked shut, I heard, clear as anything, Diana's croaky voice. Always a little too late.

'Bye, Sarah!' Always a little too late.

I gripped my bag and walked in silence, listening to the echo of my mother's voice. Matthew and Sam strode along either side of me, also silent. As soon as we were three or four double doors away, I stopped, grabbed Matthew's sleeve and pulled him to a standstill. His face filled with concern. He touched the back of his hand against my cheek.

'Are you OK?' said Sam.

I started to laugh. 'Sam, I don't remember Diana ever looking as happy as that! Ever! And do you know what? I'm absolutely starving! Does this place serve non-residents?'

Sam's brown eyes shone with relief. 'Of course.'

'Well, in that case, *silly boy*, would you like to join me and Matthew for lunch?' I hugged Matthew's arm. 'I suddenly feel the need to eat for two!'

'Me too,' said Matthew, hugging me back.

*

Lunch in the conservatory was full of good appetite, summer and expectations. I thanked Sam for his friendship and lack of professionalism and was delighted to learn that he had agreed to advise Annabelle on a project regarding Victorian lunatic constraints. As our plates were being cleared for dessert, I remembered Diana's crumpled paper parcel, stretched into my bag and pulled it out. 'Shall we take a peek at Sarah's present?'

Sam sat back and folded his arms. 'I'd open that carefully if I were you. God knows what's in there. Some of them are a bit batty in here!'

I tugged away the twisted tape and peeled open the brown paper. The first thing I discovered was a small, disintegrating rag doll, missing one baby button eye and all of her hair. 'My God,' I said. 'It's Raggedy!'

Sam looked concerned. 'I ought to mention this cache of hers to the cleaning staff. Is there anything else?'

'Yes, there is!' I peered into the parcel and pulled out a squashed red mitten, something wrapped in a frayed, paisley headscarf and a small pile of school photos tied with a grubby piece of ribbon. I pulled at the ribbon end and released a record of my infant school years and, among them, a fragile note from a little girl to her mother which consisted of uneven kisses and a badly scrawled 'Sarah'. I set them all down on the table and turned my attention to the scarf, peeled back the paisley and uncovered a thick bundle of thin, blue envelopes tied with a length of string.

'They're airmail letters!' I said, easing them apart. They were still sealed, unopened, unread. I turned the top one over to reveal an address written in bold, looked up but said nothing.

'What is it?' asked Matthew.

'They're addressed to *Sarah Clark*. At my mother's house.' I rubbed my thumb across the postage stamp. 'They're from Australia.'

I quickly put them and the photos back into my bag, lifted the frayed paisley to my nose and then squashed it down on top of them.

I looked at Matthew and smiled. 'We'll read them when we get back home.'

Then I moved my raggedy doll to one side to make way for the large portion of Greystone summer pudding that was coming my way.

HAMPSTEAD: SIXTEEN MONTHS LATER

'Is she actually eating any of this? I bet if you scrape it all off her and me and the chair and the floor and stick it back in the bowl, there'll be none missing. Coco want more?'

Matthew made another attempt to persuade a spoonful of mashed banana into our daughter's mouth.

'If it gets any worse we'll have to redecorate. Come on, Coco, sweetheart. I'll buy you a pony of you don't spit this mouthful back at me.'

He glanced across at me and frowned.

'You OK? What's the …? Fantastic! No pony today, Coco!' He grabbed the tea towel and wiped slop from his sleeve. 'Perhaps she doesn't like banana.' He looked at me again. 'Sarah, has something happened?'

I shook my head. He threw down the tea towel and got to his feet.

'Sarah, you're worrying me. Say something. What is it?'

I looked up into his green eyes and knew I could keep it inside me no longer.

'Matthew, I pushed him. It was me.'

Acknowledgements

Thank you, Louise Jarvis, Olivia Kiernan, Debbie Wiley, Diana Holmes, Val Hunt and Davy Fennell for reading and re-reading and for your creative support, encouragement and precious friendships.

Thank you, Jenny Berry, for the loan of your name … I'll be hanging on to it for the time being.

Thank you, David Headley, for advice, for believing in and bettering the world I created, and for being an inspirational and inspiring agent. Without your patience and persistence this would not be the book it is.

Thank you so much, Rebecca Lloyd for your editorial, linguistic and literary wisdom.

Thank you, John, for staying the course and watering the plants when the editing got tough.

And … thank you, Leo Malan, for really believing in me.